Meadowlark Downs

By E.J. Gambles

MEADOWLARK DOWNS

First edition. August 1, 2025.

Copyright © 2025 E.J Gambles.

ISBN: 979-8998852404

Written by E.J Gambles.

This book is dedicated to my children, who have inspired the characters in this series.

"Even from the beginning, that was the problem. People liked pretty things. People even liked pretty things that wanted to kill and eat them."

— **Holly Black,**

Chapter 1: Florida Exodus

Gravel pelted the side of the grey Impala as it weaved violently, hitting the shoulder of the deserted highway. Laraline shook herself awake and tightened her grip on the steering wheel. She had been fighting against sleep for well over an hour. However, slumber would remain a distant stranger since their lives had devolved into a waking nightmare. She nervously glanced over at Willet and mouthed an apology. *I'm sorry,* escaping from under her breath.

An irritated voice erupted from the back seat. "Jesus ma!" The last turn had jostled Adelie from her uneasy rest.

Laraline repeated her confession, a bit louder this time. "I'm sorry, I thought you were asleep?"

"I was."

"I guess I'm pretty tired myself."

Willet, who had been silent, yawned before finally responding without looking up. "Mama, why don't we just pull over, you've been driving all night."

Laraline's eyes darted nervously into her rearview mirror. The road still appeared to be quite empty. She was about to release a sigh of relief when she noticed the sky. It was foreboding with dark clouds, that seemed alive with activity. She wasn't taking any chances.

"Not just yet!"

Her two passengers gave one another a confused glance. Addie abruptly sat up, pushing her sweaty face against her sister's headrest. Her bright ginger hair was matted, sticking to her moist cheeks. She exhaled a deep frustrated sigh over Willets's shoulder. Her hot breath smelled of rest stop garlic chips and beef jerky.

Willet gave her sister an irritating grimace and leaned forward so she wouldn't get sick. She turned her focus on the agitated driver. "We don't know where we're going, mama."

Her mother snapped back from behind the thick blond mane framing her face. "That's because I didn't say."

Willet's response was quick, "Do we have a destination, or are we going to just drive around aimlessly like a trio of gypsies?"

"Is that supposed to be clever?"

"Well, how are we supposed to react, you tell me?"

Addie interjected from the backseat. "Seriously!"

Laraline was growing irritated. "Watch your mouth, you two. I'm still your mother!"

Willet immediately folded her arms, and stared ahead, with a slight pout. She tilted her head out the window and looked at her reflection in the passenger mirror. She then gave herself an angry scowl, as the wind fanned her black curly hair across her dusky complexion.

Despite getting only a few hours of sleep, Willet was surprisingly alert. There weren't many cars on this particular stretch of road and for the last few hours, it was as if theirs were the only vehicle left in the world.

Willet sighed and lazily gazed at the endless landscapes of dry brown fields that passed. The occasional structure would break up the monotonous scenery, ancient shacks, and ramshackle barns bleached grey in the heat of the day. With the forbidding clouds overhead, the depressed structures almost reminded her of lonely graves in the field. Willet turned away from the window, as she fought the urge to cry again.

The car was uncomfortably silent. The mood seemed to match the world outside. From the back seat, Adelie folded her arms and leaned back making farting sounds with her lips. She glared intently at the back of her mother's head, trying to process her abrupt anger.

As if sensing the discontent she had created with her family, Laraline took a few deep breaths to calm down. "Look, I know this is difficult for you two. But I promise, we are almost there!"

Willet was now staring at her mother. "Almost there?"

Laraline, feigning confusion, responded. "Excuse me?"

"You said almost there, which would imply that we: in fact, have a destination!"

"Willet, I'd rather not discuss, where we may be going."

"You don't trust us?"

Adelie huffed from the backseat. "I wish we had stayed in Key West."

"Look, I know it may not make sense, but I need to do what is best for our family."

Willet mumbled under her breath. "Family, that's a crock!"

Laraline pretended not to hear her daughter's frustration. "Look I know it doesn't seem fair, but I promise you both, as soon as I am able, I will tell you more."

Willet mumbled. "And the plot thickens."

Laraline's irritation was starting to build again. She couldn't blame them. They needed some downtime. It would probably be safer if they were off the road anyway. "Fine, there is an exit in about two miles. Why don't we stop and get a room? We can rest and then I can get you girls something to eat?"

Adelie quipped from the back seat. "As long as I can get out of this car, my butt is sore!"

Willet glanced back at her. "So is my nose, do you mind leaning back, so I don't have to smell your rancid meat breath."

"Perhaps you should stop breathing!"

"What happened, did you fart?"

"Willie, you're such a dork!"

"Mama, you better tell Addie to stop calling me Willie!"

Adelie batted her eyes coyly, at her older sister "Or what Willie!"

Suddenly Willet turned completely around on her knees, with her fists clenched. "Or you won't make it to your next birthday, Ginger fish!"

"Mama, tell Willie to stop!"

Laraline now found herself screaming. "Ok, both of you, cut it out or so help me I'll run us off the road into a creek, or a pond, or whatever body of water I see next, and then we will all drown together!"

There was a long awkward moment of silence before the car exploded with laughter. All three of them were almost in tears from the unexpected outburst of madness.

Adelie exclaimed. "Jesus, Ma!"

Willet stuck her head out the window again and the warm sunny breeze snatched her breath. She took a deep breath all the same, and suddenly she had a revelation. "Hey, I smell seagulls!"

Laraline smiled. "Well, we aren't far from the ocean."

Willet grinned out loud. She prided herself on her keen sense of smell. Not to be outdone by her sister, Adelie pointed to a sign that read EXIT 14, one mile.

"Is that the exit mamma?"

"Yes sir!"

As the car drifted to the right lane toward the exit, Willet caught a glimpse of a frumpy hitchhiker in a raincoat standing on the edge of the shoulder. The strange drifter held a large yellow umbrella above their head. She couldn't see their faces because of the dingy hood from the raincoat. Willet glanced back as if disturbed. "Is it supposed to rain today?"

Laraline pondered the question. She obviously hadn't noticed the peculiar-looking hobo on the side of the road. "Why do you ask?"

In her mother's paranoid state, she thought it best not to mention him. "No reason."

Laraline gave her a questioning glance to which Willet sheepishly responded. "Just curious."

The image of the hitchhiker had triggered a flickering memory of the funeral itself. She was in that itchy black dress standing alone. Her mother was at the casket trying to calm Adelie down. It was raining that day at the gravesite. She remembered all the black umbrellas. There were so many umbrellas. She quickly sat up straight, and took a deep breath, shaking herself from the painful memory.

Willet turned back to get another look at the strange hitchhiker. The side of the road was now empty. Her head darted side to side frantically scanning the back window behind Adelie. All she could see was the road behind them. There was no sign of anyone. A chill went up Willet's spine. Had she imagined him? It wouldn't have been the first time she had seen such an odd image. She had the urge to mention the current apparition to her mother but thought against it.

The road was almost vacant as the car slowed to a crawl. Laraline spotted an abandoned couch sitting on the right shoulder of the exit. It was a rickety black felt loveseat. It appeared to be completely hand-sewn and covered with tiny seeds.

Willet's eyes widened at the surreal image. "Please tell me this isn't our exit."

Laraline shrugged. "I guess someone placed it out for pick up or trash!"

Adelie took a hard look before responding. "No one is gonna want that nasty thing. It's probably infested with all kinds of bugs."

Laraline corrected her. "You would be surprised what people may snatch up, given the opportunity!"

As they coasted by, Willet could see the backside of the couch was covered in thick cobwebs. A single large grey feather dangled in the mound of fuzzy threadlike madness. The car continued down the exit ramp until they came to a sign. "Moonlight Inn, Next Right"

Chapter 2: Postcards from the Moonlight Inn

The Moonlight Inn was a vintage-looking hotel that had been very popular in the late 1960s. Now it was just an old and outdated relic. It had the typical bungalow style. Its dayglo retro-futuristic chic furnishings were very dated. The exteriors were a sickly lime green. Depending on your perspective, this was either eye-catching or a simple eyesore.

The interiors were just as bold with large oval-shaped floor model televisions and bushy orange carpet with polyester lime curtains that matched.

Laraline's current money only allowed them to occupy the deluxe single, but that was quite the experience in itself. The nightstand even had a violet lava lamp. The only thing Willet could see missing was pink champagne on ice and a brass waterbed. The bed was full-sized, and the couch folded out. Adelie immediately plopped onto the center of the bed, and within a few moments was fast asleep.

Willet instinctively stretched out on the couch and pulled out her pocket sketchbook. She stared up and studied the popcorn that littered the ceiling. Adelie was snoring rather loud now. Between breaths, Willet could hear her mother in the bathroom whispering to someone on her phone. She was not able to make out the words or the conversation. It was another of her mother's recent mystery calls.

There was always a hint of mystery surrounding her parents' affairs. However, ever since her father died, it had gotten extreme. Just three weeks after his funeral, her mother quit her job, emptied the bank accounts, packed them up in the car, and drove down the road. Here they were, two months later, and almost out of options.

Willet could always tell when they were getting close to the ocean. She could smell the seagulls. Something about the scent of damp wings. It was one of the ways her mother said she was special. It did help that her father was a seaman. At an early age, she became familiar with the scent of the sea. However, it didn't explain the other talents she had begun to develop.

The bathroom door popped open and drew Willet's startled gaze. She hadn't even realized she had fallen asleep. She must have been more tired than she realized. Before she had time to react, her mother was kneeling beside her. Her long dirty blonde hair was now tied up in an elegant bun and she had changed her clothes. She was now dressed in a dark blue dress suit. She looked as if she were going to an interview. A feeling of uneasiness overcame Willet.

"Mama, are you going somewhere?"

Laraline whispered into her ear, like a soft lullaby. It felt as if she were trying to lull her back into a sleep state. "Shhh, I've got to step out and take care of some business. I'll be back in a few hours. Stay in the room and don't answer the door!"

Willet turned to face her mother who was now heading toward the door. Despite her proper appearance, she looked strained and tired. It wasn't that long ago when she seemed so youthful. People would mistake Laraline for Willet's older sister, or her young aunt.

Father's death had taken a toll on Mother. Yet there was something else. She was hiding something from them. Her behavior was unfamiliar to Willet or Adelie. Willet blurted out her concern, which she had dared not confess around Adelie. "Are we in danger, mama?"

Her mother stared blankly at her, as she stood at the entrance of the open door. It was as if she were thinking of a proper response. This made her silence even more terrifying to Willet.

"Not at the moment, just keep the door locked and watch your sister. I will bring you guys back some takeout!"

Laraline quietly shut the door behind her, without really giving any thorough explanation. Willet lay on the couch intently listening to her mother's footfalls gradually disappear down the hallway. She naturally started to entertain several thoughts.

Where is she going? What business did she have this time of day? Who was she talking to on the phone? Where were they headed anyway?

Gradually, Willet focused on her mother's cryptic response about them being in danger.

Not at the moment. What the hell does that even mean?

Willet lay on the couch and listened intently, waiting for the moment her mother cranked up the car and promptly sped away. Willet had the urge to hop up, run to the window, and watch her mother drive away. Instead, she closed her eyes and listened.

She sometimes would close her eyes and focus on the incidental sounds of the world. The clanking of the keys. The short nervous breaths of her mother. The key unlocking the door. The sounds beneath the sounds, which the ordinary world doesn't seem to hear.

She remembered when she was very young. Mama, Addie, and her, would spend hours on those rainy autumn nights listening to the sounds beneath the sounds. Autumn was one of Father's busy seasons, so he was at sea a great deal throughout the spring and fall. Listening was one of their secret games. They would often play this when the weather was foul. It was one of the only games that Mama kept secret from their father.

Father.

Willet felt the heaviness in her sigh, as she was transported back to his wake. There were only a handful of people there that she actually knew. A few of them were his coworkers. The rest were strangers. Laraline had the body cremated, and so they spent several minutes looking at a decorative vase.

He may not have been good at playing certain games, but he and Willet had a special bond. They both loved the sea.

Mom and Addie were not fans of the water; neither of them ever learned how to swim. No matter how they tried, it just didn't seem to work. That was the one way that Willet differed from her mother and sister. For some reason, Willet felt an uneasy calm while submerged under water.

As for Addie, water seemed to be her Achilles heel. Once father had to save her from a public swimming pool. She was trying to impress some other kids and slipped and fell into the deep end. She sank like a rock. She was so embarrassed that she didn't leave the house for about two weeks.

Yeah, Father really loved the sea. Perhaps that was why he became a fisherman. Laraline always joked that Langston was her guardian water nymph. He would keep them safe from the water and feed them from the sea. Now that he was gone, who would perform this role?

There was a low grunt from the bed. Adelie was stirring. However, knowing her sister's sleeping habits; Willet figured she would be out for at least another hour or so. Willet scanned the room, as she was growing tired of the popcorn ceiling; so far, she had counted 4097 tiny balls. She turned her position on the small couch until she was lying directly on her right side, facing the room. She wrapped her hand underneath the seat cushion.

It was one of those actions, which was instinctual. She liked the feel of the cold underneath a pillow. She hated to feel hot. Her whole family tended to be hot-natured. Something was soothing about her fingers brushing a smooth cold surface. It seemed to relax her a bit. She allowed her fingertips to stroke and dig underneath.

No sooner had she done this, than she felt the crumpled, folded pamphlet. It was one of those advertisement brochures, which every hotel has near the front desk. Since they waited in the car, they never got to see that part of the hotel. Their mother secretly got the economy single room to house three guests. Willet wondered if the hotel would have a complimentary breakfast, but she knew she wouldn't be able to find out.

As she unfolded the pamphlet, it became apparent that it was an advertisement for a small nearby town. She remembered the name popping up a few times on some highway signs. Willet read the name aloud to herself as if it meant something.

Meadowlark Downs, New Maine's oldest coastal town.

As she continued to read, she became intrigued. *Wow, it's less than 20 minutes away. Why didn't we just drive there instead of this hole in the wall? As close as this is, she should have noticed it on the map. It's a fishing port. I knew I smelled seagulls.*

As she read more facts, she grew tired again. *Hmmm, it's also the oldest bird sanctuary in the coastal United States. Population 2037. Boy, that is a small town. How old is this brochure? It's three years old! Oh my god, is that the last time this room was cleaned? OH, HOW DISGUSTING!*

She immediately dropped the brochure on the floor and wiped her hands on her pants, as if they were any cleaner. She made a mental note to formally go to the bathroom and use soap when she got up. Driving around in all that heat had made her a bit sweaty and tired.

Chapter 3: Familiar Aromas

Laraline made her way to Linnet's Diner at the corner of Renfrew and Martin Street. Linnet's almost felt like neutral territory for Laraline as she stepped inside the door. The familiar aromas filled her nostrils. It was like entering a time warp. The place looked almost the same. However, the town itself seemed a bit alien. There was so much development, but she immediately felt a sense of hope as she made her way to a nearby booth. The waitress was a young girl with pigtails and thick eyebrows. She was smiling as she approached the booth.

"Welcome to Meadowlark Downs, we don't get too many strangers here!"

"Yes, well I'm not a stranger."

"Really? I'm sorry, I thought I knew everyone here."

"It's ok, I've been gone for a while."

"Much too long."

Laraline quickly turned her head and acknowledged the sullen voice. "I didn't think you would show!"

"Are you serious dear, I should be offended!"

"I mean no disrespect, it's just that it's been so many years that I..."

"Forget it, water under the bridge."

The older woman, dressed in a long blue skirt and matching suit jacket, wore a blue fedora with a pink plumage poking out. Her red hair was tied up in a bun, but it was obvious it would be very long if it was let loose. The waitress wore a startled expression as the woman approached the table.

"Tori, how about two cups of oolong tea, put it on my tab."

"Yes Miss Adler, right away!"

The young girl quickly rushed to the kitchen. Laraline greeted the older woman with a neutral yet polite hug. They both were testing the waters, sizing each other up. As they both sat down, several other people turned to look at the older woman.

Laraline noticed the additional attention immediately. "I forgot what a big deal you are here!"

"Well, it comes with the territory, literally!"

"You know, I can pay for my own tea!"

"I swear you haven't changed a bit, Lynn!"

"How do you mean!"

"You're still as proud as ever my dear!"

"I apologize if I offended you, Auntie, I'm just not used to..."

"No apology for being proud, that's how you were raised. Why don't we just suspend the empty pleasantries and let's get down to business. What kind of trouble are you in my dear?"

"Is it that obvious?"

"We haven't heard a peep from you in almost 11 years."

"It wasn't my choice."

"I know Lynn, I'm not blaming you. It is what it is."

Laraline paused before answering. "Langston died about two months ago!"

"Yes, we heard. How are you holding up dear?"

Laraline took a deep breath and sighed. "It's been hard!"

"So sorry."

"Wait, how did you know?"

Eveline looked at her oddly but didn't answer. Tori returned at that moment with two cups of tea. As soon as the cups were brought, Eveline lowered her head and began to speak a chant that Laraline hadn't heard in years.

"Yetik Arke thankful bounty!"

Laraline sat silent, slightly uncomfortable. Eveline looked up when she was finished.

"Aren't you going to pray?"

"We don't pray in our household."

Eveline paused. "Since when did you abandon your faith?"

Laraline's response was cold. "When it abandoned me!"

Eveline responded sharply. "Perhaps outside influences converted you."

"Go ahead and say it!"

"Say what?"

"None of you approved of him!"

"I wasn't going to say anything. I didn't have anything against him personally. However, you were both from two completely different worlds."

Laraline just nodded silently. "I've heard this old song before."

Eveline sighed. "Just tell me what you want dear."

"I want to ask for sanctuary."

"Dear, you don't need sanctuary, you will always be family."

"Sanctuary for my daughters!"

Eveline Adler was silent. She now understood the gravity of the situation and took a sip of tea instead of answering. Her long delicate fingers extended beyond the cup. The thick black ring she was wearing reflected flashes of sunlight on Laraline's face.

Laraline suddenly felt sick in her stomach by the other woman's silent response.

"Look, I wouldn't have asked, if I'd had another choice. These are my children, your nieces. They are both beautiful girls. Just because they have their father's blood, you don't have the right to invalidate them."

"Look, I never said a word."

"That's the point!"

"I was afraid this day would come."

"We have nowhere to go, and I believe we are in danger!"

"Danger, what kind of danger?"

"I don't know exactly, sometimes I can sense things.

The door opened and an old man walked inside with sunglasses. They exchanged suspicious glances, as he passed by their table. Laraline took a deep breath before continuing.

"Recently I've been seeing things. There are still questions concerning Langston's death."

"Well, you've always had good instincts Lynn, for the most part. Where are your girls now?"

Laraline took a sip of her tea before she answered. "Close."

"Ah, the protective mother hen!"

"I'm not stupid, I know the minute we hit town, their scent will be recognized immediately, and they will be easy prey!"

Eveline took another sip of tea. "I need to talk to my sister about this matter, and then I will relay it to the Bransons."

"Branson, that's a name I have not heard in ages. Will this complicate the truce?"

"Not any more than what it already is."

"Of course."

"My dear, your concern shouldn't be with Avis and his unruly brood, but your Aunt Sirenna."

"Do you think she will agree?"

"Well, Sirenna is a bit like a loud dog. Regardless, bring the girls tomorrow around 4pm for supper."

"Supper? Are you sure?"

"You do still remember the house?"

"Auntie, please!"

"I was just checking. Everything should be sorted out by the time we finish supper."

"Thank you, Aunt Evie!"

"Don't thank me just yet, if I know Sirenna, she will want a quid pro quo!"

Laraline let out a labored sigh. "Like what?"

"I'm sure she will let you know, my dear."

Chapter 4: The Waking Echo

The clearing in the forest was covered with autumn leaves. The ground was a red and orange carpet with patches of green showing through. Walking over the crunchy floor, she noticed that the leaves gradually morphed into feathers. She was treading through a literal ocean of feathers, barefoot.

The farther she walked, the deeper they got. At one point she was knee-deep in discarded damp feathers. Almost impulsively, her hand reached out and grabbed at a random clump of feathers at her knees. They were large and vibrant. At close inspection, it appeared as if every single one had been hand-plucked from a live carcass. Several of the plumage tips were covered in dried blood, and in some cases, bits of flesh were still attached. In fact, the sky seemed to be raining feathers of red, yellow, orange, and brown. The breeze was slightly chilly as she got her barring on her surroundings.

About twenty yards at the edge of the clearing stood a woman adorned in a gown covered in white ruffled feathers. This startled Willet. The woman's face was pale, almost white as she got closer. So faded was her complexion that her facial features were almost nonexistent. The thing that drew Willet's attention were her eyes. They were black pools of night, an empty darkness. It was as if she contained no soul to speak of. Her lips were equally black and callous, as her tongue obscenely protruded outward to moisten the dryness.

As they made eye contact, the other seemed to beckon. Willet felt an uncontrollable urge to approach her. The black lips hid a slight grin at the corners, as she waited patiently. Her arms stretched out in Willet's direction. The other's long bony fingers reached out in her direction. They were almost talon-like in their appearance. A chill swept up Willet's spine.

A large draft of feathers parted the ground between the two. There was now a clear open path, exposing the naked red dirt beneath. The ground was blood red, as if violent crimes had been suddenly exposed from beneath an ocean of feathers. The ground was damp and squishy to her feet. Her toes were stained crimson as she crossed the threshold to where the strange woman stood.

Suddenly a voice from within her spoke, defiantly, against her own body. She stopped walking toward the feathered nymph. She looked directly into the other's face and verbally responded. "No!"

Shock animated the woman's face. Even from her lifeless eyes, there seemed to be a glint of discouragement. The edge of her mouth curled in a kind of coiled grimace. A measured sense of rage overcame her face, as from under the surface, a low gargling growl started to emerge from her pale throat.

Instinctively, she began to back away from the wood nymph. No sooner had she begun to distance herself from the situation, the other opened its mouth and began to scream. At first, it was a low guttural growl. However, it very quickly morphed into a long high-pitched squeal.

The sound was so piercing that Willet had to cover her ears. At first, it almost resembled a screaming bird in pain, then gradually changed into something like a woman's scream. When Willet opened her eyes, she could still hear a faint remnant of screaming. She rose from the couch in a daze. The scream trailed off. In that moment, she wasn't sure if the dream had awakened her, or an actual scream had woken her. As she came to her senses, the room was silent. The only difference was Adelie. She was now awake, sitting up looking just as perplexed. Her long red hair draped over her sweaty confused face. She eyed Willet in a panic.

"What was that?"

Willet had a pit in her stomach. "You heard it too?"

Perhaps there was a real scream. She rose to her feet as she looked about the room. She was almost sure the sound came from one of the rooms to the left of them.

Adelie was afraid. "Where's mom?"

"She stepped out. She went to bring back some food."

Willet eyed the door, as she hurried across the room to the window. The sky outside was dim, the night was quickly approaching. The parking lot was empty, save for three cars. A sky-blue Volkswagen, a dark velvet red Oldsmobile with feathered flames on the side, and some souped-up lime green monster truck. Mom's car was still gone.

Willet could still sense something. She wasn't sure. She looked back at the door and an eerie feeling overcame her. A voice deep inside spoke.

That direction!

She was sure Adelie could sense it too, but she lacked a curious nature. Willet quickly strolled across the room. She unlocked the door and stuck her head out. There was a familiar scent in the hallway. It reminded her of the woods. Where was that smell coming from? It was not a strong smell. The daily odor of old bleach and stale cinnamon air fresheners dominated the air. It was the scent beneath the scents, which was unusual.

She closed her eyes and inhaled. A light breeze of the hallway air conditioner chilled her ears and face. There was something else. She could barely smell it. It was very subtle and slowly dissipating. She was going to lose the scent.

"What are you doing, Willie?"

Adelie was standing at the door now, with her arms folded, and she was shivering because of the cold air.

"I'm taking a peek and stop calling me Willie!"

"I don't think this is a good idea. I think we should just stay here quietly and keep the door locked until Mom gets back!"

Willet, of course, ignored what she said and countered with, "Hey, keep the door locked, I'll be right back."

"Back? Where are you going?"

"I'm just going to check the walkway. I'll be right back!"

Willet was out the door and down the hall just as she heard the muffled voice of Adelie say something. She had to get going quickly to pick up the scent. It was already starting to fade, so she had to hurry. As soon as she had first opened the door into the hallway, she could smell the familiar scent of something wild. Like an animal.

Now that she was walking down the hallway, she was starting to smell it clearer. The scent behind the wild scent was also familiar but in a darker way. She could smell the slight hint of fresh blood. This intrigued her.

She was like her father in that respect. She was fearless, according to her mother. At a time like this, she would say it was stupidity. There was the slightest germ of an idea, near the back of her mind. It told her that her current actions might be a tad reckless. Here she was, alone in a long dark hallway, in a seedy coastal motel, investigating the scent to a mysterious scream.

As she headed further, she was able to pick up the scent again. She was getting closer. She wasn't wrong, it was fresh blood. She knew that sweet pungent smell very well. Around the scent was an even stronger smell of something else wild. As she passed the doors, she read the numbers to herself, 124, 126, 128. When she got to 130, the scent was the strongest. She stopped in front of the door.

This is where the scream came from! Now what Sherlock?

No sooner had she come to this sobering realization, than she felt movement from the other side of the door. Whomever it was had become aware of her presence. A male voice whispered from behind the door.

"I think someone's at the door!"

A woman's voice responded, "Are you sure?"

Willet panicked and quickly ran back down the hallway, to her room. The door was still open, as Adelie hadn't yet got up to lock it. Thank heavens for her inept laziness. Willet quickly ran inside and quietly pushed the door shut. She even put the deadbolt on. She then slid down against the door, trying not to hyperventilate.

"What's going on?"

Willet had her finger over her mouth emphatically. "Quiet!"

Adelie reacted immediately. She curled up in the corner of the bed clutching her covers, wide-eyed and visibly shaken. The room was suddenly silent and for a moment, Willet thought that everything was ok. She had probably overreacted, she told herself.

Then she heard the footfalls in the hallway. They were definitely coming from the direction of room 130. They were faint, but Willet could hear the sounds behind the sounds. The impatient breathing from the nostrils. The deliberate pace of the boots silently walking, followed by a strange fluttering sound.

Perhaps they are just leaving the room. They could be just leaving.

However, these hopes were quickly dashed, as she could hear their footfalls stop right in front of her door. Whomever they were, they were just waiting right outside the door. The scent of wildness filled Willet's nostrils. That familiar aroma of fresh blood tickled the air again. Willet winced in fear almost gagging, as she could taste the metallic flavor.

It was the guy from room 130. He was standing right outside of the door. She could hear a hint of controlled breathing and beneath that; she could hear the sound of slight rustling again.

What do they want?

Willet and Adelie were as silent as church mice, as they waited. At one point she could feel someone pressing their ear against the other side of the door listening.

He wants me to know he knows!

The faint sound of a woman's voice hissed down the hall. "Let's just get out of here!"

There was a sudden shift in mood as if the one at the door was acknowledging the comment. Willet was just about to exhale relief when there came an obscene ripping sound sliding down the front of the door.

Willet winced in horror, as Adelie began to reach for the phone. Suddenly the sound stopped. Other than that, there was complete silence. There was no way to be sure if someone was still outside the door.

Both girls stayed frozen for several minutes, debating whether to get up and check the door. At one point, Willet thought she heard some activity in the parking lot. However, she was too afraid to move.

Adelie held the phone in midair as if debating whether to call. Neither girl was certain if the stalker had left their door yet. Several minutes passed before the dial tone started to beep. Adelie's eyes widened in horror, as she quickly clicked the sound off. She could feel Willet looking at her accusingly.

Adelie responded by mouthing the words. *Still there?*

Willet had to admit, she had no idea. Whoever this guy was, he was a lot harder to read than most. She carefully rose to her feet and looked out the peephole. The hallway looked empty. The thought entered her mind, why didn't she just look out earlier, to see who was scratching at the door?

Cause he would have anticipated that you idiot!

Willet still wasn't completely sure he wasn't just waiting at the side of the door. Perhaps the scream was harmless. It didn't necessarily mean anything. If that was the case, then why was she and her sister hiding in a hotel room with the door locked?

Perhaps she should call the front desk and report the incident. They could not have been the only ones to hear that scream. Perhaps someone already reported him. Maybe this person just got a complaint and thought I reported him. *Crap!* When Willet's brain started to go, there was no stopping her.

Adelie bolstered her courage and this time audibly addressed Willet, who was crouching at the door, like a caged cat.

"Is it safe?"

"I dunno, maybe."

"Who was it?"

"The neighbor, a few doors down."

"What did you do to them?"

"Nothing, I didn't even knock on the door!"

"What?"

"They heard me at the door, and they literally came after me!"

"Oh my god. I wonder if they murdered someone over there!"

"That thought entered my mind!"

Adelie turned back to the phone and pressed a button.

"What the hell are you doing?"

"I'm calling the police!"

Willet was quick with her reflexes, as she leaped like a cat across the room. Her hand was on the receiver in a flash, as she snatched the phone from her sister.

"Think, all we have is a scream. It could have been as innocent as two people being intimate. I mean there was a woman with him because I did hear a woman's voice too!"

"You don't believe that. I know you, Willie!"

"What I believe, and what we can prove are two different things. However, we could call housekeeping and say we are concerned about the neighbors."

"Maybe we should wait till mama gets back, maybe she'll know what to do."

"You really think Mama's going to fix everything? She's done a stellar job so far!"

At that moment, the door handle turned slightly. Willet quickly cupped her sister's mouth and pointed to the door. Someone was trying to get inside. The door clicked open until it snapped against the chain. Adelie's voice wavered. "Who is it?"

"It's me. Open the door Adelie!"

"Mama, is that you?"

"Of course, who else could it be?"

Willet was silent, as Adelie went to unlock the door. The temperament of her mother's voice sounded a bit abrasive. She was beyond irritated. She was pissed.

Perhaps she heard what I said about her, right before she came inside. Maybe it was the errand she had run or the meeting didn't go as planned. Whatever the reason she seemed rather aggravated. Well, at least the weirdo from 130 appeared to have left the hallway!

Adelie popped open the lock and Laraline stepped inside with two bags of warm takeout. She took two steps inside and plopped the bags down on the bed. The bed that Adelie had ruffled.

No sooner had she relieved her cargo when she scanned the faces of both girls. "Ok, now what is the meaning of the door?"

Willet was in defense mode. "What?"

"We don't have the money for room damage!"

Both Adelie and Willet looked at each other in confusion.

Adelie was back to her usual vocal self. "What on earth are you talking about, ma?"

Laraline walked and pretended not to see their shocked expressions. She passed Adelie and pulled the door wide open for the girls to see the source of her irritation.

Willet gasped in horror as the front of their room door revealed four distinct slits dug into the wood of the door alongside the keyhole. What was scary to Willet, was the fact that the arrangement of the markings very much resembled claw marks.

Chapter 5: The Last Supper

As the girls explained what had happened while she was gone, Laraline's expression drastically changed. It became more somber and concerned. Willet could hear her mother's heartbeat. It was manic, and she was definitely bothered. As they finished their tale, Laraline calmly rose to her feet and looked sternly at both girls.

"Ok, Wait here."

"Mom don't!" Willet reached for her mother instinctively.

"Don't worry, I can take care of myself. A lot more than either of you two may realize."

There was something different about her demeanor. Even the gaze in her eye was almost alien. Her pupils appeared dilated and her eyebrows course and thick. In a low gravelly tone, she almost hissed at her children like a venomous snake. "Keep the door shut, I'll be right back!"

As she reached to pull the door shut behind her, her fingers seemed long and menacing as her long nails gave the slight appearance of talons. As the door closed, there was a deafening silence in the room. Willet was sure Adelie witnessed what she had, but neither spoke of it. Instead, they listened to the hallway nervously waiting, anticipating, and wondering what their mother could surely do.

Out of the silence, they heard an expected knock on the neighbor's door.

Willet was nonplussed. *Is she actually going to confront them? What is she going to say? Excuse me sir, but your screaming freaked out my two geeky daughters. How embarrassing!*

So, they waited in anticipation to hear a response at the door, ...and they waited ...and they waited some more.

Luckily for Willet, there wasn't a response. Whoever had been there was long gone. According to what Mom said, it was just as well, on the off chance they were criminals or something. There was such a dark mystique about the room's occupants, and Willet had no idea what they had looked like.

When their mother returned, she appeared normal again. Her eyes seemed as warm and inviting as ever. Her hands seemed thin and soft, not long and menacing. However, her demeanor remained changed. In fact, after that evening, everything was about to change.

Willet would always remember that last night at the hotel. It would be the last glimpse of the normal life she'd had while her father was still alive. Laraline unpacked the takeout bags, and they all began to partake of Asian rice noodles and tofu. Willet had decided earlier that year she was vegan, and the idea of animal flesh was gross.

Willet looked about the room and before she realized what she was saying, the words just popped out. "I wish Daddy was here!"

Laraline looked intently at her daughter and cleared her throat. "I do too."

Adelie had just slurped up a very noisy-sounding noodle when she thankfully changed the conversation. "So, what's the plan tomorrow, ma?"

Suddenly an uncomfortable expression overcame Laraline. Willet recognized that look. Whenever she had some bad news, she would start off with those five cryptic words. It was how she informed them about their father's death.

Laraline cleared her throat. "Girls, we need to talk."

Adelie could sense the fear in her mother's voice. She could also see that she was trying to hide whatever she was dealing with.

"About what mama?"

"About us and what our plans are going forward. I didn't want to say too much until things were more concrete."

Willet interjected. "Is this about the business you had today?"

Laraline gave her a nod. "Yes, dear. I had to see a woman today, who has promised to help us."

Willet glared at her mother "Help us! Are we in some kind of trouble?"

Ignoring Willet's outburst, Laraline continued to explain. "She has a place we can stay, but I need you two to be open and not make waves. They can be a bit religious and there are a few rules."

Willet groaned. "Great, are they Amish?"

Adelie looked up from her food. "Where is this place?"

"Actually, it's not far from here. There is a small hamlet called Meadowlark Downs."

Willet perked up, as she recognized the name from the brochure she had found earlier that day while napping. She looked over at the couch to see if she could find the pamphlet. However, in all the excitement, she forgot where it was.

Laraline continued, "We will be heading there tomorrow afternoon after checkout!"

Adelie appeared disturbed. "So, we travel halfway around the world to live in a strange remote unknown village."

"It's remote and strange, compared to the outside world. But it's far from unknown. I grew up there."

Willet seemed overwhelmed. "Who are these people?"

"The woman I met with was one of my aunts."

"So, we have family. Why didn't you tell us? I thought you said you were an orphan."

"My parents died when I was still an infant, so my aunts took me in and raised me."

"You've kept that a secret, all this time!"

"It's not that simple. I had a falling out with my family, so I left and promised never to return... until I talked to Aunt Evie yesterday. I thought she wouldn't even see me."

"What happened?"

Laraline was quite candid. "They disapproved of your father!"

It was silent as both girls took in what she was saying. Willet's mind flooded with questions, but before she could ask, her mother changed the conversation. When Laraline was done talking about something, she was done. Her father's voice popped into her head. *When momma is done talking, let it go, until the time is right!*

Almost intuitively, piggybacking on Willet's internal conversation, Laraline added. "Enough about tomorrow. Tonight, we have two more orders of Moo Goo Gi Pan and a single order of vegetable Lo-Mein to get through. Come on, eat up girls. This is our last official supper of road trip takeout!"

Chapter 6: Welcome to Meadowlark Downs

M eadowlark felt remarkably ordinary, at first glance; it had a rustic almost aristocratic feel. Most of the streets were brown and tan cobblestone, as thick plump shrubbery adorned the sides of the walkways and building fronts. Every corner seemed to have an antique oil-fueled streetlight. The buildings were vintage rustic brown and red English Tudor-style structures peppered with pale or off-white trim.

This place was entrenched in old money. The type of money that spanned not only decades but centuries. The residents were dressed well, yet simple and casual. Adelie noticed they were really into earthy colors. As one of her interests was fashion design, she would know. There seemed to be a distinct air of self-importance among the residences that they passed. Father would say they were pompous. On a certain level, he would be right, but there was something else.

As they rode through the town, Willet and Adelie could feel the vibe immediately. Under the surface, it felt like an invisible veil covering the entire area. There was an instant feeling of deception. As the crappy-looking Impala drifted down the fancy exotic streets, many residents stopped to stare. Driving this car, they might as well be wearing signs that said "poor, low-class strangers". Adelie and Laraline wore brave faces, smiling and pretending not to notice. Willet was a bit more confrontational. She would stare back and occasionally glare. She was used to being labeled "inferior" in school and had acquired tough skin.

However, there was something a bit different here. She recognized that many of the looks were cold and indifferent. They were obviously being judged by the car, but there was an expression

28

behind the stare Willet couldn't quite decipher. It was almost as if they weren't surprised. It felt as if their arrival was almost expected.

As they reached the heart of the town, Willet began to recognize a familiar scent. It was the wild animal smell from the hotel. *Oh my god, that creep is a resident of this town.* She stuck her head out the window to get a better whiff. Where was it coming from? The Impala reached a roundabout. As they made their way around it, Willet realized that it wasn't coming from any one place. In fact, from what she could tell, there were hints and variations of that scent in every direction. *Perhaps it's a popular upstate body wash or cologne!*

"Willet, what in the world are you doing hanging out of the car?"

"I thought I could smell that weirdo from the hotel!"

"Please get back inside. You look ridiculous!"

"I don't give a flip about what any of these stuck-up morons think about me!"

"Well, I do, sit back down!"

She uneasily complied, as she was forced to remain seated. With her arms folded she started to speak in a very loud and obnoxious manner about her mother. "The red queen is very insistent!"

Laraline rolled her eyes. "Please stop that, Willet!"

Adelie chimed in next. "Yeah, you ain't no poet, Willie!"

Willet glared at Adelie. "Shut your dumb pie hole!"

After they passed beyond the roundabout, Mother slammed on the brakes. "Please, you both promised me."

Adelie quickly acknowledged, "Yes ma'am."

Laraline looked at Willet, who was now, brooding. "Willet!"

"I'm not joking. I could smell that creep. He is here, in this town!"

Instead of trying to reassure her daughter as Willet had expected, Laraline's response was unexpected. "Well, I'm sure you did, you have an incredible gift, as does your sister. However, that doesn't change anything!"

"Yes, it does, it changes everything!"

"No, it doesn't. You have a faceless man, whom you don't know who he is. At the same time, he has never seen anyone in this car. This man, you believe, may or may not be involved in something nefarious. Does that about sum up your concerns?"

Her explanation was so practical that Willet could do nothing but sit quietly and contemplate what was just said. She was right, there was no way of knowing what they had "actually" heard.

"Could you please try, Willet?"

She dryly responded. "Ok."

Laraline quickly changed the subject. "Well, what do you girls think of this place?"

Willet looked about in silence with uneasiness on her face.

Laraline glanced at her. "There is the cutest little coffee shop around the corner called Linnet's. When I was your age, it was the local hangout place."

Adelie quickly chimed in excitedly. "Does the whole town look like this?"

Laraline looked back. "Like what?"

Willet interjected. "Like a historical theme park ride."

Adelie finally decided. "I like it, it's cool!"

Willet turned to the back seat. "You have such an economy with words!"

"Thanks!" Adelie looked around oblivious of the sarcasm.

Willet shook her head at the realization that her comment went completely over Adelie's head. Just as quickly as the diss on her sister evaporated, she turned her attention to their route. Her mother suddenly declared as they turned right onto a street called Blue Jay Way, "We're very close!"

"Hey Mama, what's with all the bird-centric themes?"

"So, you noticed."

"You can't help but notice, we are in a town called Meadowlark, we came in on Martin Boulevard and we just turned onto Blue Jay Way!"

Adelie perked up, her interest piqued. "Noticed what?"

"That the folks here are obsessed with birds. Look at all the street names and historical points."

Adelie's response was quick. "Well, you did say it was a bird sanctuary?"

"Yeah, I guess so, but..."

Adelie snarked at Willet. "Why you gotta make something out of everything?"

Laraline was suddenly cross, it was out of the norm for Adelie to be the aggressor with her sister. Usually, Laraline would have perceived this as simple bickering, but there seemed to be a sincere feeling of unease with Willet. This wasn't the usual issue with her life, as her dramatic nature seemed to thrive on. Without even thinking, Laraline snapped at Adelie.

"Leave your sister alone!"

Willet was unusually silent. She didn't even try to defend herself, which was strange. Instead, she just looked ahead at the road in a nervous stupor.

Adelie suddenly turned to her mother. "What is that building?"

"It's a Masjid Temple."

"What religion is that?"

"It's hard to explain. But there are a lot of different types of churches here."

"What do the aunties worship?"

"That's a bit complicated too."

Chapter 7: Greywood Manor

At the entrance of the estate, a large iron gate stood thickly covered with generations of thick coarse ivy that weaved in and out of the long metal spires. The vegetation was so overgrown that one could forget that the gate was originally see-through. Two matching bronze owls stood on the very top of the gate doors. For Willet, this was probably the most distinctive characteristic of the entrance to the entire estate. They almost felt sphinxlike, as they sat perched some 18 to 20 feet high, gazing down at them in the car. From this distance, they seemed to be quaint figurines. However, they were probably closer to human sized.

Willet approximated the actual size, as there was a third owl that stood upright, by the side of the gravel road. The hulking figure stood about 8 feet high and sat at the entrance of the gate. Laraline pulled the car up beside the large bronze owl. On its chest sat an intercom and some buttons. She reached her arm out of the window and quickly pressed one of the buttons.

There was an immediate click, followed by a low buzzing sound. After she had done this, she waited. It was quiet. Adelie mumbled from the back seat. "Maybe nobody's home."

Willet corrected her. "They're home alright, they are just curious about the odd lifeforms at their gate."

Adelie's response was quick. "What are you talking about?"

Willet just looked up at the two owls, who almost seemed to be malevolently smiling down at her. Suddenly there was a voice through the intercom. It sounded old and gravelly, like an old woman who was inconvenienced at having to answer the buzzer at all.

"Yes. Please state your business."

"My name is Laraline Swift, I have..."

However, before she could finish, the voice on the other end cut her off.

"Yes, Lady Adler has been expecting you, please wait for the gate to come to a complete stop before driving your vehicle inside Miss Swift."

"Yes, thank you."

Willet mumbled under her breath. "Wow, how rude."

With her announcement, the gate began to slide open with a dull rumble. The car advanced gradually in compliance. As they passed, Willet looked up at the owls, as if she expected them to flinch. They slowly coasted beyond the threshold, as Willets's focus turned to the vast grounds before them.

It was as if they had stepped into another world. As quaint and aristocratic as the town itself felt, the Greywood Estate was almost alien in comparison. Ahead of them stood a rather imposing structure. Adelie leaned forward until she was almost between both her sister and mother in the front. Her jaw dropped as she saw the actual size of the home.

"Mama, this is a frickin' mansion. What is wrong with you, why didn't you tell us our family is rich?"

"Addie please!"

Willet was also surprised at the sheer size of the Greywood Estate. It was a three-story dwelling that stretched the length of about three large homes with multiple entrances. However, it was also quite old. The entire exterior was constructed with large grey stones. Large archways and exaggerated walkways embellished the outside aesthetics, giving it an almost castle-like vibe. As they coasted down the main cobblestone drive, the girls studied the unusual landscaping that made up the grounds.

Willet carefully eyed the number of peculiar owl statues that littered the grounds. By the time they reached the main entrance, she had counted about nine, not including the two on the gate, and the large standing intercom. If the town wasn't bird centric enough, then this place would suffice.

Laraline finally came to a complete stop and took a deep breath. Willet glanced over at her. Her mother appeared afraid. She reached over and touched her mother's hand to convey some reassurance. She couldn't know what it would be like to be at odds with her entire family, nor did she want to know.

Adelie was already out of the car in a tethered excitement. She was oblivious to the emotional drama back inside of the car. Instead, she was focused on the steps that led to the front door. The entrance was majestic with two large wooden arched doors with actual golden knockers, thus adding to the castle feel.

Laraline smiled at Willet as if trying to reassure her that she was ok when she finally noticed Adelie ascending the steps. Laraline glanced over at Willet.

"I guess your sister has quickly gotten accustomed to the idea of being here."

Willet raised her brow playfully at her mother. "Kids!"

Laraline called after her. "Wait for us, Addie!"

Adelie's response was typical. "Hurry up guys, I'm dying to see inside!"

Adelie reached the top and ran to the door to get a closer look. The double doors were beyond magnificent to her. The wood was dark mahogany with large golden knockers that resembled a pair of bizarre female faces. So expressive were the faces, that they could be mistaken for either convulsing in pain or pleasure, it wasn't clear.

Both doors were flanked with what appeared to be large bronze wings that extended from the door handles up to the frame itself. It was the kind of place that demanded reverence.

Adelie scrunched her face against the sidelights to the right side of the door. The glass was embossed with patterns resembling lush flowers and there appeared to be a frosted tinge. It was kind of hard for Adelie to see anything. She quickly pressed her ear against the sidelight.

Laraline grew impatient. "Stop that, you're going to smudge the glass. Aunt Sirenna is a bit particular about her home!"

However, Adelie was oblivious to her words. As they rushed to join her at the top of the steps, a most curious feather caught Willet's eye. It was a rather large blue feather with yellow spots just lying on the steps. She reached out and plucked it from its resting place on the second to the last step. She held it up to the sky to get a closer look. She had never seen such a large feather. It was brilliant and practically translucent, as a wave of blue light flashed across her face. As she lowered the feather, something caught her eye.

On the third floor, in a window at the right corner of the estate, a curtain closed. Someone was there, watching. Willet felt a chill up her spine. She was about to address the matter with her mother, however her mother seemed preoccupied.

Adelie was notorious for her selective hearing: and was exercising this gift with such mastery that one had to wonder if she were truly deaf.

"Adelie, I know you're excited, but I told you to get away from the door! Answer me now!"

Instead, she responded as if her mother hadn't spoken. "I think I hear birds inside!"

"You heard mama, get off the door, retard!"

Willet took her left foot and gave Adelie a swift kick in her bum, knocking her to her knees a few feet from the door. Willet then quickly stood in her place. She pulled at the doorknocker, letting it fall with a deep echo.

Laraline's eyes blazed at Willet in disapproval.

Adelie rose to her feet confused. "Ouch, what the heck!"

Willet leaned over her. "Earth to moron. While you were flippantly extolling the marvels of the rich, we were gathering all the luggage, including your sorry bags!"

Adelie's teeth were now clenched. "I have your moron here!"

"I dare you!"

Addie's hand was clenched in a tight fist and about ready to swing at Willet's face when the front door suddenly began to creak open. All three visitors stopped and turned their attention to whoever was now at the door.

A small, frail-looking woman poked her head out. She was about Laraline's age, but she carried herself as if she were much older. She was dressed in a formal black dress and her hair was tied up into a bun but was obviously very long. "Yes, how may I help you?"

"Yes, Ms. Weever?"

"Lady Laraline, is that you?" Almost immediately, the formal coldness gave way to a warm embrace by both parties. Willet felt a little better for her mother.

As the two stopped hugging and the older woman apologized. "Pardon me. I didn't recognize you at first. It's been such a long time. Where have you been keeping yourself?"

"The Florida Keys."

"Well, let's take a good look at you, lass."

Ms. Weever stepped back and finally caught a glimpse of Willet and Adelie.

"Whom have you brought home with you, dear?"

"These are my daughters."

"Children?"

Laraline nodded, prideful as a peacock, allowing Ms. Weever to continue to fawn over the revelation.

"My, it has been a long time. I have two daughters around the same age. They would get along well. Will you be staying with us for a while?"

"Well, I'm not sure."

"You're more than welcome. Oh, you can just leave your bags here, I will have someone fetch them. Follow me!"

She opened the door wide, allowing all three visitors to enter. As they entered, a wave of emotions flooded Laraline, almost knocking her backward. Images and memories that she hadn't wanted to remember came rushing back.

The grand foyer was a large room that connected to a long hallway. To the left of the hallway stood a tremendous stairwell leading up. The floor was black and white peppered marble. Rouge-colored walls surrounded them on both sides, while several important artworks littered the length of the long hallway that led to the rest of the downstairs.

The small woman was almost an inch shorter than Willet and about the same size as Adelie. Seeing her daughters standing next to this woman, Laraline realized how quickly her children were growing up. One day they will be women with their own lives, concerns, and troubles.

Within moments of entering, another older woman similarly dressed, ran up to Ms. Weever. She was out of breath as she tried to explain something to her obvious supervisor.

"Ms. Weever, we have a guest at the front entrance."

"You're a little late Mrs. Broom, they are all here!" Ms. Weever stretched her hand in the direction of Laraline.

"Mrs. Broom, this is Lady Swift and her family. They are guests of Lady Adler this evening!"

"Yes Ms. Weever. Nice to meet you, Lady Swift!"

Laraline corrected her. "Mrs. Swift, if you please."

"Mrs. Broom seemed confused. "If you please milady, but I thought..."

Mrs. Weever quickly cut in before Mrs. Broom was able to finish.

"Their bags are on the front porch, fetch them and bring them to their designated rooms."

Adelie murmured excitedly to herself. "Rooms!"

Willet immediately recognized Mrs. Broom's voice from the intercom. Over the intercom, she sounded cold and harsh. Now she was almost weak and groveling face to face. Willet glanced at her profile as she passed by, almost immediately she noticed the most peculiar eyepatch on the woman's left eye. It was thick and completely covered her socket. Slightly peeking out from underneath the gauze appeared to be a couple of thin vertical scars. Willet could smell a hint of fresh blood from the eye patch. It was a fresh wound.

She thought about similar marks she had seen on the hotel door the day before. Her heart suddenly raced. It was too much of a coincidence. For a moment, she wondered if Adelie or her mother noticed the scars. She was lost in thought when she heard her name being spoken as from a dream.

"Willet!"

Suddenly she realized that the others had made their way down the hallway, while she was left still standing at the entrance. Her mother was impatiently summoning her. "Willet, stop lagging!"

Willet quickly sprinted down the long hallway. The squeaky soles of her sneakers seemed to echo up into the manor's unusually high vaulted ceiling.

As they made their way to the entrance of the dining room, they passed a large glass wall. This was a separate room filled with several small trees, bushes, and various kinds of shrubbery. Willet was immediately intrigued, as sounds of chirping seemed to emanate from within.

"What is this place?"

Ms. Weever nodded, and for the first time gave some recognition to Willet.

"This is Greywood Manor's private bird aviary. Perhaps Lady Adler can give you a tour after supper. She is most pleased with it. It took her almost 25 years to construct!"

Adelie triumphantly quipped. "I told you I heard birds!"

Laraline pushed her daughters along as they both were starting to fall behind again. Ms. Weever was at the end of the hall in a large doorway. She waited patiently for them to catch up.

Chapter 8: Dinner Is Served

When they entered the large dining room, there was a feeling of sudden anxiety. Several other formal-looking guests were already seated at a long great mahogany table. Silver and glass-encrusted fine China covered the entirety of its length. All of this is in anticipation of some grand meal that was promised to all the attendees.

The rest of the room was shrouded in shadows. Flickering candles sat snuggly in hidden enclaves on the sides of the surrounding walls. The warm patches of candlelight gave the massive room the eerie ambiance of a dramatic theater house.

Adelie marveled that she had so many relatives whom she had no prior knowledge of. Mrs. Weever led them to their seats. Willet eyed her mother's interactions, as she greeted the various family members she bypassed. Most of them she greeted with a polite nod and cordial smile, while a few she gave a stern look.

Who were these people she had chosen to leave? Unlike most people, Willet was familiar with auras. These particular people were quite unusual to read. She noticed her mother make eye contact with a woman who was sitting on the left end of the table.

Laraline seemed relieved when she spotted the woman, as both acknowledged each other with a smile. The older woman held out her hand to Laraline as if to give support. Willet noticed the odd mood ring on the queen's left hand as she grasped her mother's hand. Before either girl had a chance to ask, the older woman leaned in and introduced herself.

"I'm sure your girls are wondering, whom all these strange people are!"

Willet mumbled to herself. *"You don't know the half of it, sister!"*

Laraline poked the child in the side. The older woman responded. "What was that dear?"

Willet corrected herself. "I mean, we were a bit curious."

"Well for starters, I'm your mother's Aunt Eveline. That makes me your great aunt, I suppose. However, if you want, you can call me Aunt Evie. After all, we are family."

A scruffy, older gentleman, who was sitting beside Willet, snickered. He leaned into her and causally spoke. "Behave now child, mind your p's and q's, you're now in the company of monsters."

Willet was taken aback by this comment.

"What?"

"Yes, look around; you're surrounded by them now."

Willet raised her eyebrows and folded her arms across her chest. "What about you sir?"

"Me? Well of course dear, we are all monsters here at Greywood Manor!"

Willet leaned closer, intrigued by this character. "What kind of monsters?"

"The ugliest kind!"

With that, he took a deep sip from a glass of red wine he appeared to be nursing. As he turned his glass up, Willet saw he had a ring similar to Eveline's. As Willet looked about, she realized that everyone at the table was wearing the same type of ring. She surmised it must be a family thing.

Of all the family, he was the only one not concerned with trying to look proper, with his five o'clock shadow, wrinkled dress suit, and the stench of stale bourbon. Willet pegged him as the family drunk. Every family had one. That one family member who was uninhibited by liquor. Willet remembered something she once heard. The sauce gives some men wings. However, for the life of her, she could not remember where she had heard it before.

Eveline hissed at the drunkard. "Merle, please!"

He continued as if she had not spoken, nodding at the young girl. "Why do you think your mother left this place?"

Eveline was growing irritated at his antics. "I think you have had quite enough to drink."

Merle glanced up, and for a moment he spoke with sincere clarity. "Have I? I don't feel quite numb enough, yet."

Adelie interrupted the awkward exchange, as she eyed the empty chair at the opposite end of the table from Eveline. "Who sits at the other end of the table Aunt Evie, your husband?"

A sneering voice answered before Evie responded. "No child, she doesn't have a husband, she's an old spinster!"

A woman with bright strawberry blonde hair sat leering at them, from the middle of the table. She was a middle-aged-looking, scantily dressed woman. She seemed to be under the illusion that she was still a teenager.

Eveline's response was quick. "Well, I had your husband and he wasn't to my liking, so I told him to give you a shot. I didn't want you to be lonely, dear Patsy."

Almost immediately, the other woman was visibly enraged. The man beside her straightened his tie and pretended not to hear the exchange. Willet and Adelie discreetly exchanged a humorous glance at the savage burn. They half expected the conversation to escalate, however it quickly diffused into dismissive embarrassment and silence.

Adelie curiously pressed Eveline. "Well, who does sit in that chair?"

"That seat belongs to my twin sister, Sirenna!"

"Twin sister, does she look like you?"

"No, we are quite different."

"What was our grandmother like?"

Eveline glanced at Laraline before she spoke.

"Oriole was a whirlwind. She was the eldest by two years and she was, as you say, the total package."

"What happened?"

Laraline gave Eveline a look and quickly interjected. "Can we change the subject?"

Eveline took her cue and continued. "Anyway, my twin Sirenna and I have been running the family business for years!"

The drunkard beside Willet snapped. "Speak of the devil, it's her royalship now!"

Willet spun around to see a tall thin woman carefully entering the room. She was dressed in a red evening gown that seemed to squeeze her every curve. She was an older woman who had the distinct features of a faded model or beauty queen. A looker even by today's standards and under the right circumstances could attract most men. Her bleach-blond hair was tightly wound up in a type of ceremonial bun called a casque. This gave her a slightly proper and pompous air.

Walking beside her was a short and stubby old woman dressed in shawls and various silk wraps. She reminded Willet of an old gypsy. Large rose-colored glasses covered her eyes. Several beads and symbols dangled about her neck. The old woman carried a knobby-looking walking stick. The type that had tree knots and carvings all over the neck.

There was a chair drawn to the right of the empty throne. It was obviously for the old gypsy. The blonde woman in red politely waited for the older woman to sit down first. She treated this older person with such reverence that her polite actions would soon contradict the behavior to shortly come.

There was a cold alluring vibe about her, like a serpent. As she made her way to the table, she tossed a curious glance in Laraline's direction. She quickly studied them, sizing up her newfound relatives.

Willet felt an instant chill in the air. As she looked at the groups' reaction, she got the sense that they were all afraid of this woman, save for Auntie Evie and the strange old gypsy woman, who was leaning back in her chair, with a rather large pipe snickering.

Willet leaned in the direction of Eveline, who seemed to be the one family member that was somewhat approachable.

"Who is that little old woman, is she your mother?"

"Arke no! That is Mother Sephora Hazel. She was a childhood nanny, and she is our house weaver."

"A what?"

"A spiritual adviser. All the great houses have one."

Willet was intrigued. "Great houses?"

Laraline cut Eveline off discreetly. "My girls don't come from this world."

"Well, dear niece, they are living in this one for the time being. You may want to get them up to speed!"

Adelie seemed oblivious of the conversation, as she looked at the quirky relatives around her. There was a young girl around their age sitting beside the woman that Eveline had words with earlier. She seemed bored and aloof.

Willet looked at both women trying to figure out the words behind the words. She knew, at that moment, her mother was still keeping a lot from them. She suddenly felt a twinge of anger and fear.

Mrs. Weever and Mrs. Broom returned to the dining area with two large serving carts. Each woman operated one side of the table. In this way, both Eveline and Sirenna received their food at the same time. Within moments, each guest was served a large silver tray, with a silver lid.

Willet looked toward the new arrival. She was obviously in charge. They didn't even serve the food until she had arrived.

Sirenna sat like some perched bird studying all her guests. She gave a few curious glances in Laraline's direction. She then locked eyes with Willet, as if she could sense the young girl watching. Willet quickly looked away.

Sirenna's deep green eyes were almost calculating, as her gaze shifted to every dinner guest. After a long uncomfortable pause, she finally picked up her glass and addressed the table.

"Welcome family and friends. Thank you for joining us this evening. For years, Eveline and I have entertained many dinners over the years, yet none as significant as this. As you know, we have finally secured the permits for the fishing rights off the boardwalk. A congratulation goes to my little sister's husband Norris for securing that impressive deal, huzzah!"

There was an uncomfortable hush, amongst a flurry of initial applause.

"What, did I say something?"

Pasty gave her big sister a patronizing look. "You know that isn't his name, I've been married for seventeen years, and still you choose to disrespect my marriage. No wonder this one left." She glanced briefly in Laraline's direction.

Sirenna motioned to the man sitting quietly by Patsy. "Sorry Norman!"

"His name is Nester!"

"Excuse me, perhaps if you had married someone a bit more interesting, I wouldn't forget the poor fellow's name. Of course, when one has to get hitched in a hurry, that doesn't give one many choices!"

Patsy mumbled something under her breath as Sirenna continued.

"Seventeen years, that is a cause for celebration. Oh, don't you have a child roughly the same age. Isn't that a happy coincidence!"

Patsy looked beet red and embarrassed. "You monster!"

"Where is dear Phoebe, now I can tell the family resemblance. I wasn't sure at first."

Merle took another sip before he blurted out. "Well, I can tell!"

"You're not as drunk as you seem brother. I believe you are right. I can tell too. I can tell by the slope of her narrow beady eyes, and she has the same pinched bottom lip as her mother."

Eveline finally interjected. "Sister, you have made your point!"

Patsy declared defiantly to the rest of the crowd

"My Phoebe is a suitable heir to the Adler Dynasty. She is of proper breeding, and she is beautiful! She already has offers from Vogue and Teen magazine!"

Phoebe, who had finally acknowledged that her name was spoken, perked up and almost froze into a model-type pose. To Willet, she reminded her of one of those cheap, glamour-shot models in the back of magazines.

Sirenna responded dryly. "Suitable, she has the intelligence of a dead fish. I sometimes try to forget that you hatched this one from your womb!"

Phoebe snapped back at the older woman. "Well, I'm still beautiful!"

"I rest my case!"

Eveline called out from across the room. "I think you're quite finished!"

"Am I, sister?"

"As many of you know, many years ago, our niece lost her way, and now she appears to have found her way back to the Greywood. She has returned as a leech, not unlike the lot of you. Give a toast to the prodigal child's return. This is almost a prestigious occasion. Huzzah!"

Everyone complied and lifted their glasses. "Huzzah!"

Laraline was visibly irritated. This was not missed by Sirenna, who seemed rather bemused by her reaction.

"You seem bothered, dear niece; would you care to say grace?"

She spoke slow and soft. "You go ahead."

Sirenna then responded. "Yetik Arke, over all your children, thanks for the blessing of these lost souls who have returned to your table. Blessed bounty!"

As soon as she finished, the whole table repeated the last phrase. "Blessed bounty!"

Laraline was noticeably silent as if trying to control herself. She finally responded, attempting to sound reserved and calm, although she was visibly shaken. "I'm not lost."

"What was that dear?"

Laraline raised her voice, trying to remain respectful. "I am not lost, nor was I lost. In the time I have been gone, I have raised two beautiful daughters."

"Yes, I noticed you invited your brood for dinner!"

Eveline snapped. "I invited them. I wanted to see my nieces!"

Sirenna responded. "Of course you did, sister."

Eveline continued to lobby. "She has come all this way, please don't embarrass her."

Sirenna's expression was cold. "She must ask!"

The room remained silent.

Laraline rose to her feet and looked at her aunt perched at the other end of the table.

Sirenna sat with her wine glass, an almost sneering grin under the surface, waiting in anticipation for Laraline to speak.

Laraline's voice wavered and cracked as she spoke. "Please Aunt Sirenna, I request sanctuary for myself and my daughters!"

"If you need my sanctuary, then you *are* lost. Why else would you come back here groveling for a place to live?"

Laraline lowered her head. "Yes, Auntie!"

"Well, I haven't decided yet, have a seat."

As her mother obeyed Sirenna's command, Willet felt rage boil in her gut. She stood from her chair and glared at the older woman. "Who do you think you are?"

Sirenna passively looked in her direction, not quite processing what was happening. "Excuse me, are you talking to me?"

"Listen Miss High and Mighty, when is it customary to insult a grieving widow? I thought you were supposed to be someone important. To my observations, you are nothing more than a common bully!"

The entire room fell silent. All eyes looked from the young waif, and back to the matriarch who was momentarily shocked. This shock gave way to incensed anger. She spoke deep and slow, her breath measured as if daring the girl to repeat herself. "What did you say to me?"

"I believe you heard me fine, Miss Fancy Pants!"

"What is your name child?"

"You already know my name, I'm sure you have made a point of studying everything about us before we even stepped onto your property!"

This response took Sirenna off guard a bit. Yet, her response was extremely calm and cold.

"Aren't you afraid of what may happen to your family? It is my understanding that the Swifts don't have many financial options before them these days."

Patsy cackled at this remark as she took a sip of wine.

Willet was unaffected, as she responded. "A threat. Why am I not surprised? I'm sure that you plan to hold that over my mother for obedience, just as you seem to do over everyone at this table."

Willet gave a cold glance at Patsy who quickly stopped, as if she had been called out again.

Sirenna could have burned holes into Willet with her eyes. "Insolence! You hold your tongue child!"

"Hold my tongue? Why, so you can slowly rip it from my mouth? I suppose I will no longer have a voice of my own, then I can become a little obedient slave!"

Sirenna countered. "A mute one would be more to my liking!"

"Sorry, I can't help you there, lady!"

Laraline finally shook herself into action. "Willet, please stop!"

Sirenna finally addressed Laraline. "So, niece, am I to believe this insolent child is one of your spawn?"

Laraline was in tears, as she saw her daughter try to buck up to Sirenna. The plan to relocate to Meadowlark was unraveling and Willet was the cause. Willet suddenly stopped talking, realizing what she had just done, yet she remained standing.

Sirenna spoke carefully to Willet as if trying to control unhinged rage. "You certainly have a lot to say. In all my years of running this estate, I have never had someone stand before me, at my own dinner table and talk to me as if they were my equal."

Willet glared back. "I am your equal!"

The room was dead silent. The two stared each other down for several moments until the old gypsy woman who had entered the dining hall with Sirenna burst out into maniacal laughter.

The old woman was almost choking with amusement by the situation.

Suddenly, like symmetry, so did Sirenna. They both looked at each other and exploded with an obnoxious cackling that chilled Willet. Like a bizarre domino effect, the entire room broke into laughter, except Willet's mother, sister, and Auntie Eveline, who had moved closer to Laraline and proceeded to comfort her, obviously trying to calm her down.

Willet looked from face to face at the table laughing at the rather absurd moment. Perhaps it was just that moment when things were so tense: you need to laugh to keep from crying. Suddenly her head was swimming at the surreal scene.

Sirenna's voice bellowed across the room. "Silence, the food is getting cold!"

The table was instantly quiet again. Everyone suddenly complied. Willet looked at how they responded, just like puppets. The entire dinner party was now eating their meals in obedient silence.

Sirenna finally addressed Willet. This time her voice was candid, yet uninterested. "Mind your manners child, we are eating. Have a seat."

Her mother echoed the sentiment with a painful whisper. "Willet, please sit down!"

Willet looked around the room confused, wondering what had just happened, yet she quietly stood. Eveline leaned in and whispered to the bemused girl. "Let it go and sit down now!"

Sirenna eyed her directly as the young girl struggled with a need to defy her. "I suggest you listen to your mother; you have already caused your family enough pain. You don't want to cause them anymore!"

This time, Willet felt a direct threat from the older woman, she looked across at Adelie, whose face was flushed, and her head was down. She looked to her mother for answers. Laraline was too embarrassed to look up. Instead, she quietly just repeated her aunt's sentiment. "Please, sit down and eat your food, Willet!"

Realizing the futility of her stand, Willet slowly sat down. She was so upset she could hardly look up.

Mrs. Weever and Mrs. Broom began removing the silver lids to expose the main course. Mrs. Broom was wearing a fresh gauze over her eye. Willet noticed that her cousin Phoebe made a point to thank Mrs. Broom for the dish. For some reason, this seemed to make Mrs. Broom visibly agitated.

Willet gasped in horror as the silver lids were removed. It was some sort of strange fish. One she had never seen before. It was similar to a Salmon, but it had what appeared to be a fleshy horn on its head. And yes, it was the whole fish, head to fins, all lying atop a bed of vegetation.

Merle grinned to himself. "I love Knook fish, and it's fresh today!"

"What is Knook fish?"

He reached into his tray and using his fingers, dug into the flesh. It almost seemed to wince.

Willet reacted. "It's still alive?"

Uncle Merle had a bloody mouthful of flesh in his mouth as he responded. "Of course, it's better that way!"

No one was looking at Willet or her family anymore. Instead, all the dinner guests were hungrily eating, as they had been commanded. They seemed like a pack of crazed animals attacking their food.

Willet glanced over at Adelie who was holding a piece of meat in her palms. Her fingers were stained red, as she turned over the dripping carcass. A pool of blood had formed on her plate.

For some reason, Willet had lost her appetite.

Chapter 9: Desserts and Other Nightly Confessions

T he dinner had started winding down and Willet was still a bit nervous from the confrontation she'd had earlier with her great aunt. She had made her stand, but as a result, her stomach was in knots, and she had barely eaten anything. She had been veering toward a more vegan diet, so she was not big on the dinner selection.

Regardless of her appetite, her mind could not focus on the meal, but on the feeling of an uneasy limbo. Because she attempted to defend her mother, tomorrow was uncertain. After a bit, Mrs. Weever came in to help clean the table.

Sirenna finally addressed her servant. "Mrs. Weever, where is Mrs. Broom?"

"Lady Adler, she had to go to the doctor after she served dinner; her eye is in a bad way!"

Sirenna sighed to herself. "Oh, while you are here, show our guests to their rooms. Let them get acclimated to our unique habitat!"

"Yes, Lady Adler!"

Sirenna turned to Evelyn. "Evelyn, I understand that you have arranged for the children to meet the headmistress at Talomore on Thursday. I believe the new semester starts next week. Perhaps a semester or so at a proper finishing school will teach them manners." Everyone seemed in shock, given Sirenna's disposition earlier. "Well, do not just stand there. We have a busy day tomorrow!"

Evelyn nodded trying to hide a deep relieved grin. Laraline and both girls hopped up and quickly followed behind Mrs. Weever. They dared not look at Sirenna as they passed, in case she changed her mind. However, Willet could feel the gaze of the old gypsy woman. She glanced up; Sirenna and the old woman were staring at her. She was terrified and quickly looked away. She heard the old woman snicker. Willet suddenly felt unsafe and wished Aunt Sirenna had expelled them from Greywood Manor after all.

As soon as they got into the hallway, Adelie ripped into her older sister. "Well, we can stay here, no thanks to you and your big mouth!"

"I'm sorry. I didn't like the way she was treating us, especially mom!"

Laraline jumped to her daughter's defense, hugging Willet close. "It's water under the bridge, sweetie! I'm just glad everything worked out!"

Laraline was still deeply disturbed by the situation. For some reason, it seemed to her, that Sirenna actually gave them a chance because of Willet's defiance. This scared Laraline.

Back inside the dining room. The two matriarchs sat alone at opposite ends of the table. Sirenna took a sip of her wine and closed her eyes. Evelyn looked at Sirenna suspiciously.

"What game are you playing sister?"

"Game? Whatever are you talking about?"

"Stop it, Laraline is family!"

"I thought you, of all people, would be overjoyed that I agreed to let that harlot niece of mine and her two lek offspring stay!"

Eveline frowned.

Sirenna caught her sister's expression and dismissed it quickly. "Oh please, they will be called worse than that when the town folk find out they are here."

Sirenna paused for a moment as if carefully considering what she was about to say before she continued. "The eldest child does share a striking resemblance."

It felt like the elephant in the room. "Is that what the night's production was all about, revenge?"

"Production! That child was trying to insult me at my own party!"

Evelyn looked at her sister candidly. "And having a pretty good go at it. She is not like her mother at all. Slinging petty insults and bullying won't work on her."

Sirenna seemed offended. "Petty! You must have me mistaken for little Patsy!"

Evelyn changed the subject. "Speaking of Patsy, I'm surprised you didn't rip into her tonight harder than you did."

Sirenna acknowledged her. "Well, maybe I'm learning to be the bigger person. I have learned to be more sympathetic with my baby sister. What about you darling, a little birdy told me that Patsy went after you again before I arrived!"

"I was very civil!"

Sirenna raised her wine glass triumphantly. "Good for you, darling!"

"If this isn't about revenge, what's it about?"

Sirenna leaned back into her chair and stared up at the ceiling. She took a deep breath and whispered to her sister. "Providence!"

By the time Mrs. Weever led the guests to their rooms, it was starting to become dusk. The time had passed by a lot quicker than they had anticipated. As she led the way to the rooms on the second floor, Willet looked upward to the third-floor balcony. Mrs. Weever, sensing the young girl's curiosity, explained.

"The Adler twins both have bedrooms on the third floor. Uncle Merle sleeps in the outside guest cottage. Mother Hazel is in the first-floor guest room. All your quarters are on the second floor."

Willet still managed to find a question that the woman had not answered.

"Is there nothing else on the third floor except those two bedrooms?"

"They are rather large rooms."

"Wow, so the whole third floor is made of those two bedrooms?"

"And the top of the aviary, as you can see."

Willet could see the thick double glass roofing with metal netting encasing the ceiling.

"The aviary divides the third floor?"

"Lady Evelyn is on the left and Lady Sirenna is on the right. That way, they don't ever really have to see one another."

"That's rather odd. Don't they get along?"

"Child, you are full of questions."

"Sorry, I just like to know what is really happening."

Before Willet had a chance to continue, Laraline nervously pressed Mrs. Weever about her concerns. "Lady Adler mentioned that my girls would be meeting a headmistress?"

"Yes. Her name is Mrs. Faulkner."

"What happened to Mrs. Peregrine?"

"She retired mum, now she teaches local prayer groups. You can meet Mrs. Faulkner for yourself if there are concerns."

"I know Rhea Faulkner all too well."

"Lady Swift, you were kids then. I'm sure things have changed since then."

Adelie peeped into the conversation. "You didn't get along with this lady?"

"Let's just say, we weren't friends in school."

Mrs. Weever tried to put a positive spin on it, as the conversation was heading in a troubling direction. "All the children in Meadowlark attend Talomore, even my daughters Daryn and Jae."

Willet looked at Mrs. Weever intently. "What is the school like?"

"Well, it's a seat of higher learning and they have choice academics and many more electives since your mum attended."

Adelie interjected. "Clubs?"

Mrs. Weever laughed. "Of course, dear child. In fact, we have proper swimming, chess, archery, fencing, and gymnastics teams."

Adelie's eyes widened. "They have archery?"

Mrs. Weever looked at Adelie. "Do you fancy archery?"

"Well, I've never done it before, but Willet can sword fight!"

Mrs. Weever's gaze turned to the moody teen behind everyone. "Is that true dear, do you fence?"

Willet quickly dismissed her sister. "Well, I took a few semesters at my other school, but it didn't go anywhere."

Laraline frowned, as she corrected Willet. "Actually, she's quite good. Ever since her father's passing, she has lost interest in many of her passions."

Willet interrupted as she walked past them. "Ok mama, she doesn't need my life story!"

Mrs. Weever chuckled to herself as she noticed Laraline sigh. "I understand. I have a teen myself."

Willet suddenly questioned them. "Where do we catch the school bus?"

"There are no buses in town."

"Shut up, no buses! Why?"

"It's always been that way, but we have trollies and a local taxi service."

Adelie mused to herself. "A taxi to school. Well, I guess mom will be carpooling with us on her way to work?"

"Thanks, girls, I love how no one even asked me!"

Mrs. Weever shut down the conversation. "Oh, none of that is necessary. You both appear to have strong legs."

Laraline burst out laughing, as both girls looked at each other confused.

Adelie impatiently quipped. "What's so funny Mom?"

A lightbulb finally went on. Willet sighed to herself. "Oh, very funny!"

Adelie still looked confused. "What is she talking about?"

"We are walking to school, Einstein!"

"Walking, we have to walk to school every morning?"

Laraline finally stopped laughing. "Hey, I walked to school when I was your age."

Mrs. Weever interjected. "My daughters must walk from Crecheland. Besides that, if you look out this window, you can almost see the tip of Talomore's Observation Tower."

Adelie's eyes widened. "The school has an observation tower?"

Mrs. Weever leaned to the side of the large hallway window so both girls would see. She pointed to an obscure block object hovering in the distance to the left. Even from this distance, she could see a hint of light flickering from the castle-like structure. Willet scanned the vast landscape to the right of the window and her eyes came across a dark mass.

"What's over there?"

"That would be the Greywood Forest, young Willet."

Mrs. Weever stepped back as she pulled a large iron blinder down over the window and sealed it shut.

Laraline concluded the conversation. "They will be fine walking. Their father pampered them a bit."

Both girls protested. "Nah huh!"

"In fact, if he were still here, he would say. No worries, Lara, I can take them, our daughters should be treated like queens." She suddenly paused and teared up as a memory pleasantly drifted into her consciousness.

Mrs. Weever reached out and touched Laraline's arm. Though it wasn't socially proper, it was necessary. "It's hard but it gets better, I promise."

They reached Willet's room first. The room was large with dark wood, so the room had a rustic feel. A single oil lamp sat beside the nightstand giving the dim space an eerie glowing vibe. The bed was a queen-size canopy, with gold velvety silk sheets. At the foot of the bed was a dark mahogany-looking chaise bench. Placed on top was her tote bag and book bag.

As Willet scanned the room, she made a fascinating discovery. "Hey, where's the dresser mirrors? I don't remember seeing any mirrors since we arrived here."

"This is Greywood house child. None of its occupants are that fond of mirrors, cell phones, or cameras, for that matter."

Willet's eyes widened. "Really, why not?"

"You'll have to take that up with the Lady Adler tomorrow. I suggest you hold your questions until the morning and get some rest."

Willet felt chilly and wrapped her arms about herself tightly. She could feel a draft, as she continued to scan her new bedroom. Her teeth were almost starting to chatter from the chill when Laraline noticed her reaction. "Are you cold, dear?"

"A little bit!"

Mrs. Weever was quick with her response. "Sorry child, these old houses weren't built to keep in heat. I think Mrs. Broom opened the windows to air out the place a bit. We don't have many visitors these days."

Mrs. Weever quickly crossed the room and promptly pulled down similar metal blinds that had also been in the hallway and locked the two windows in the bedroom. Realizing that she had just seen the woman lock up the last set of windows, she inquired.

"Do you latch these up every night?"

"Each and every night!"

"Why?"

"As you noticed, we are near The Greywood. Sometimes some of its wildlife wanders about this way at night, so make sure you always keep these closed at night!"

"Wildlife? What kind of wildlife?"

"Raccoons, mice, snakes, bats... you know the typical culprits."

Willet thought of the strange blue feather she found on the steps. "Any birds?"

"On occasion."

"What kind?"

"Not any you would care to encounter, miss. Besides, the blinds keep out the extreme cold breeze. It won't be nearly as brisk tomorrow night! Just keep the blinds shut after sunset and they are not to be opened again until sunrise. Lady Adler is very insistent about that."

Willet defiantly asked. "Is that an order?"

Laraline popped her daughter's head. "Willet!"

"Let's just say, if you plan on staying, you must follow the house rules!"

Mrs. Weever seemed a warm and personable person; however, her demeanor seemed a little guarded and bothered as she discussed the rules about the blinds. Willet felt there was more to her explanation, but she was too tired to argue.

Willet looked at her mother. "So, this is officially our new home."

Laraline nodded slightly. "Looks that way, kiddo. This is actually my old bedroom when I was your age."

"Really? Wow, it smells like you!"

Laraline turned pale and suddenly seemed sad.

"Mom, are you ok?"

"Yeah, I'm fine."

"Sorry about my outburst at dinner!"

"Don't be, you said what I really needed to express."

"But you couldn't, because your job is to protect us, even if it hurts you?"

Laraline touched her daughter's face. "How did you get to be so wise?"

Willet could feel the chill bumps on her arms, and she quivered a little. Her mother seemed so fragile. "Mama, how come you never talk about grandmother?"

Laraline seemed a bit taken aback by the sudden question. She was close to giving some sort of response when Adelie impatiently huffed at the door. "Mama, I'm tired."

"Well, that's my cue. You sleep well tonight."

"I'll try, love you, mama."

"I love you, my little one!" With that, Laraline kissed the top of her forehead.

Willet cautiously made her way into the room. Mrs. Weever shut the bedroom door behind her. Now that she was alone. She made her way to the bed and sat down. She was curious as to what the other rooms looked like. However, the sandman was already tickling her eyelids. She stretched her arms out, her legs dangled off the bed and she took a deep breath and exhaled slowly. It had been a long, strange week. She thought briefly of the situation at the hotel before her attentions were drawn to the décor of the room and the bed she was lying on.

She eyed the strange canopy that surrounded her. It resembled painted weeds or vines. On every other leaf, small-carved birds with outstretched wings adorned the canopy edges. Even though birds fascinated Willet, she was no expert. However, she was sure the birds on her bed canopy were sparrows.

She closed her eyes and thought about her father. This was the first adventure she was about to embark on, that he would not be a part of. A tear bubbled to the surface of her eye and slid gently down her cheek.

Chapter 10: Moments

At some point that evening, Evelyn made her way up to Laraline's bedroom. She silently stood at the door observing Laraine unpack her clothes. "I'm so glad you're home."

Laraline turned with a weary smile. "Jeez, you startled me. How long have you been standing there?"

"Sorry, I was just making sure you guys were ok."

"I truly forgot how difficult that woman can be."

Eveline sneered. "No, you didn't."

Laraline had tears in her eyes as she laughed out loud. "No, I didn't!"

"It's ok, I've had to live with her all these years!"

"What about you, Auntie?"

"What do you mean?"

"Hasn't there been anyone else, in all that time?"

"A lady never tells."

"You really are a lady, Auntie."

"So, you haven't told anyone about Langston?"

"I kept the details out of the paper. I didn't want the girls to ever find out what condition his body was found!"

Evelyn seemed concerned. "But are you sure?"

"When I identified his body, a smell was all over him. I remember that scent from when I was a child. Meadowlark has that same distinctive smell, especially the beach area."

"Why? It makes no sense!"

"Perhaps, it was a hate crime. Our marriage was very controversial at the time."

"I can assure you, your exploits have long been forgotten. That was far too many years ago. If that was the case, wouldn't the girls have been targeted?"

"Well, there have been times recently, where I have felt as if we were all being watched and followed."

"Which is why the sudden cross-country road trip. From what you have described, it could be a blood shamma at work." Mother Hazel wouldn't know more about such things.

"You always told me to trust my instincts. I know the girls can sense something. Though they won't say, especially Willet. She feels everything. She's more attuned to the world than I ever was. She is even starting to have dreams."

"How old is she now?"

"Willet turned seventeen a few months before her father passed."

Evelyn added, "And Adelie is fifteen. Your Willet is near the age of her blooming cycle."

"I believe it may have started already. When she was about seven, I think. It began for a few months, then it suddenly stopped. Of course, she doesn't remember."

Evelyn furrowed her brow. "That's quite premature, usually it doesn't start until a female reaches the fertile ages of sixteen to twenty."

"There is nothing typical about Willet!"

The two laughed quietly as the whistling of the wind could be heard outside. Laraline turned uncomfortably to Evelyn. "Is she a lot like my mother?"

"Why do you ask?"

"Come on, I have seen the pictures, they could almost be twins Auntie."

"That's ironic, even Sirenna remarked on it earlier."

"Do you think that's why Aunt Sirenna let us stay?"

"Well, your mother was an unusual creature, even Sirenna looked up to Oriole."

"I know so little of her. All my life I have tried to be a good mother to my girls, but I don't know what a mother is supposed to do."

Evelyn's face was drawn and tense as if she were holding back tears. "There may be similarities, but still, I have never heard of a blooming cycle starting at seven, then stopping and resuming ten years later."

"Well, I can't be sure, it's just she was in so much pain. We dismissed it as growing pains, but her spine had started to cause her chronic issues. She started showing signs of being ultra-sensitive to sound and smell. In fact, the smell of blood makes her ill. She became a vegan this year because of her digestion issues."

"Any trouble sleeping?"

"For years!"

"What about her dreams?"

"She won't talk about them."

Evelyn gave her a knowing glance, as she touched her shoulder. "Well, seventeen is a difficult age for all Adler women."

"You're telling me. I often wonder what may have happened if I had never given birth. I wonder how different my life would have been."

You can't beat yourself up. It was the wise choice at the moment. That adoption helped the family secure some holdings in Bangladesh."

"Bangladesh, is that supposed to make me feel better?"

Evelyn grimly responded. "No, not at all, you were a child yourself."

Laraline's eyes were puffy as she continued to speak. "I think about him sometimes, I will lie in bed and just imagine holding my baby boy.

"Last I heard, the adoptive parents had relocated to France."

"Well, I'm sure, they were paid off handsomely. Sirenna was always generous with her payoffs."

The shutters outside the window snapped, and there was a distinct flutter that quickly dissolved. Both women stood silently listening to the wind outside. Evelyn sighed as the weather eased a bit. "Well, the night is upon us."

"Don't worry, the kids are asleep, and all the windows are locked, I double-checked."

"They don't know?"

"Perhaps tomorrow, this is a lot to spring on them."

Evelyn folded her arms and paused for a few moments before responding. "It's none of my business, but I really think you should teach your daughters who they are before someone else does."

Laraline quickly responded. "You're right, it's none of your business."

It got awkward and quiet until Laraline changed the subject. "What's happened to Uncle Merle? He seems a bit off."

"Well, his health is not good. We're pretty sure it's diastasis."

"Oh no!"

"It's in the early stages, but I think he has kind of given up. Sirenna told him he was cursed."

"Of course, that woman is some piece of work!"

"Hey, that woman is still my sister and your aunt."

"I'm sorry, she's always been at me, even as a child I never thought she much liked me."

Evelyn didn't have much of a response. "Well, your aunt has had a hard life."

Laraline wisely changed the subject. "Auntie, doesn't diastasis run in the Branson bloodline as well?"

"Yes, it does. Do remember Branson's late wife Meadow?"

"Not so much, I was too young."

"Well, his daughter-in-law, from what I understand, is in stage three!"

"Oh my."

"Yes, that family seems to be cursed."

Laraline glanced over at the locked metal blinds of her bedroom window. "And we aren't?"

Chapter 11: A Quiet Family Evening

A vis dug his fingers into his thinning white hair. He took a deep breath and continued to watch the large glass tank in anticipation. At first glance, it resembled a world globe. The tank itself was a perfect sphere, almost 20 feet in diameter. It sat atop a square wooden platform a third of its size. If one stood looking down, it almost appeared as if the tank was floating in the middle of the room.

Shahaf had bought the tank and directed the installation shortly after Lady Branson's death. At first, the idea seemed a bit surreal. However, over time, it became a treasured ritual. Shahaf's wisdom of worldly alchemy and the weaver arts, in general, was only surpassed by his need for perfection. Hailing from Bangladesh, he was also able to acquire the rarest items.

Tonight was no exception. He promised Avis that this would truly be a rare one. However, the match was about to start, and things were still in some disarray about the Branson estate. Excepting Shahaf and Avis, no one else was present.

Branson watched the weaver work diligently to make sure the tank and its participants would be ready. "Are these players from your private stock, Shahaf?"

Shahaf adjusted the curtains on the tank to make sure no bright light was peaking inside to cause any premature disturbance. "No sire, these are imported. Which reminds me, speaking of imports, you wanted me to inform you when they arrived in town."

Avis arched one well-groomed brow. "When?"

"They arrived this afternoon. I will, of course, keep you informed of any new developments."

"I am concerned about everyone honoring the sanctuary."

"That is a possibility, my lord."

Suddenly Aquila pushed the door open and entered the family game room. Tonight, she wore a grey eyepatch that matched her grey gown and a diamond-studded choker with black lace inlay. She always dressed to the nines on any game night. By birthright, she was the eldest and should be the head of the family. However, due to the accident, her younger brother Avis took over that mantle.

She had naturally become his second lieutenant. Aquila was every bit as powerful as Avis and some may say even more ruthless and cold. Because of this, she was thought of as the invisible face of the Branson dynasty. This opinion would not at all displease her. However, having to take orders from her little brother did ruffle her feathers a bit.

Shahaf whispered to Avis discreetly. "We can discuss the matter at another time."

Aquila stopped, eyeing both men suspiciously, and hissed. "Dirty little secrets?"

Avis tried to ignore her comments, instead, he greeted her presence. "Good evening to you, Aquila."

She reluctantly replied. "Brother. Shahaf."

Shahaf nodded from the shadows. "Your perfume is quite unusual, Lady Aquila. Is it Jasmine?"

Aquila quickly responded. "Please tell me that is not your pathetic attempt at flirting. Why did you ever hire this third-world hack, Avis?"

Shahaf looked slightly offended as Aquila continued her tirade. "Well, I'm here, when is this going to begin?"

"Glad to see you in your usual pleasant mood, sister!"

Before she had time to shut the door behind her, Ephron slid in behind her. He was wearing a dark grey suit and looked as stressed as usual as he pushed his way inside. Of all the Bransons, he was the most ordinary-looking. He handled most of the public relations work for his father these days.

"Father, I looked everywhere. I cannot find Gavin."

"He'll be here, he never misses a match. That's more than I can say for Jonas."

Ephron suddenly paused in ponderous thought. "Where is Jonas?"

Aquila lifted a long cigarette holder to her lips. She had a passively saccharine stare as Ephron glanced at her. He looked as if there were some unspoken words he wanted to say.

She responded to his stare. "He's up a tree."

"What do you mean, he's up a tree?"

"The large oak tree on the edge of the road, I believe that's where I saw him."

Avis's interest suddenly peaked. "What's he doing up a tree?"

Aquila took a deep puff as if she were tasting a vintage wine. She gently exhaled a thin stream of smoke before responding. "As far as I could tell, I think he was trying to hang himself."

Avis reacted. "Hang himself?! What, in the name of Arke, are you talking about woman?"

"He had a rope about his neck, so I assumed that was his intention."

All the color drained out of his face, as he turned to Ephron. "Could you check it out?"

"Right away father!"

Ephron ran down the hall and out of the room. He had become a surrogate parent of a sort to his younger siblings. A role that he fell into after the death of their mother. Avis wasn't particularly paternal. His business and many indiscretions kept him absent from everyday family affairs.

Avis turned back to Aquila slightly irate. "It didn't occur to you to try to stop him?"

"Well, I figured you have two other sons."

"And neither of them is fit to become an heir." Raven sneered as she entered the family game room. The younger of two fraternal twins, by three whole minutes, she was visually striking with her dark crimson hair and alluring features. She was something of a provocateur, as she strolled in scantily clad in a black leather body suit, with a matching top hat.

Avis noticed her attire, but as the father of three teenagers, he had to pick his battles. "What are you wearing?"

She stood up proud, flaunting her attire, and quickly changed the subject. "So, what are we talking about?"

Avis raised his eyebrow. "We?"

Aquila turned to her niece. "We were just talking about your half-wit brother."

"Which one?"

"Touché, niece!"

Avis was growing tired of his sister's voice and answered Raven himself. "Aunt Aquila says she saw Jonas trying to hang himself!"

"Well, it wouldn't surprise me. Everyone at school thinks he's a weirdo."

Avis pondered Raven, with her thick black eyeliner covering her entire eye sockets. He gave a subdued grunt at the irony of the situation. He mumbled to himself. "What is taking Ephron so long?"

Aquila took another sip from her smoke. "It may take a moment to cut him down, dear brother. He may have to chew the rope if he didn't have a knife."

"To think, you used to babysit my children!"

From the bay doors, Arnold Letch came in, escorting a slightly bemused young man with golden bleach blond hair. Gavin had the most delicate features with intense piercing green eyes.

Because of this, he was naturally Lord Branson's favorite child. However, he would never admit this publicly. "Gavin, I knew you would be here. You never miss our special family time."

The young man gave a warm smile. "Of course not, father."

"My boy!"

Gavin confidently strolled across the room, politely addressing everyone. "Aunt Aquila, Shahaf, and dear sister!"

Raven ran up and embraced her brother tightly. If it were not for the family lineage, one might mistake them as a power couple. There was an uncanny familiarity with the twins.

Letch bowed before Avis and extended his arms out to his sides in reverence. Avis slightly returned the gesture. As soon as they were done. Letch responded to Gavin's claim.

"Well, he almost didn't make it tonight. This one is now on house arrest."

Avis rarely questioned anything Letch said. After all, Arnold Letch was a five-figure salary lawyer. He had been on an exclusive retainer for the Bransons for almost four years.

"House arrest? How is he supposed to get back and forth to school, and make his fencing tournaments?"

"We worked out a 7 to 7 curfew. We'll talk about all the logistics later, Lord Branson."

Gavin pulled himself from Raven's grasp. "You worry too much, father."

Avis reached out and embraced Letch. "Thank you, Letch."

"Just doing my job Lord Branson."

"Nonsense, have a seat and join us. You're family!"

Letch didn't seem particularly happy to be invited, as he was not a fan of game night. However, he would never admit this to Lord Branson himself.

Raven threw him a seductive look. "Please have a seat beside me, Uncle Archie."

"Please don't call me that."

Gavin gazed in Shahaf's direction. "So, what is for dessert tonight Master Shahaf?"

Aquila rolled her eyes. "Please don't encourage his long-winded explanations."

Gavin countered. "I love to hear him speak."

Shahaf glanced at the young man, who was staring intently at him. "Well, tonight we will have something quite special, young Gavin."

Gavin leaned into his father. "Father, I think I saw Jonas and Ephron up in that tree, by the rock garden."

Aquila snapped her fingers. "Oops, wrong tree! Well, you live in the country long enough, every tree starts to look alike."

Avis tried to ignore her flippant comment. "Don't worry about that, your brother is just upset."

Gavin looked confused. "Which brother?"

Raven took off her shoes and proceeded to put her legs across Letch's lap as if he were just part of the furniture. She leaned toward Gavin and responded. "Guess."

Gavin had a puzzled stare. "Upset about what?"

Aquila responded as if speaking from the ether. "Jonas is like his mother, a bit too artistic."

Gavin snarled at her like a snake ready to strike. "You dare use your poisonous breath to utter anything about my mum!"

"Our little sociopath is offended. What do you intend to do? Cut out my tongue while I'm asleep, little sprout?"

Gavin was cold, but he retained a pleasant smile "Don't tempt me, auntie!"

Raven hissed excitedly. "Game night just got real!"

Before Gavin had time to respond, the door opened and Ephron walked in with his arm wrapped around the shoulders of a young man. Gavin turned his attention to the young man who appeared to have a noose around his neck. He had matted curly black hair and dark eyebrows.

"What happened Jonas?"

Jonas came in and sat down beside his brother. "I was trying to commune with the dead and Ephron stopped me!"

Ephron popped the side of his head. "You almost killed yourself, you idiot!"

Avis's voice was stern. "For Arke's sake, why son?"

Jonas mumbled. "You wouldn't understand."

Raven leaned over to where Jonas sat. "What's it like being dead?"

"Do I look dead?"

"Totally."

"You're one to talk sis. I mean what's that crap all over your face, you look like a raccoon!"

Raven's eyes burned with rage. "I wished he had left you up there dangling in that tree, so the crows could peck your eyes out!"

Avis finally stood with complete irritation as his voice boomed loudly across the vast parlor. "Can't we just all get along for five minutes?"

The room was silent as if shocked by Lord Branson's outburst. Ephron leaned into his father discreetly. "I can't stay too long."

Avis inadvertently responded out loud. "Why not?"

Aquila was intently trying to listen, as Ephron whispered in his father's ear. "Meena is having a bad day."

Just 20 minutes?"

"Ok, but I have to go after that."

Branson was like a kid, as he clapped his hands together eagerly. "Great, Shahaf we are more or less ready."

Up until this time, Shahaf had been relatively quiet. He often remained a ghostly observer. The best weavers were. However, he finally spoke amid the chaos. "So, let the games begin?"

Like a Vegas magician, he finally removed the thick curtain from the round tank. The crowd watched in anticipation, as the lights within the tank suddenly became vibrant. The interior was now visible. A large husk of a branch protruded up from the floor. On the branch, sat a mammoth horned owl. Its eyes glistened in the low fluorescent lights from above. On the other side of the tank sat a large wooden box. Whatever was inside the box was fluttering and shaking about. It was ready to be free.

"Welcome, friends and loved ones, for another edition of game night. You may recognize this beast to our right as one of our endangered species on loan from the new Essex Bird Sanctuary. Our reigning champion is our great horned owl, Mr. Stuffins."

The sound of boos directed at the beast filled the room with such a fever that Shahaf had to wait till the noise eased to continue. When it finally did, he cleared his throat and continued the presentation. He strolled over to the other side of the tank, where the large box was shaking even more now.

"Tonight, she will go against a new group of challengers. They have been patiently waiting inside the box all afternoon. Who may be bold enough to take the title from the vicious might of the monstrous Stuffins? Would anyone care to guess?"

Raven yelled loudly. "Giant gofer rats who eat owl meat!"

Gavin glanced at Aquila with a cocky smile. "Could it be some of the local visitors from our own Greywood?"

Aquila gave him a dark scowl. The very suggestion enraged her.

Avis chimed in with his guess. "A seed vulture."

Shahaf smiled with his arms outstretched. "Very good suggestions, however, you are all mistaken. Today our guests hail from overseas. For your approval, a murder of Indian crows."

He pulled the latch of the wooden box. Almost instantly, a quartet of large black crows exploded from within and charged at the anticipating owl. They were black as coal and their sleek shiny wings gave them an almost perverse presence. They screeched at the owl, as they surrounded it from a distance. They were checking out their glass prison. However, the animosity they held towards their natural enemy outweighed their desire for freedom. They looked about at their captors with seething contempt. They were aware of what was happening. Gavin seemed to be growing impatient, as was Avis.

Avis looked at Shahaf. "Why aren't they fighting?"

"Patience, my lord."

It was as if the crows heard Avis's complaint. Suddenly the first crow tore at the right cheek of Mr. Stuffins as it flew by. The next two dive bombed the owl and barely missed as it ducked. The fourth hovered in midair flapping its violet-black wings and waiting. It seemed to look and stare directly into Jonas's eyes. Jonas felt it was smiling. One of the dive-bombers made a second pass and struck the left side of their adversary's face. The crow dug its beak into the soft iris of Mr. Stuffins eye. It screeched in horror and immediately snatched the crow from the air with its powerful beak. A splash of blood hit the glass in front of Raven and she screamed in delight.

"Brilliant!"

Mr. Stuffins held the crow down with its hooked talon, ripping into its adversary's back. With its savage beak the owl began to savagely pluck the wings from its body. The crow screeched and flailed in pain. It tried to turn and writhe away from underneath, but the owl was too strong.

Mr. Stuffins seemed to give Raven a hard look with its good eye, as if angered by the girl's reaction. It proceeded to rip the crow's throat out as if it were a rag doll. Raven began to chant in unison with Aquila, "Rip it off! Rip it off! Rip it off!"

This of course did not happen, as the owl was interrupted by another attack. The first crow struck the owl's belly with its beak, knocking it backward. While the fourth finally dove and began to peck at its neck. The fourth crow then returned to the scene of the crime where its brother had just been nearly decapitated, determined to attack the wounded eye. The crow flew to the left of the owl, now that it had a blind spot. The owl darted its head about. With its good eye, it tried to anticipate where the attack would come next. However, the black bird was quick. This time, digging deeper into the owls bleeding eye socket.

The owl tumbled over, off the branch, hitting the soft cage flooring on its back. Its talons released the limp carcass of the crow in the process. The remaining three crows were like bees that the owl swatted at with its massive wings. It struggled to get to its feet as it was vulnerable on its back. The murder of crows continued to mob the owl as the crowd outside of the tank cheered on. Ephron looked at his sister who seemed bummed that the owl did not finish pulling off the crow's head.

"Remember little sister, there are strength in numbers."

Mr. Stuffins finally rose into the air out of desperation. The three remaining crows violently hung on. Scratching and tearing simultaneously at its blood-stained torso.

Jonas looked about the room. Everyone violently cheering. Their faces seemed contorted by their excitement. Gavin pressed his face against the glass and started laughing so loud that Jonas got up from his chair.

No one noticed him discreetly leave the room as the battle was nearing the endgame. Although the ritual of game night had pretty much saved his family from tearing itself apart, he felt just as disenfranchised as ever. Ever since his mother died, he was having trouble connecting with anyone in his family. She was the only one he had truly felt connected to. Gavin at least made shallow attempts, but that was pretty much Gavin, shallow. As he looked from his family to the wild beasts in the tank, he realized there was not much difference between either group, except for the glass between them.

Chapter 12: Waking Dream #2

I t always starts the same, high above the trees, soaring against the crisp autumn wind. Below the vast forest beckoning, whispering for her presence. Her body gradually descended, as if in a trance.

She passes over the treetops catching a glimpse of her shadowy silhouette below. At that moment, she can hardly recognize the shape. A mighty wingspan seems to engulf the very sun from the trees below. Small forest animals scurry in anticipation of her arrival.

Vines begin to whip and snap hard against her. The trees take their que from the vines, and long branches beat at her about the face and stomach, ripping and tearing at her wings as she tries to land in vain.

She is pulled downward, now a captive of the forest, or more so, something within the forest. The more she struggles, the bloodier she gets. She surrenders and falls downward, ripping through the branches. Flocks of black birds scatter like bugs into the wind. She hits the ground on what appears to be a mound of leaves. The forest floor is covered with autumn leaves. It is like a sacred lush carpet that coats the ground underneath.

She rises to her feet, realizing that her wings are now blood-stained tatters. They flake apart like dried yellow newspaper. A single leaf from the underbrush blows upward past her face. However, at close inspection, she realizes it is not a leaf, but in fact a feather. The entire carpet of the ground is actually covered with thousands of such feathers. All red, gold, orange and brown hues lie in lush piles, all along in a colorful walkway through the forest.

She reaches down and gathers a handful, realizing that she is now earthbound, and this is a bleak reminder of what is no longer hers. At a closer glance, she can see bits of flesh attached to the ends of several of the feathers. Suddenly a few yards in front of her a mound of feathers starts to form, and mount into a thick, yet tall pile. She watches in amazement as the pile of feathers start to solidify. The feathers acting as some sort of cocoon.

A figure starts to emerge from within the pile. First, an arm claws its way out, then another. It is as if she is to bear witness to some sort of bizarre birth. As more of the body started to emerge from the feathers, there is a strange recognition of this over developed newborn. The woman who is always there waiting for her. Who is this strange woodland creature: pale of pigment and adorned in a white madrigal feathered robe. There are variations in the sequence of events, even some of the details altered, but always they confront one another in this place. She and her doppelganger. She speaks not in words but opens her mouth and screams.

It was right before dawn, when Willet awakened to the strange sounds of fluttering outside her window blinds. At first, she thought it was still part of the dream, until she realized she was sitting up in her own bed. She looked about the room. Strange shapes and objects seemed to be leering out at every corner, in her new her alien landscape of a bedroom.it seemed, A few hours earlier, the bedroom seemed so elegant and quaint.

There was a slight scratching sound at her window. She darted her attention to the closed blinds. She could only image what was on the other side. The words of Ms. Weaver about wildlife from the Greywood, echoed in her mind.

Willet sat motionless in a cold sweat for several minutes, listening. She squeezed at her pillow tightly, wishing it were her teddy bear. Mr. Claude was such an unusual teddy bear, as it seemed to be the same material as bean bags are made of. Because of this, it made him soft and squishy.

Willet was prone to fidgeting and moved her fingers a bit nervously at times. Because of this, she would cart Mr. Claude off everywhere. Mr. Claude was a casualty of the sudden exodus from Florida.

Actually, there were other things lost in the move. She thought about the last pair of boots that she had just purchased. She was suddenly irritated at the thought. There was a chorus of chirping birds. Willet glanced at the blinds. They were calm and silent. Light was starting to peak in now. The sun was starting to rise. Willet took a deep breathe and hopped out of bed. The chirping was loud, so loud. Was she the only one to hear them. As far as she knew, her mother and sister were still asleep.

She slowly walked over and released the blinds. Morning light exploded into the room exposing all the normalcy of the rooms interior. As Willet looked out her window, she could see the large, picturesque view of the town and trees, yet the scene was bare of wildlife. Even the animals must still be asleep. What about the birds she heard earlier at her blinds. Had she imagined them. She scratched her head and looked back at her closed bedroom door.

Willet was wide awake and decided to explore. The chirping started up again. It was now consistent. She finally surmised they were coming from the aviary downstairs. As she made her way down the winding stairwell to the bottom floor, she looked at the various doors shut closed along the way. A thought entered her mind; she wondered where strange Uncle Merle was located.

Willet subconsciously headed to the vast glass dome. Even though she could see the door closed, there were sounds of activity behind the door of the aviary. She took a deep breath and pushed the door open.

The room was unlike anything she had seen. There were at least half a dozen tall trees stretching toward the glass ceiling, bushes and vegetation grew along the walls, and there was the distinct scent of moisture. The room was humid inside and tiny bits of water droplets were collecting on the glass frame. As she peered about the leaves to search for a bird, she heard a familiar voice. "Why are you creeping about this time of morning?"

She turned towards the voice and saw Aunt Sirenna squatting barefoot on a moss-covered landing by a gurgling pool of water. Sirenna's hair was no longer in a bun and she wore a black nightgown. Her extremely long white hair was down to her sides and her eyes were glowing green. Her stare was almost inhuman as she studied the young girl.

Willet's heart almost jumped in her throat. However, she refused to be intimidated.

She looked directly at Sirenna's face. "I couldn't sleep."

"Bed not to your liking, child?"

"You know, I do have a name."

"Yes, of course you do, however it is of no consequence to me."

"Whatever."

Willet turned away from her and was about to leave when she found herself face to face with a massive white owl. It stood on a branch hovering slightly over the doorway. The owl had large black talons that were aged and menacing. Willet cleared her throat as she stood perfectly still.

"Does it bite?"

"She has no interest in you, child. Unless you choose to become threatening."

As soon as Sirenna finish speaking, the large bird hissed at Willet.

"Will it let me pass safely?"

"Dadu doesn't care for being called *it*. She is very sensitive."

Willet acknowledged the bird while trying not to make direct eye contact. That was something she once remembered reading about predators.

"Sorry if I offended you, Dadu. May I pass?"

Almost instantly, the large beast stopped hissing. Willet slowly made her way under the large curious bird as it silently watched her, studying her every move carefully. After a moment, the great bird flew up into the dome rafters.

Willet took a deep breath and put her hand on the door. Before she turned the latch, Sirenna's voice called after her.

"So why did you feel compelled to come here, of all places?"

In a moment of self-reflection, Willet spun round. "I thought the birds might relax me a bit."

For one moment, Sirenna started to speak in a manner and depth Willet did not think possible for the older woman.

"Yes, being in their presence is a bit like a church sanctuary. There is such brutal honesty and reverence in their purity. Sometimes just watching an entire flock's circadian movement is spiritual.

Of course, the moment did not last as Willet, humming with curiosity, changed the mood. "Why are the blinds shut every night?"

"Are you asking me a question?"

"I believe that's what it's called."

"What did Ms. Weever tell you?"

"She said it was to keep out the wildlife from the forest."

"There you have it. Sounds reasonable."

"Not to me!"

"Then perhaps you should ask your mother about such things."

Sirenna rose to her feet and slowly walked across the mossy floor to the shallow stream. "Oh, I would love to continue our discussion, but alas, I must cut our conversation short, I have a previous engagement."

Ms. Weever entered the room. The servant was carrying a large red towel, which she hung on a branch beside Sirenna. Willet was puzzled. It was not until Lady Adler started to disrobe that Willet realized she was about to bathe in the stream. She quickly turned her head, slightly embarrassed. Willet shuffled back toward the closed door and left the large dome room.

It felt slightly chilly out in the hallway. Her arms formed goosebumps as she made her way from the aviary across the cold marble floor. The aviary acted as some sort of greenhouse or glorified sauna in retrospect. For a moment, Willet had the urge to return; even though her great aunt was inside the bowels of the glass dome bathing. To say that Sirenna was a strange bird was an understatement.

The sun was now shining through the windows. The light drew Willet to the large maple front door. As she reached for the handle, she was afraid the door would be locked. Would she be trapped in this mausoleum of living artifacts? Auntie Sirenna being the most curious. To her surprise, the door clicked open and a stream of sunlight poured inside across her face. Even the sliver of daylight was holy and inviting to her, as she carefully walked out onto the front porch and closed the door behind her.

Chapter 13: How to Make Friends and Enemies

A s Willet explored the estate grounds, she gazed across the landscape. She took a deep breath and exhaled. It felt like being in a foreign country. The vast land stretched until it disappeared in a misty horizon. She could hear the morning sounds as she strolled across the thick grass barefoot.

The wet morning dew tickled her toes. The sensation was strangely calming, as she inhaled the fresh country air. She could taste a hint of the ocean, as she exhaled. She curiously looked about trying to figure out which direction the ocean was.

Greywood itself was a vast wonderland of aristocratic excess. There were pools and gardens. Near the back garden was a large chessboard field made of different square patches of grass with a gazebo in the center. The dark grass and light grass made the whole of the naturally constructed chessboard.

The edge of the board ran into a patio, adjacent to a small bungalow that Uncle Merle had claimed as his quarters. This quaint dwelling connected to the large and roomy garage situated at the edge of the circular driveway that led back into the entrance.

Willet mused to herself. *Adelie would get a kick out of this!*

Willet scanned the massive field around the estate and made a curious discovery. All along the edges of the property, she noticed that all the owl statues were standing erect, facing out. In fact, it seemed as if every statue sat strategically every 20 yards from one another.

Willet did a 360-degree turn to see where they stopped. She discovered the entire estate seemed to be enclosed and surrounded in a perfectly planned circle.

She spied one of the large bronze owls near the edge of the front lawn. It stood about 5 yards from a matching set of wicker lawn furniture. In front of the owl, she could see a wall of mist in the distance. She moved in the direction of the owl until she was standing right beside the statue. It stood at least three feet above her and this intrigued Willet. She walked around to face the statue. She studied its large omnipotent eyes. There was a kind of surreal creepiness with all the statues.

She took a step back to get a better look when she felt something brush her ankle. Startled, she looked down. Laying there was a single large black feather. It was unusually large, like the one she had found on the steps the day before. She eagerly snatched it up. However, this one was different from the first. It was thick, oily, and sticky. Almost as quickly as she picked it up, she allowed a light breeze to carry it from her grasp and into the air. Willet watched it drift across the field until it was out of sight. It left quite a bit of residue on her hand. She had to wipe her hand on her pants.

Gross, it even had a strange bizarre gamey smell. It was a scent she was not familiar with, but one she would, unfortunately, become acquainted with.

A delicate wind tickled the back of her neck. The breeze felt a bit like icy fingers. Willet suddenly had the strange sensation that she was being watched. She turned and looked in the direction of the mist. She saw nothing. She grabbed a handful of her long dark curly hair and wrapped it in a ponytail: using the faded blue hair tie that had become a temporary bracelet until she could unpack.

Without thinking, she quickly began to straddle the mammoth figure. The cold damp metal numbed her bare toes as she climbed. Soon she was sitting on its back. Her legs wrapped around its thick neck as she peered over its head. She was able to get a better look at the morning fog in the distance.

She squinted her eyes as she peered ahead. After close inspection, she soon realized the mist was covering a large body of trees. There was a forest within the mist. Willet realized what she was observing. This was the clump of woods that Ms. Weever was pointing to in the darkness last night. It was the place that she called "The Greywood".

It still was impossible to view it accurately. It had to be at least half a mile away, yet it contained a presence that permeated across the entire landscape. The thick fog seemed to be seeping from the very heart of the woods. A sudden gust of wind whispered past her. For a moment, she thought she could hear her name in the breeze. *Willet!*

She answered instinctively. "Is someone there?"

She waited for a response, but none came. She sat atop the statue for quite a while, almost frozen with nervous fear. She must have been sitting there almost 10 minutes, transfixed on the mist when she heard a soft voice from behind. "My mum says The Greywood is haunted."

Willet whipped around at the sound of the unfamiliar voice. It startled her to the point that she slid off the top of the great owl. She stumbled, but caught her footing, as she looked up at the visitor.

A few feet to the left of Willet stood a tall dark olive-skinned girl with braided hair. She was wearing faded jeans, a tied-off plaid shirt, brown cowboy boots, and chewing a wad of purple gum. Willet slowly responded." Jesh, you kind of startled me."

"Sorry, it's not every day you see someone sitting atop the ikons."

"These are ikons?"

"According to lore, they are supposed to be really old. I think they are older than the house itself."

"Well, they're so cool looking, I couldn't resist."

"You must be one of the new Adler girls going to Talomore this upcoming semester."

"Who are you?"

"My mum works for the Adlers, and she was talking all about Sirenna's dinner party last night. Of course, I'm not supposed to say anything. So, we didn't have his conversation!"

Willet looked suspiciously at her. "I still don't know your name."

The young girl extended her hand out to Willet. "Sorry, I'm Jae Weever."

"Ms. Weever is your mother?"

"Yeah!"

Willet cautiously embraced the girl's palm as she introduced herself. "Well, my name is Willet Swift, and I may be related, but I am not an Adler."

"You're not?"

"We just got here last night. This is actually my first time meeting them."

"What do you think?"

"Hopefully, we won't be here too long."

"Don't you want to belong to one of the most important families on the East Coast?"

"Well, not really."

"My, my, my. Where is your mother, sleeven?"

A condescending voice interrupted their conversation. A young woman approached the pair. Willet recognized her cousin, Phoebe, from dinner. She didn't realize just how pretty the girl was. The dining room had been dim and foreboding, not the most flattering light for anyone.

In the bright light of day, Willet could see she had bold catlike eyes and full lips. These features were framed by her long straight blonde hair and perfect hourglass figure she was all too aware that she possessed. She even moved like a cat across the thick grass in her black diamond studded heels. She had a painful-looking scowl on her face, and her focus was on Jae.

Jae responded without turning around. "She is off today, so watch your mouth!"

"If you don't like my words, then leave. This is family property!"

Jae calmly turned to confront her. "Make me."

Willet's eyes furrowed as Phoebe cracked her knuckles to appear intimidating. Her cousin was pushing a confrontation. This was the first time Willet had enjoyed a pleasant conversation since they first arrived in town, and now Phoebe was messing that up.

Willet glared impatiently at Phoebe. "Hey, I'm talking to her, she can stay as long as she wants!"

Phoebe crossed her arms defiantly. "Well, I don't like her kind and want her to leave."

Before Willet could speak, Jae folded her arms and snapped back. "What are you going to do about it, you cheap blonde pip?"

Phoebe became enraged. She raised her hand in the air and charged. It was as if she were going to strike Jae across the face. Her fingers were outstretched and her long thin fingernails arched.

Instinctively Willet countered. Her hand reached out and without thinking snatched her cousin around the throat. There was a strangling sound as Phoebe fumbled about for air. Willet's fingers had become long enough to extend around her throat. Her nails were now long and talonlike. Willet's eyes were suddenly glowing dark green as she responded to Phoebe in a tone that could only be described as menacing. "Why don't *you* leave?"

Strange muscles in her forearm bulged, as she flung her cousin away. Phoebe flew backward several feet and tumbled against the nearby wicker lawn chairs. The whole scene was reminiscent of a bowling ball, striking a few spare pins. At first, Willet chuckled at the image to herself.

Phoebe quickly stood up in complete shock. Her attention was now on Willet. Her face revealed a bloody nose. There were also dark marks on her neck that resembled scratches. Not believing what had just happened, Willet suddenly felt ashamed of finding humor in the attack.

"My god, did I do that to your neck?"

Phoebe instinctively raised her finger to her neck and immediately felt the bruises. Her eyes bulged in horror. She almost seemed to be on the verge of crying.

"What did you do to me?"

"I'm so sorry Phoebe. I don't know what happened."

Phoebe's mood suddenly turned from hurt back to anger. "You will be sorry, you freak!"

"It was an accident"

A frantic voice echoed across the yard. "Phoebe, keep away from those horrid children! Come to me at once!"

If Willet had to guess, it sounded like Patsy calling. The tone was that of a pissed-off mother who had just witnessed her daughter manhandled. She probably didn't see the event that led up to the altercation. She was the type that wouldn't believe it, even if she saw for herself.

Willet located the source of the voice. It came from the black car at the edge of the driveway entrance. Pasty stood leaning against the hood with dark sunglasses staring in their direction. Willet looked away, as she could feel the woman's eyes burning into her skin. Now she felt like a criminal.

Phoebe began walking away, desperately trying to hold on to a sliver of dignity. She looked back at Willet. "You had better remember what side your bread and butter is, cousssin!"

She then glanced at Jae with her bloody nose. A single drop of blood touched her full lips. She menacingly licked the blood away. "I'm not done with you, sleeven!"

Jae sarcastically smiled. "Great, let's do lunch!"

Phoebe stomped off angrily in her mother's direction. Within moments, both mother and daughter were heading to the house on foot. Patsy tried to comfort her child, but Phoebe snatched away from her mother as if irritated by her touch. As they walked to the house, Patsy glanced back at Willet with utter contempt.

Willet sighed deeply in frustration. "Oh great, that is all I need."

"Sorry."

"I already didn't make the best impression on them last night. My mother is going to be so pissed when she finds out what I did this morning."

"You're right, you're not like an Adler."

"Gee, thanks."

"Well, if it's any consolation, thank you for saving my ass, I owe you. If you want, I can tell your family she was trying to attack me!"

"Yeah, that was completely insane how she just went after you. What was that word you called her anyway?"

"Pip?"

"What does that mean?"

Jae sheepishly answered. "Well, it's another term for an escort."

Willet folded her arms and raised her eyebrow. "So, you called her a whore. That explains a lot."

"She has been looking for an excuse to get me anyway."

"Is she like, your nemesis?"

"It's a bit more complicated than that!"

"Well, what's the story?"

"Nothing. Really!"

"Hey, come on. You said you owe me. Well, I want to collect, now."

"What did you say your name was again?"

"Willet."

"OK, Willet. Pheobe and I never really got along, but things really went south after what I would like to call the Gavin Branson incident."

"Gavin Branson incident? That sounds intriguing."

"It's a pretty tedious teen drama. The real issue is, she is under the unfortunate delusion that she is his betrothed."

"Did you say *betrothed*? What century is it here?"

"Well, this is a very old community entrenched in the traditional ways!"

"Yeah, no school buses!"

"What?"

Willet unfolded her arms and began to move about with a thick English accent. "Never mind. You were talking about the betrothed maiden Phoebe. I do like how the word betrothed rolls off one's tongue."

Jae looked puzzled. "Oh. Ok?"

"First, who is this, Gavin?"

"Gavin Angel Branson is one of the most popular guys in school. She is totally in love with the jerk, but he doesn't even know she exists. Anyway, he asked me out last semester to the spring dance."

"Oh, the clouds are beginning to part."

"We went out once. That was all. The funny thing is, I don't even think he was interested in me. Regardless, she has had it in for me ever since."

"Wow, that's a lot of drama I just stepped into."

"Regardless of what I called her; she has always had a bit of temper. Just yesterday morning she attacked one of my mom's coworkers. She tried to scratch her eye out, just because she accidentally stepped on her shoe."

"Oh, are you talking about Ms. Broom?"

"You heard about it already?"

"Not exactly, but Ms. Broom was wearing an eye patch when we first arrived!"

"Jae's eyes widened. Shut up. She really must have done some real damage to her!" The entire situation started to make Willet feel a bit uneasy, so she made an effort to change the subject. "You mentioned that this Gavin guy is a jerk."

"Well, he is a Branson. It comes with the territory. He has a twin sister, who is even worse if you ask me!"

Willet glanced back toward the front entrance of the house. A crowd of the family had gathered, including her mother and sister. Her mother was desperately waving for Willet to come.

"Oh god, I see my mom. I have some explaining to do!"

Jae glanced over creating a shade over her forehead with her hand and blocking out the morning sun from her eyes. "Yeah, I see what you mean!"

"Your mother said that you guys walk past here on the way to school?"

Jae sheepishly responded. "Me and my sister walk past here, by way of Crecheland."

"Perhaps, Addie and I can join you on your walk to school?"

"No, I mean Crecheland is the poor side of town."

"And?"

"Adlers don't normally fool with us crèche folk too much. It's not really socially proper."

"Like I care!"

"You should care."

"Why?"

"Well, if you need to know, the Bransons and Adlers are the town's most powerful and wealthy families. You are like royalty now. You can't be friends with just anyone without ruffling some feathers. It's all about social status here."

"So, you're telling me, I have inherited a group of snobs and bigots? Toto, we're definitely not in Kansas anymore!"

Willet's reference elicited a giggle from Jae.

"Well as I said earlier, I'm not an Adler. I'm a Swift and we don't care what side of the track you live on, as long as you can dodge the train."

Jae chuckled. "That's pretty clever!"

"My dad used to say that to us when we were younger. I don't know what made me think of that."

"He sounds pretty cool. Where is he now?"

Willet was nonchalant as if she were discussing the weather. "Oh, he went and died on us, so we had to move away, and come here to live. Wow, that came out really insensitive, didn't it?"

"Um?"

"You don't have to answer that."

Jae didn't know how to respond, or if she was even supposed to answer. She quietly replied. "I'm so sorry about your dad."

"It's ok, I don't seem to be myself. I feel like Alice in Wonderland but I'm not able to wake up."

"Wonderland?"

"Sorry, I was thinking outside of my head again."

"Yeah, well, you don't appear strong enough to handle your cousin: much less throw her."

"That is what I'm talking about. I have never done anything like that before. I'm feeling very queer as of late."

Finally, Jae leaned forward with a puzzled expression on her face. "Do you always talk like this?"

"Like what?"

"Like you're reading from a play or something!"

"Unfortunately, I've always been a bit melodramatic, it gets on my sister's nerves!"

"Well, it's very..."

Willet jumped in with her exaggerated face, suggesting possible words to complete Jae's sentence. "Weird? Strange? Bizarre?"

Jae finally finished her statement. "Quirky!"

"Quirky. All of this and my rating is just quirky?"

"Don't worry, I think quirky is pretty cool."

"Does that mean we can all walk together to school?"

Jae chuckled. "If you can survive the wrath of Phoebe and her mother, I'll see you next Monday, Willet Swift."

At that moment, Laraline's voice cut through the morning air with the classic primal call to any kid in deep trouble. It sounded impatient and urgent. "Willet! Come here this instant!"

Willet didn't even bother to glance up. Instead, she sighed, resigned to her fate, and bid farewell to Jae. "Well, I'd better go. The natives are getting restless!"

"Good luck, and thanks again!"

Chapter 14: The Phoebe Crane Affair

"**I**'m sorry, I really didn't mean to throw her. In fact, I have no idea how I did it."

As Willet tried to explain what happened, Sirenna and Mother Hazel glanced at one another, discreetly observing the exchange. Willet tried her best to make amends. Unfortunately, her victim was inconsolable.

"Well, I don't accept your lek apology!"

Eveline was stern. "Watch your language, child!"

Patsy came to her daughter's defense. "How dare you chastise my Phoebe. She is the victim here!"

Eveline looked to Sirenna, who was now dressed in a silk Asian kimono. She had a non-committed look on her face, as she shrugged. The large white owl was also present. It was perched on a railing close to Sirenna, intent on listening to what its mistress had to say.

"I told you what could happen if they came. It hasn't even been a full twenty-four hours."

Laraline stepped in to confront Patsy and Phoebe, who were facing down her daughter.

"Look, she apologized, Auntie Patty. Willet is typically not a violent person."

"What do you call those bruises? My Phoebe demands justice. Look at her face and neck!"

Phoebe almost burst into tears, playing the victim card on cue perfectly. Willet found herself glaring at her staged performance. Eveline tried to calm her younger sister.

"It's just a few slight bruises. She is young and resilient."

"Slight bruises! She's a fashion model, her face is her bread and butter."

Willet's voice cut the air. "What is a lek? I know it's an insult of some sort, but what exactly does it mean?"

Phoebe stopped sobbing long enough to gloat at her cousin's ignorance. "That's what you are, your blood is tainted with impurity!"

Willet felt her sweaty fingers ball into a fist. "I should have smashed your face."

"Mother, do you see how she is?"

Willet was beyond reproach as she continued. "Whatever! For the record, I couldn't care less about whatever little names you call me. Lek or Sleeven, makes no difference to me. I'll still kick your ass if you ever touch me."

The entire group got deathly silent. Mother Hazel, who had remained silent til now, took a sober step forward to address her.

"Where did you hear that word child?"

Willet was instantly intimidated but stood her ground. "What word?"

"Sleeven. That is not a commonly used word where you come from."

"Cousin Phoebe called Jae a sleeven."

Phoebe shook her head as she violently denied it. "No, I didn't, she must have misunderstood me!"

"You said it twice!"

"You're lying! I swear I didn't!"

Phoebe suddenly looked afraid, as did her mother. They both looked around at the rest of the family. The smell of fear was powerfully apparent. Suddenly the focus was not on Willet. Now Willet was even more curious as to what the word meant. Sirenna murmured under her breath, as her angry gaze landed in Phoebe's direction.

"Insolent offspring."

Mother Hazel eyed Patsy with a deep scowl before turning to Willet earnestly. "Please, explain what happened exactly."

Patsy quickly interjected. "No, I do not wish to hear lies from this child!"

Sirenna passively answered. "Then leave, but your daughter must remain here for interrogation."

Pasty whispered softly. "No."

Mother Hazel touched Willet's shoulder with her wooden cane. "Explain what transpired."

Willet dramatically recounted the sudden attack and the verbal exchange between the two girls, before Willet had interceded. As Patsy listened, she grew enraged.

"This is madness, I demand justice!"

Sirenna corrected her. "Phoebe has been warned about her loose tongue before. Everyone knows she is far from innocent in this matter."

Mother Hazel snapped her staff against the floor. "Silence! According to the Asclan lore, both parties could air their differences in combat until one yields or falls."

Laraline loudly protested to Sirenna. "I don't believe what I'm hearing, they are just children!"

"You knew our laws and customs before you decided to humble yourself, and set foot back into this abode, niece!"

Mother Hazel continued to speak as if reading from a text. "I say in one hour's time, both parties enter the Aviary, ready to do battle!"

Laraline gasped. "Are you all insane?"

Eveline interjected. "Perhaps, a little more time would allow both parties time, to properly prepare."

Sirenna responded. "How much time would you say?"

"What about three days?"

"Nay sister, this matter must be swift. No pun intended."

Laraline blurted out. "I can't believe you want them to fight!"

Willet suddenly reacted. "Fight, we're supposed to fight each other like in a ring?"

Phoebe was deathly silent, and her eyes were uncomfortably wide. "Mother?"

Eveline turned back to Sirenna. "That is my point. Neither child knows what is actually happening!"

Sirenna shrugged. "That is the mothers' burden, not ours."

Phoebe's expression was of fear. Whatever pain she was having was momently forgotten. "Mother, is this real?"

Patsy waved her hand dismissively. "They are just having a lark, they don't expect you to fight darling. Isn't that right?"

Eveline continued. "Neither child has the apparent knowledge of their heritage, to evoke the spirits necessary to protect themselves properly. That would not be very sporting."

Serena looked at Mother Hazel for approval. The older woman shrugged in response before she slammed her cane as if it were a gavel.

"Ok, they have two days to prepare. If the grievances remain, they will meet again here to conclude this dispute."

Phoebe looked at her mother with fear in her eyes. There was an uncomfortable silence. Sirenna clasped her hands together. "Ok, now that is done. My tummy is rumbling. I think it's time for breakfast."

Patsy was frowning, displeased, as she followed Sirenna down the hallway. "Tell my daughter this is not true. Tell her this is utter nonsense."

Phoebe was close behind. Eveline had no doubt they would try to suck up to Sirenna for favors concerning vengeance without a fighting match.

Willet looked to Eveline. "What just happened?"

Eveline was chuckling to herself. "I bought you a little time."

"Time for what?"

"That would be up to your mother."

Willet looked back at Eveline. "Why don't you just tell me?"

"According to our customs and laws, until you become of legal age, the mother is completely responsible for you. Your lore or any knowledge must be withheld unless the mother gives her blessing. No one can assist you unless Laraline has given her blessing."

Laraline eyed Eveline. "I know what you two are up to and it's not funny. I am her mother and that counts for something."

Eveline looked harshly at Laraline. "You may not like the truth, but it may save them both."

Laraline became visibly upset, as she hurried to the stairs. She was in tears as she climbed the steps that led up to the second floor. Adelie was now standing close to her sister looking very confused, when Willet called after her.

"Mama, what is she talking about?"

She got halfway up the steps and paused. Without turning, she called down to her daughters. "Come upstairs girls, we need to talk!"

Chapter 15: Regarding Willet

A lthough the aviary was where Sirenna and sometimes Evelyn would go to unwind, the study was the designated war room. It was where important business and sensitive matters could be discreetly resolved. Where the aviary stood in the eastern view of the sun, the study sat at the western end of the estate.

At first glance, the impressive study was a historical library. Dozens of old manuscripts and first editions sat indiscriminately beside one another in large teetering shelves that rose to the ceiling. A grand marble table sat in the middle of the room, flanked on either side by two rustic crimson leather wingback chairs on either end. Down each side were smaller matching leather chairs. In the center of the table sat an unusual mirror-tiled world globe. Each land mass was proportionate to their size and embossed in gold leaf.

Sirenna made her way to the right side of the table and sat in the large wingback chair. The other wingback was obviously Eveline's seat. There was an underlying innate respect that the twins had for one another. In some ways, they functioned a bit like a married couple. As brash and unflinching as Mother Hazel was, she had great respect for the natural order and codes of the house. She exhibited this by sitting in one of the smaller chairs.

Though Patsy had been in the study several times, she had never spent a significant amount of time there. She had yet to understand certain protocols. She quickly showed her ignorance by making a beeline for Eveline's chair. Mother Hazel snapped her staff in front of her, thus obstructing her from sitting. Before she had time to react, Sirenna explained.

"You cannot sit there."

Phoebe was standing right behind Patsy and quickly answered for her mother. "Why not?"

Sirenna looked sternly at her younger sister without bothering to acknowledge her daughter. "Can you silence this thing of yours, Patsy?"

With much sugar, Patsy asked her pouting daughter to comply. "Phoebe, please dear, I need to talk with your auntie!"

Phoebe's response was quick. "If it's about me, I think I have a right to hear!"

Mother Hazel turned to Patsy. The old woman seemed visibly irritated by the manner in which she had answered her mother. However, she responded. "She does have a point."

Sirenna seemed unconcerned either way. In fact, she did not seem as if she cared about any of it, to Patsy's chagrin. Sirenna was nursing a headache that had been growing since she had taken her morning bath.

"I don't care as long as I don't have to hear her lips move!"

Pasty cleared her throat, as she built up the strength to address Sirenna. "Is there any way Willet can be punished?"

"Punished for what?"

"For the pain she inflicted on my daughter, she tossed her like she was a rag doll. Look at her neck. Those marks will have people talking!"

"She could always wear a scarf.

Mother Hazel's look of surprise seemed mildly put on. "Why Patsy, I didn't know you were so concerned about local gossip!"

This is a serious matter. I really don't think..."

Sirenna suddenly interrupted her younger sister, as she went into a tirade. "Look, I've had about enough of what you think. You're lucky I don't trounce your child myself! Especially after she willfully maimed one of my employees. We still don't know if Ms. Broom will be blind. Who do you think must pay for doctor bills and any possible lawsuit?"

Patsy and Phoebe stood like wide-eyed deer intently listening. Sirenna's voice was calm now, yet there was an aura of contempt as she continued to speak.

"Do you realize your daughter is putting every one of us in jeopardy?" She leaned back in her chair and closed her eyes. "Soon they will come after us with pitchforks and torches!"

"Isn't that a bit mellow dramatic, things are more civilized than that, Sirenna!"

Sirenna paused for a moment and looked out the window at one of the sitting gardens below. The sun was shining vividly on the gardenias below and flickering on the back of a large bronze owl that stood amongst the vegetation. "If you only knew, and now you want a favor from me!"

Patsy suddenly perked up. "Let me remind you that Phoebe is in line for a marriage proposal from one of the Branson heirs."

Mother Hazel scoffed. "Poppycock."

Patsy narrowed a glance at the old woman as if she were offended. Sirenna then used the sudden breach in polite diplomacy to speak quite candidly.

"That's not what I hear. From what I understand, young Gavin's tastes run a bit closer to the exotic. It appears as if he has grown tired of your Phoebe's flavor, as of late!"

"That's not true. I mean, all couples have their minor growing pains!"

"He hasn't called on her in almost a year. To my understanding, a courtship this slow and uneventful is bordering on comatose. Wouldn't you agree Mother?"

Mother Hazel was smoking a long pipe in her mouth as she looked at Patsy with red rose-colored glasses and nodded. The old woman took a long puff before she responded candidly.

"Perhaps she's frigid."

Sirenna strangled the laugh that threatened while trying to keep a straight face. She turned to the old woman who never broke a smile. "Mother, you're simply horrible!"

Patsy turned red and stomped off, finally disgusted. Phoebe looked confused before finally following her mother. Soon the laughter died down and both Sirenna and Mother Hazel were alone.

Sirenna leaned closer to the old woman. "Little sisters and their demands."

Mother Hazel looked at Sirenna. "How long are you going to let our guests believe in all that nonsense about ceremonial battles and such?"

"I do miss the old ways. We've gotten too modern for my tastes. I'd be amazed if either of them actually agreed to such a match. You see how afraid they were."

Mother Hazel sucked her pipe before she answered. "I think you're having too much fun."

Sirenna leaned back in her chair again. "Seriously, if Willet and Phoebe had a fight, who would be bested?"

"Hard to say really. Phoebe is pure-blooded and knows how to fight dirty, a skill she learned from you, of course."

"I don't know if I should be offended."

Mother Hazel rubbed her wrinkled fingers over her cane. "However, this Willet is a wild card. This sprout has a lot of sand in her gut. She even tried to buck up to you, my lady."

"Well, she doesn't know me yet!"

"Oh, she knows exactly who you are, and you know this. She is not afraid of you Sirenna. In fact, she is the only one in this house to openly defy you. That takes a lot of strength and this intrigues you. Which is why you haven't sent them all packing."

Sirenna denied. "They are family who have fallen on hard times, I am duty-bound to help."

"When has love and sentiment ever swayed you?"

"True, I don't have much affection for anyone, especially kids. However, I am getting old. If the house of Adler is to survive, we must adapt and endure."

"Ha ha ha, you don't mean a word of what you are saying."

"You lecherous old hag, perhaps I should chop you up into tiny little pieces and feed you to the dogs."

"We don't have any dogs, you already had them shot last month!"

"I did, why?"

"You said, and I quote, the dreadful beasts wouldn't stop howling!"

"Oh yes, I had all but forgotten."

"It's so unfortunate."

"I have been meaning to replace them. I've seen a few extra feathers around the grounds as of late. Tomorrow, I will put a note out to remind Ms. Broom to purchase three new dogs who crave the flesh of horrible old weavers but will not whine and pester all night."

Mother Hazel calmly adjusted her glasses. "Ms. Broom is having her eye surgery tomorrow, remember, she won't be here."

Sirenna took a sip from her glass and in frustration bellowed down the hallway in hopes that Patsy may still be within earshot. "Patsy, thank your horrible offspring again!"

It remained silent for a few moments before Mother Hazel cleared her throat and whispered to Sirenna, who had finished her glass. "What are you plotting Sirenna?"

"Plotting?"

"I've been training you since you were 17 years old. I can tell when you're about to take a breath."

Sirenna coyly replied. "Whatever are you talking about?"

Mother Hazel was grinning behind her glasses. "Purred the hungry cat to the baby bird."

"Ok, I was thinking. Even though she has tainted blood, with some refining, she could almost be a suitable option for either of the Branson boys."

Mother Hazel leaned closer. "Avis is not going to let you anywhere near his docks, even if he agrees to nuptials. I'm not sure if he would agree to a mixed marriage. Besides, you made such a stink about Laraline that it would be a bit hypercritical to push one of her daughters off on the Bransons."

Sirenna sat silently stewing. She took a sip of her drink as the old woman leaned back into her seat with a counter thought.

"However, Laraline and her children do seem to be friendly with Evelyn."

"And why should I care, Mother?"

"Because Evelyn is the only one in this family who Avis trusts. Laraline's arrival may prove to be a valuable bargaining chip in trying to broker a deal with Branson."

The room was suddenly uncomfortably silent. It felt as if Mother Hazel had just spoken some perverse idea into existence. Sirenna fawned a teaspoon of guilt.

"Well, I couldn't do that to Patsy. The poor dear has put all her hope into a possible marriage, thus creating a union between the two great houses. That would break her heart. As much as I loathe her presence, it would weigh upon me to know that I had betrayed my word on this one matter."

"No, it wouldn't!"

"How can you say that? I am the one who pushed for her marriage to... what's his name?"

"Nester."

"I am the one who pushed her to have a daughter instead of a son. I have asked so much of her, what kind of big sister would I be if I broke this one promise?"

"The same kind you have always been, wretched and deceptive!"

"I hope you fall out of an open window from the third floor."

"I don't travel on the third floor."

"You're like Patsy in that respect. What kind of faigal is afraid of heights?"

"I'm not afraid, I'm just too old to sustain such a significant fall."

"Of course, the fall would tenderize you a bit for the new hounds I intend to buy!"

"I stand corrected."

"Why would you say such horrible things? I love my sister Patsy."

"Because you know that I know, that if a marriage between her Phoebe and either Branson boy materialized, your dominance over her would end very quickly."

' "What do you see?"

"She would most likely fight to become the head of the Adler dynasty. She is the only one here who would openly advocate for this. She would well be within her right. If she were able to pull off such a feat as ending the war. Could anyone deny this?"

"You're wrong, family is loyal."

Mother continued without missing a beat. "No one would openly go against you. There would be a vote, completely democratic of course, but if given the choice of a hidden ballot, I suspect she would defeat you easily. There would be the exceptions, of course, Eveline and a few other sycophants, but you would lose."

"And who would you cast your vote for, old woman?"

"I would gladly unseat you dear!"

"I should slit your throat for your heresy, this very moment!"

"Why, because I offer you truth and counsel?"

"Truth and counsel! Is that what you call it? Your words are like knives, and every day I am treated to longer and deeper blades into my flesh!"

"Dear Sirenna, you are beautiful, smart, and quite cunning. Very few pupils can match me in a battle of wits, however, given the choice, I would gladly invite a fool on the throne instead. With a fool, there is always someone else in charge. A fool is only a figurehead."

"Are you saying my beloved baby sister is a fool?"

"Absolutely."

"Well, it's hard to argue the fact, so this is about power!"

"The illusion of power means nothing to an old woman like me. You should know me by now!

"What is this all about?"

Mother Hazel ignored her and spoke frankly. "If I may offer some advice, I would be cautious about how you treat your niece and her daughters. I suspect they may play a bigger part in your future."

"Have you seen this, yourself?"

"Not exactly, but there are signs and hints."

"Riddles, why must you always speak in riddles?"

"Because the future is always in motion. It is not always clear. However, sometimes important players can become very clear if you recognize them."

"You speak of this willet!"

"This is no ordinary child, and you know that, Sirenna."

Sirenna didn't respond at first, when she did speak again, she was ponderous. "She asked me about the blinds this morning."

"What did you tell her?"

"It's not my job to inform her of all the dark, evil things lurking about in the night shadows, that's what mothers are for."

Chapter 16: Know Thyself

Willet and Adelie quietly made their way up to their mother's room. During most conflicts, Adelie was passive and quiet. Willet, on the other hand, was more confrontational. When Willet reached the doorway, she was almost in shock when she noticed that Laraline had pulled out a suitcase and had begun packing.

"What are you doing mama?"

"Packing our things, we're leaving. It was a big mistake coming here. I know that now. I cannot believe what I let them put you through."

"Where are we going now?"

"I'm not sure. I have a girlfriend upstate. I can try to reach out to her when we get on the road."

Willet folded her arms defiantly. "You're dead serious!"

Adelie looked confused as she backed away from the doorway. Willet, on the other hand, was pissed.

"Yes, it was a big mistake to come here, but that is beside the point, we are here now!"

Laraline focused on willet. "I thought you were the one, who didn't want to be here, in the first place. There is no pleasing you."

"Cut the crap mama."

"What did you say to me?"

"We went through a lot of crap to get here; we can't just keep running."

"Are you insane, you want to deal with all their sick mind games or the possibility of fighting your cousin?"

"Not really, but she is not unlike the dozens of other mean girls who decide they don't like me because of what I'm not. I've had to deal with bullies since I was six years old!"

"Willet please, I know you're trying to help, but you don't understand!"

"No, you don't understand. You don't realize what life is really like for me and Addie. You live in this dream world where things were perfect for us until Daddy died. It's always been hard. It just got worse after he died."

"Willet, you don't know what could happen here, just pack your things."

"Then explain it Mother and stop running from everything."

"They're starting to rub off on you. This isn't you."

Willet suddenly found herself yelling. "Perhaps it's you who are just like them, with your hidden agendas and mistruths. All my life, there have been secrets surrounding us."

"They will destroy you, Willet!"

"And what are you doing to us now, mama?"

Laraline was taken aback by her candor. She stood frozen as Willet chastised her.

"All these lies and secrets are strangling us. Don't say I'm exaggerating. We don't even talk about Daddy anymore. I buried my father almost five months ago and I do not know how he even died. It's now this taboo subject. We bring it up and you change the subject or tell me not to dwell on bad things. Well, I miss him."

Adelie came inside the room with her hands covering her ears. "Please stop fighting!"

Laraline instantly fell to her knees and started to cry. "I miss him too."

The suitcase she was packing tumbled to the ground and all the clothes spilled out. Adelie ran to her mother trying to console her. Willet joined them and soon they were all embraced on the floor. It was the first group hug they had shared in almost four months. Laraline held them tight while whispering the words. "I'm so sorry, I didn't realize!"

They spent the better part of that morning on the floor, remembering the late Langston Swift. Laraline told them several stories about when the girls were young. She discovered she was pregnant with Willet, and they decided to run away and start over, as Sirenna wasn't very sympathetic to mixed marriages. Aunt Evelyn was the only one who did not treat him ill.

Willet was blunt as she asked. "So, they didn't like that he was African-Caribbean?"

"Well, that didn't help, but the real issue was, no one wanted me dating a sleeven."

"Sleeven, that's what Phoebe called that girl Jae."

"You won't find it in Webster's dictionary; it's an old word from our families' native tongue."

"Well does it mean?"

Laraline looked troubled for a moment before she responded. "Translated today, it would mean human."

Willet laughed off her mother's odd joke. "No serious, what does it mean?"

"Willet, I'm telling you the truth. My family didn't like the fact that I fell in love and decided to marry a human."

A queer look went across Willet's face. Her mother's bizarre joke had caused her to chuckle.

"Ok, I'm confused, they didn't like Dad because he was human. Then what are we?"

Laraline put her hand on her daughter's hand and sighed. "That is a bit complicated, dear."

Ok, wait a minute. Just take a deep breath and count to three before you respond. One. Two. Three.

Willet's eyes widened. "What the hell do you mean by complicated?"

"Watch your language, young lady!"

"Don't young lady me!"

"I'm trying to tell you the truth, I thought that's what you wanted!"

"You just told me I'm not human. Are you insane? Please stop lying!"

"I'm not lying."

Willet broke down in tears. She crumbled into a ball on the floor.

"Why won't you just tell me the truth?"

Adelie looked at her sister, then her mother. Finally, she quietly turned to her mother. "Are we like aliens or something?"

Willet snapped at Adelie. "Shut up, don't encourage her lies!"

Laraline sat down beside her daughter. "This is the truth you have been waiting to hear. I'm sorry if it's not what you wanted, but it is the truth!"

"Stop talking, I'm not listening anymore. I'm going to lay back down in my bed, and when I wake up, none of us will speak of this conversation."

Evelyn stood at the door looking down at Laraline kneeling beside a young girl with her hands covering her ears. It was like déjà vu for the older Adler. "Can I try to explain the situation?"

Laraline threw up her arms in frustration. "Do you think you can do better?"

"Well, I don't think I can do any worse."

"Have at it, then."

"So, do I have your blessing?"

Laraline stood stewing. "Fine, whatever!"

Evelyn politely turned her attention to Adelie and Willet then clapped her hands. "Please come with me girls, I want to show you something."

Willet's face was puffy and swollen as she rose to her feet and coldly responded. "What?"

"Just come with me, I think you will find what I'm about to show you quite fascinating."

Adelie was suddenly intrigued. "What are you going to show us?"

Evelyn whispered to the young girl with a mischievous look. "That would be telling."

Chapter 17: That Ole Time Religion

They followed Evelyn down the hallway, to the second set of steps that led up to the third floor. As all four entered her bedroom, there was an instant scent of mint and wintergreen spruce. The entire room was dressed in shades of blues and greens. A lush aqua-blue carpet covered much of the wood floor, with matching curtains and a couch. The bed was in the corner of the room covered by soft green linens. As Evelyn walked across the room, she motioned to the Swift family. "Please come and sit, make yourselves comfortable."

Willet, now calm, headed to the large sofa with her sister. Laraline was at the door waiting. For the first time in quite a while, she seemed calm as well, almost at peace, as she waited to hear what Aunt Evie would say.

Willet scanned the massive suite. "So, this is your bedroom?"

Adelie added. "If this were my room, I would never leave!"

Evelyn answered playfully. "There are days when I don't."

Willet turned her attention to Evelyn's bed. She noticed that on the floor there were a few scattered feathers. These were identical to the blue and yellow spotted feather she had found outside on the steps when they had first arrived. Before she could ask where they came from, Evelyn had returned with a large, oversized book. She seemed excited as she sat the book directly on Willet's lap. Willet looked up in disbelief as Evelyn showed her treasure.

"I appropriated this from the study, in anticipation of your families' arrival. Just look!"

The book itself resembled a thick, leather-bound scrapbook. The cover contained some bizarre symbol that reminded her of a pair of wings with an infinity sign in the middle. Under the symbol were some strange markings or letters, that Willet surmised were some kind of foreign language.

She gently touched the golden embossing that outlined each character in the title. She looked back up at Evelyn in a curious manner. "I can't read this."

"This is in our native tongue; I don't even think your mother still remembers."

Laraline rolled her eyes and then crossed her arms from the doorway. "Of course, I do."

Adelie looked up at her mother. "Well, what does it say, ma?"

Laraline obliged. "Blessed bounty!"

"That's all Lynn?"

Laraline looked at Evelyn. "Well, this is **your** show Auntie!"

The older woman cleared her throat and began to speak in an imposing voice as her demeanor changed. She moved behind the sofa to see the book from the girls' perspective.

"Well, the symbol on the front is the universal Asclan."

Adelie repeated the words. "Asclan?"

"Yes. It's pronounced with more emphasis on the first syllable."

"Hey, it looks like the engraving on your ring."

"What?"

Willet finally interjected. "She's talking about your mood ring."

"We call them divining rings. We all wear them publicly. It's how we can quickly find one another in the world."

Adelie quickly corrected her. "Momma doesn't wear one."

Aunt Evie leaned close to Adelie. "No, she doesn't, that is because she doesn't want to be found."

"Is that the only way to find each other?"

"Of course not, it's just the most direct way."

Adelie rubbed the cover of the book with her fingers. "What does the symbol mean?"

"It's similar to the holy crucifix in sleeven Christianity."

Willet finally jumped into the conversation. "So this is a bible?"

Eveline corrected her. "The Bible."

Laraline clarified. "It's the bible of our people."

Eveline continued. "Of course, I'm not as crazy about this edition. This is a fifth edition. For my money, the third edition is the most comprehensive. However, this one is more contemporary I suppose."

Willet interjected. "I think I remember Mother Hazel making mention of the Asclan earlier."

"I assume you are familiar with the traditional sleeven story of creation?"

"Of course, in the beginning, God created the heavens and earth. He did this in seven days."

Eveline cupped her hands to her cheeks. "Yes, we definitely have our work cut out for us."

"I take it, that's not what you want to hear."

"In faigal doctrine, the creator is known as the Mother Prime."

Adelie chimed in excitedly. "Like mother nature?"

"As I was saying, in the beginning, when Mother Prime forged the cosmos and all the celestial realms. She also constructed the Ethereals, as well as sleeven in her image."

"What are Ethereals?"

"Ethereals act as emissaries to all the spiritual and physical realms. Sleeven will sometimes refer to them as angels."

Adelie eagerly nodded. "Yes, I know what angels are."

"Why am I not surprised?"

"After the eventual fall of sleeven, Prime bayed a third of the Ethereals to remain, safeguard, and observe. Hundreds of legions stayed. Arke led one of these legions. Little did the Ethereals realize that their service in this world was to be an extensive servitude. A servitude as babysitters to sleeven-kind."

"Ethereals were essentially immortal. However, they began to die out as they were now stranded and no longer impervious to sickness and death. The longer they remained, the less they remembered who or what they were. Driven mad, many procreated with sleeven and other wild beasts to secure their survival. This created all manner of abominations that began to populate the various dark corners of the realms."

"Arkes' dwindling legions remained steadfast and pure, and because of this obedience, Mother Prime sent for Arke. Many of Arkes' brethren had retreated into the other realms, away from Prime's creations. Mother Prime sealed these doorways to the other realms and charged the legions of Arke with their eternal guardianship."

"After receiving this news, they were disheartened and broken. Every day they remained; a piece of their essence was forever lost. One day, they could very well succumb to the wickedness of our brothers. Arke went before Mother Prime and pleaded their case. Mother Prime sat in deep contemplation at their words."

"In the end, a vertriste was offered to the legions of Arke. They were given a blessing to acquire one single creation. It was agreed that Arkes' legions would be allowed to pass their seed on to the birds. Of all the world's inhabitants, the bird is the only one with complete reverence for the sky. It is the only creation that remembers where it came from, so it would never forget."

"It was also agreed that the gift of first light would be gifted to the strongest amongst the legions' offspring, to protect against the shadows. Arke names this new offspring the faigal, the new watchers of the skies. To this day, our people flourish across this world!"

Willet looked unflinching at Eveline before she spoke. "You're saying we come from birds?"

Eveline huffed. "Well, if you need to simplify our linage with sleeven understanding."

"Sounds like some demented fairytale. I think I like Adelie's alien theory better."

Laraline was bemused at her quick response. "I know how this must sound."

"I don't think you really do. So, you're telling me everyone in this house is an angel-bird thing?"

Evelyn corrected her politely. "We are Faigal."

"My bad, faigal. So, everyone here is a faigal."

"Ms. Broom and Mrs. Weever are sleeven kind."

"If everyone believes this bird creation jazz, where are your wings?"

"We are not bird people, we are flesh, blood, and wings."

"What's the difference?"

Evelyn looked accusingly at Laraline. "See, that's why it is so important to learn the Asclan at a much younger age. One is more accepting and open to the truth. When one reaches an older age, the mind is more jaded and closed to new perspectives!"

Willet interrupted Evelyn's chastisement of her mother. "That still doesn't explain the lack of wings!"

Laraline looked at Willet impatiently. "We hide our wings!"

Adelie turned her attention to Laraline. "Do you have wings, mama?"

Laraline, with her arms still folded, gave her a wink. "I may have a couple of wings tucked away somewhere."

Adelie's eyes were wide. "Let's see them, can you actually fly?"

Willet was quick to dismiss this. "Of course not. She can't fly, dork!"

"How do you know?"

"The next thing you will tell us is that dragons are real."

Evelyn scoffed. "Ridiculous, the Verithraxus have been banished for at least four hundred years."

Willet rolled her eyes. "Are we quite done with fantasy hour? I'd like to go back to my room?"

Laraline's impatience was growing. "That quite enough of this attitude, Willet!"

"Look, even I do decide to accept this truth, as you put it. How do I reconcile this with myself? If my father, as you all are so quick to point out, is not part of this little club. Where does that leave me and my sister?"

Evelyn was sober as she continued. "I won't lie. This situation is more difficult for you two, considering your connection to the human world. You are considered a lek, among our people, a half-breed. There is a level of prejudice you would have to endure. You would have to work harder to prove your worth among the faigal community."

"Prejudice amongst the higher evolved life forms, image that. What about ordinary people, how do they feel about us?"

"You're referring to Sleveens. Very few know of our existence. Those that do, fall into two camps. Some are sympathetic; while many others are threatened by our very existence."

"How is your existence a secret to humans? That makes no sense, how could they not know about something this big."

"Well until now, you had no idea yourself."

"So human and faigal look that much alike?"

"Only on the outside, our internal makeup is quite a different story. However, to your point, no two races can cohabit without any crossover. We have been very influential on greater sleeven society over the centuries. Faigal culture has informed fashion, art, clothing, literature, government, science, and military."

"What influence has man had on you?"

"I'm sure there have been a few, but I can't seem to recall them."

"Typical."

"Well, speaking from a non sleeven point of view, I can only speak to what I know. We even inform the basis of religion. I mean there are versions of the Asclan available in many new age bookstores and coffee shops around the world.

"How is that even possible, I still don't get why people haven't discovered you, I mean if they're selling your bible.?"

"When most sleeven hear the word faigel, they think of a religious term, like Baptist, Amish, or Muslim. Very few actually know the depth of our biological origins. The Asclan is advertised as a kind of Wicken coffee table book or some sort of nonsense, because of the inclusion of basic shammas."

"What are Shammas?"

"Spells."

"Like real spells?"

"Of course."

"So, you can do magic like witches and wizards?"

Evelyn rolled her eyes. "That's one thing I wish we could influence more. The sleeven desire for vulgar barbaric terms such as witches."

Willet finally piped up. "Do you have proof of any of this?"

"Proof?"

"Anything to back up what you're saying besides this old book!"

"You're talking about wings again, aren't you?"

"Of course I am."

"Perhaps we have evolved from having wings!"

Adelie quickly pointed to the floor. "What about all the feathers on the floor by the bed."

Evelyn seemed embarrassed. "Do not make mention of a female when she is molting, it's considered rude and improper."

Willet rolled her eyes. "You cannot be serious, they're just feathers!"

"In our culture, feathers are sacred. It is as if one were exposing him or herself."

Laraline, who had been silent, finally interjected with a serious motherly tone. "Girls, most ordinary humans can be very reactionary with anything they don't understand. You need to understand that we have to be very careful. We can't have any slip-ups. It could be rather dangerous to be exposed to this world with wings."

Willet nodded as if the weight of what she had to say was crucial. "Well logically speaking, I guess that makes sense."

Noticing Laraline's successful exchange, Evelyn backtracked her last comment. "Perhaps later I can show you my full bloom."

"Bloom?"

"My open wingspread."

"Really?"

"Sirenna is the one with a more extraordinary plumage, that is why she always spends so much time in her aviary. She loves to bloom."

"Later? You can't give me anything now. I mean no offense, but this book still hasn't made this a conclusive reality."

"Well, on the back page of the Asclan, there are some old pictures and in particular, a newspaper clipping!"

Adelie flipped to the back of the book and snatched a folded news clipping spread of an old black and white photo. The article title simply read **Worlds Fair, Chicago**. There was a photo spread of events at that time. Many of the pictures were of festive crowds around the so-called technological wonders of the future.

Evelyn motioned toward the second photo near the bottom. In the foreground stood some sort of encased glass tank. A winged humanoid dangled from some wire cords behind the glass. The image was grainy and unclear. Willet angled the picture as if her perception would change what she was seeing.

"Is that what the wings look like?"

"That's not real, we destroyed the original corpse."

"Destroyed?"

"Well, we can't have any real proof of our existence. As I said earlier, that would be catastrophic."

Evelyn tapped her finger on the tortured figure in the picture.

"What we have here is just smoke and mirrors. That is not what I wanted you to see. Look carefully at the crowd below."

Willet leaned in to get a closer look at the photo. At first, she did not see anything. Just an assortment of strangers marveling at the strange exhibit.

"What, I don't see anything."

"Look a bit closer."

Was there some puzzle she was supposed to notice? All she saw was a crowd of ordinary people. She was about to give up when she noticed a young Uncle Merle standing with another woman. Merle looked quite different from the drunkard at dinner. He was dressed in a suit and was clean-shaven, but it was definitely him. She looked at the woman beside him. Suddenly she realized who she was looking at. She looked back up at Evelyn looking down at her.

"Hey!"

"Yes, the woman beside him is yours truly."

Willet looked back down at the photo. This time she focused on the young girl beside him. She did look familiar. She could not place her until Adelie gasped.

"Momma! Is that you?"

Willet took a double take of the photo, as Laraline confirmed. "Yes, I had always wanted to see The World's Fair."

"How old were you?"

"I believe I was sixteen at the time."

Willet looked harder at the photo and behold, it was the younger version of their mother. She looked up at Laraline who was still near the door. She then looked back at the photo. The date on the clipping was 1930.

"That was so long ago, how is this even possible!"

Laraline searched for a scientific answer. "Faigal metabolism is quite different than sleeven."

"That would make you how old?"

Laraline folded her arms as if insulted. "Old enough, young lady!"

Adelie perked up. "Are you immortal?"

Evelyn quickly answered. "Far from it, we get old and sick, just like all Mother Prime's creations. We just do it a bit slower."

Willet turned to her mother suddenly. "Did father know or was that something you kept from him too?"

Laraline looked at Evelyn coldly, before walking across the room. She knelt before her children and touched both their faces.

"Listen, I never kept any secrets from your father. He was a good and decent man, who knew what he was getting into. We were equals in our marriage and in life. That was one of the things I detested, the secrets in my family!"

Laraline felt a familiar presence behind her and quickly added. "Which is why we had to leave here, isn't that right Aunt Sirenna!"

Sirenna was suddenly at Evelyn's door. She was dressed in a bright red jumper and matching red and pink cape. She wore dark pink sunglasses that concealed her poker face.

"Your mother finally decided to teach you about the birds and the bees. With the emphasis on birds, I assume."

Laraline responded with an uncharacteristic bite in her tone. "In light of recent events, we thought it best."

Sirenna was unflinching as she bit back. "It's about time you came to your senses niece."

Laraline impatiently sighed. "What exactly do you want, Auntie?"

"I'm going to town to pay Ms. Broom's astronomical doctor bill, and shop for some more watchdogs, among other errands."

"What happened to the old dogs?"

Sirenna quickly avoided the subject. "That's beside the point. I thought our young guests may be a bit stir-crazy and want to get out to see the town."

Laraline wondered if this was a peace offering or if she was up to something. Sometimes it was hard to read Sirenna.

Laraline suspiciously probed. "Just you?"

"Merle is driving. Don't worry, it's too early for him to start drinking."

Even though the house's atmosphere appeared to settle into a semblance of what constituted normalcy, Willet nervously interjected. "What about my fight with Phoebe?"

Sirenna laughed loudly. "Don't be ridiculous. There won't be any fight. Do you want to go to town or not?"

Laraline had mixed feelings after her aunt's behavior. However, Sirenna had the respect of a mob boss around town, so she knew the girls would be, at least physically safe. Perhaps it was what they needed to break up the stress of the day.

Sensing her apprehension, Sirenna impatiently added. "They are in safe hands."

Laraline looked back at her daughters. "Do you wish to get out?"

Adelie quickly squealed. "Heck yeah!"

Willet looked at Sirenna pensively, as the older woman stood smiling at her. She almost seemed to be studying them from behind her shades. Willet gave a solemn answer. "Perhaps."

Laraline turned to Sirenna. "What time will you be back?"

Sirenna looked up from her glasses. "Really Lynn?"

"Yes, really!"

"Before dinner, I suppose."

"I guess it would be good for them. Mind your aunt and be polite to your elders, girls."

Laraline and Sirenna both looked pointedly at Willet. She noticed this and quickly chimed in with a coy response. "Yes, mother dear."

Willet was pouring it on a bit thick and it wasn't lost on Sirenna. "Well, I'll have Merle bring the car around. Come on children. "

"Wait, let me talk to them a moment first."

Suddenly it felt uncomfortable. Laraline looked like a stern parent who wanted privacy to deal with her children. There was almost an unspoken standoff for several moments. The aunts wanted to hover, making sure their will was enforced properly. The single mother had to push the point, that these were still her children.

Finally, Sirenna relented. She walked away from the door and headed down the hall toward the stairwell, apparently unconcerned. Evelyn was now the third wheel and quickly anticipated their need for a private moment. "Please shut my bedroom door when you're done. I don't want Dadu to tear up my room."

"Yes, Auntie."

Laraline waited several moments, listening for the tell-tale sounds that would indicate Sirenna and Evelyn were both downstairs. "Neither of you are to speak a word about any of this in public. We all must blend in with society if we are to remain safe."

Adelie nodded. "Of course, mama, not a word!"

Willet was still on the fence with her acceptance of this truth, but the behavior of her mother was convincing. "Mom, relax! Why would we even bring such a crazy story up? I'm not an idiot."

"Just promise me. It's forbidden to speak of such things among humans."

"What would happen if someone did?"

"It would not be good for either party, faigal or human!"

In that moment, Willet had a kind of mini epiphany. "Which is why you had to leave home!"

"Willet."

"Ok, I promise, not a word."

"Thank you."

Laraline quickly changed the subject. Willet felt this seemed to be the meat of what Laraline wanted to discuss. She leaned closely and lowered her voice.

"You may hear some things from your great aunt, and she may ask you questions. Just listen and don't ask questions. Don't give any information about yourself other than simple answers. You both know what I mean."

Both girls had graduated into becoming teenagers and had mastered the calculated art of evading direct questions and authority disinformation. At this age, it seemed to be their specialty. Adelie could even use the bubbly innocent stare, which she seemed to have perfected, to give the impression that she was a bit ditzy or a complete airhead.

They both nodded in unison as if they were going on some covert mission or at least that's the way it felt to Willet.

Laraline added. "Above all, trust your instincts."

Willet looked at her mother's face. "You don't trust Aunt Sirenna, do you?"

"She won't let anything happen to either of you. If I thought that any harm would befall you, I would not let you go with her!"

Willet rejected the deflection. "That's not what I asked."

"I know what you asked."

"You don't trust her?"

Willet found her mother's response quite peculiar. "I trust you."

E.J GAMBLES

Chapter 18: On The Town with Auntie

Sirenna led them to a purple Cadillac with bright whitewall tires. Dark-tinted windows shielded them from the outside world. Uncle Merle's involvement in the current travel plans was predicated on the fact that he was the only family member with a valid driver's license.

Patsy lived down the road in her own little world, and neither sister had bothered to learn to drive. To be fair. Evelyn did have a permit, and though it had expired, at times she would make small trips when necessary. Truth be told, if it were not for the mobility issue, it is uncertain how much involvement they would actually have had with their younger brother.

Adelie called shotgun with the intent of not sitting with her creepy aunt, as she had started to refer to her, so she sat in the front with Uncle Merle. Willet could not blame her sister, after all, being the youngest, she wouldn't normally be able to sit in the front seat.

In light of her public showdown with Sirenna, Willet was pissed to be in the backseat with the woman. As she climbed into the back, she just knew this was going to be a very long, quiet ride and wondered if she should have stayed home with her mom.

Willet sat behind Uncle Merle so that Sirenna could take her position of authority in the back passenger side of the car. Willet noticed Aunt Sirenna eyeing Merle's driving and the dashboard. She chose to ignore Sirenna's domineering manner and looked out the window.

"Watch your speed, Merle, all we need is for you to get another ticket!"

His response was usually silence. He rarely spoke unless he was drinking. Instead, he glanced in the rearview mirror at Sirenna who was studying his measured behavior. He was not drunk like he was the night before. However, he did look a bit disheveled. Willet supposed he was nursing a hangover.

Willet had her hands in a tight ball, as she looked about the car and out the window. She glanced at one of the owls near the perimeter as they passed. She was starting to drown out the world when Sirenna finally spoke.

"So, your mother cautioned you about your wicked auntie."

Willet tried to act surprised. "I don't know what you are talking about."

"We have all afternoon together. Lies do not become us, nor do they protect us, and sometimes, they can even destroy us."

This slight directed towards Laraline was not lost on Willet, however, she couldn't deny her aunt's cryptic words. At the moment, it was as if this old woman was offering an olive branch to Willet, who acknowledged her gesture cautiously by changing the subject.

"Why aren't there any mirrors in Greywood?"

"There are a few."

"I didn't see any."

Sirenna folded her arms. "It's important to minimize the risk of allowing any more cracks and other openings to spread."

Willet had no idea what her aunt's statement meant, but it was stated in such a matter-of-fact manner, all she could do was politely nod. Willet turned back to the window in utter bewilderment.

They had made their way down Blue Jay Way when she finally turned to Sirenna with a concrete concern. "You said there wouldn't be a fight between Phoebe and myself."

"Highly Doubtful."

"How do you know?"

"Are you afraid of her?"

"No, not really."

"There is a wildcard factor you may not know about her."

"What would that be?"

"If Phoebe was interested in fighting, she would have struck you back when the altercation first happened. The moment was lost. Understandably, most people avoid conflict. They run from it, even if it means they live subservient to the whims of others. For all practical accounts, your cousin is a coward."

"Are you saying, she will just let it go?"

"You already know the answer to that."

"A surprise retaliation is the wildcard factor?"

Sirenna nodded. "Very good, in some ways a coward is more dangerous. She would most likely have you attacked or beaten, by someone she or her mother has hired. That way, no one gets their hands dirty. That is the aristocratic way of doing things."

"Is that how you prefer to do things, the aristocratic way?"

"Sometimes. However, I don't mind getting my hands dirty. I don't mind conflict!"

"Some might say you enjoy conflict!"

"As well as you do. Do not underestimate the power of conflict. Without it, there is no change, not really. That is the only reason I am the longest-ruling matriarch of the Adler dynasty. The members of this family may hate me, or find my methods disturbing, however, no one else wants to make the hard choices!"

Willet quickly called out her righteous indignation. "Like throwing a widowed mother and her two children out on the street."

"Believe me, I've done far worse."

"I don't doubt you have."

"You are a lot like me in that respect."

"How?"

"You aren't afraid of conflict either. That is a rare asset. Even with the limitations of your blood lineage, you have the ability to get pretty far in life."

"Limitations?"

"We all have them."

"I know you think my human blood is a limitation. However, you're wrong. In fact, I'll bet it proves to become a great asset."

Sirenna glanced out the window as if bored from the conversation. "Well, we can agree to disagree."

They had driven about a half mile down the road when Merle pulled up to the curb. On the roadside, an ancient-looking flatbed truck was parked beside a large fenced-in pasture. The truck itself was very nondescript. It did not seem to have an actual color, as it was so old and most of the color was worn away.

The truck's cab had a large bulky bundle covered carefully and tied down with a large blue tarp. Two men were discreetly tying down a large blood-soaked burlap sack underneath the tarp. At first, when Merle pulled up, both men seemed nervous until he rolled down the window. They seemed to become more at ease as they recognized who was in the car.

"Merle Adler, is that you?"

"What seems to be the trouble, fellas?"

The slightly older guy tipped his straw hat and put his hand on his hip. "Them varmints got a whole bunch of my goats again. That's the fourth time in two weeks!"

"Oh my, didn't your dog stop them?"

"Well, Goliath chased after one of them but he never came home. I fear they got him as well."

Sirenna impatiently leaned forward with her shades at the bridge of her nose. "Merle, why have we stopped?"

"Sorry sis, but Mr. Dunn has had some troubles with the night visitors."

Ira Dunn stuck his head inside the window. "Sorry to disturb ya Lady Adler, but I was wonderin', did you have any issues last night?"

"No, it was a surprisingly uneventful evening." She threw a hard glance at Willet. "However, I am going to town to replace the dogs, yet again."

Dunn turned to face the forest, he then hacked and spat a wad of whatever he was chewing on, before replying. "Wow, they're getting' real brazen. Mrs. Lance, down the road, lost her 400-pound seed bull last month."

Merle, who wasn't much of a talker, finally interjected. "Isn't she the one with all the cats?"

"Yeah, they lost a few cats as well."

"Oh my."

Sirenna mumbled to herself. "Well, a few cats is hardly a tragedy around here!"

"So, are these your grandchildren, Lady Adler?"

"Grandnieces. I'm taking them into town for a bit. If you excuse me, we need to get going. Vero is supposed to drop by sometime today. If you want, I can tell him to stop by your place as well."

"I'd be much obliged, Lady Adler.

"Well, good day gentlemen."

Merle abruptly sped off, as he could feel Sirenna growing impatient. Willet looked back at the truck. The burlap bags sat peeking out from under a thick tarp. She looked at Sirenna who was now filing her nails. "What was that all about?"

"What do you mean?"

"He said something killed his goats?"

"Just wildlife."

"Why did Uncle Merle refer to them as night visitors?"

"One thing you will soon find out about Uncle Merle is that he is very theatrical. I believe he even attended some theater classes in Essex. Isn't that right little brother?"

Merle cleared his throat. "All the world is a stage, and all the men and women are merely players. They have their exits and entrances, and one man in his life plays many parts."

Sirenna gave a subtle clap as Merle pretended to bow. "Thank you, thank you!"

Willet inquired about the passage Merle chose to recite. "So Shakespeare is a human influence?"

Merle and Sirenna gave her a queer stare.

"What did I say?"

Merle seemed insulted as he corrected her. "Shakespeare was a faigal. Everyone knows that."

Willet did not know exactly how to respond. Instead, she remained silent. The rest of the drive to town was awkwardly quiet and heartbreakingly serene. Fortunately, for Willet, they were nearing town. She could see the observation tower of the school getting closer.

Sirenna cleared her throat. "Do you see that building on our left?"

"Yeah, I guess so."

"That is Talomore Academy. You will both be attending starting in the new semester. Your appointment is in a few days."

Willet remained silent but politely nodded. The building seemed massive to her. It looked more like a college than a secondary school. She recognized that tower. Mrs. Weever tried to show them the school from the hall window. It's funny how different things look, in the light of day.

Willet glanced at the vast parking lot and was reminded of the transportation issue they faced. "So, why aren't there any buses in town? It doesn't make any sense. I mean there are cars everywhere. Is it something based on religion?"

"It has more to do with our inherent faigal nature. Public transportation lumps everyone together equally. That, to put it simply, will not do."

"What is wrong with that, some would say your reasoning is elitist."

"We are territorial beings and there are many different lineages among us."

"You mean like different species?"

Sirenna was slightly insulted as she tried to explain. "We are not animals!"

Willet quickly tried to diffuse the hot topic. "I didn't mean to insult!"

Sirenna took a deep breath and continued. "We have very instinctual adversaries within our own kind. The public transportation would have to be large enough to allow room to dissect and separate the various clans."

"As an Adler, your spirit lineage is the great horned owl. The Branson spirit lineage is the carrion crow. Even in nature, the two groups do not integrate well. The owl and the crow are mortal enemies."

"Birds of a feather flock together."

"Exactly!"

"In the world I come from, that is called segregation."

"You think you can dissect us with typical sleeven self-righteous hypocrisy. Just because your sleeven have given it a word, doesn't mean you are not above exercising and manipulating its mechanics for your desires. Whether you believe it or not, it is a necessary evil of the physical world."

Willet couldn't really argue the point she was making. On the surface, it was cynical and depressing. She decided she was tired of talking to her aunt. It wasn't helping her mood at all.

They had gotten close to their destination and Sirenna suddenly turned her attention to Adelie. "What is one of your favorite things to do?"

Adelie was shocked, as it was the first time someone addressed her directly since she had arrived in town. "Are you talking to me?"

"Of course, you're Merle's silent copilot."

"Are you trying to butter me up?"

"That depends"

"Depends, on what?

"If you like to go shopping!"

Adelie's eyes glowed with excitement. "It is one of my favorite things!"

"I thought so. I can tell by the way you put your attire together."

Sirenna leaned forward to the front seat to get a better look at Adelie. Willet looked at her own clothes, feeling a bit like a plain Jane.

Sirenna responded with more honey. "You should come with me on Saturday. We will make a day of it, if you wish!"

"Sounds good to me, as long as it's ok with momma."

"We'll see what we can do. In the meantime, would you hold on to this for me?"

Sirenna extended her gloved fist forward and placed a wad of money into Adelie's lap.

Willet watched in astonishment as Sirenna easily seduced her sister. Adelie was grinning from ear to ear, as she picked up the money and began to count. The car suddenly stopped beside some strange municipal building. It resembled a temple by the roof, but it had an office vibe on the outside.

Sirenna sat silently and waited for Merle to get out and open her door. Willet looked around carefully trying to get a bearing on their location. Adelie turned around in her seat to face Sirenna. "So where are we going shopping first Auntie?"

Sirenna was curt and suddenly emotionless. "Turn around in your seat Adelie, that's not very ladylike."

The young girl slowly complied as Willet mumbled under her breath. *pathetic!*

Adelie was about to reply to Willet but stopped when Merle pulled Sirenna's door open. A wash of white light temporarily blinded the girls. Sirenna adjusted her sunglasses in response, as she climbed out of the car. Both girls followed behind. Willet imagined she was climbing from a dark coffin. As her eyes adjusted to the day, Sirenna finally responded to Adelie's question.

"Well, I will have to take a raincheck today, perhaps you could do me a favor and share that money with your older sister. While you two go exploring the town, I have to run a few errands!"

Willet was uneasy. "You're just leaving us?"

"I have adult matters to take care of. You see where we are parked. There are some shops over there on Martin. There is also a local diner across the street. I will meet you there to pick you two up around four!"

Willet watched in disbelief as Sirenna and Merle headed into the municipal building. All they could do was watch them disappear. At the last minute, Willet realized a crucial fact that she was missing. She yelled in their direction. "What is the name of the diner?"

Adelie's face fell. "What do we do now?"

Willet looked at her little sister holding a handful of twenties in her fist. She promptly snatched the bundle from her and put it in her pocket.

Adelie quickly protested. "Hey!"

"I'm still in charge when mom is not here. We will use one of these twenties and give momma the rest. Willet handed a single bill back to Adelie who proceeded to snatch it back from Willet and put it in her pocket.

"Just don't lose it."

"I'm not stupid!"

Normally Adelie would fight tooth and nail about something like taking money from her. However, Adelie wasn't stupid. Willet would gladly explain how she acted around Sirenna and she didn't want her mother to know that. Willet finally looked at her sister.

"Are you hungry?"

"Very!"

"Come on, let's see if we can find that diner."

Chapter 19: The Perfect Chocolate Milkshake

The main road in Meadowlark was Martin and it pretty much stretched the length of the town. Today the Swift girls traveled the same stretch of road, visiting a variety of tiny specialty shops, the kind that littered most small tourist towns. The strange thing about Meadowlark was there seemed to be no obvious visitors.

As Willet led Adelie down the quaint sidewalks, there was a prominent vibe. This was a small town and outsiders had to pay their dues. Most people did not acknowledge the girls, even when they openly greeted them. It was kind of disheartening as they made their way through waves of cold and indifferent stares. It was beginning to feel as though they had made a mistake coming to town until Adelie spotted a small café on the corner of Renfrew and Martin.

"Can we stop there and get some food?"

Willet looked at the sign for the café. It was one of those upscale mom-and-pop diners.

"I guess so."

As they made their way across the street, Willet picked up a familiar scent. It was the smell from the hotel. She looked about in search of a person with that distinct smell. She froze in the middle of the crosswalk and scanned her whereabouts nervously.

"Willie, what's wrong?"

Not wanting to alarm Adelie, by reminding her about the scary hotel tenant, she brushed it off.

"Nothing, I was daydreaming."

The moment they entered the café, Willet felt more at ease. The gentle aroma of bread and herbs filled her lungs. The place was not quite crowded but seemed to be mildly busy. They waited at the front beside a sign that read, **PLEASE WAIT TO BE SEATED.**

Willet was starting to feel a bit hungry. It wasn't as if she had eaten that morning. With all the drama with Phoebe, she had neglected to eat, and the night before she wasn't excited about the meal, so she was well on her way to malnutrition.

She found herself curiously staring at the plates of food that had been served on the other tables. Everything looked very appetizing. After a few minutes of salivating at other people's food, a young girl with pigtails finally strolled up to them. She wore an apron and had a warm smile.

"Welcome to Linnet's Diner, please have a seat ladies!"

"Is this the only diner in this area?"

"This is the only diner in town. Don't like the vibe?"

"We're supposed to meet our great aunt at a diner on Martin."

"Then please have a seat, you are at the right place."

Willet purposely led Adelie to the closest window seat. This way she had a vantage point of Sirenna's car. It was at a distance, but still in their line of sight. She was pretty sure this was the diner that Sirenna was talking about, however, if she didn't show up, she could see the car. Her mother's words about trust entered her head.

The girl with the pigtails returned to the table with two menus. "Hello, I'm Tori and I will be your server today."

"Yeah, do you have any vegan options?"

The waitress paused for a moment as if processing what Willet just asked. She then pointed down to a decorative square at the bottom of the menu. This section is pretty much all we advertise, but if you think of something else you'd like, the chef will try to accommodate."

"Ok, thanks."

"You know, if you're not feeling the dairy thing, we have an incredible chocolate milkshake with Oat milk that is to die for!"

Adelie nodded. "Yeah, that sounds good!"

Willet continued to look at the menu before adding other items. "Ok, can I get the vegetable rice noodles, a large garden salad, a large plate of French fries, and two large milkshakes?"

"Hungry much?"

"Extremely."

"Where are you guys from?"

"Another world called Key West!"

"Wow, I always wanted to go to Florida."

"Yeah, I miss it sometimes."

"So, you moved here?"

Willet corrected the server. "My mother moved us here, to be close to her family."

"Well, that sucks."

"That's the adventure that is my life!"

"What's your name?"

"Willet Swift and this is my little sister Adelie."

"Well, my name is Tori Ingram and in addition to being a professional in culinary hospitality, I am a junior at Talomore Academy."

Adelie eyes widened. "That's the local school, what's it like?"

Tori resembled a bubbly pixie with red pigtails, as she dramatically responded. "Horrible, have you seen it?"

Willet nodded. "Yeah, on the way here."

"Doesn't It remind you of some medieval dungeon, especially with the large tower in the middle of the quad?"

Willet cracked a smile at Tori's animated explanation. It was the first time she remembered smiling in quite a while. Tori continued in a most exaggerated manner. "I will be a senior next year. I only have one more year to endure that prison."

"Well, we have to meet the headmistress to see where we are going to be placed!"

"Headmistress Faulkner isn't human. I swear I think she is some sort of lizard!"

Willet felt a bit uneasy, as Tori made the lizard comment. Perhaps it was just a flippant comment about some mean teacher. However, now she was ultra-sensitive about the remote possibility that she wasn't completely human herself.

Tori continued her small-town grilling. "How old are you?"

Adelie cleared her throat. "Well, I'm almost sixteen."

Willet answered cautiously. "I just turned seventeen."

"Great, you will probably be in my grade. I'm glad to see some interesting people are finally moving here. I can't wait till I graduate. I'm going to Georgetown, which is far away from here!"

An older woman's voice boomed from the back. "Tori, get back to work or you can go on a permanent break!"

Tori jerked from the threat and frantically answered. "I was just getting their order; I'm on my way!" Before she left, she gave a devilish look. "To be continued."

Adelie giggled. "She seems nice."

Willet noticed Adelie looking out the window. At that moment, she was reminded how much older Adelie appeared. She looked like she was the same age as Willet from first glance. At the tender age of 15, she was overly developed and had turned many a guy's head. Willet herself had taken a different path in the growth department.

Until quite recently, Willet was flat chested and thin as a rail until last summer when everything changed. She had suddenly just blossomed outward. It was a very uncomfortable feeling, when adults, who had seen you grow up as this quirky little tom boy who loved to read, are suddenly eyeing your womanly parts a little too much. Willet had gotten lost in her own thoughts as she dazed out the booth window.

She started to wonder where Sirenna and Merle disappeared to. Were they still in that building? Willet looked hard at the building behind the car. From this angle it had the appearance of a large temple. It even had gabled arches in the entrance. For a moment, she pondered if it was some sort of faigal church. Her eyes scanned up toward the building's spire when she suddenly felt lightheaded.

Tori returned to the table. "Your food should be ready in a few minutes."

Willet glanced slowly up at Tori. "Can I get a glass of water, I feel a little sick?"

"Yeah, you don't look so good!"

"I don't think I ate enough today."

"Well, if you can hold on, I think your salad is about ready."

As soon as Willet started to eat the garden salad, she started to feel a little better. A few minutes later Tori brought the rest of the food. Both girls didn't bother talking, as they tore into the food as if they hadn't eaten in days.

Tori came back around with the check after things had settled down. Willet was quick to comment on their server's suggestion. "You're right, that milkshake was delicious!"

Adelie was animated. "It was the bomb, if I weren't so full, I'd get another!"

Tori exclaimed. "Yeah, I would like totally get one every day!"

Willet quickly cut into the conversation. "Hey, is there any place to hang out around town?"

"Do you drive?"

"No, my mother isn't big on us driving!"

"Well, this is a small town, but if you don't have a car, it can be frustrating. Luckily, I have a car of a sort, so I can drive down to Van Warren. It's nowhere like Key West, but it is a pretty cool place to hang!"

"Van Warren, where is that?"

"Van Warren boardwalk. Everyone hangs at the beach when school is not in session."

Willets's eyes widened. "I love the beach."

"You know a group of us are headed there, for the annual end-of-summer bash Saturday. Both of you should join us. We should have plenty of room."

"Really, that sounds great. I have to ask my mother."

Adelie had been sitting so quietly that Willet had almost forgotten she was even there until she entered into the conversation. "What time does it start?"

Tori shrugged as she addressed her. "Whenever people show up. Things usually don't start kicking till about 5."

Willet glanced back at the building. A large lime green truck coasted by the window. Willets's eyes widened as she saw it pass. There was instant recognition. She knew this truck from the Moonlight Inn parking lot. He does live in this town. This wasn't a figment of her imagination.

She suddenly hopped up and ran out of the booth. She pushed through the front door and out onto the sidewalk. She looked in the direction that the truck went, however, the street was vacant. There was no traffic in either direction.

Chapter 20: Incident on Martin Blvd

Willet found herself in a sudden panic. Her creeping fear had manifested into a sickness. A cold sweat covered her so that she began to have chills. Adelie quickly joined her outside on the sidewalk.

"Willet, what is wrong with you today, you didn't pay the bill?"

"Crap!"

Willet quickly reached into her pocket and shoved a couple more twenties into Adelie's fist. "Here, quick, give this to Tori. Tell her I got sick and had to step outside."

Adelie, not wanting to alienate the first person around their age that connected with them, quickly obeyed Willet without question. She ran back inside and waited for Tori to return to the table. After a few moments, both Adelie and Tori joined Willet on the sidewalk. By that time, Willet was kneeling down, as if out of breath. She felt a wave of nausea as she steadied herself.

Tori knelt down beside her with genuine concern. "Do you think it was something you ate that made you sick?"

"I don't think so. I've been feeling odd even before I started eating. It just got worse."

"Do you need a doctor or something? I can call if you want."

"I think I just needed some fresh air!"

"What happened?"

A crowd had started to gather around. She remained in an uneasy state. Willet suddenly felt dizzy and claustrophobic, as strangers started to enclose her out of morbid curiosity. She was about to scream when a voice boomed from beyond the crowd. "What seems to be the problem?"

A tall, but balding man dressed in a light grey uniform pushed his way through the huddle. Willet struggled to focus on him, as she felt an immediate dizzy spell and everything got blurry.

Adelie quickly explained. "My sister ran outside and got sick!"

Willet tried to rise but stumbled and fell on her butt, as she tried to sound lucid, but found herself slurring. "Are you a sheriff?"

The stranger knelt down beside her. At t his moment, she could see he had a thick mustache and rather coarse expression. "Something like that, I'm Constable Fletcher."

The officer extended his hand. "And who may you be miss?"

After much concentration she blurted. "Willet Swift."

"Ok Miss Swift, you want to explain to me what is happening?"

"Well, I was in the diner. I had just finished eating, when I thought I saw this truck, I ran after it and then I felt really dizzy."

Constable Fletcher looked up at Tori. "Did you see anything, Miss Ingram?"

"No. She suddenly ran out, and when I came out, she was on the ground."

The officer addressed the crowd in a large booming voice. "That will be all, people, please move along, you too Tori!"

As soon as the crowd started to dissipate, the officer turned back to Willet. "You said you ran out after a truck. What truck?"

Willet tried hard to focus. Unfortunately, she blurted out what was going on in her head.

"It was the green truck from a nightmare. When I got out here, I didn't see it, anymore!" Willet immediately realized how odd her explanation sounded.

The cop must of thought so too, as he began to treat her quite differently. "I see. Miss Swift, I'm going to ask you some personal questions and I need you to be completely honest!"

Willet was suddenly intrigued and scared. What question was he going to ask?

"Miss Swift, are you currently under the influence of any narcotics, or have you been drinking?"

"Drinking?"

Adelie interjected defiantly. "My sister hasn't been drinking, she just got sick!"

The officer quickly turned on Adelie. "So, you are the younger sister?"

"Yes, I am!"

"Where are your parents?"

"What?"

"Perhaps, we should call both your parents down at the station, I don't remember seeing either one of you around here before."

Even as the world was spinning, Willet was starting to fume. "What are you getting at officer?"

"This is a small town, and we don't like any trouble! "

Willet was about to get upset when a familiar voice snidely addressed the constable. "What on earth are you doing, Fletcher?"

"Ms. Adler, these are matters that don't concern you!"

"These matters are my great nieces, and it very much concerns me, constable!"

His eyes widened in horror, as he realized whom he was harassing. "Your nieces?"

Sirenna stood hovering and pointed down at Willet. "Why is she on the ground?"

"Sorry, Ms. Adler I had no idea who she was!"

"Did you put a hand on her?"

"Absolutely Not, Ms. Adler, I saw her on the ground, she said she got dizzy and fell.

"And your solution is to harass a child because they felt dizzy? Thank heavens she didn't pass out. I suppose she would have been arrested if she had."

Fletcher had now taken off his hat. "Ms. Adler, they didn't say they was with you!"

Adelie response was quick. "You didn't ask!"

"Did you ask them any questions about who they were? It's quite obvious you didn't, or she wouldn't be here still on the ground!"

"I'm so sorry. We just had another missing person right outside of the town limits, at that hotel on exit 14. They called it yesterday."

"Your investigations do not concern me, idiot! What does concern me is how you have shamed my family with your suspicions and incompetence!"

"I'm really sorry, Ms. Adler!"

"I'm not the one you harassed!"

The constable's demeanor was suddenly subservient. Willet recognized similar behavior from her mother, the night before. For a moment, she felt sorry for the guy, even though she enjoyed hearing Sirenna rip into him!

He quickly knelt down to apologize. "So sorry, Ms. Swift for the confusion. I deeply apologize for jumping to conclusions. If you wish, I can escort you and your family to the doctor, or home if you wish."

Willet nodded in acceptance, as she was too sick to respond. Sirenna answered for her instead, and her answer was quite different.

"Escort, do I think I want you following us home like a little lost puppy. I think you have done enough for today!"

Suddenly, the caddy pulled up to the curb. Merle was at the wheel waiting impatiently. His fingers drummed furiously on the dash. Sirenna barked at the officer. "Constable, open the door and help her inside. That is the least you can do."

Yes, Ms. Adler.

Fletcher did as he was told. He pulled open the door and carefully lifted Willet under her knees and slid her onto the seat. Adelie moved to the other side of the car, so she could join Merle in the front.

Fletcher tried in vain to appear more personable. Sirenna saw his efforts, and this pissed her off even more. "I didn't realize you had additional family, Ms. Adler."

"These are Laraline's children. You do remember Laraline?"

"I think that was before me."

Sirenna ignored him as she stood at her door and waited. Fletcher quickly dashed to the other side of the car and opened up her door. The older woman briskly slid into her seat and waited for the door to be shut. As he complied, she rolled her window down to respond to the obedient officer.

"Oh, that's right, you're the new constable that took over from Hanson."

"Yes mam, this will be my third year here in Meadowlark."

"Well, I preferred your predecessor, at least he wasn't a total moron."

With that, she rolled up the window in Fletcher's face. She then carefully adjusted her sunglasses and leaned back in her seat. "Get us out of here, Merle!"

Chapter 21: The Dog Whisperer

As soon as they drove off, Sirenna pulled off her gloves and set them on the seat between her and Willet. "It appears you two had a bit of excitement!"

Willet was short with her answer. "A tad."

Sirenna tilted her head down. "Please tell me you're not going to get sick in the car?"

Willet was a bit insulted, but too sick to say anything.

Sirenna turned to the front seat. "So, Adelie, did you do much shopping?"

"Not a lot."

"Perhaps next time."

Adelie realized that Sirenna had no intention of taking her shopping. She just wanted to see her reaction when she offered. She turned around and silently stewed in her seat.

Willet looked at Sirenna curiously. "How far away are we from the beach?"

Sirenna seemed puzzled. "The beach? Why are you asking about the beach?"

"This is a coastal town, so we are near the ocean."

"From what I've heard, it's not very far."

"You haven't been there?"

"I have no need of the beach."

"So you live in a coastal town and you've never been to the beach?"

"I never said that, why are we even talking about this?"

Willet got straight to the point. "Because. I would like to see the ocean."

"You should talk to your mother about such foolishness. I have had enough of this subject. I have had enough of any more verbal discourse in this car. I require silence."

145

Adelie's eyes met Merle's, who glanced over at her. Adelie carefully whispered. "Why is she so angry?"

"Shhh, she is just tired."

"She sounds so unhappy."

Sirenna quickly responded. "I said silence!"

Sirenna got so unusually prickly, that the mood in the car was uncomfortably silent for the remainder of the trip home. Willet had to bite her lip so as not to say another word. This sudden behavior made Willet even more curious. This wasn't like the confrontation at dinner. Sirenna, for the first time, seemed really upset, even vulnerable. Willet could not be sure, but through Sirenna's sunglasses, she thought she saw a tear stream down her face. This was hard to confirm, as Sirenna was facing the window.

Willet realized that she could almost remember the way back to the estate. After all, it was an almost straight shot. She thought about her mother and what she was doing. An irrational thought entered her head. What if her mother had packed up and left while they were gone? She and Addie would be stuck living with this horrible woman beside her.

She still felt a bit dizzy, but the feeling was less if she stayed still. In her clear mind, she thought about something the sheriff said. He mentioned something about a missing person, and a nearby hotel, right outside of town. He could very well be talking about the Moonlight Inn. Maybe something did happen. Perhaps they had inadvertently witnessed a crime after all.

Willet had plenty of time to contemplate the situation after she got back. Especially after her mother learned of the whole near-fainting incident, she was sent to her room to rest until dinner. With Willet in bed, Adelie decided to hang around with Evelyn and Laraline. Sirenna was in a mood and had locked herself up in her atrium for the evening.

Adelie's bonding time with Evelyn and her mother didn't last long, as she soon became bored. She began wandering around and discovered the massive chess board built near the back lawn patio. The board itself was formed from grass squares that stretched about the same length as a tennis court. The actual chess pieces were carved into the likeness of large white owls and black crows. Adelie didn't know the rules of the game, but it didn't really matter.

She walked up to one of the owls and realized that it almost reached her shoulder. She wrapped her arms around the base of the bird and lifted the piece. It had to weigh about twenty pounds but, she quickly dropped it back down panting as if it weighed a bit more.

Uncle Merle was standing a few feet away with a drinking flask in his grip. His attention was on Adelie dragging, lifting, and maneuvering the pieces about the various light and dark green checkered lawns. "Do you know how to play?"

"Not really."

"I could teach you one day, it's not hard. I taught your mother when she was your age!"

Adelie was not in the mood to learn. "That's ok."

Since he was no longer on the clock, Uncle Merle had fallen back into his bottles. He just sat in the backyard gazebo feeling sorry for himself. He still had his dress clothes on from the morning meeting; however, he had removed his shoes so he could feel the soft grass under his feet.

Adelie was playing outside for a while when a large grey truck appeared over the horizon. It was heading toward Greywood Manor estate. The gates were open from earlier. It had been an unusual day for the Adlers. As the truck pulled into the drive, Evelyn and Laraline came out to meet the driver.

Vero Ingram was the local harbormaster, but he would do the occasional odd jobs about town to supplement his varied income. One such job was deliveryman. Since he owned one of the larger vehicles in Meadowlark, any urgent items needing to be shipped locally, he could usually accommodate.

Vero had settled in Meadowlark almost 30 years ago. He was an immigrant who fled from Greece after a civil war broke out. Many of his family had elected to stay behind. Only a few cousins eventually made it out. With help from Avis Branson, his pregnant sister was eventually awarded citizenship. Vero was able to adopt 2-year-old Toridora Valencia, who was facing possible foster care after her mother's untimely death.

Evelyn recognized the large burley fellow immediately. "Vero, what brings you out this way?"

"Sirenna and her rush delivery."

"What rush delivery?"

"Her dogs."

"Oh yeah!"

"How come you go through so many dogs?"

Evelyn just nodded as he continued to grill her. As intimidating as Vero looked, he was quite the opposite. He was soft-spoken and rather sensitive for a guy. She knew his chastising came from a place of concern for the animals' welfare.

"I think this is the eighth order of dogs within the last ten years. Usually, they last a bit longer."

Evelyn sheepishly changed the subject. "Have you met my niece Laraline?"

"Laraline, this is Vero, he is the harbormaster." She discreetly leaned to Laraline's ear.

"If you have any questions about Langston, you could ask him."

"Hi, I'm Laraline Swift, nice to meet you, sir."

"Likewise, I understand that you just returned to Meadowlark."

"My two teenage daughters and I just arrived yesterday."

"I have a daughter, she works at the local diner."

Laraline struggled to understand his words, through his strange thick Greek Midwest accent.

Evelyn interjected. "You know his daughter Tori, from Linnet's. She waited on us the other day."

Laraline eyes registered sudden recognition. "Yes, such a sweet girl."

Vero continued with the surface pleasantries. "Heard about your loss, I'm so sorry."

"Loss?"

"Your husband."

Laraline was taken off guard that he knew. "How did you hear?"

"This is a small town. Langston was a good guy and very well-liked."

"Thanks so much, I didn't know you knew him."

"He was a regular fixture in these parts."

"What do you mean, regular? We have been living in Florida ever since my daughter was born."

"That may be true, but at least twice a month he ran his schooner about a mile outside of the pier. "

"When did this start?"

"A few years ago."

Laraline had the most peculiar look on her face. "When was the last time you saw him?"

Vero suddenly looked a bit bothered by her line of questioning until Evelyn had to explain to him. "He had been missing for several days when they found his remains aboard his boat, apparently it was found adrift about a hundred miles northwest of the Florida Keys."

"Oh, I didn't know how it happened."

"I'm just trying to find out what happened."

Vero finally answered. "I think it was mid-Spring when he was last up this way."

Laraline still seemed unsure. "Are you sure it was his boat?"

"The Lenore is the name of schooner, is it not?"

Laraline answered dryly, as if she were disappointed by the revelation. "Yes, it is."

"Well, I don't know too much more. I didn't talk to him that day. He did pick up a shipment the week he disappeared."

"Do you know from whom?"

"I will have to check my log. I think Branson signed the release."

Evelyn signed reluctantly. "Really."

Laraline looked horrified as she shared a troubling glance with her.

"Look, I don't mean to be short, but my truck is starting to smell like dog piss. I need to get them out. They're getting antsy."

Evelyn nodded. "Please, don't let me stop you."

Laraline looked over at Adelie who was a few yards away playing around with some Cardinals. A huge bird gathering had congregated in the center of one of the gardens, on the ground near the back of the house. "Adelie, can you tell Sirenna that her dogs are here?"

"Now?"

"Yes, now!"

"Where is she anyway?"

"She's in the aviary."

Adelie didn't answer as she had become completely enchanted by the birds once again.

"Adie, did you hear me?"

"Ok, just a moment."

"No, now!"

Adelie stomped off toward the house mumbling about being disturbed. She looked back twice to see if her mother was watching. As soon as she was out of range, Laraline turned back to Evelyn.

"I can't believe that my husband was doing jobs for the Bransons!"

"Perhaps it was indirectly."

"It was that monster who killed my mother."

"They never could prove that."

"I bet he had something to do with Langston's death as well. It would explain the condition of his body."

Evelyn sighed. "I highly doubt it."

"Why are you defending him?"

I'm not defending him, I just think there is a more logical explanation. What reason would he have to murder him? You and Langston were on the outs with Sirenna, and he didn't really know either of you!"

"Even so, I still think he may know something. I don't trust that family, they have done so much evil over the years to us."

Evelyn corrected her. "As have we to them, we are not innocent in our dealings with them."

"What are you talking about?"

Evelyn relented as she could see Laraline was growing irritated. "Nothing, so I guess we should probably talk to Avis."

"Will he meet with us, I mean as you said, I've barely talked to the man!"

"He will meet with me."

"You have always been the peacemaker. I don't know how you manage. I mean, even living with Sirenna! That takes strength."

"She is my sister. We grew up together. I know things about her and watched her deal with more pain and suffering than you could even fathom. I suppose she has seen me deal with things equally as horrific. That is what makes a family!"

Laraline was silent.

Evelyn continued carefully. "So, if I set up a meeting, you must watch your mouth."

Laraline impatiently answered. "Ok!"

"No, ok is not enough. There is still an uneasy truce between me and Avis. I do not need you tearing everything apart, in the heat of the moment. Do you understand?"

Laraline saw the concern on her face. "I understand."

"Good, I will reach out to him."

"What is the deal with the dogs? Merle says Sirenna shot the last ones because they were making too much noise?"

"Do you truly believe that?"

"I guess I don't know what to believe anymore. It's not like she is not disputing the rumors."

"Let's just say the dogs aren't working as well as they once did!"

"What happened?"

"Can I trust you to keep a secret?"

"You know you can."

"This is the truth. She took a shotgun to both dogs' heads!"

"Then it is true!"

"The truth is not always what it seems."

"You just said she killed the dogs with a gun."

"The problem is not what I said, but what I didn't say."

"Now I am confused."

"It was about four in the morning when she found both dogs whining. They had been attacked and mangled beyond recognition. She was merely putting them out of their misery."

"Oh my god, what happened to them? "

Evelyn threw her a knowing look. Laraline glanced back over her shoulder. She found herself staring at the foggy mist of the Greywood. She walked a few feet until she was at the perimeter. "I wish that place would just burn to the ground."

"That won't change the curse."

"I guess it won't, it will just have to run its course."

"You know Uncle Merle got lost in those very woods when he was a child. They didn't find him till after dark. I remember it like it was yesterday. He was so terrified. He never spoke of what he saw to this day. Something in him changed that day."

"His drinking problem?"

"No, his drinking started after he lost Marisol. It was as if after he came out of the forest, he was just a bit more fragile."

There was an uncomfortable silence. As both women looked at Merle passed out on the gazebo floor. Even though he was the one male heir of the Adler clan, he would never be considered for any position of authority.

Adelie suddenly came out of the front door, frantic. She had been crying, and her face was reddish. Every few steps she would blurt out a single word. "Mama!"

"Adelie, did you tell Sirenna about the dogs?"

"Mama come quick."

"What's wrong hon?"

"It's Willet, I went to check on her and she is burning up! Her skin is like fire and I can't wake her up!"

Chapter 22: The Fever

Mother Hazel spent most of her days in her tiny guest room on the first floor. The dimly lit room was adorned with a multitude of burning candles and incents. Originally recommended by Mother Gertrude Pence, Sephora was placed under a contract by Ronan Winton Adler. Ronan was a well-established weaver in his own right who wanted a nanny to teach his daughters, Sirenna, Oriole, and Evelyn, the old ways. With three heirs, the chances of one of them becoming a weaver were great.

He had been grooming Oriole to be his successor. Her other two sisters, Sirenna and Evelyn were aware that Oriole was highly favored. She was quite gifted and extremely striking. By the time she came of age, she had many hopeful suitors. Because of this, Mother Hazel had to become a protective parent. Though Mother Hazel never had offspring of her own, the Adlers had, over time, become like her own.

Mother Hazel was meditating that afternoon. She was somewhere near a trance state when she sensed that Sirenna had returned. However, there was something different. There was another presence. It was like a shadow that was trying to make itself known.

She could feel the energy, but there seemed to be no motive or thought. A weaver's powers grew over time. However, there were still limitations even for Mother Hazel. Only a select few were ever chosen to be weavers. Even Sirenna, as talented as she was in the arts would never be more than a garden variety enchantress.

It was a dying art among the faigal. It seemed with each generation, more of the faigal forgot about the ancient arts. To most of the younger generations, weavers were simply seen as holistic doctors who practiced parlor tricks.

Behind closed doors, in the echelons of power, the ancient arts were crucial to survival in the faigal world. Even Avis had to resort to importing a weaver from across the world. Only those royal families who could afford and manage the company of a weaver were considered to be of any importance.

Evelyn always had potential or at least that is what Mother Hazel had always felt, or at least she had the temperament. Even on a Namvula aptitude test, she scored within a 20-point range of a tempest, the highest order of weavers. However, her interest in the arts seemed to take a backseat to family concerns.

So, when Evelyn called for Mother Hazel within an hour of dinner. There was the slight hope that she had questions of enlightenment. However, on this occasion, Evelyn sounded frantic and concerned. "Mother Hazel, come quick!"

Mother Hazel first assumed that Sirenna had been attacked by the new dogs and needed medical assistance. Since she had been needling the watchdogs, it made sense.

However, her voice was coming from upstairs. Sirenna always spent her evenings in the aviary. Not wanting to exhaust her energy needlessly, she responded. "Is this important?"

"It's urgent!"

"What is it?"

"Please!"

Because of her age, Mother Hazel hated going upstairs, so much so, that she hadn't actually been upstairs in almost 9 months. This had caused much contention for the sisters. If they were in need of her council, everything had to be on the bottom floor. Which is probably why Sirenna started to spend the majority of her time downstairs in the atrium. Mother Hazel couldn't remember why she chose to come upstairs the last time. It seemed like it was something urgent, but she couldn't quite recall.

The steps were much larger than she remembered. Every time she ascended one, she would curse out loud. Her aggravation was growing with each step. To be fair there was an elevator at the end of the hall. Unfortunately, the entire situation was a catch twenty-two. She could take the elevator upstairs, then again, the elevator wasn't that quick.

At some point around the second flight of steps, Evelyn came to Mother Hazel's aid to quickly escort the older woman up to the second floor. On the way, she updated her on the situation that had started to develop.

When she arrived, Laraline was sitting beside a bedridden Willet. Adelie sat at the end of the bed with her arms folded, staring down at her older sister. As for Willet, her eyes were closed and her skin was wet and clammy. Her breathing was shrill and labored. Laraline looked toward the old woman as she made her way to the doorway.

Mother Hazel dismissed her sickness at first. "It looks like she is going through her first cycle!"

Evelyn corrected her. "That's what I thought but her mother says she already had a first cycle, when she was very young!"

"Perhaps it didn't quite finish, it does happen, delayed blooming."

"When does it ever cause unconsciousness?"

Mother Hazel glanced at Evelyn in disbelief. Then with her walking stick, she hobbled over to where Laraline knelt.

"When did this happen?"

"It was suddenly, she was feeling sick earlier today!" '

"How much earlier?"

"A few hours maybe."

Mother Hazel looked at Evelyn. "Was she unconscious when you found her?"

"Adelie found her, but I would say maybe an hour."

Mother Hazel reached out to touch Willet's forehead, almost immediately she recoiled her hand from the heat. "Sweet Arke, I need a large bucket of ice immediately!"

Laraline quickly ran out of the room toward the stairs. Adelie looked to the old woman, as soon as her mother left. "Is she going to be ok?"

"How old are you child?"

"I'm almost sixteen."

"Go help your mother."

Adelie quickly followed her mother, at which point Evelyn moved beside Mother Hazel. "What do you think?"

"Still working on it, I can't get close enough to tell. I need you to start a bath. The colder the better!"

Evelyn quickly obeyed, as she ran to the bathroom. She got a steady stream started as Laraline and Ms. Weever returned carrying a large trough filled with ice. Adelie soon followed with another smaller ice bucket. Hazel surveyed the scene. "Ok, bring the ice bucket!"

Adelie nodded and carried her container to the bed. Mother motioned to her. "Pour it on her face!"

"On her face! Won't that hurt?"

"This is life and death. Do it now!"

Adelie was quick and dumped her contents on her sister's face. A wave of steam erupted from the contact. Hazel, without missing a beat, motioned at Laraline. "You two put the rest of the ice in the bath. We need to cool her down. She is having trouble regulating her own temperature."

Laraline was now in a panic. "Is she going to die!"

Mother Hazel was frank. "Well, she is young and healthy, she has that going for her."

Evelyn was at the door and motioned them inside. As soon as the sound of ice pouring hit Hazel's ears, she called loudly. "Everyone grab a limb, we need to do this fast, she's going quickly!"

Evelyn and Laraline quickly lifted her torso. Even with wet clothes, she was very hot. Mrs. Weever grabbed her thighs and readjusted her position, as the heat caused her to flinch. Adelie, realizing she didn't have a limb, ran to make sure the door was open. As soon as they got to the edge of the tub. They all sort of gave her a toss. They immediately recoiled their hands and waved them about in the air, as if they had touched hot bread.

Willet dropped below the surface of the water, as an explosion of steam erupted from the tub. For several seconds the entire bathroom was a fog of steam. Suddenly there was a high-pitched scream. Willet lifted up in horror. Her eyes were now open and completely black. Laraline gasped at the sight of her daughter.

Suddenly Willet started to speak in a very strange tongue, Mother Hazel was quick and extended her hand and clenched the young girls forehead. She then shoved Willet's face back down below the icy water's surface.

Laraline instinctively reached out to stop Mother Hazel, but Evelyn caught her hand. "Do not interfere. If you want to save her you must let her do her job. She knows what to do!"

Mother Hazel used her weight as she knelt over at the edge of the water. Almost instantly, the old woman started to see images. Willet was projecting images from her dreams. At one point Mother Hazel screamed and recoiled her hand. The palm of her hand was blistered and red. Willet's head bobbed up and this time her eyes were closed. Mother hazel was out of breath, as she mouthed the words. "We need a lot more ice!"

Chapter 23: A Plague of Fishes

The town was not prepared for the storm that would fall upon them. It was, for the most part, an ordinary sunny afternoon. It was at least three hours till sunset, so the warm daylight bath was a typical reality. The dark clouds began to form out of nowhere. A few drops of hail started bouncing like tiny pebbles on the shops' roofs and beach docks. Droplets of rain sprinkled to give the illusion of seasonal normalcy.

When the first fish dropped down on the large sky roof of the aviary, Sirenna heard the thud. Her first thought was that it was a random bird. After all, it was still daylight. She saw the bizarre shape flopping about. She quickly ascended the highest branch, to get a closer look. It lay on its side heaving the acidic air. Its black iris rotated about in a circular motion as if it were trying to look at her.

Hail tapped about the ceiling as if someone were trying to put seasoning on the fish. She couldn't tell what kind of fish, but it was alert yet slightly confused.

A second fish fell a few feet from the first. This one slid down the side of the glass dome roof. It slowed down as if its own slimy body had created enough friction to sustain it, on a more vertical glass surface. A third and fourth fell almost on top of the first one. Sirenna quickly ran down the staircase. Just as the thundering of dozens of fish started to tumble down on the entire Greywood Estate.

On Martin Street, there was a traffic jam, as fish dropped during the 5 o'clock traffic. A few car windows shattered, as fish dropped like bombs onto the town. Tori had to run back into the diner, as she was suddenly pelted by fish!

Down the street, at Ambrosia beauty salon, Pasty and Phoebe were in the middle of getting facials. It was an early girls' day at the salon, to get their minds off the horrible incident earlier that morning. A large gust of wind blew in the front window. Hail and random fish poured inside. Though neither was hit directly with any of the fleshy debris falling inside, they were almost trampled by the crowd and chaos that ensued as they ran from the salon. At one point, both mother and daughter ran into the street, unaware of the condition of the weather. Only then, both were knocked to the ground with waves of raining fish.

Over in Celandine Springs, Avis and Aquila were hosting a business dinner for a possible merger with Ukrainian investors. They had booked a private patio at the Davenport, an upscale hotel near the Van Warren Boardwalk. They were in the middle of the second course when the roof caved in from the weight of falling fish. Shards of broken glass poured down and around Avis and his company.

Shahaf, who was in the hotel lobby, became aware of the commotion when several hysterical people from off the street came inside. The tall Mediterranean fellow ran to the entrance of the sliding doors, to see what the commotion was. By the time he reached the street, the initial flood of fish had stopped. The ground was littered with piles of dead and dying fish. He quickly knelt and picked one off the ground. It was burning hot to the touch. He immediately dropped it back down on the pile. He blew on his fingers as it flopped about atop of its dying brethren.

No sooner had the storm stopped raining fish, than the fever that had overcome Willet suddenly dissipated from whence it came. Her eyes remained closed, but her breathing was more steady and controlled. Mother Hazel rose to her feet. Mrs. Weever and Laraline poured the last of the ice onto Willet. "That should be enough, her fever has broken!"

"What do we do now?"

"Put her in bed and let her rest."

"What was happening to her? Was it the blooming?"

"I will have to get back to you on that, this is beyond my current knowledge."

Sirenna scrambled into the doorway. All eyes looked in her direction. Her lips pursed in astonishment as she examined the bathroom scene. "I was about to say you missed all the excitement."

"No, we didn't. Willet fell into a heat-induced coma. We have been pouring buckets of ice on her for the last twenty minutes to dispel the heat."

"She's sick still?"

"What do you think?"

Sirenna countered to Evelyn. "I thought perhaps it was food poisoning, they ate at that greasy little dive you like to frequent."

"You mean our dive?"

Laraline stayed on Sirenna's first comment. "What was the excitement that we were supposed to be missing?"

"For the last ten minutes, it's been raining fish!"

Adelie's eyes grew very round. "Fish! You mean like, real fish?"

"The entire yard is covered with dead fish!"

Adelie and Mrs. Weever both dashed to the window to get a first-hand look. Evelyn joined them and gasped at the scene. "Great goodness, it's an omen!"

Willet lay asleep as the entire group went downstairs to see the yard. As soon as Adelie got to the door, she pushed it wide open and gasped at the scene. Just as advertised, the entire yard was covered with fish. Fish covered every conceivable space. The green grass was nonexistent.

Laraline quickly chased after Adelie. "Wait, Addie, don't touch anything!"

Evelyn, Sirenna and Hazel slowly followed to witness the aftermath. By the time Mother Hazel got to the front door, she could hear a gentle hissing.

Adelie exclaimed loudly. "What's that sound?"

Mrs. Weever exclaimed. "It's like their all cooking, they are so hot!"

Laraline looked about the horizon at the hundreds of fish. I wonder how far it rained.

Mother Hazel looked suspiciously at Sirenna. "When did this start?"

"Right after I took a look at the dogs, and then I came inside. By the way, the canine choices are getting rather slim. We may need to mail order next time."

Mother Hazel impatiently prodded Sirenna. "Then what?"

"Oh, I just poured myself a glass of something, and sat in my aviary, when all of a sudden, it started."

Evelyn was looking intently at Hazel as she interjected. "About the time we started to pour ice on Willet!"

Mother Hazel then nodded. "So, would you say the storm suddenly stopped within the last two minutes?"

Sirenna looked back uncomfortably at both women who were studying Sirenna. One of the dogs had gotten loose and was trying its best to eat at a fish nearby.

"I suppose so, I came up to tell you what had just happened!"

They could hear Laraline's footfalls squishing around as she had made her way into the middle of the yard. She was looking down the road in both directions, as she was mumbling under her breath. "Crazy, I think it rained over the entire town!"

Suddenly, Uncle Merle came from around the side of the house. In all the excitement, no one had realized that Uncle Merle was drunk outside, under the gazebo. He was holding his stomach and head. He mumbled under his drunken breath, as he maneuvered the steaming pockets of fleshy earth, barefoot. "I drank too much, I keep seeing fish."

Laraline turned toward the two on the porch. She had the look of someone who needed reassuring. Evelyn had not seen that look on her face since she was child. Laraline's eyes pleaded for reason, as she verbally voiced what was on everyone's mind.

"What is happening?"

Mother Hazel cautioned both women. "Don't breathe a word of Willet's affliction until we find out what is happening!"

Sirenna looked at Evelyn and then back at Mother Hazel.

"What?"

"Do I have your word?"

Sirenna looked confused. "What are you saying?"

"Promise me!"

For the first time in quite a while, the twins answered in complete unison. "We promise!" Sirenna quickly engaged the old woman. "Now what is this about, Mother?

Mother Hazel cryptically whispered. "I believe, somehow, that Willet caused this storm."

Chapter 24: A Bridge Over Troubled Waters

• • • •

THE MARTIN BRIDGE WAS notorious for its sheer length and for the fact that it was the only way to cross the Greywood without traveling on foot. To the casual traveler, the bridge was a beautiful scenic route, 35 feet above the forest floor that encompasses the land between Meadowlark and the beach. It was a necessary evil to drive the bridge en route to get to Van Warren, Celandine, and most of the elite tourist destinations.

If you didn't take the bridge then you could go on foot. Although, few would choose to trek across 200 acres of untamed forest to travel either to town or the beach. Of course, you could travel around the entire perimeter of Meadowlark and avoid the Greywood altogether. It would tack on at least an additional 2 hours of driving time, however, as opposed to the 21 minutes if you were to take Martin Bridge straight through.

Jonas preferred to skateboard on the bridge, especially after six o'clock, most cars had reached their destination by then. There was the occasional supply truck, or joy rider out on the town, yet for the most part, the road was empty.

After the biblical rain, as it would become known, Jonas was struck with the curious urge to explore the aftermath. Many of Meadowlark's residents were currently doing the same. Instead of looking around town, Jonas was drawn to the bridge around the Greywood.

This foreboding stretch of road had been dubbed the Bermuda Triangle of Meadowlark, as a large number of tourists and even a few locals ended up missing without a trace. It was seen as a curious folk anomaly until someone important went missing.

The new town constable, Martin Fletcher tried to remain impartial. The demands of local business and political leaders put pressure on him to be more than a friendly face, and figurehead. They wanted a strong deterrent against the influx of decaying Western values. That was the political platform that was suggested for him to run on for his upcoming campaign. His mission was to end the disease that had seeped into Meadowlark, like several small towns around the country.

Strangely enough, his jurisdiction did not include Greywood, as it is a protected wildlife refuge. At present, Constable Fletcher's efforts seemed rather futile. How do you curb the statistically bizarre nature of Greywood's mystic?

As Jonas drifted down the narrow pass to where the shadows dwelled, it was almost as if the sun had been swallowed up. He headed deeper into the arched lane of trees that hid the road from day overhead. Not too many fish ended up on this road. Most were tangled and skewered up in the numerous branches that stared down at the young man.

It was deathly silent, as he pushed his skateboard along the edge of the fenced roadway that separated any passenger from the edge of the great abyss below. It was as if the storm did not even touch this area at first glance. Jonas could see a mound of fish had broken through the branched barrier and collected onto the edge of the right side of the bridge.

Jonas was about to get excited about the possibility of seeing the landbound aquatic specimens up close. His excitement was quickly dashed, as he realized that there was a wake of vultures feeding on the pile of fish. There were five of them, with large black greasy feathers.

However, as he took a better look, he stopped short.

What he saw wasn't birds at all. They had big black vulture bodies, but their heads were like children. Precisely baby heads sitting atop the body of a vulture! They were obscene and surreal at the same time. They snarled and grunted, as they fought amongst themselves over the bounty that lay before them.

Suddenly, one of them started to sniff its humanoid nose in the air. Its chubby cheeks winced in a perpetual pout as its tiny delicate nostrils flared and found a strange new aroma. They had picked up the young man's scent. Jonas was still a distance away and the fish scent was so pungent that they didn't know which direction he was coming from.

They hadn't seen him yet, but it wouldn't be long. He quickly backed up, away from the scene. He continued to retreat until they became tiny blurs. He didn't realize how nervous he had felt until he exhaled a deep breath of relief.

He had heard the rumors about the creatures for years, yet he had never actually seen one, much less a group of them, up close. Luckily, they hadn't seen him and he was now far enough away so that he would probably be forgotten.

It was soon approaching sunset and he didn't really want to be out on the road with those things about. He had long passed Martin Bridge and was about a half mile from where Sabine Street crossed Martin Street when it became dusk. He was now breathing normally as he looked ahead at the fork that led back home.

He glanced up at the early moon. It was high in the sky. Suddenly, the feeling of dread overcame him. There was a pungent scent because of the fish. By mid-morning everything would spoil and begin rotting.

He looked up toward the sky again and this time his heart sank. Seven tiny dots were heading across the sky. They were in flight now and heading towards him. Jonas quickly ran to the left side of the road. He eyed a nearby patch of unkempt shrubbery. Without hast, he dove under the extended branches to conceal himself somewhat. Hopefully, they hadn't seen him. He could hear the flutter of wings as they passed overhead. He half expected them to attack.

Fortunately for Jonas, they were preoccupied and weren't looking for him. They were indeed searching. They had picked up another scent. They were definitely heading somewhere. As Jonas continued to hide, he watched the strange flock veer to the left toward Blue Jay Way. He wondered to himself who they would be calling on tonight.

Chapter 25: Night Visitors

Willet's eyes opened to the sweetest humming she had ever heard. It reminded her of when she was a toddler, and her mother would sing her to sleep. It took her a moment to adjust to the fact that it appeared to be night. The world was dark, even as she sat up, all she could see was a dim kerosene lamp beside her bed. She sat up and felt a wave of nausea. She felt achy all over.

She soon realized she was in her nightgown. What had happened? The last thing she remembered was lying down before dinner, which she obliviously missed. Why didn't they get her up? She turned her torso to sit up and felt pain all over.

She realized her arms, chest, and face were covered in various creams. She could feel the thick sticky consistency on her flesh. She touched her cheek and quickly winced in pain. Her entire body was sore. It appeared that flakes of her skin were peeling. Was she sunburned?

She was in the beginning stages of a full-blown freak-out when she heard the humming again. It wasn't a dream. She looked around her room, yet no one was there. She called out. "Is someone here?"

The humming paused for a moment, then started back up. The sound was so sweet, that Willet was compelled to rise to her feet. Everything felt stiff, but as the humming continued, the calming effect was numbing her pain. However, she could not see where it was coming from. Willet looked to the window. They were closed and latched, but the singer was outside. She quickly raced to the window and called. "Is someone there?"

There was a pause and suddenly she heard her mother's voice. "It's me, sweetie."

"Mama, is that you?"

"Yes it's me, I've missed you so!"

Willet moved her hand to open the latch when a wave of putrid death filled her nostrils. She almost threw up in her mouth. She stumbled back gasping. She could almost taste spoiled fish in her mouth. Something about the scent helped to wake her up. Willet covered her mouth but stayed at a distance. "What is that horrible smell?"

"Please come to me."

"Why are you outside?"

"It feels so good outside, my sweet dear."

"What happened today, I don't remember anything. Why am I covered in sores?"

"You got very sick, but mama is here now, to take care of you."

"Something feels strange."

"I'm locked out, please go downstairs, open the front door, and let me in, quickly dear!"

"Who did it? Was it Aunt Sirenna?"

"Yes, she refuses to let me inside."

A sudden rage overcame Willet, as she quickly made her way out of the room. The entire mansion was dark and quiet. It was definitely very late. Did Sirenna really lock Laraline out of the house? As she got to the steps, she struggled, as she was weak and achy. Yet somehow, she was able to harness enough strength to make it downstairs.

Willet could see the front door, and there was a slight movement in the sidelights. How had she made her way down to the porch, so quickly?

The voice was now frantic. "Hurry. Let me in before she hears!"

"Why did Sirenna lock you outside?"

"I'll tell you as soon as you open the door, hurry it's cold."

Willet reached for the nob but then paused. There was something queer about her last statement

"I thought you said it felt good outside, why are you suddenly cold?"

There was silence.

"Mama?"

"Please let me in dear. Just open the door. I can see you in the sidelines through the window. You're almost there."

Before Willet had a chance to react, a stern voice boomed from behind her. "Stop, do not open that door!"

Willet turned, startled. It was Mother Hazel in her shawl and full dress. She was holding her cane in one hand and a kerosene lantern in the other. It was probably the first time she had seen the old woman without her sunglasses. "That is not your mother outside!"

Willet turned back to the door. This time a feeling of fear started to permeate all over her. The voice outside sounded irritated. "Let me in!"

Willet stood defiantly as she quickly backed away from the door. "No, go away!"

There was an abrupt change in the voice. It now sounded deep and raspy. Other voices joined with it, in a similar chorus. "Let us in child, we are hungry!"

"I said go away!"

"*We are so hungry for faigal flesh. I can smell her young sweetness. She is new meat.*

My sisters and I need to feed. Let us inside."

The voices were replaced by violent scratching at the front door as if some wild animal were trying to break its way inside. The door banged a couple of times before it settled back into silence. Willet found herself gasping for air, as the situation too closely reminded her of the incident, at the Moonlight Inn.

Before she had a chance to speak, Mother Hazel answered for her. "They are now gone!"

Willet's eyes were wide with disbelief. "What were they?"

"Those are our nightly visitors; the reason we keep all the windows and doors locked!"

"They almost sound human."

"That's a relative term around here!"

Mother Hazel motioned to Willet. "Come with me."

Even though she found the old woman intimidating, she felt strangely compelled. Willet followed after her, down the long dark corridor. Mother Hazel continued to speak, as she hobbled past the bizarre paintings that covered the walls. "The earliest sleeven accounts refer to them as harpies."

"Harpies are things of myth."

Mother Hazel chuckled. "Myth? You have a lot to learn about your world."

"What do they want?"

"They wish to devour us, of course!"

Willet wasn't sure if she was serious or not, but of all the Adler clan, she seemed to be the least humorous one. They came to a small black wooden door at the end of the hallway. The old woman pulled out a set of skeleton keys and began to jiggle one of them into the old lock. She paused and turned around to address Willet.

"Whether you realize it or not, a curse has been placed on the Adler bloodline."

"A curse?"

"After what I just witnessed, it makes sense why you got so sick."

Willet coughed into her pajama sleeve. "I don't know why I got so ill."

Mother Hazel studied Willet intently before she spoke again. "I need to ask you something rather important. Since you have been here, have you noticed any unusually large black feathers lying about the grounds?"

"Yeah, outside by the ikons."

"Did you touch them at any point?"

Willet was suddenly uneasy as she remembered the previous morning picking up a black-grey feather with an odd smell.

"Yes, I found one and picked it up to get a closer look."

"For Arke's sake, it's damn near impossible to keep those feathers off the lawn. Where is it now?"

"I dropped it and it blew away!"

"It belonged to one of our night visitors!"

"Oh gross!"

Mother Hazel reached across a nearby table and picked up one of the random feathers lying around. It was olive green, with hints of red on the edges.

"That's the funny thing about a feather; it looks so delicate and fragile."

The old woman suddenly held it up to Willet's face. "Look at the arch, in the middle it has but one function: to push air. This allows for flight. Yet all these tiny threads extend out into hundreds, if not thousands of deceptive and sophisticated strains into one single accord."

She then dropped it in Willet's hand, before continuing her lengthy explanation.

"The harpy wings are covered with an oily residue. When you touch that feather with your fingertips, that film absorbs into the pores of your skin and immediately starts to seep into the bloodstream. It begins to poison the blood upon contact."

"Poison! I've been poisoned?"

"I'm telling you; you were deathly ill. You developed a fever that spiked so high, it began to burn you from the inside. You had to be submerged in an ice bath for several minutes to get your fever down!"

"I can't believe I was poisoned."

Mother Hazel gave a solemn half smile. "If we had gotten to you any later, it would have resulted in paralysis and then death."

"So that's why I'm covered in this cream and I feel like I have a sunburn?"

"Unfortunately, there is one caveat. Because your blood has been poisoned, it can't be unpoisoned. You are eternally connected to the harpies."

"What does that mean exactly?"

"That means they can sense your heartbeat. Wherever you are or wherever you go, as long as you have breath left in you, they will hunt you, to the ends of the earth."

"What can I do?"

"We are all victims of this curse. Ironically, your mixed blood would have made you exempt from this persecution. That's probably why your mother wanted you far away. It doesn't even matter. They know your scent now."

"Scent. That's why Sirenna bought the dogs!"

"Their nightly patterns are so sporadic, some nights they don't even come near. Fortunately, the dogs will always tell you if they are near. A dog can't stand the smell of a night visitor."

"If they only want to eat us, what happens when we are all gone?"

"In theory, they would cease to exist. However, over the years they have expanded their appetites."

"How did this get started?"

"You mean the curse."

"Yes, please tell me about this infamous curse!"

"Every important faigal house is vying for the possession of the first light."

"Yes, Auntie Evie mentioned that earlier."

"There is a text in the Arke and the Old Testament where it describes the creation."

"Yes, Genesis!"

"The first light referenced is not actual daylight, it comes before daylight. The seven tribes of Ethereals that remained on earth were each given a piece of this light as a gift, for remaining in servitude on earth. The faigal have been fighting over control of the piece that Arke had in his possession ever since. The House of Adler has possessed this very artifact for almost 120 years!"

Willet's eyes widened. "You mean it's here now? Where?"

"Hidden in plain sight."

Willet furrowed her brow.

"Whoever has this light is the target of jealousy and desire from every other house. The harpies are, simply, a by-product of this jealousy.

"You mean they were created by your peers to destroy the House of Adler?"

"In a manner of speaking."

"How?"

"As important as this subject may seem to you, there is something more crucial to the future of our family existence. That is why I have asked you to join me here."

"If it's so important, why talk to me?"

"When we were trying to exercise the fever from your body, the entire town experienced an unusual phenomenon. It rained fish down, in biblical proportions, at the same time your fever climaxed!"

"Fish?"

"Yes, as we speak, there are thousands of dead fish lying around the estate and the town."

"Is that the weird smell coming from outside?"

"Trust me, the odor will be even more unbearable by midday tomorrow."

"I still don't understand what it has to do with me."

"I don't believe you do. I think that somehow, in your fevered state, you manifested the storm we experienced."

"That's insane! I don't have any power. I can barely keep my clothes in order."

"I've noticed."

Willet wrinkled her nose. "Thanks!"

"I don't believe you truly think you have any power."

'It was probably just a coincidence."

"Well, in any case, I wish to have you tested."

"I'm not sure I like the sound of that."

"She will simply ask a few questions and stuff."

"It's the *and stuff* that worries me!"

"You're afraid?"

"Heck yeah! And who is this she, some quack doctor?"

"She is one of my sister mothers."

"Look, I'm feeling relatively better, why do I need to be looked at by another witch?"

"We are not witches. I trained for over 70 years to become a weaver. Do you understand?"

There was a silent pause before Willet spoke again. "Yes."

"The problem is the entire house bore witness to this anomaly. Sooner or later, everyone will draw their conclusions about how to act on and what to do about you."

"What do mean, do about me? I would expect that from Sirenna, but my mother and Evelyn aren't like that."

"Power changes people. Especially the fear of someone having too much power."

"That's crazy. I'm a nobody."

"Those are the most dangerous sort."

"Now I really feel sick."

"The plan is, I will let her check you and declare you ordinary, regardless of the outcome. That will diffuse any fear or uncertainty toward you and protect you."

"Why would you do this, what in it for you?"

Let's just say if she sees something, then you may need to learn to defend yourself from far more than a few harpies."

"Like who?"

"There are three other great faigal houses here on this continent, one right over the hill."

"Are you talking about the Bransons?"

"Yes, you have heard of them."

"Just bits of rumors and gossip."

"The Bransons are one of our oldest feudal enemies. Lord Avis Branson is the controversial head of their dynasty. His second in command is his half-sister Aquila. Some believe she should be the rightful heir, and she knows it. If she ever takes over, we are in trouble. She is bold enough to start a war.

He has four heirs who stand to inherit his vast empire. The oldest is Ephron, a spoiled narcissist whose marriage with a sickly wife gives the illusion that he has a soul. Some say he has a wandering eye and likes his bottles.

The second is the middle child, Jonas. He will be a senior at your school. He's a bit of a black sheep. People speculate that Avis is not his true father, including Avis himself. He seems like an outsider, a Branson by name only.

Then there are the youngest heirs. The twins, Gavin and Raven, are around your age. Both are cold and as ruthless as their aunt Aquila and twice as sadistic.

There are also two weavers in Lord Branson's employ. They come from House Ortega, but are mainly in the shadows. We don't know much about them. All we know is that they alternate duties bi-annually. Half the year Mr. Shahaf represents Avis. Of the two he is more visible, and the current weaver."

"You mentioned another weaver?"

"Yes. Mother Nashca is apparently a close cousin of this Shahaf. We don't know a lot about her other than she is the replacement when Shahaf is gone."

"Wow, how do you know all this information if you are enemies? Do we have spies?"

"Evelyn went to school with Branson and they have maintained a cordial relationship throughout the years."

Willet interjected. "Keep your friends close, and your enemies closer!"

"Good, you learn quickly. Even though many sleeven are bent on faigal genocide, some of your deadliest adversaries could be faigal, even family!"

"What about Aunt Sirenna? Should I worry about her?"

"I'm talking about her."

"I thought you were close to her."

"I love Sirenna like a daughter, but my allegiance is to the House of Adler first!"

"Is there anything else you can tell me?"

"You have a lot of questions. I have something that might help."

Mother Hazel finally stood and hobbled over to a shelf. She pulled out a small green hardback book. She made her way back to Willet and handed it to her.

"What's this?"

"You have an inquisitive nature. Take this book, read and study, but tell no one. If you have questions, you know where I will be." Quite abruptly, she began turning off lights and ushering Willet out into the hallway.

"Wait, what do I do now?"

"Go back to bed, it's getting late."

"Bed? How can you sleep with all that is happening?"

"I usually just close my eyes."

Mother Hazel started to shut the door on Willet, and then suddenly paused. She stuck her head through the crack of the door and whispered. "Remember, we never had this conversation." Then she closed the door.

Chapter 26: The Plot Thickens

"What was all that commotion yesterday afternoon?"

Meena was now sitting up, seemingly alert. The spotting on her face was the same. At least it hadn't gotten any worse. Ephron stroked her auburn hair. It was usually full, bright and radiant. However, at the moment, it was sweaty and matted as his fingers work to untangle the clumps of unkempt hair.

"It's nothing, it rained a few fish yesterday."

"Did you say fish? Like real fish?"

"Yes, fish."

"How peculiar?"

"Yes, it is."

"I mean really, this is a fishing port and Lord Arke sends fish to rain on us?"

Ephron nodded at the irony. "It is odd when you put it in those terms."

"What kind of fish?"

"Stop asking so many questions dear, you need to rest."

"That's my problem, I'm always resting. How could I miss an event like a fish storm because of napping? It makes me sound a bit pitiful."

"You know it's not that simple, dear. Your condition requires you to save your strength."

"Piss on my condition. I want to live life. Especially if I don't have much time left."

"Meena, don't talk like that. You're strong, and you're going to get better!"

"I don't know, your mother was a strong woman."

"Silence."

Just the mention of Meadow Branson was unnerving to him. Meadow Branson had become a taboo subject, to the point that her name wasn't even uttered anymore. Ephron took a deep breath.

"I'll tell you what, if you get enough rest, maybe we can go somewhere this weekend."

"What about the beach?"

"Meena. the sun is blistering for your skin."

"I will stay in the shade. I have a big umbrella. Oh, please, I so love the beach. The sunlight makes me so happy."

Ephron folded his arms and sighed. "Perhaps."

"Remember how much I used to love to swim?"

"Yes, you were the best, before you became ill."

Just the mention of how things were before, made Meena feel depressed. She glanced over at the bedside table. There was a montage of their wedding pictures. The entire reception took place aboard the Elysium. As she considered the photo, she could hardly recognize her old self. She looked over at Ephron who usually seemed aloof these days.

"Do you still love me, Ephron?"

Ephron was silent as he took in her question. "Why would you ask such a question?"

"Sometimes you act as though you can't stand me."

Ephron ignored her complaint. "You know, it's about time I do your hair. What would you like today? Pigtails?"

"My hair always looks atrocious when you touch it!"

Frustrated, Ephron huffed and got up. "Well, have the house girl fix your hair, it's starting to stink."

"Please don't get upset Ephron. I know you do so much for me."

Ephron stomped out of her bedroom, pretending not to hear. It had been almost one year since they had shared a bed and another two since she was well enough to be intimate. He felt guilty about how he had started treating her. He was growing tired, and she could tell. They were practically newlyweds when she got sick, and now he was spending his days waiting for her to die. It wasn't fair.

Diastasis was a death sentence among his people. As her health deteriorated more every year, she grew less motivated to even keep up with her hygiene. He couldn't blame her. When his mother was sick, there were entire days when she did not stray from her bed.

He made his way to the bathroom and turned on the faucet. Ephron splashed his face with cold water. As he looked up at himself in the mirror, he didn't recognize himself. He was growing numb to everything lately. Meena, the love of his life was responsible. He hated feeling this way, but he was angry at her.

He was tired of trying to be a good husband, loving, polite, and faithful. With her current situation, it felt impossible to even try. However, she would be heartbroken if she ever discovered any of his improprieties. It would destroy her. Lately, he had been fantasizing about cutting his wings and diving into the ocean. Just allowing the water to overcome him. He was deep in thought when suddenly the house girl knocked on the bathroom door.

"Master Ephron."

"Yes, Millie."

"You have a visitor."

"It's kind of early. Who would be calling at this time of the morning?"

"Lady Branson. What should I do? She wants to come inside."

Ephron rolled his eyes and clenched his jaw when he found out who his guest was. He took a deep breath before he answered. "Tell her I will meet her on the patio, I'm on my way out."

He was about to say goodbye to Meena, but he suspected that he would find her in tears. His last comment was a bit insensitive, but he wasn't ready to sit and spend fifty minutes counseling her and consoling her about how she was the most important person to him. He would wait till after he got to work. He was too stressed to deal with the drama.

It would be easier to send some flowers and make a nice dinner for them. His phone was already flooded with calls about the town cleanup. Even Mayor Van Warren left a spirited message for him. *"No one wants to vacation in a city infested with fish, flies, and gnats!"*

He would have to deal with this before his father was contacted. The last thing he wanted was Daddy to clean up his mess. Arke knows Avis had his hands full with Gavin's exploits these days.

He had all but forgotten that Aquila was waiting for him on the front patio when he headed out. She was dressed in a silk black gown with a low cut neckline. Her hefty cleavage was on display, accentuated by her black diamond choker. She was patiently waiting, as he made his way outside. She stood so her good eye could study his reaction. She could sense his irritation.

"So, I'm not even invited inside now!"

"Morning Aunt Aquila. What brings you around this early, the rooster hasn't even stirred!"

She strolled up to Ephron, blocking his path. "I missed you. Don't you have a kiss for your dear auntie?"

Ephron was aggravated. "You dare come to my home like this. My wife is probably at the window right now!"

"Scared the misses will discover our dirty little secret?"

"Why are you here?"

Aquila's eyes became cold and serious. She turned her head so her eyepatch was visible. "I am still waiting for my package!"

For a moment, Ephron looked confused as to what she was referring to, then recollection hit. "Look, I'll call Gavin when I get to work. You made this arrangement with him!"

"Then you shouldn't have suggested Moonlight Inn. Usually, when I order merchandise, I expect prompt service!"

"Look, the whole thing with this crazy fish storm kind of put everything behind."

"You're just like your father; excuses define your character."

Ephron put his hands on his hips and took a deep breath as if trying to control his growing irritation. "I think it's time for you to leave, auntie!"

"I want that package tonight, or I may come back here tomorrow and wait for you to bring it here. I'm sure Meena and I will have lots to talk about."

"You wouldn't?"

"Try me."

Ephron shrunk back in horror, as she called his bluff. Aquila was no one to go against unless you were going all the way. Ephron obediently responded. "Yes, mam!"

The indiscretion with Aunt Aquila was embarrassing and bad enough, but these other matters were troubling. The last thing he wanted was to piss off Aquila.

"Come on, let's not be enemies. I have plans for you, big plans!"

Aquila extended her hand and gently caressed his tightened jaw. "All you need to do is be a good little boy and play along."

Chapter 27: Breadcrumbs

The road crews were out early trying to figure out where to dump 200 tons of dead fish that lay basking in the September sun. The county commission suggested landfills, while others said that burning them would be the only efficient way of clearing out the flies and gnats that were starting to infest the town. Still, another suggestion claimed that the solution would be to just dump the fish back into the ocean, where they had most likely come. As Laraline and Evelyn headed out mid-morning, one thing was clear. The aroma of rotting fish had become unbearable. There was no place one could drive to in town that didn't reek of dead fish. Even Laraline's car smelled of the sea as a few dozen fish had settled on the roof and hood and remained there overnight.

Usually, she would roll down the window and enjoy the air. However, at the moment even this simple gesture could have questionable and regrettable consequences. As they headed across Martin Bridge to Celandine Springs, Laraline had a flash of a memory. She was very young, and she was running through the woods. From what she had known, this had to be a dream or false memory. The very idea of playing in the grey woods was ridiculous.

She was about to ask Evelyn but thought against it, as they were nearing their destination. They ran into road crews redirecting traffic. Trucks were loading large lawn bags filled with dead fish onto multiple trucks.

In the parking lot of the Davenport Hotel, a single maintenance person in an orange jumpsuit was spraying down the road and parking lot with a soapy green disinfectant. The fish had long been removed from this side of town, however, the scent still lingered.

Avis was at the entrance waiting when they drove up. He nodded in recognition as they pulled in. Right beside him stood a rather tall, dark-skinned man. Laraline whispered. "Who is that guy?"

"That is the obedient Mr. Shahaf. He is the Branson house weaver."

"You don't like him?"

"Not necessarily, he's charming enough. There is just something about him a bit off, and I can't put my finger on what it is."

Evelyn suddenly leaned into Laraline. "Let me do the talking, and please hold that tongue of yours!"

As the two women left the car, Evelyn extended her arms out to the sides and nodded toward Branson. He paused and made the same gesture before speaking. He sounded quite jovial as he addressed her. "Evelyn, you're looking well!"

"You're looking, well, rounder."

"What can I say, I'm an emotional eater."

"Do you remember my niece, Laraline Swift?"

Avis carefully studied her before speaking. "Yes, I remember you as a child, I haven't seen you much, even before you left town."

There was an uncomfortable silence as Branson seemed unsure of what to say next. "Oh, where are my manners, this is Shahaf Ortega, my associate."

Laraline was coy. "Associate?"

Shahaf answered her question. "Yes, I have been in Lord Branson's employ for several years now."

His eyes were dark, intense and a bit seductive. He reached his gloved hand forward as a cordial greeting. Laraline slowly accepted it, as she studied a curious fork tattoo on the base of his neck.

Avis continued to speak. "How many years has it been now?"

Laraline cleared her throat and bluntly addressed him ignoring his query. "Yeah, can you tell me anything about my husband's death?"

The abruptness caught Avis off guard. "Excuse me?"

Evelyn quickly interjected. "She recently found out her husband was in this area during the month before he died. She is anxious to find answers about his death."

Avis nodded at her explanation. "Yes, such a regrettable loss!"

"I understand he worked for you."

"Well, not exactly. He worked the entire dock from Celandine to Crecheland. He worked the circuit. He even did some work in Virginia Beach and Myrtle in the warmer months. I spoke with him exactly twice, I believe."

"When was the last time you spoke to him?"

"Wow, my memory is not as sharp as it used to be. If I had to guess, maybe about nine months ago. I introduced him to Arlis Greenbaum."

"Who is that?"

Evelyn answered Laraline's question. "He is a local business leader in Crecheland."

"Why did you introduce him?"

Avis was beginning to look cross, as she blankly asked question after question. He impatiently responded. "Because they wanted to meet each other."

Laraline was about to speak again when Shahaf quickly cut her off and stepped in front of Avis. "Remember to whom you are addressing, young lady. For this line of questioning, perhaps you should find the local constable, Lord Branson is quite busy."

Before she had time to respond, Shahaf quickly led Avis back into the hotel lobby. Evelyn threw Laraline a look.

"You catch more flies with honey!"

"What does that mean?"

"It means the world is not this black and white box, which you can place all of us inside."

"What did I do?"

You are holding on to this idea that the bloodline of the Bransons' is so evil. You can't be cordial enough to someone who could help you find information about your husband to actually get to the information!"

"Look, I didn't mean to upset your good friend."

Evelyn's reaction was sudden as she slapped Laraline across the face. "You know, I may not have been a fan of your husband, but the one thing I can give him credit for; he wasn't big on judging folks. How did he ever deal with you? You shame his memory!"

Evelyn quickly walked off to try to smooth things with Avis. She left Laraline in the parking lot still in shock. When she caught up to Avis, he was waiting at the elevator. Before he could say a word, she blurted out. "I'm so sorry, she has been under a lot of stress lately."

"I felt like I was being interrogated like a common criminal. You're the one who asked me to get him some work in the first place. I was doing you a favor. Why don't you tell her that?"

"She has a lot of pride, she would never forgive me, besides that, it's not like you haven't done horrible things."

Avis nodded. "That's fair enough."

"I do need to ask you something for myself."

"What is it now?"

"We discussed sanctuary, for Laraline and her two children."

"Yes, and I have agreed to the terms requested."

"I just wanted to be sure, because it appears yesterday her oldest child was infected by an unworldly fever, that almost ended her life. You wouldn't know anything about this?"

Avis inhaled. "Look, the sanctuary has been honored on my end, I promise."

Evelyn nodded. "Thank you. Well, we need to get going."

Avis finally added. "I almost didn't recognize Laraline."

"Time flies."

When Evelyn reached the parking lot, Laraline pulled the car up to the entrance. She anticipated some reaction from Laraline, as she opened the car door Evelyn immediately apologized.

"Laraline I'm sorry, I put my hands on you. You would never done that!"

"Auntie, as much as I think the past is behind me, the more I realize it's not. I treated Avis unfairly, as well as you. I'm so sorry for my behavior. If you wish, I could go back and apologize."

"Don't worry, everything will work out."

"I admire you, auntie. You have always been a peacemaker. Do you remember Arthur Dell?

"Wow, that's a name I haven't heard in years. Wasn't he a friend of yours?"

"Absolutely not! He was a bully!"

"Really?"

"He would literally terrorize me at school every day, until you confronted him and his mum, by inviting them over for tea. I was so embarrassed. I couldn't show my face in school for weeks."

"I'm so sorry, I meant well."

"Don't be, by the end of the year, he invited me to the prom."

"What happened?

"I said no, of course, I still couldn't stand him. But your efforts changed things."

"Well, thank you!"

"I should take a page from your book."

"Hmm, what ever happened to Arthur?"

"How am I supposed to know?"

"Why didn't you ever get married and have any children? I can understand Sirenna, but you?"

Evelyn had a somber stare as she responded. "Well, it just wasn't in the cards for me."

Both women embraced before Laraline put the car in drive and sped off. From the window, Shahaf could see the car speed off. "They're gone sir!"

Avis looked up. "She looks so much like her mother. Speaking of family, where is my sister?"

"You mean half-sister, sir?"

"I think she is trying to undermine my authority again."

"You don't believe she is honoring the sanctuary, sir?"

"What do you think Shahaf?"

"Aquila has been busy building allegiances and growing connections. I wouldn't be surprised if this was some power move, sir."

"I think I would like to have her publicly flogged."

"You can't do that anymore, sir. There are laws."

"Really? How disappointing."

"Besides, the last thing you want to do, is give her more ammunition. You're not as popular as you once were. Don't underestimate Aquila. She is cunning and hides all her cards. However, she is also greedy. She will eventually slip up."

"Enough about my troubles. How is your lovely cousin, Nashca, doing?"

Shahaf looked away from his lord. "She is still in exile from her lands."

"I desire to see her again."

"Very soon sir."

"That's what you keep telling me."

Shahaf moved across the room to gather his ledger. "I will write another letter to her with haste, sir."

"Please do so. I have grown quite lonely since the Swifts arrived in town. I don't mean to infer I wish you gone. You have been completely loyal."

Shahaf stood by the hall mirror with his palms clasped together. "I understand sir. Sometimes a little feminine energy is needed to feel complete."

Chapter 28: Mother Sister

The Mother Sister arrived at the Greywood Estate that afternoon. Mother Hazel had been waiting for her arrival. Mother Sister Elyria Rivera was extremely tall. Her white hair was long and flowing. Even her eyebrows were white. Her thin delicate features illuminated her eyes that were a light emerald green.

She wore a long flowing dark royal blue gown. The gown was so long she almost appeared as if she were floating. She carried a long grey staff with several engravings etched along the side.

Adelie was in Willets's room when the Mother Sister and Mother Hazel entered. The tall woman glanced at Adelie with eyes that seemed to glow. "This must be the younger sister."

Mother Hazel concurred. "Yes. Where is your sister, Adelie?"

Adelie stared blankly up at the ghostly woman. "Are you looking for Willet? She is in the bathroom; she should be out in a moment."

The Mother Sister nodded. "Could you excuse us? I need to talk to your sister alone."

Adelie responded. "Is she in trouble?"

The bathroom door suddenly opened, and Willet stepped out. She had just finished washing her face. The tall white-haired woman was not lost on Willet. She immediately addressed her visitor.

"Hello. May I help you?"

Mother Hazel cleared her throat. "This is the Mother Sister. She has come to evaluate you."

Willet extended her hand out to shake the woman's hand. The Mother Sister looked down curiously at the young girl. Willet uncomfortably dropped her hand. "Sorry, I guess you aren't into physical touch."

The Mother Sister sort of bowed down slightly, as she extended her arms to the sides before the young girl then abruptly rose back up. Willet looked at Mother Hazel, confused about what to do. The old woman nodded for Willet to follow the visitor's lead. Willet awkwardly did a bow and extended her arms. For a moment, it appeared as if she would lose her balance. She then stood up and did a salute.

The Mother Sister looked puzzled at Willet without speaking. Just as the silent exchange was ending, the strange woman turned to Mother Hazel. "I see what you mean."

Adelie stood perplexed as she noticed the woman's hair. "Why is all your hair white?"

Mother Hazel almost appeared embarrassed until her superior answered Adelie. "Well, I and all my sisters look quite similar, where I come from.

Willet noticed she had a rather soft monotone voice as she spoke. She looked to Adelie and quietly spoke. "I need to speak to your sister alone now."

Mother Hazel quickly ushered Adelie by the arm. "Come on, we need to give them some time alone."

Adelie was about to protest when the Mother Sister gazed into her eyes. Adelie nodded in response. "Yes, mam!"

As soon as the door was shut, Willet looked up at the tall, strange visitor. The woman immediately approached her like some intrusive alien. She stopped about two feet from Willet before politely addressing her. "May I ask you a question?"

"I guess so."

"What are your thoughts about what Mother Hazel has told you?"

"I'm not sure what to think."

"That is understandable."

Willet clasped her hands together. "So, when do we start the test?"

The Mother Sister proclaimed. "We are finished."

"How is that possible, you didn't even ask me anything about myself?"

The woman stood up straight and looked at the door. Almost immediately, Mother Hazel reentered with Adelie close behind. Mother Hazel knelt before the woman. "Yes, Mother Sister?"

"We are finished here today, Sister Mother."

"Yes, Mother Sister."

"Your sire is downstairs?"

"Yes, Sirenna is in the aviary, do you wish to see her?"

"Not really, I have what I need. Mother Sister Pence will reach out to you."

"Allow me to walk you out Mother Sister."

"Thank you, Sister Mother."

The two weavers abruptly left Willet's room. Both sisters stood looking after the women completely perplexed. Adelie finally turned to Willet.

"So, what was all that about? Did you fail or pass?"

Willet glanced out the window at the two women walking down the driveway. "I really don't know?"

"I hope our interview with the headmistress is that easy!"

"Ugh, don't remind me."

Chapter 29: Linnet's Diner

The next day, Linnet's was swamped. It almost seemed as if half of the town had come to eat. Tori Ingram was called to work an extra shift due to the high volume of customers. Mayor Van Warren, fearing the aquatic debris effects on local tourism, had crews out early, so by midday, most of the shops and sidewalks were cleaned up.

Of course, most residential areas were still infested with rotted fish. That was the reason a great many of the town's residents elected to spend the better part of the day in town, away from the overwhelming fishy neighborhood smells. What this meant for Tori was that a lot of the town's more colorful inhabitants converged on Linnet's at roughly the same time.

Thelma and Herb Lutzes were an elderly couple that had retired to Meadowlark almost 16 years ago. They normally just got coffee, a bran muffin and cantaloupe chunks. Of all Linnet's patrons, they were one of the most pleasant.

Across from the Lutzes were the Peregrine sisters. Delores and Violet Peregrine were rarely apart. Tori didn't know too much about them other than they were big in the religious community. They always came across like two snobby biddies to Tori.

Jonas Branson was there when she arrived. He had probably been locked out of his home again. It happened often. One would think that belonging to one of the richest families in town would make life easier. Tori approached his table, which was near the front window. "Is that a good book?"

He was startled as if he had been deep in thought. "It's informative."

Tori was just making small talk and had no idea what he was reading, and didn't care. "Yeah?"

193

He responded as if he had just read some startling revelation. "I don't think I want to be buried. I think I want to be mummified."

"Ok, well do you want to order any food, or are you just getting away from the fish siege?"

"It isn't a siege!"

"No, then what is it then?"

"It's the end of days."

He sat drinking a hot cup of green herbal tea while reading a book about mummification. He had gotten through the seventh chapter, when in walked Phoebe Crane. She was wearing overly large sunglasses which appeared to be covering bruises. She was obviously trying to remain inconspicuous. She stood at the entrance peering around as if she were looking for someone.

Tori gave up on Jonas ordering anything and approached Phoebe. "Do you want a seat, Colombo?"

"No, I don't!"

"Well, you can't just loiter."

"What do you mean? I'm just standing here, not bothering anyone!"

"That's the definition of loitering."

Phoebe protested. "Oh, well that's a stupid rule."

"Are you looking for someone?"

"Absolutely not!"

Finally, Phoebe spotted Jonas and waved. He looked around as if in complete shock. Had she mistaken him for someone else? Before he had time to react, she hurried past Tori and stood right in front of his table. "Do you mind if I join you?"

"Yes, I just want to..."

She cut him off as if he was not even speaking. "Great, we need to talk."

Jonas trailed off. "... be by myself."

"What was that?"

Jonas sighed. "Oh, nothing."

"Where is Gavin?"

"I'm not my brother's keeper."

Phoebe laughed out so loud that the Lutzes gave her an odd stare.

Tori returned to the table. "Do you want a menu?"

"Why do you keep bothering me?"

Jonas looked at Phoebe impatiently. "You do know that if you hang around, and don't buy anything, that's loitering."

Phoebe mused. "Is this a conspiracy?"

Both Jonas and Tori were silent as Phoebe started to vent. "Stop accusing me of loitering! I'm being sociable! Speaking of social, where is Raven? I've called her four times, but she has yet to answer."

"She doesn't like phones."

"Really? Weird."

Tori moved away toward the Lutzes table. She leaned over with the coffee pitcher. "Do you want me to top you off, Mrs. Lutz?"

"No, thank you, dear. I've had more than I should already."

Herb Lutz interjected. "Can we get the check, Tori?"

Tori reached into her apron pocket and pulled out a small white ticket. "Got it right here sir." She laid it down on the top and he quickly snatched it up. Thelma addressed the young girl.

"My, it's so crowded today."

"Yeah, everyone is freaking out about the fish storm."

"I've never seen anything like it before."

Herb laid down a couple of bills on the table as he rose to his feet. "Yeah, it's a sign of the times!"

Tori turned back to him just in time to see the tip he had left. "Thank you, so much Mr. Lutz, you didn't have to, sir!"

"Nonsense!"

Then Mrs. Lutz said the most bizarre thing. "If we had been able to have children, I think I would have a daughter as sweet as you."

Tori didn't know how to respond. They were a nice old couple who as much as they enjoyed each other probably regretted not having a family. Tori waved bye, as they headed to the door. She then heard a shrill voice from behind.

"Waitress, can we get the check, while we are still breathing?"

Tori moved around to see Violet Peregrine glaring at her. Tori quickly reached into her pocket and placed the ticket on the table. With her long gangly fingers, Violet slid the ticket across the table. She took a suspicious glance to confirm that the price was right.

Tori suddenly recognized Alouette Heron coming in the door and used it as an excuse to get away. She could tell it was her, from the shape of her hair. She always wore a 50's vintage beehive. Alouette had discreetly come by to pick up a takeout order for her mother.

Many a boy would have given their right hand just to be seen walking with her. Alouette was easily one of the most striking girls in Meadowlark. She had a quiet elegance about her that was very reserved. In any case, this added to the mystic.

"Good morning Alouette!"

"Hi Tori, my mother ordered the baked ziti."

Tori didn't have any issues with Alloute. She was one of those pretty girls who didn't have a lot of friends because people were so intimidated by her looks. She was also strangely popular because of the mystique around her. Tori felt sorry for her because she always seemed a bit lonely. She recognized that awkward shyness about her that was misinterpreted as graceful aloofness.

"Yeah, it's right here. You doing ok?"

"I'm ok, just busy rehearsing."

"When is your big dance audition?"

"Not until the spring."

"Try not to worry."

Alouette had her head down but made a point of looking up and giving a friendly smile.

"How much do I owe you?"

"It's on the ticket."

"Oh thanks."

She carefully reached into her purse and pulled out an envelope containing a handful of bills that she began to peel through. Several of the patrons had noticed her presence and were intently watching her pay the bill.

"Here you go, keep the change."

"Thanks."

Sensing that eyes were on her, she quickly collected the food container and hurried to the exit. Tori turned back around to the main dining area. Several patrons quickly turned back to their plates, busted by Tori's sharp eyes. When she returned to Jonas, Phoebe had insinuated herself into the booth with the poor boy. However, as Tori returned she quickly disengaged with him, trying to seem as if she had been bored.

"Well, what did she say?"

"Who?"

"Alouette!"

"Are you serious, she was picking up food."

Most of the popular girls, such as Phoebe, had a morbid obsession with Alouette. They were jealous of her, yet so fascinated by her, that they tried to study her. It was as if she were some celluloid movie star. She definitely had that iconic celebrity look. The problem was everyone knew Alouette was destined to be a star, except for Alouette.

Phoebe whined. "But what dish?"

Tori impatiently put her hand on her hip. "The order was baked ziti."

Phoebe exclaimed. "Well, I think French food is so last week."

Jonas snidely responded. "Well, since Ziti is Italian, I guess she is in the clear."

Tori was almost fuming with impatience. "Look, are you going to order Phoebe?"

"Do I need to tell my mother you're harassing me? I will have you fired before your head can spin."

Tori, aware of Phoebe's temperament, quickly diffused the situation by appealing to her Achille's heel. "Hey, what happened to your face?"

"My face?"

"Yeah, it looks swollen. Are you sick?"

Before she had time to respond, Jonas picked up on what Tori was doing. "She's right, around your eye is a bit red."

Suddenly Phoebe looked distraught and panicked. She was already wearing sunglasses. Nevertheless, she quickly pulled a scarf up around her face.

"Don't look at me!"

Phoebe had sustained injuries on her face from her altercation with her cousin Willet, though it wasn't common knowledge just yet. Most likely because school hadn't started yet.

At that moment, Gavin walked through the door. He was his usual smirking cocky self. Whatever one may feel about his personality, Gavin was usually smiling. He was one of the few genuine heartthrobs around the school. Because he knew this, he had his pick of female admirers. Most of the teachers and authority figures secretly hated him, as did a lot of the town, but he was very popular amongst his peers.

In a recent school poll, he and Alouette were voted the most beautiful young people in Meadowlark. It was unusual for Gavin to come into the diner alone. He strolled through the entrance. He slid past several customers waiting and made his way into the main dining room.

Gavin approached the table, and Phoebe immediately glowed. Almost instantly, Phoebe tried subtly flirting. "Hey Gavin, we were just talking about you."

Tori looked confused. "We were?"

Gavin smiled like a wolf looking at an innocent sheep. "Hey gorgeous, where have you been hiding girl? I love that blouse."

Phoebe sheepishly blushed and giggled. She stood up, so he could get a better look at her form-fitting designer clothes. She was about to say something she deemed clever when Gavin asked the unthinkable.

"Hey, are you sick?"

The paranoia quickly returned. "What do you mean?"

"Your scarf and glasses..."

He did not get to finish as she blurted out. "Don't look at me!"

Without warning, she pushed past him and ran out of the diner, crying. Leaving Jonas and Tori laughing so hard, that they could scarcely contain themselves.

Gavin looked confused. "Did I miss something?"

Jonas dismissed the situation. "Nothing, I'll tell you later."

"Why don't you tell me now?"

"It's not important, what's up?"

"Let's go, we need to get you back home."

"I thought you were grounded from driving?"

"Who says I'm driving?"

Gavin pointed across the street at a dark red velvet Oldsmobile. A suspicious and familiar blond woman with glasses sat in the driver's seat. Jonas took a good look and shook his head. "You're playing with fire."

"What can I say, I love getting burned."

"Come on, we have to get going."

Tori leaned in. "What about my tip?"

Gavin tossed a crumbed bill on the table. "Don't drink the green tea. It will give you gas."

Tori rolled her eyes and left the table.

Jonas rose to his feet, pulling up his coat. "Are we in a hurry?"

"Well, I got a lot going on this evening."

Jonas glanced back at the red car. "I bet you do."

"No, I got this thing I promised to do!"

"Oh no, the last time you had a thing, you got picked by the cops."

"Don't worry, it's just a delivery for Auntie."

They both headed out the door into the street, as Constable Fletcher watched curiously from afar. He passed them on his way inside the diner. He stopped to see them both cross the road to where their ride was parked.

"Constable Fletcher, are you keeping on watchful eye on things?"

"Mayor, what brings you to this side of town today?"

There was nothing especially remarkable about Mayor Van Warren. He had a reasonable head of hair, a medium build, and his features were rather non-descript. However, being born a Van Warren and his financial pedigree was anything but ordinary.

Van Warren quietly joined Fletcher on the sidewalk, as he surveyed the aftermath of the storm. He wore a signature grey overcoat and brown leather gloves to keep his hands warm. He had a concerned look as if he were truly troubled.

"Well, when it rains sea life on your town, one is compelled to investigate. Is that what you are doing constable, or are you harassing children again?"

"That was an unfortunate misunderstanding!"

"I got a call from Sirenna Adler. She said you all but accosted her niece on this very sidewalk. Wasn't it just last week you held a prominent businessman's son illegally without bail, and today I find you actively spying on that same boy? That's harassment."

"That kid is a sociopath and he is into something, I can feel it in my bones!"

Van Warren put his hands into his coat pockets. "I hope you are not getting too attached to our town Fletcher."

"Is that a threat?"

"Fletcher, you can't keep harassing the local town folk and expect to win reelection!"

"I may remind you that our duties extend to all of Meadowlark's residents."

"What are you getting at, constable?"

"There are more than just two families that make up this town, you may try to remember that, Mayor Van Warren!"

"How dare you talk to a public official with such disrespect!"

"I apologize Mayor, but it doesn't take a genius to see there is something wrong here in this town, and don't tell me this is just a small town. On my desk, I have a stack of unsolved cases of missing infants and small children. They date back over 70 years!

Most of the eyewitness reports describe everything from big black birds, tentacle monsters, and a phantom woman with wild hair sporting multiple appendages.

Sounds ridiculous save for the fact that I have two zip-lock bags of black feathers collected at multiple crime scenes. The local farmer, Ernest Kelly, was out hunting and found a ripped onesie in a pile of animal excrement that the pathologist still doesn't know what kind creature it came from.

I have another stack of missing-person cases. Girls between the ages of thirteen to seventeen disappear without a trace. According to my statistics, Meadowlark averages about three missing persons a year for the last 15 years. That is a lot for a town this size."

"Do you need more men? We have a flexible budget."

"More men? I have a box of cold cases that documents angel sightings, ghost sightings, and strange animal sightings from and around the Greywoods. Woods that are protected as some sort of wildlife refuge. Yet, when I try to access what kind of animals are protected, a page comes up that says, classified. I have been requesting clearance for 8 months!"

"Constable, what are you getting at?"

"Just listen, I have several farmers claim that the very wildlife in those woods, that is being protected, is responsible for the repeated livestock mutilations they have reported every spring and fall solstice for as long as they can remember, and wait for it, yesterday, it rained fish on just this town.

I called all the surrounding towns, Jasper, Engiles, and even Monticello. No one else within a 100-mile radius has reported a biblical fish storm. The only other time there was something like this, it happened some 300 years ago. When the town was annexed by the purchase of several properties by certain familiar family dynasties."

"Are you investigating the Adlers and the Bransons?"

"They seem to be the one variable in the town's unusual phenomenon."

"Are you saying they made it rain fish?"

"No, I'm saying that I feel that somehow, they are connected to everything in this town!"

"Careful where you tread, Constable. If it weren't for those families, you wouldn't have a job, and neither would I."

Chapter 30: Heart to Heart

Willet spent the better part of the day resting in her room and reading the notebook Mother Hazel had given her. It differed a bit from the explanation that her mother and aunt had given her. This notebook filled in some blanks as it was written in shorthand. Although much of the writing was in the faigal language, a lot of it was translated into English.

She was able to pick out various faigal words and phrases. She wasn't quite sure of the pronunciation. One of the things she was able to learn quickly was the order of class systems within the ranks. There were the commoners, then nobles, and at the top, the royals.

The most fascinating thing she read about were the several notes about weaving and magic. Most faigal could perform some minor spells. The more advanced spells are called shammas. All faigal can hide their wings instinctively. They do this to hide themselves from the human population.

Some are predisposed in the art of shammas. Some study to become proficient in basic herbal medicine, spiritual cleansing, and spells that are more sophisticated. These faigal are called weavers. They tend to live isolated, devoting several hours to prayer and meditation. These weavers belong to a collective order calling themselves the Namvula.

The Namvula house the most advanced weavers who train all others in the art of weaving. There were also several passages about a phenomenon of weavers whose abilities are so connected to the earth that they are simply called tempests. Their existence is quite rare. However, their powers are so great, that many faigal fear them as deities themselves. After this most of the passages got a bit wordy and were hard to understand. Especially in the section about laws and rules.

Willet quickly turned to the section on grooming and physical body health. This section went into detail about blooming, shedding, and wingspread. Willets's eyes widened. There were diagrams showing several sketches of seemingly humanlike people with large wings protruding from their shoulder blades. They had clawed fingers and exaggerated features such as tufts of feathered hair, elongated noses, rounded eyelids, and sharp teeth!

I wonder if I have ever met someone before who wasn't human.

There was a knock at the door. Willet was so startled that she jerked up. She quickly closed the notebook and shoved it inside the pillowcase. She then sat up, as if she were just waking up.

"Yes, who is it?"

"It's your mother."

"Give me a minute."

Willet hopped out of bed and began to straighten her pillow and make the bed, so no one would have a reason to mess with her bed and find her book. As soon as it resembled what it did the day before she cleared her throat. "Come in mama."

"I just wanted to check on you and see how you were feeling."

"I'm ok, a little sore."

Laraline had a mournful expression on her face. "Mother Hazel told us about last night's visitation. I'm so sorry."

"Did they ever visit you?"

Instead of speaking Laraline nodded, as if it were too disturbing to discuss.

There were so many questions Willet wanted to ask, but in light of her mother's emotional state, she felt it better not to dwell on the issue, so she was glad when the subject was changed.

"I heard about your meeting with the Mother Sister."

Willet just shrugged it off. "Oh yeah, whatever that was. At first, I thought she was going to tell me I was this badass weaver."

"Personally, I'm relieved. Weaving is more trouble than it's worth."

"Do you have any powers?"

"Wow, I've never heard it referred to in those terms. I'm a mother and that is the greatest superpower."

"So, you were ok, giving up everything to live in the human world?"

"Didn't you like Key West?"

"Yeah. But giving up life with magic and money for a fisherman is, you know..."

Laraline didn't let her finish. "Trust me, life with your father wasn't ordinary. I can appreciate how exciting the idea of this may seem to your eyes, but you don't know what it was like growing up."

"What about Grandmother Oriole?"

"According to my Aunt Evelyn, my mother had such gifts, and it drove her mad. I gather she had just given birth to me, and she was in a bad place. She fell into a deep depression. She started to hear voices and see visions, which is common, especially for a new mother. One morning after listening to voices all night she was convinced to go outside. She headed into the Greywood and was gone all night. The next morning, they all went looking for her but they never found her body."

Willet found herself tense. "What about your father?"

"I never knew him. All I know is that he was a nobleman." Laraline was almost in tears. "You do not deserve this. We tried so hard to keep you from the curse, Willet."

Willet changed the subject before she could get emotional like her mother. "Hey, where's Adelie?"

"She and Aunt Evelyn were in the garden earlier. I don't know what may have happened to you if it weren't for her. She is the one who discovered you, unconscious."

Willet looked out of the window. "Wow, I guess I owe her!"

"Also, there is something I want to discuss with you."

"I'm all ears."

"Well, Ms. Broom officially quit this morning."

Willet put her hands in her pockets and cocked her head. "I can't say that I blame her."

"Do you know something I don't?"

Willet forgot that she was privy to gossip from Mrs. Weever's daughter Jae. It wouldn't be wise to spread such things, as it was probably in confidence. Instead, she played it off.

"No, I was just saying."

Laraline looked at Willet suspiciously before she continued. "Well anyway, we need money, and I was thinking about it. I could pick up her slack and run a few errands, just until I find something."

"You want to be a servant to that woman after she debased you at dinner?"

"No, I would be assisting Sirenna in any capacity and helping Evelyn with a few things."

"Aunt Evelyn asked you to do this?"

"No, I asked her!"

"I don't understand."

"I don't either, but I see how everyone in town reacts to her. It's not out of fear, or obligation, but out of respect. She commands a respect Sirenna could never understand."

"Well, it seems that you like spending time with her."

Laraline thought for a moment. "Yeah, I do. She is almost like the mother I never had.

Willet removed her hand from her pocket and gave a bow.

"Then you have my blessing, as long as it's temporary."

"Well, thank you, good madame. I'll try to make you proud. Seriously, Willet, I just want you and Adelie to be happy."

Willet whispered melodically. "Well, whatever will be will be!"

Laraline grinned as they both broke into song. "*The future's not ours to see, que sera, sera!*"

After a unison chorus, Laraline shook her head. "Boy, that brings back memories."

"I remember you would sing that to me whenever I had a nightmare."

"Do you still have them?"

"What?"

"Nightmares. Of course, you wouldn't tell me if you did."

"Everybody has bad dreams."

"You never did like to sleep, Willet. Why is that?"

"Maybe, I never trusted what may be hiding in the shadows."

The witching hour, somebody had once whispered to her, was a special moment in the middle of the night when every child and every grown-up was in a deep, deep sleep, and all the dark things came out from hiding and had the world all to themselves.[1]

Roald Dahl[2]

---

1. https://www.azquotes.com/quote/347770?ref=scary

2. https://www.azquotes.com/author/3576-Roald_Dahl

Chapter 31: Once Upon a Midnight Dreary

The large velvet red Oldsmobile slowly coasted down the road onto the large bridge. The lights were off, so as not to advertise their arrival. The car looked very familiar. She had seen it before.

I see a red car with flames on the side. Why is that familiar? I've seen this car before. I don't know these people or this place, but I feel it's nearby. We are on some bridge. Am I dreaming this? Is this real?

The car came to an abrupt stop a few yards in front of a strange glowing light. Almost instantly, the bright light started to move in the direction of the car. From the darkness, an older woman emerged to greet the driver. She was dressed in black and wearing an eyepatch over her right eye. She was carrying a lantern in her left hand. Her other hand was free, as she motioned for the driver to get out. Two people were sitting in the car. One was a young man and the other was a studious-looking blonde woman with glasses.

The older woman began to speak. "I had almost given up on you showing up tonight!"

The young man emerged from the passenger side. "I didn't think we were late."

"Time is of the essence!"

."I just made bail the other day; remember. I had to wait until things cooled down."

The older woman looked at the driver suspiciously. "Who is that with you?"

"She's cool, she helped me with this one."

The older woman held her lantern higher to see the driver's face more clearly. "Mrs. Faulkner, you should watch the company you keep."

The blonde decided to remain in the car. Pulling up her glasses tightly, she puffed a cigarette. As she exhaled, she responded. "Are you done talking to me?"

The older woman ignored her comment and turned to the young man dressed in a dark grey hoodie. "Where is my package!"

"It's in the trunk!"

They can't see me. I'm standing right here with them, yet none of them can see me. Why am I here?

They both walked around to the back of the car. He then proceeded to unlock the trunk. It was hard to see what he was doing, as she was at a distance from them. She did notice the woman behind the wheel looked irritated and nervous. She wasn't happy about whatever he had gotten her into. You could see it on her face.

Finally, he lifted an extremely large bundle from inside the trunk. Because of its weight, he let it drop to the ground. Almost instantly, there were forceful movements and muffled sounds as if someone was trying to speak or scream.

Oh, my goodness, there is a person in that bag.

A chill went up Willets's spine as she stood, as a passive observer. Whomever these people were, they had kidnapped someone and bound them up in plastic and there was nothing she could do but watch helplessly.

The older woman inquired. "Did you have any trouble?"

The quiet woman at the wheel suddenly wasn't very quiet, interjecting between puffs of her cigarette. "Someone was there!"

"What?"

The young man quickly corrected her in a threatening tone. "Shut your mouth or I'll shut it for you!"

"What is she talking about?"

"Nothing much."

"Explain now!"

"It's just that this one is a bit of a screamer."

He gave the bundle a swift kick. There was a muffled sound followed by coughing. The older woman was almost threatening as she repeated. "What happened?"

"It's no big deal, someone from one of the other rooms heard her scream, and they were creeping around the door. But they didn't see anything."

"Who were they?"

Oh no, these are the creeps from the hotel, and they are talking about me!

"I didn't see, but I caught her scent."

"Her?"

"I know the scent of a woman, and she had a curious one."

They are totally discussing me!

"How do mean? Was she human, was she faigal?"

"I'm not exactly sure."

"What do you mean?"

"Look, it's getting late; do you want the damn thing or not. My plans didn't entail us spending the evening out here."

"Ok, but if you lead a trail back to us, I will gut you!"

"Relax, whoever they were, she was scared, I made sure!"

"Well ok, let's have a look at the goods."

They both jerked the package upright and began to unwrap it, right in front of Willet. They were unaware of her presence so far. Willet took a couple of steps closer to get a better look.

The package was an almost naked young woman. She had duct tape covering her mouth. Her hands were bound in a similar fashion behind her back. As soon as she was completely uncovered from the bag, she suddenly leaped away. That's when Willet beheld her back.

Two tremendously large brown wings emerged and stretched out from her shoulders. The wingspan extended out at least 10 to 12 twelve wide. Her feathers were so large and very similar to the blue feathers Willet had seen on the steps, on her first day. Willet stood

in awe. It was true. Everything her mother and aunt had told her was
true.

Even in the young woman's distress, there was an elegance about
this creature. She quickly flapped her wings twice and it almost
looked like she might get somewhere, as she had risen a few feet
above the car.

Without warning, the young man unsheathed a large sword-like
blade from his side and leaped into the air after her. He took one step
on the car hood and dove up, so he was almost eye level with the
fleeing faigal.

He brought the blade down on the left wing, almost slicing it
clean off. The young woman gave a muffled screech through the duct
tape as her body violently descended. She immediately dropped to
the ground and collapsed on the road. The older woman yelled at the
young man. "Finish the wing!"

He quickly complied, as he ran to the fallen faigal. He straddled
her back and with his freehand, he pulled back against the broken
wing. He then started to vigorously cut on the slice he had made
previously with his blade. There was a snap. She instantly writhed
backward in unconscious pain.

Willet could see a single tear in her eye as she leaned backward
before passing out. Willet's heart sank in her chest as he finished
cutting her left wing completely off. Willet released an emotional
scream into her hands. It was a loud and booming echo across the
road. The young man looked about confused as if he might have
heard Willet. However, it was followed by complete silence.

Willet yelled at herself internally. *They can hear you, idiot. Shut
up, or you'll be next!*

The old woman snapped at him. "Can't you keep her silent?"

The blonde behind the wheel looked puzzled. She knew the
unholy scream didn't belong to the unconscious girl. She mumbled
under her breath. "That wasn't her."

The young man rose to his feet and put his blade back into its hidden holster. He had a crazed grin on his face as the older woman approached. He must have surmised Willet's scream came from his fallen prey at his feet. "I told you she was a screamer!"

The older woman with the eyepatch seemed to be glaring at the young man. "Hurry, while she is still unconscious!"

They both began to drag the helpless girl across the road onto the edge of the bridge. It didn't make sense to Willet what they were doing until the others started to arrive. A small flock of strange birdlike creatures ascended down on the very railing where the dangling body lay. These creatures were birdlike in the fact that they had wings, feathers, and claws. However, they had the heads of people. Willet gasped in horror at what she was seeing.

These things were like oversized vultures with human heads. These weren't just ordinary human heads. These were the faces and heads of infants complete with bald heads, fat cheeks, and innocent eyes with playfully malevolent expressions, hidden behind pupils black as coal. Most infants don't have teeth, but these beings seem to have tiny fanglike mandibles dripping drool out of their bright pink puffy pouty lips.

This must be a nightmare!

The older woman acknowledged their arrival. "My children are famished. They are almost skin and bones. Well don't worry, Mother has brought you a little snack."

The faigal girl had started to come to, noticing the committee of strange birds all perched patiently waiting. Her eyes widened as she realized what was happening. She was trying her best to scream for help through her sweaty tape muzzle.

The older woman gently knelt beside the young girl and kissed her forehead. At that moment there seemto be so much compassion for the young woman that Willet thought she may have changed her mind. The older woman whispered, "Blessed bounty."

Suddenly, she lifted the wounded girl with her legs and tossed her headfirst over the railing into the darkness below. Almost instantly, the strange bird flock quickly descended into the darkness after the fallen package.

The obligatory sound of something heavy falling and crashing through small trees and bushes, erupted into the night. Willet recoiled from the disturbing sound. Without missing a beat, the young man turned to his elder impatiently.

"How many more of these trips are necessary?"

"Look, you already are being handsomely rewarded. Your skills using the crissum are unmatched. I will make it so you cannot be defeated by any other crissum in a duel ever."

"Are you sure?"

"Fresh meat has arrived in town. Hopefully, there won't be many more of these excursions. Why, does it bother you?"

The young man paused. "I knew this one, she was a classmate."

"Do you feel remorse?"

"Maybe it is because she was faigal, I didn't give the matter much thought."

The older woman folded her arms. "So, do you have an opinion on the matter?"

"When it comes to death, not really. It's just all these missing people are starting to attract attention."

The older woman cautiously looked about the perimeter. She noticed the severed wing still lying in the road and it was involuntarily twitching. She snapped her fingers to the woman in the car. "Get out and get that thing off the road!"

"Are you talking to me?"

"Why are you here, little girl?"

"That's what I keep asking myself!"

"Help us clear all the evidence."

"I didn't hack off the damn thing!"

"No, you just watched him do it, without saying a word!"

Finally, the young man threw down his cigarette and stomped it out. "Get out and help!"

The blonde gave him a controlled glare before she responded. "Fine"

She hopped out of the door and slammed it shut, showing the aggravation she felt at their treatment of her. She paused, as the amputated wing seemed to jerk away as if sensing her closeness. She lunged forward and grabbed the bloodied appendage. As soon as she had secured a firm grasp, the older woman motioned. "Hurry, chuck it over the rail"

She impatiently hurried to the edge of the bridge, holding the tips of the appendage, avoiding the bloody areas. She carefully lifted it and flung it sideways over the rail. It landed in a group of branches right beside the railing. It was snagged onto the claw-like branches holding it up. She was about to panic when the wing suddenly slipped and tumbled downward until it was out of sight.

She was quite grossed out about the entire situation. She took a deep breath, then heaved and a stream of steady vomit chased after the appendage. As she lay doubled over the railing, her companion seemed concerned as he approached her.

"Are you ok?"

She paused as if she were trying to get a bearing on her condition. She then wiped her mouth off and rose to her feet before responding. "Do I look ok?"

He reached out for her, but she slapped his hand away. She then made the proclamation. "Good frickin' night!"

She stomped off and headed back for the car. He started to follow her but got sidetracked as he noticed a handful of random bloody feathers lying on the ground where he initially cut the girl. He fell to his knees and frantically began to scoop up the feathers.

The one-eyed woman cheered him along. "Yes, hurry! Get rid of everything before someone comes along!"

Willet stared at the spot where the girl was attacked. She held in her desire to scream again. as the participants in this crime headed back to their respective cars.

The small black Mercedes coasted back down the road. The driver of the red Oldsmobile wasn't about to wait for her companion to return to the car. The second he opened the door; she began to pull off. He quickly flung himself inside and slammed the door. Within moments, the entire bridge was empty and silent.

What had Willet just witnessed? Perhaps this was just another elaborate nightmare like the ones that seemed to plague her recently. It had the same strange dream logic. However, this felt different in almost every way. Willet looked about in wonder.

How is it that they didn't see me but they heard me?

Out of the darkness, she heard a shallow scream, then it abruptly stopped. Willet glanced in the direction of the bloody railing. It was coming from the direction where the faigal had fallen to her ultimate fate.

Willet found herself walking in that direction despite herself.

If this is a dream, I really need to wake up!

She was about a yard from the railing when a bloody hand reached up grasping. Willet jumped back out of instinct. She helplessly watched the talon-like fingers grasping frantically on the railing trying to find a place to pull up. Just as quickly as it rose, it let go and disappeared below as if it were being pulled back down.

Willet felt her throat and vocal cords betray her with another scream.

Leave her alone!

Her voice echoed down into the blackness below. Up until now, she was just an unseen observer. She was unnoticed. That was until now. Familiar voices from below the bridge emerged from the darkness below.

"Who was that?"

"Is that mother?"

"Mother, is that you?"

"That's not mother's voice, it sounds younger!"

"It sounds fresh and delicious!"

Willet stumbled backward as the voices grew louder. Three great big baby-headed birds hopped up on the railing to investigate. Willet was closer now and could see them more clearly. They all looked identical. They could have been triplets or clones. They, curiously, resembled the one-eyed woman, if she had both eyes.

They were sniffing about like feral dogs in heat. There was a wildness about them that was very off-putting. Especially when Willet noticed that their mouths were blood-soaked. She had disturbed their feeding.

One of them landed on the road, a few feet from where Willet stood. It weaved its head about as if it were trying to smell the air. It was trying to pick up a scent. It spoke in a deep gravelly childlike voice. "Who disturbs feeding time?"

It can't see me, but how did it hear me?

Willet continued to back away from the bridge where the others were. The wayward creature continued to hobble down the road looking for her. Willet finally made it several yards away from the bridge. The bird creature poked its head forward and studied the area carefully in her direction.

"On my, is that you sweet meat. Have you finally come to offer yourself to us?"

Willet was in a panic, and for some reason, it was looking right at her.

How is this even possible?

"My, you look so young and tender. I can't wait to taste you."

As Willet continued to back up, down the road, two bright lights appeared on the horizon coming from the direction of the bridge. The headlights caused all the other night visitors to scatter back into the shadows, save for the lone pilgrim who was after Willet. It seemed oblivious to the approaching vehicle.

Willet saw the opportunity before her. She just had to preoccupy the damn thing long enough. She lowered herself down toward its level. She moved to the edge of the road and began to briskly move backward. Maybe she could keep it preoccupied, yet just out of its reach.

"What are you up to meat?"

The truck was now about forty yards away.

"You can't hide from me, I can see you, sweet meat."

Willet snapped back at the approaching harpy. "Why would you ever want to eat me? I would surely give you severe heartburn."

The truck was about twenty-five yards and the beast started to move quicker. Its neck extended as it began to snap at the air near her. It hissed at her with its cute, but menacing baby lips.

"Why are you teasing us, we came to your home, but you wouldn't let us in, and now you are here."

Willet suddenly realized that she needed to get that thing in the air. It was the only way for her plan to be effective. "I think you are too fat to use your wings. I guess they are just for show."

"What did you say?"

The truck was 10 yards away. She had to act fast. "That's why you have to waddle about on the ground like a pregnant toad. You're too fat to fly after me!"

Its face turned red and it became so enraged it looked like it was pouting. Its lips poked out and it started to breathe hard as if it were trying to calm down. "Shut up!"

"What's the matter, are you going to cry?"

"I'll show you!"

The engaged harpy bared its tiny fangs as it leaped into the air at her head. At the same time, the large semi-truck raced through an unseen Willet. She felt an uneasy feeling, almost like being on an amusement park ride, as the truck zoomed through her ghostly presence.

As for the harpy, it wasn't so lucky. It was immediately struck by the side of the truck's grill. There was a loud harsh crunch as the harpy was knocked across the side of the road. The truck cleared through her as if she were mist. Willet rubbed her hands over her body quickly making sure she was ok. She looked behind her, as the dark silver delivery truck passed by, oblivious of what it had just hit.

Willets's thoughts went to her attacker. Where did it end up? Willet searched the side of the shoulder until she found the wounded beast. Its torso was bleeding out and its breath staggered. The creature's left wing was mangled as it lay on its side very still.

Willet knelt down in front of the wounded harpy as she taunted the dying beast. "You know, I don't think you are going to make it, meat."

Spittle came out of the creature's mouth as it tried to speak. "What kind of trickery is this?"

"It's the Swift curse."

"Swift Curse?"

"When you sisters come for your body. Tell them what I have done to you. Tell them that I will do the same to all of your family if don't leave me alone.

It hissed through a mouthful of thick blood. "You're lying!"

"Then why are you dying?"

Willet was about to continue needling when she saw several familiar dots flying in the sky. They were still at a distance, but they were searching for their fallen sister. Even if they could not physically see her, it would be better if she were not around. She quickly darted across the road into a grassy field with plenty of distance between her and the harpy roadkill. They would smell her soon.

How far am I from my home? I know this is Martin Street, but how far down is the bridge from the turn at Bluejay Way? How do I get back? What has happened to me? Perhaps, I am actually dead.

After walking for a while, she suddenly felt quite tired. Her eyes were starting to get blurry and her arms felt weightless. She made it another twenty feet before she collapsed in the tall grass. She turned over on her back before she looked up into the sky and whispered.

"Please make this stop."

Chapter 32: Just Another Dream?

Willet woke up startled. *Had she fallen asleep? The sun was up. Had she slept the entire night outside, without incident? Where were the harpies?*

However, as soon as her eyes adjusted, she realized she was in her bed. She was still wrapped up in covers. She scanned her bedroom and breathed a sigh of relief. She looked up at the ceiling through her canopy and started to laugh aloud. She thought about the absurdity of her nightmare. She rose to her feet and stretched. The notebook dropped to the floor. *Crap!*

I forgot I was reading the thing before I went to bed.

She was about to pick it up when she heard a strange sound outside her bedroom window. A twinge of fear immediately returned. A chill went up her spine and she slowly contemplated her next move. Willet moved across the room with the resolve of a cat as she opened the shutters. She half expected to see the harpy from last night, bloody and deranged.

She popped the window open, and her heart beat faster in anticipation. The only thing to greet her was the bright sunlight. She squinted her eyes until they adjusted to the day. Out her window stood a truck on the lawn. It was removing the last of the dead fish.

She breathed again. *Get a hold of yourself. It's just a truck picking up those nasty fish.*

She thought about what Mother Hazel had said about her and the fish storm. She began to chuckle to herself. She was starting to believe the old woman. She walked back to her bed and knelt to pick up the book when Adelie popped into the doorway.

"Morning sleepyhead!"

Willet discreetly folded the book into her covers. That was a conversation she didn't want to have with Addie. To call Adelie a big mouth was an understatement. Adelie could not keep a secret. It was so frustrating not being able to share things with her. As much as she wanted to talk to someone about what was happening, Adelie was not an option.

Willet tried to act normal. "I'm up."

"How are you feeling?"

"Other than some weird dreams, I feel ok."

"What dreams?"

Willet almost said too much but quickly walked it back. "It's not important."

It got awkwardly silent as Willet struggled to fill the silence with another subject as engaging as nightmares filled with murder and madness. Finally, she hit on something. "Hey, I never thanked you, Addie!"

"For what?"

"For being my sister and watching out for me. I heard you are the one who found me passed out."

"That's my job, Willie."

"I would be dead if it weren't for you. So, I owe you."

"Well, you were pretty gnarly looking!"

Willet feigned being offended. "Shut up!"

They giggled and hugged each other. It felt nice for a change. They were just sisters today. Tomorrow they very well would be bitter rivals, but not in this moment. The days were always smoother when they weren't at each other's throats.

As Adelie pulled away, Willet had an image of the murdered woman with wings. She shook her head uncomfortably as if trying to shake the painful image of her dream before it replayed in her mind.

Adelie touched her head. "Are you ok?"

"Yes, some of the nightmares I had got to me. They felt so real."

Adelie mused. "Did you sleepwalk too?"

"What do you mean?"

"Look at your feet!"

Willet looked at her feet. They were covered with dried dirt.

"What on earth did you dream last night, Willie?"

Willet opened her mouth to try to deflect the question with another excuse, but her dirty feet had left her dumbfounded. She pulled back the bedspread to reveal dirt-stained sheets where her feet had been.

Unfortunately, Laraline interrupted their reflections on any possible explanation. "Hey, you two get ready. Your appointment with the headmistress is today."

Willet tried to act surprised as she blocked the view of her bed. "Is that today?"

"Look, I know this is unusual for you girls."

"It's downright stupid, why do we have to meet some uptight ninny, before we go to school?"

"That's enough of that. Your great aunts went through a lot of expense to organize this meeting."

Adelie probably felt the same, but typically, it was Willet who seemed to want to buck authority. Willet was about to introduce a counterargument when her mother noticed the muddy sheet.

"Willet, what in all that is holy have you done?"

"What do you mean?"

"Evelyn has had those sheets in the family for years."

"Mama, I promise I'll wash them myself."

"That's not the point."

Adelie interjected into the conversation, which was heading south for her sister.

"Willet is sleepwalking again."

"When did this happen?"

As expected, the focus shifted from Willets's utter irresponsibility and callousness to therapy concerns to help whatever was troubling her. It was a bittersweet victory, as there was some element of truth to her need for therapy. In reality, she could have very well have slept walked. It would explain so much.

Evelyn had Merle pull the car around for the meeting at the school. Evelyn elected to take the girls herself and have Merle drive, even though Laraline was a capable and legal driver. Laraline would be running personal errands. Besides, the background history of a bitter rivalry between schoolmates Laraline and Rhea Faulkner could make things awkward.

Evelyn also insisted that she talk to the headmistress instead of Sirenna. Evelyn didn't want her sister to resort to bribes or strong-arm deals when it came to the children. She believed that they should be able to stand on their own merits.

Besides that, Uncle Merle had run out of his prescription for pain medicine. Whenever he was out of medicine, he tended to drink more. Evelyn had been working on him for days until she could finally convince him to get a refill.

Since the meeting was so formal, Sirenna insisted that both girls wear appropriate attire to make the best first impression. When both girls headed to the car in matching black and white uniform-style dress attire, Evelyn almost broke down in tears.

"You two remind me of when Laraline was in school. You both look absolutely stunning; however, it would help if you were smiling."

Laraline who had walked out with the girls responded with a sympathetic scowl. "I think that's the best you're going to get from these two."

Laraline was about to get in the car when she noticed that Adelie was chewing gum and mysteriously her blouse had been unbuttoned two buttons lower than she approved. "Adelie, come here dear."

"What's wrong?"

Willet slowly strolled to the caddie. Her mind was elsewhere, yet she still managed to hear the innocent protests of Adelie. There would be a power struggle for Adelie to show cleavage and for Mom to cover it up. Willet was almost to the car when she noticed the parked truck again. A flash from her dream popped into her head. This trunk was the same type of truck. It was a silver delivery truck.

It could be the same truck. Even if it was, I probably saw it around town and put it in my dream.

Suddenly Willet changed direction and found herself approaching the truck. She was hypnotically drawn to the large vehicle.

What am I doing? This is crazy. She was on the side of the truck and proceeded to walk to the front. She just had to ease her mind.

If this was the truck, then I should see something that would indicate that. Actually, it looks a bit smaller.

She got to the corner of the grill and saw nothing. She breathed a sigh of relief. She noticed that the driver walked past her and got in on the other side of the truck.

Oops, I checked the wrong side.

By now, she was confident it wasn't the trunk from last night. She quickly strolled across the front to get a quick glance at the other side. She wanted to be sure. Her confident pace quickly faded as she saw the grill on the driver's side was slightly damaged. A few of the grill plates were dented slightly and had created a blood-splatted crevice.

Willet gasped as she moved closer to the grill. There was an indention and a deep crack with something poking out. What was it? She impulsively reached out with her fingers and tugged at something looking like a string. She pulled the string, realizing it was a strand of hair.

Without warning the driver blew his horn at Willet. Startled, she jumped back, dislodging a clump of debris from the hole in the grill. A clump of hair and bloody feathers dropped at Willet's feet. She screamed in horror at the revealing discovery.

The driver hopped from his cab and ran to the young girl. Laraline and Adelie quickly joined them. The young driver seemed confused, as he tried his best to explain.

"I was about to pull off when I saw her just standing there. I didn't mean to freak her out!"

Laraline nodded at his explanation and quickly grabbed her hysterical daughter. "Willet dear, what were you thinking?"

She was so upset, that all she could do was point at the bloody grill and the obvious roadkill debris that had fallen to the ground. The driver responded trying to feign a bit of guilt.

"Yeah, I hit a bird or something last night driving across Martin Bridge. I hate traveling through those woods. If it makes you feel better, I'm sure it died quickly and didn't suffer much."

Willet mumbled. "No, it wasn't slow. It definitely suffered."

Laraline looked horrified at her comment. "Willet!"

However, she hadn't heard her mother. Her focus was on her disturbing epiphany.

Laraline nervously smiled. "I'm sorry sir, she hasn't been well."

Willet snapped back in a frantic rage. "Stop making excuses for me, I'm not this fragile thing. You don't understand, it's all real! I saw them. They kidnapped her and then they killed her, and she had these wings, such beautiful wings."

By this time, Evelyn had come to join the gathering. Willet, who had become hysterical, had to be physically moved out of the way of the truck. The driver had a blank expression as if he did not know what to think.

As the truck pulled off and headed down the main road, Willet had started to calm down. Laraline was holding her and stroking her forehead. Evelyn sat behind them rubbing Willet's back. No one seemed to know what to say. Even Uncle Merle looked concerned, as he moved from the front seat of the car to the rear bumper. He pulled out a cigar and nervously puffed. In the dead silence, Adelie finally commented on the situation.

"Does this mean we don't have to go to our appointment?"

Chapter 33: The Interview

Rhea Faulkner was finishing her cob salad and cucumber sandwich. It was one of the few consistent pleasures that she felt she had at this station in life. As headmistress over the Talomore dormitory, her responsibility left little time for a personal life. The job itself was not a problem. It was all the politics that came along with the job. Whenever you run a school that services select members of the upper crust, they always have demands.

Their demands could include a call at 11 p.m., requesting an emergency meeting about an incident you were not informed of, or demanding one's presence at an all-day function on a weekend, in exchange for the funds for new textbooks.

Talomore was originally named after the famous 13th-century alchemist of the same name, Fredrick J. Talomore, a faigal and self-proclaimed humanist. After spending the better part of twenty years traveling around the world, he felt it was his duty to create a school of higher learning. On the surface, it aimed to offer the highest levels of the world's greatest faiths including religion, alchemy, herbalism, chemistry, and science. It was one of five major institutions that catered to the faigal population, unbeknownst to the humans who were allowed to attend.

As it was, her 11 a.m. meeting was already 6 minutes late therefore allowing her a little more time to savor her lunch. She would, of course, down this meal with half a cup of grapefruit juice and a teaspoon of honey.

She was about to head to the restroom to refresh herself when there was a knock on her office door. Her secretary, Ms. Young popped her head inside the door. "

"Headmistress, the Swifts have arrived."

She quickly looked at her watch before responding. "Show them in."

Because of the mayhem that ensued earlier that morning, the plans changed and Laraline decided to join them. This made everyone uneasy except for Willet, who didn't care if she was accepted or not. Even though they were assured that the interview was a formality, you never could tell.

Evelyn was the first one inside, Adelie and Willet soon followed, and Laraline entered the office last. Almost immediately, there was a recognition that Rhea and Laraline knew one another. Before she had time to react, Evelyn bowed slightly with her arms extended to her sides. Rhea was more awkward and stiff, as she half-heartedly complied.

Adelie and Willet looked at one another bemused. This awkward greeting was so strange to them. The headmistress quickly rose, yet her eyes never left Laraline. Tilting her head down and looking coldly over the rim of her reading glasses, she addressed Laraline. "Laraline Adler! My, what brings you back to town?"

"Good morning, Rhea. It's Laraline Swift now."

Ms. Faulkner folded her arms. "You do realize you're 6 minutes late. We do not abide by tardiness here at Talomore."

"Yes, we're sorry, we had a last-minute emergency."

"Ironic."

"What do mean, ironic?"

"Well, that about sums up your own school history, a series of last-minute emergencies!"

Laraline could feel the rising animosity from the woman behind the desk. "I see."

"We are adults now; I was merely making an observation."

"Well, you haven't changed a bit, Rhea. You look almost the same, in fact, I believe that is the same dress I last saw you in when we graduated!"

Evelyn stood up in an attempt to diffuse the growing tension. "I may remind you both, that this is a meeting about these two children. Perhaps their mother and I should make ourselves scarce."

Ms. Faulkner nodded. "That would probably be wise."

Laraline mumbled in response. "I suppose so."

Evelyn clapped her hands. "Good, we'll leave you to it. Sirenna will be back to pick them up and see how it went. She's very interested in their success at this wonderful institution."

Ms. Faulkner cleared her throat and uncomfortably nodded. "She is? Well, of course."

As they left the office, Laraline looked at Evelyn. "What was all that about Sirenna picking them up? She's not even coming."

"Ms. Faulkner is afraid of your Aunt Sirenna!"

As soon as both women were gone, Ms. Faulkner eyed the girls. "So, before we begin this interview, do either of you have any questions?"

Willet raised her hand.

Ms. Faulkner produced a tight smile. "Good, politeness, that is an important virtue here at Talomore. You will both notice that when your aunt came in, she greeted me in the traditional bird of peace bow, as I did the same greeting as well. All students will always address his or her instructors with this greeting. Respect is key here."

"Yes, miss."

"You may call me Ms. Faulkner."

"Ok, Ms. Faulkner."

"Good, now what is your question?"

Willet had the most innocent look as she proceeded. "Why do you hate my mother?"

The tight smile on Ms. Faulkner's face turned into an uncomfortable grimace. As she looked at Willet's expression she recognized the calculated question and its intended function.

Adelie quickly raised her hand before the headmistress had a chance to respond. "Where is the toilet, I think I got to pee?"

Chapter 34: Auction

Coventry Gallery House had advertised for months about the exclusive auction. It would highlight the weapons from ancient civilizations. This international exhibit was from the Brome Levi collection. Levi, a fabled general from the fifth century, supposedly fought in some of the world's most important military campaigns.

Sirenna had been anticipating its arrival, even since Lillian Finch leaked the news to her last spring. The Adler twins both pushed the town of Meadowlark to host this important showing. The mayor finally relented after learning that several royal representatives from overseas had expressed interest in attending.

If the Bransons were the technological innovators for Meadowlark, then the Adlers were the curators of the arts and education markets. Some of these markets could be very financially lucrative. Not that there wasn't a certain amount of that with Branson's prestige.

However, this division of economic enterprises helped to ensure the delicate truce between the Adlers and the Bransons. It was a sort of symbiotic existence, where everyone understood their role.

It seemed that of late, Lady Aquila Delilah Branson had been pushing that line, especially in the eyes of Sirenna, whom she could hardly stand. Things became more antagonistic when Aquila unexpectedly showed up at the auction without any prior invitation.

That morning, Councilwoman Finch arrived at the Greywood estate to pick up Sirenna and Mother Hazel. They were to witness the collection firsthand before the public could fawn and clammer over its riches.

Usually, Mother Hazel kept out of such public matters. However, Evelyn was suddenly obligated to be present at an orientation meeting with the headmistress from Talomore earlier that morning and there was a scheduling conflict. The private viewing was for the elite and Sirenna was not disappointed.

The crowd was small but enthusiastic. A distinguished gentleman wearing a thin silk robe, matching blue pants suit, and a warm smile, approached Lady Adler. He had white curly hair and matching sideburns. Sirenna almost scrambled over her words as she rushed to greet him.

"Lord Demarkis, I'm honored you could make this event."

"Thank you for your invitation. it's a marvelous collection from what I can see, Lady Adler."

"Please, make yourself at home."

He nodded as one of the many servants came to gather his coat. "Where is your charming sister?"

"She had a previous engagement. Are you here alone, sir?"

"That's debatable."

"Excuse me?"

The regal gentleman extended his arm in the direction of a young couple. "You know my niece, Lady Valerian, and her betrothed, Sir Lucian Bragg."

Sirenna's eyes fell upon the elegant pair. The woman had long blonde hair tied up in a casque. Her features were strong and athletic, yet elegant. She wore a gold gown with classic faigal slits along the back. It was draped down to the tips of her Jimmy Choo's. Her ample cleavage caused Sirenna to blush.

"Lady Valerian, I had begun to think you were a bit of a recluse. I don't believe I've seen you in Meadowlark before."

The young woman beamed at the young man holding her hand tightly. "Well, this one here is so obsessed with the States, it's the only time I get to see him, unless I travel abroad."

The young man wore a green gown with the blackest boots. His hair was kempt in the traditional style, offset by his curious five o'clock shadow. He gave the impression that he lived hard. He dressed the part, but the look didn't seem to fit him. There was a hint of impropriety about him that reminded Sirenna of her great-nieces. She faked pleasantries by extending her hand and bowing toward Bragg.

"Lady Adler, you look ravishing as ever. If I weren't betrothed, I would let you keep me as a pet for your seductive whims." There was polite chuckling from the group, but the comment was awkward at best.

Despite how improper it was or how awkward, it solicited a blush from Sirenna, as he was rather pleasing on the eye. With his dark features and captivating eyes, Lucian Bragg wasn't the type to wed, he was the type to enjoy before considering nuptials.

She quickly walked back his comment. "Not that I would, especially considering the lovely maiden at your side."

Valerian welcomed the compliment with a faint smile and nod. "Thank you, Lady Adler."

As if oblivious of what he had said. He grinned at a slightly bothered Valerian. "She is something. She is a perfect ray of sunshine. I do believe she is the only thing keeping me sane in these times."

"So, why are you here in the States?"

"I'm an old friend of Lady Koko."

"Tuledge?"

"It's not what you think. We're just good friends. There are also many good folks on this side of the pond."

Valerian interjected. "My Lucian is a people person."

Sirenna glanced at Lord Demarkis, who was silently embarrassed by the admission that her betrothed was friendly with a notorious madame. Lady Adler tried to respond, but the words came out sounding queer. "Just like your uncle."

Valerian's expression changed as if struck by the comment. Yet, she nodded.

Bragg responded. "Well, I'm no saint."

Valerian mumbled under her breath. "Neither is he."

At that moment, Mother Hazel approached the group. She nodded politely as she scanned the energies. "Saint Sebastian, welcome to Coventry House."

Lord Demarkis nervously corrected her. "Just Lord Demarkis here."

"Don't be shy, a member of the ministry is rarely so beloved by their own people. Hell, your more liked than that chubby Eskar you work for!"

Lord Demarkis gave an uncomfortable smile. "Where is the bar?"

Mother Hazel pointed with her cane. "It's over there. Just follow your nose. I'm sure you know how to find that type of spirits, Lord Sebastian."

He nodded coldly. "Lady Adler, give my regards to your sister, Evelyn." As he drifted away, the conversation went from awkward to uncomfortable. That was usually how things went with Mother Hazel in social gatherings.

Sirenna tried to salvage the dialogue. "So, this is Valerian and her betrothed, Lord Bragg."

Hazel grinned from beneath her sunglasses. "Aren't they a lovely couple. Valerian, I was beginning to think you would end up an old maid."

Bragg glanced uncomfortably at Mother Hazel before Valerian spoke again. "Well, it's nice meeting you."

Mother Hazel glanced at Valerian. "What type of interests do you entertain? I've heard you're quite an expert at weapons."

"We were just heading in the direction of the weapons display." Valerian gave Mother Hazel a curt nod as the couple drifted back into the crowd.

Sirenna turned to Mother Hazel with a pointed look. Mother Hazel feigned innocence. "What? Did I say something wrong?"

Sirenna had her arms folded as she eyed Mother Hazel. "What was all that about?"

"What?"

"Stop being obtuse."

"They are a sweet couple."

"You don't think they will last?"

"No chance in hell!"

"Oh, come on. Let's mingle."

Sirenna moved about the crowd in her velvet red gown with a fuzzy plum coat and matching leather boots. She slid on her signature shades as Mother Hazel followed closely into the main gallery. Sirenna's eyes scanned the scene, as if bored. Her mood changed when she noticed Aquila Branson in the crowd.

"Oh my, what on earth is that vile creature doing at my auction?"

Before Mother Hazel could respond, Aquila must have sensed their stare because she began to head in their direction. Sirenna gritted her teeth as she approached.

Aquila wore a form-fitting black evening gown, with a V-line to accentuate her cleavage, which was quite a bit less than subtle. Her black eyepatch was adorned with rhinestones that matched her 4-inch heels. They seemed to give the illusion that she was floating as she casually made her way right in front of Sirenna.

Aquila did a most graceful bow, with her arms extended. Sirenna greeted her as well, as she silently sighed. Both women rose at the same time before any words were spoken.

Aquila was the first to break the ice. "Lady Adler, such a small world!"

"It's a bit too small for my tastes, Lady Branson."

"I rather like what you've done with all this old, dusty stuff. It all looks so squalidly quaint and old-fashioned."

"Speaking of old-fashioned, that is quite the outfit. I hope you don't catch a cold. You seem to be spilling out of your dress."

"It's funny you should mention cold. A little birdy told me that one of your young visitors has been ill. I hope that's not the case."

Mother Hazel arched her eyebrow. "What do you mean, ill?"

"It's just, I never see them out and about. Of course, if they are city children, sometimes the wildlife is a bit much for outsiders to take. When I first arrived in town, I thought this country's air was unbearable."

Sirenna responded under her breath. "As we did of you when you arrived."

"It's amazing what one can get used to. Eventually things do change, though, whether we are ready or not, a storm is coming!"

Sirenna folded her arms as she faced her down. "Is that a threat?"

"Is that what you heard? I'm sure I meant no such utterance, milady. Just a poor choice of words on my part!"

Sirenna hissed under her breath. "And dress!"

Aquila leaned into her rival. "Excuse me, did you say something?"

Sirenna quickly responded. "I was just saying it's so easy to **SEE** how you could have made such a **blindly** foolish comment!" Sirenna made a point of staring directly at Aquila's eyepatch as she continued. "Oops, I guess I have done it myself. I think I can see your point a bit clearer now."

Aquila's teeth clenched as she forced a smile. Mother Hazel, feeling the tempers between the two start to escalate, interjected, "Lady Branson, why don't you get a refreshment and browse around? Lady Sirenna and I have matters we need to attend to quite urgently."

Aquila nodded and moved just as abruptly to another crowd of people. Mother Hazel escorted Sirenna to an empty room around the corner. As soon as she made sure the door was shut, she turned to Sirenna, who was now fuming.

Mother Hazel pointed her cane at Sirenna's face. "That tongue of yours is venomous, and it's going to get us all in trouble!"

"I have a good mind to make her strip to her underwear and pluck every feather from her scrawny carcass. How dare she come here and threaten me at my own auction!"

"Sirenna, your mind tricks won't work on that woman."

"She is in blatant violation of the truce; I would be within my rights to break her neck."

"This is what she wants, for you to react."

"Why is that a bad thing? This is a public place, in the middle of the day, and on my turf."

"Sirenna, I have been telling you for years, Avis is not the one to watch out for."

Sirenna grunted in response. "Blind hag!"

"One thing I do find curious. Did you notice the black choker she was wearing?"

"She always wears that thing. She is a fashion-limited cyclops."

"Listen, I do not believe that is a choker at all. What if it's a binding ring? It's just dolled up to make it look like a common accessory."

Sirenna eyes widened. "I don't know."

"When I was young, I knew several women like her, who wore similar chokers to hide the various neck brands they received for disobedience. Why else would Avis export this mysterious Mr. Shahaf?"

"She wouldn't be that emboldened, would she?"

"All I know is that if she does indeed have a brand on the back of her neck, then it is a sign that she has been excommunicated."

"If that is the case, why is she still practicing?"

Mother Hazel held up her hand. "Calm down. Lower your voice."

"They already have a house weaver under employ. Having two practicing weavers in one house is against faigal law and Namvula protocol."

"Well, we don't have physical proof she is still practicing."

"What about the fish storm? Isn't that proof enough?"

"I don't know if she was responsible for that."

Sirenna seemed irritated. "I know you think Willet can somehow do such things, but she is a lek. She is not capable of anything like that; with such diluted blood, she would not have the strength."

"She is strong enough to defy your will."

Sirenna was almost sulking at the prospect. "Shut up, witch."

"Regardless of what you think about Willet, Aquila is not going to be that obvious. Besides, she doesn't have the kala to affect the weather; only a tempest can wield such power.

One thing is certain: she seems to know that someone was sick. That would seem to imply that she has a hand in the curse on Willet. We may be able to surmise who is behind our nightly curse.

Chapter 35: Connections

After a long introduction of Talomore's history and expectations of upperclassmen and underclassmen, Willlet had zoned out into a hazy stare. She found herself studying the strange lines and wrinkles on Ms. Faulkner's face. She had also deduced that Ms. Faulkner had quite recently had a mole removed from her extensive collection of bumps and growths about her neck and chin.

Adelie had positioned herself at a slight angle so she could take a catnap. The older woman seemed oblivious to Adelie's slight, steady snoring, as she blathered on about tradition and such institutional nonsense. Willet was about to follow Adelie's lead when the receptionist knocked on the door, startling her to full attention.

"Ms. Faulkner. I know you are in a meeting, but your sister is here to see you."

"Tell her I'm busy."

"I told her, but she insists it is rather urgent."

Ms. Faulkner leaned back in her chair and sighed. She sat with her eyes closed for several moments as if she were thinking. Finally, she opened her mouth after deliberating.

"Tell her to give me a few minutes, I was just wrapping up."

As soon as the woman left, Ms. Faulkner got to the crux of her interview.

"Well, this is the deal. We at Talomore have opened our doors to sleeven and faigal alike throughout the years. I have been made aware of your unique situation. We don't get a lot of mixed children here."

Willet's eyes narrowed, and she could feel a hint of rage building in her. "Typically, we have those attend most of their classes with the regular faigal population exclusively. However, you both have spent the better part of your life in human society, so you naturally are ignorant of basic faigal norms. There are moral and philosophical

240

differences among our races. Had your mother been more responsible, you wouldn't have these handicaps to contend with."

Willet took a deep breath before speaking. "I may not be an adult, but I do have feelings. When you discount me as if I didn't matter just because of some beef you had with my mother, it still hurts."

Ms. Faulkner shook her head as she held her hand out.

"That is what I am talking about. The sleeven in you is much too emotional and attached to the idea of what others may think. You have a great deal to learn, but you seem to be a forward thinker, so it may not be futile."

Willet passively mumbled. "Gee, thanks!"

"I think I will place you both in Ms. Faber's room. She works with the younger classmen still struggling to find their place in society. If you two can adjust, perhaps we will consider putting you with an upper-class instructor."

"I'm going to be in the same room as my sister?"

Adelie popped up from her nap with a stunned expression. Her eyes looked red and strained as Ms. Faulkner continued.

"Even though you are both half breeds, I don't have to tell you the importance of amenity amongst your human peers. You are not allowed to discuss or share your true lineage as it will be grounds for automatic expulsion."

Adelie repeated the warning in her own words, which was a quirk that drove Willet insane. At times, it felt like a constant echo.

"So, we are not allowed to talk about ourselves with anyone human."

"That is correct."

The headmistress then handed two large manila envelopes to Willet. She carefully took the thick parcels and rose to her feet. Ms. Faulkner remained seated as she continued her very impersonal script.

"You shall need a parent or guardian to sign the following papers before the term starts next week. Just have your mother or aunt come by to sign off."

Willet responded with an air of attitude. "I'll make sure my mother comes."

Ms. Faulkner completely dismissed Willet's mood, as she had become quite numb to the sensitive nature of her students. "Well, that concludes our business today. You can let yourselves out."

Both girls looked confused at the sudden abruptness of the situation. Adelie looked back and shrugged. Willet stood and tried her best to be civil under the circumstances.

"Well, thank you for your time, Ms. Faulkner."

Instead of acknowledging Willet, she glared at both girls coldly.

"You may leave now."

There was an awkward silence as Ms. Faulkner lowered her head and began to straighten up her desk. Both girls left her office and found themselves in the waiting room. The receptionist was busy typing and didn't stop when the girls stood awkwardly by her desk.

"Please take a seat, girls, your mother said she would be back shortly."

They sat down and waited for someone to come by and pick them up as the receptionist continued to work, oblivious of their presence. The phone started to flash a bright red without any sound. Adelie thought this was curious, however, she recalled that her mother didn't care for a ringing phone either. Her family home didn't have many phones, so she deduced that faigal were sensitive to loud ringing.

Things had just settled down when Willet could almost hear a low thumping sound in her ears, it was fast and steady and a bit unnerving. She scanned the room and noticed the older blonde woman with sunglasses flipping through some pulpy teen fashion magazine. She appeared completely bored, yet anxious at the same time. The thumping seemed to be coming from her.

Am I hearing her heartbeat? Why? She is very nervous. It's beating really fast.

There was nothing particularly striking about her, if she saw this woman on the street, she would blend in with the scenery. There was an inherent blandness about her. Not necessarily unattractive, but very unassuming.

However, Willet found herself staring at her. There was something familiar about her. It didn't make sense, but she had the sense that she knew this woman. At some point, the woman must have sensed Willet's stare because she looked up. "Why don't you take a picture? It will last longer!"

Willet was startled. "Sorry, you looked familiar. I thought, perhaps we had met."

"If that is some lame pick-up line, I don't go that way. I like boys!"

"No, it's nothing like that, I'm not either...never mind!"

Willet put her head down, embarrassed, not really understanding her own actions. She was acting creepy and had no explanation. *Why was I staring at her? I must be going crazy. It's not as if she killed someone or something.* Then Willet's mind triggered. She glanced up at the woman again.

It was her! I didn't recognize her at first, but it's definitely her!

Suddenly, the receptionist put the phone down and addressed the blonde. "Ms. Faulkner, your sister will see you now."

An image of the blonde woman in the red Oldsmobile popped into Willet's mind. *She was the driver, and the older woman with the eyepatch referred to her as Ms. Faulkner.* In a split second, the entire incident replayed itself behind Willet's eyes. The older woman's words toward the blonde were etched in her mind. *You'd better watch the company you keep, Ms. Faulkner!*

Willet shook herself from the memory just as the blonde walked past them into the headmistress's office. Willet was intrigued. As the door shut behind her, Willet arched her ear to the wall so she could hear.

It was silent for a moment, but then she heard the headmistress speak. "You have two minutes."

"Look, I know how you feel about me coming around."

"Kestrel dear, this is my job. I have a reputation to protect. I can't have you coming around with your... dramatic issues. Ever since you met that Branson boy, your life has come undone. I told you to stay away from that family."

"Ephron still loves me, I know it in my heart!"

"How many years ago was that? You were both still in school. He's moved on and is married!"

"Rumor is she doesn't have long."

"Listen to yourself. What has happened to you? I don't even want to know the rumors I'm hearing about you and his younger brother."

"It's complicated!"

"No, it's not! He is not only a minor, but also a very popular student under my watch. What would happen if people found out about my sister running around with one of my students? My career would be over!"

"It's not what it seems. The entire thing is a sham. It's all for show. What they call the right type of gossip!"

"The right type of gossip for whom? It makes you sound like one of those cheap pips in Crecheland."

"He is helping me gain access to Ephron. You think I'm crazy?"

"I never said that."

"It's in your eyes, the way you talk to me, like I'm an idiot."

"Seriously, I have a lot of work to get done for the new semester. Can't this wait?

Something happened last night."

Silence. There was no comment from Ms. Faulkner. Willet could picture in her mind the heaviness of her sister. The blonde broke down into tears. Willet could hear the extensive sobbing through the door. At that point, the voices became whispers. There was a series of short verbal exchanges that Willet could not make out. The last thing she heard was the headmistress exclaim, "My arke, what have you gotten yourself into now?"

It was at that very moment that Willet heard her name called as if from a dream. It was enough to shake her concentration.

"Willet!"

Willet finally looked up, startled. Her mother was standing at the entrance with her arms folded. Adelie must have long gotten to feet because she was impatiently waiting behind Laraline at the door.

"Come on, Willie!"

Willet rose uneasily to her feet as she greeted her mother. Her mind was still perplexed by the circumstances that were unfolding behind the doors of the headmistress's office. She was still trying to listen until her mother started to grill them.

"So, how did it go?"

"It went."

"What does that mean?"

"Lets just say, the headmistress is not a big fan of the Swifts."

Laraline looked bothered by her daughter's tone. "Did something happen?"

Willet quickly realized she was potentially opening a can of worms, decided to downplay the rude encounter. She dismissed her mother's concern by stating the facts. "Oh, you have to sign some paperwork for classes next week, but that could be done later."

Her mother was suddenly excited. "Good, that's wonderful news, we should celebrate. You are now officially in school."

Willet gave a final glance at the headmistress's door as they left. She was dying to know what was being said. She thought she had a pretty good idea anyway.

Adelie looked around, concerned. "Where is Auntie Evie?"

"She is waiting in the car downstairs."

As they headed out of the dimly lit building and into the daylight, Willet felt a certain kind of sickness. The revelation of what she had just witnessed was staggering. She walked the campus of her new school, trying to get familiar with the layout.

Soon, she came to the student activity board. It looked like a cluttered collage. There were so many advertisements, personal items for sale, or needed signs, official dates of tests and open houses, party and event dates. This was a living pulse of the youth. Perhaps this is how she and Adelie could keep up with everything happening for their age groups. Near the right corner, a particular flyer caught her attention.

Back-to-school beach bash. Call Tori for details.

There were several tiny strips underneath that displayed the number. Willet quickly ripped off a strip and put it in her pocket. Adelie ran up to the board and quickly became engulfed by the amount of teen information.

"Wow!"

"Take a look, Addie. This is our refuge from total boredom."

Laraline finally caught up with them both and was trying to catch her breath. Before she could speak, Willet was pointing at the beach flyer. "Mom, I met this girl the other day. Can we go to her beach party?"

"Party?"

"This is the girl we met at the diner. She was really nice."

Addie nodded. "Yeah, she's cool!"

Laraline weighed in. "Well, I guess you guys are getting a bit bored hanging around with us old folks.

Adelie emulated snoring sounds in her mother's ear.

"Well, get the number and I'll see."

Willet removed the strip from her coat pocket to show her. "Already did."

Laraline looked bemused. "When is a good time to call?"

Willet perked up. "We could call her at the diner for details. I know she is there now."

Laraline immediately dismissed the idea. "No, bad idea. Never call someone at their job, unless it's important."

"It is important!"

Adelie looked at her mother curiously. "Mama, speaking of phones, do the aunts not have a phone? I mean, since we have been here, I don't remember seeing one."

"Well, it's not that they don't, it's just our people aren't really big on phones and a lot of technology in general. I, however, love my phone."

"How do they even get in touch with people?"

"Specters."

"What is that?"

"It's another word for a familiar."

"Auntie Sirenna has a familiar? You mean like a witch?"

"No, I mean like a specter. We prefer the term weaver. To call a faigal, a witch, would be an insult."

"Well, I don't remember seeing a black cat around."

Laraline chuckled to herself. "You haven't seen any black cauldrons either."

"What?"

"Never mind, it's because she hates cats, as do most faigal. A specter does not have to be a cat. You get to choose. Sirenna has a great white owl."

Adelie frowned. "I don't remember seeing anything like that."

"Well, Dadu is shy around strangers. After all, we are very new here."

Adelie pondered for a moment. "Well, I like cats."

"Your father liked cats, as does your sister. However, Mommy is not crazy about them, so we never got one."

"So, a specter is a lot like a pet?"

"Kind of, except you do not own them. It's more of a partnership. However, you do get to name them. Aunt Sirenna has had her specter for a long time. It watches over her, protects her, and gives her messages."

The young girl's eyes widened in amazement. "Messages, what kind of messages?"

Laraline now had a devilish grin as she leaned in close to her daughter's ear. "They're more like secrets that are whispered from one specter to another. When I was a child, I was told that there is no location in the world beyond seven whispers away."

"So, these pets are like international cellphones!"

Laraline sighed. "Your generation lacks the magic of romanticism and wonder. I suppose that's why weaving is a dying art."

"Mama, did you ever want to become a weaver?"

"Believe it or not, when I was your age, I thought it was all rather boring."

"Boring! You must be joking?"

"Yeah, it sounds ridiculous thinking back on it."

"It sounds like there was so much going on when you were a kid. How did you even keep up with all this stuff?"

"Easy, I left home and didn't have to think about it at all."

"What?"

"Sometimes ignorance is bliss."

Laraline and Adelie continued walking. However, Willet was still standing at the board. Something had caught her eye. It was a slightly covered missing person flyer. The photo immediately resonated with Willet. It appeared to be an image of the very faigal Willet saw murdered the other night, but it was dark. She read further to get more description. The girl's name was Ryn Stowe, and she was seventeen.

"She was my age?"

She was a brunette with brown eyes and a height of 5'9". She was last seen on Thursday around 10 p.m. driving a lime green Jeep with plate number FD5367 on Martin Road West. Anyone with any information, please call the Meadowlark Police Department.

Willet gasped. "She has a lime green truck. All this time, it was her truck."

Willet's doubts about this being the same girl in the flyer were laid to rest. There were too many coincidences.

"Willet, hurry up!"

Her mother was impatiently calling from the parking lot. Willet looked ahead and quickly ripped the flyer off the wall and shoved it in her pocket, then ran down the steps into the parking lot.

When they got to the car, Aunt Evelyn was sitting on the hood.

"Everything ok, Auntie?"

"I just got really tired, it's my nap time, you know!"

Adelie turned to her mother. "Do all faigal take naps?"

Laraline frowned. "Why do you ask such a strange question?"

Adelie protested. "I don't think it's strange."

Evelyn responded, "Neither do I. I think it's a valid question. It's only by asking questions that we learn about one another. Actually, I don't know the answer to that question. I understand your sister is an authority on birds."

Evelyn motioned towards Willet, actively trying to engage her in the conversation. She was in her own world again. The group dismissed it as her zoning out.

However, Willet was, in fact, staring up at the observation tower. It stuck out over the town like a strange, unearthly beacon. The tower had vintage-looking oil lamps that hung on the parapets near the top railing. Perched there was a rather large crow. It crooked its neck, as it looked down at her. She felt that the crow seemed to be watching her intently.

A feeling of paranoia overcame her as she crawled into the backseat. Something was happening to her in particular. She needed to talk to someone, but she didn't have many options. Suddenly, she blurted out, "Is Mother Hazel at home?"

The entire car looked over at her sudden outburst. After a moment, Evelyn answered.

"Actually, she is taking my place in Celandine Springs with Aunt Sirenna. There is a gallery show tonight."

"Celandine Springs? Where is that?"

Laraline turned to the back seat to face Willet, who was buckling herself in her seat. "It's the ritzy community on the beach."

Willet looked concerned. "Well, how long does it last?"

Evelyn responded. "You will probably be long asleep by the time they return. There are a lot of items they need to go through."

Adelie furrowed her brow. "Why the sudden interest in Mother Hazel? I thought she gave you the creeps."

Willet rolled her eyes at her sister. This was exactly the reason she didn't share things with her sister. Adelie had a big mouth. She immediately tried to gloss over Adelie's comment.

"Hey, we are all living here together; besides, she's kind of fascinating in a way."

God, I hope they bought that!

Laraline smiled earnestly. "Well, is there anything you want me to relay to her. Whatever you want to tell her, I can just let her know?"

Willet just stared at her mother, trying to figure out how to respond.

Mama, if you only knew.

Evelyn looked around at Willet. "Yes, what do you and Mother Hazel have to discuss?"

Willet responded with a coy response. "Well, we could always discuss the weather."

Chapter 36: Traps

When Jonas arrived home, he immediately noticed Raven. She was perched on top of the old wooden split fence by the edge of the driveway. Her back was slanted downward, and her arms curled across her knees. She was dressed in a thin black tank top and cut-off blue jean shorts. She wore a black top hat on her head that shielded her eyes from the afternoon sun. She was barefoot, and her tiny toes clawed into the base of the wood railing she sat upon.

Her head darted about the entire yard, silently searching for something. Raven was hunting. Not wanting to disturb her, Jonas whispered in her direction.

"What are you looking for?"

She seemed not to hear, so he repeated his question. "So, what are you looking for?"

She dryly replied. "I heard you the first time."

"Then why didn't you answer?"

"Because I'm busy hunting vermin."

"What kind of vermin?"

There was a loud clanging snap near his feet. He anxiously looked down to see an empty steel trap less than eight inches from his left sandal.

Raven calmly responded. "Cats."

Visibly irritated, he responded. "What cats?"

"Any of them. The neighbor down the lane has dozens of disgusting cats, and they sometimes wander over here. Then there are all the ones in the Greywood."

"Father told you before about such talk."

"Oops."

"You do realize I could have lost my toe if I had taken another step."

"That would suck for you, and then you would have to change your name to something like stumpy."

"That's not funny."

"Please, you're not going to get all emotional and whiny, are you?"

"That's all you can say?"

"What can I say, you can't make an omelet without breaking a few eggs."

"What does that even mean?"

Without lifting her head, Raven raised her arm slowly and pointed to a large black lawn trash bag across the yard. It sat a few feet away from her, haphazardly tied. From a distance, he could tell it was far from empty. "What's in that bag?"

"Egg shells."

Jonas mocked her. "What's the matter, can't catch a kitty cat!"

She lifted her head with her glazed stare. She was not smiling, but her eyes gave the impression that she was. She gently pursed her lips together and whispered confidently to her brother.

"Not yet."

Jonas felt a chill as he cleared his throat. "By the way, Phoebe called for you again."

"I was wondering what was up. We don't normally have a reason to converse this long!"

Jonas sighed as he looked for a secure path back to the house.

"Whatever."

"What did she want?"

"How am I supposed to know? She's not my friend."

"Friend, I never said she was my friend."

"Then why do you hang around with that loser?"

"The question is, why do I allow her to follow me around?"

"Fine, whatever."

"You do realize that is the second time in our brief but illuminating conversation that you used that word."

"What word?"

"Whatever."

"What?"

"You used the word, whatever."

"I was not aware."

"If you use the same words over and over, you can come across as special needs!"

"Fine."

"However, in the interest of time and the eventual end of this boring conversation, let me answer your burning question. The answer is, she amuses me."

Jonas had momentarily forgotten his question at this point. "Amuses you?"

Raven pressed her fingers to her mouth to warn him about the noise level. She then carefully reached behind her back and removed a large crossbow. She closed her right eye and moved the bow about, scanning the plush weeds beyond the fence. There was a quick swishing sound as she released the arrow. There was a sudden squeal as the arrow pierced into the forehead of a jackrabbit that had leaped midair from the tall thicket. It abruptly tumbled back into the deep grass.

Jonas folded his arms. "That's not a cat!"

"Shut up."

Jonas smirked. "You said she amuses you."

As if from deep thought, Raven continued. "Oh yes, Phoebe loves to prattle on and on about some of the most insignificant nonsense. She is like some stray cat that follows one around for food. Perhaps I will grow bored of her, and I may catch her in one of my traps!"

At this point, Jonas didn't care what she was saying. It seemed like everything that came out of her mouth these days was bizarre. He made sure not to use whatever when he responded to her. "Nice."

"I thought so."

"Well, do I need to watch the yard for traps?"

"Well, since I don't quite remember where I placed them, it would be advisable!"

Jonas nodded and proceeded to delicately maneuver the grassy patches of the lawn. A slight chill went up his spine as he passed by the dead rabbit that had fallen victim to her arrow. As he made his way up the walk, he noticed his Aunt Aquila's black Mercedes.

How in the world did she manage to get by all of this?

Arnold Letch was standing on the porch looking down at him. Jonas locked eyes with him for a moment before turning back to Raven. "Are you eyeing my little sister?"

"You don't care for me, do you, Master Jonas?"

"I never said that."

"You didn't have to; it's in your body language."

"My brother Gavin is the friendly one. If you're looking for a friend, talk to him, solicitor!"

Letch looked at him curiously. "I know all about you. Jonas, the brooding middle child. The angry child. The sad child. This routine is getting rather tedious."

"What do you know about me?"

"Not any more than you know about me, I suppose."

Jonas played off his introspective comments and changed the subject. "Why is my aunt here?"

"Your father requested a private meeting with her today."

"What about?"

"As I just stated, the meeting is private."

"Then why are you here? Shouldn't you be slithering about on the front lawn?"

Before there was time to answer, Jonas heard his father calling for Letch. "Arnold, your presence is greatly needed."

The lawyer straightened his tie and took a deep breath. "Well, I guess that's my cue!"

Jonas wasn't letting him get away without one more shot. "Getting ready for your hot date?"

Letch rolled his eyes at Jonas before he proceeded down the massive grey marble hallway to the dining area. When he arrived, Aquila and Branson were sitting opposite one another at the end of the longer black ivory table. The mood was rather tense as he entered. Aquila glanced up as Letch entered.

"Well, brother, your sleeven stooge has arrived, can we begin?"

Avis leaned into the table with a very concerned look. "What have you been up to, sister?"

"Whatever do you mean?"

"I do not have time for your games!"

"Life is one big game, perhaps you could clarify."

Avis leaped from his chair and across the table. His hand was around her neck within seconds. Before Aquila had time to react, he shoved her down on the ground and was practically on top of her. His anger was so great that his large, grey black wings ripped through the back of his shirt. A black tuft of feathers started to emerge on top of his hair. His fingers became as claws as his eyes glazed over into those of a bird of prey. "Is this clear?"

Aquila's eyes bulged as she struggled for air. "Crystal."

He released his grip and stood over her as she struggled to her feet. Finally, she spoke out of confusion. "Why should you care about a mother and her two half-breeds?"

"They are mere innocents in this equation."

Aquila stood up right, trying to adjust her dress, and her hair that had gotten a bit disheveled in the tussle. She was still breathing hard when she countered his logic. "Brother, there is bound to be some collateral damage in any war of this sort."

"Is that what this is? A war? I was under the impression that both families were at a respected stalemate."

"Is that what you thought?"

"Evelyn Adler came to me, and we made a vertriste, no harm would befall her niece and her niece's children. I gave her my word."

Aquila countered. "Yes, which makes this perfect. I made no such promise, and they are oh so vulnerable!"

"And so are we! I have three children who attend the very same school. What is to stop them from retaliation? Suppose they kill Jonas, or hunt down Raven, or Gavin! I guess I should just chalk that up to collateral damage as well."

Aquila snapped her finger. "About Jonas, does he even count as yours?"

"I'm serious."

"Perhaps you have allowed these children to make you weak, brother."

Avis bared his teeth as his wings fully bloomed wide to show his irritation with her disrespect. "I have spoken, you will honor the sanctuary, is that clear, Lady Branson?"

Aquila could see in his eyes; this wasn't the moment to force a confrontation. Avis was certainly capable of horrific acts if pushed. She would give him the high road today as she softly mumbled under her breath. "Yes."

He had the appearance of a madman on the edge. "What? I didn't hear you!"

"Yes, Lord Branson. May I take my leave now?"

He exhaled quietly as he calmed himself. His wings folded, and he closed his eyes. He took several short breaths before he answered. "You may go."

Aquila had to contain herself in his presence. Humbling herself before her younger half-brother was painful. She winced as the anger bloomed, flooded by the situation. However, she knew she needed to exercise patience. She took a deep breath and bowed stiffly before him, then took her leave.

By the time she reached her car, she was fuming. She clenched her teeth and slammed her palms against the hood of her car. She looked back at the entrance of the Branson Estate and hissed. "Bastard, I'll show you." She would have to speed up her timetable.

Chapter 37: The Experiment

When Mother Hazel returned that night, she could sense things were off, though she didn't know exactly how. On the surface, everything seemed normal. Sirenna was zoning out in her aviary. Uncle Merle was drunk in his room. Evelyn was in bed, quietly reading poetry, while all their other guests were asleep, in their beds for the night.

When the mother entered her room, she first lit her night lamp, so she could see the wall of wooden dolls sitting and smiling at her. It was as if they were waiting for her to return home, so they could go to bed. Mother Hazel addressed them. "Couldn't sleep children, well no matter, I've returned now."

She was about to turn off the light when she sensed movement behind her in the corner. She swung her cane around at the intruder. Willet was quick and snatched the end of the cane.

Mother Hazel smirked. "Very good reflexes, you have been studying!"

"You knew I was near?"

"I could smell you from outside the door, no offense."

Willet responded by sniffing her armpits.

"Well, let's have it. What has happened? You wouldn't come down here sneaking about unless something was amiss."

"Something happened last night that I can't explain."

"Night visitors, you'll get use to them, we all do."

"No, something even worse."

"I'm intrigued, go on."

Willet presented her yarn about dreams, kidnappings, murders and harpies. She even told the mother about the crow and the flyer of the dead girl. Willet rambled on trying to make the whole thing seem more coherent.

When Willet finished, Mother Hazel sat silently for several moments, as if taking in what she had just heard. The old woman finally cleared her throat and began to respond. "Well, that's quite a story?"

"You do believe me?"

"So, I guess you think I have all the answers."

"Well, don't you? What does all this mean?"

"I'll let you know when I have more information."

The old woman is definitely hiding something!

Willet had to remember that Mother Hazel was still a faigal with possibly alternative motives. She would need to tread carefully. "So, who were those people on Martin Bridge, because I have no idea who they are?"

"The woman with the eyepatch sounds a lot like Aquila Branson, half-sister of Lord Branson. The boy is probably her nephew, Gavin."

"Well, I figured out who the blonde woman was myself. Her name is Kestrel Faulkner. She is the sister of my new headmaster! From what I can tell, she is involved with Gavin, which is totally gross."

"My, you have been busy."

"That leaves the murdered girl. I believe I saw her jeep a few days ago at a hotel just outside of town. I saw it again on the same day I got sick, but someone else must have been driving it because today I saw this. I'm sure this is her in this photo. Her name is Ryn Stowe."

Mother Hazel glanced at the crumbled flyer that Willet placed in her hand. The old woman squinted her eyes before placing the paper down on a nearby coffee table.

"Well, I don't know this girl, but many young faigal have been disappearing around town for a while."

"Should I go to the police?"

"If you go in person, they may find out who told them."

"How?"

"The same way you found out who they were."

"Are you serious?"

"You are exercising faigal power, believe me, Aquila can do the same. If you start poking around, it won't take her long to figure out what you've been up to child."

"You said exercising faigal powers, you mean like a weaver?"

Mother Hazel ignored her. The old woman seemed very uncomfortable at this idea, so Willet changed the subject. "So, did I witness the past or something?"

"No, it appears that you were in the present. You drifted your spirit from one place to another."

"Drifted? You mean like astroplaning?"

"It's complicated."

"Let's just say for a moment that I drifted. Why to a bridge in the middle of nowhere where I've never even been?"

"Well, sometimes one can be so sensitive that they are spiritually attracted to unusual disturbances. A drifter can be triggered by sights, sounds, smells, and touch."

"Yeah, but I didn't know they would be there."

"Perhaps your spirit did."

"That makes no sense to me!"

"Ok, let's try something."

Mother Hazel reached out on the nightstand and handed back the missing person flyer to Willet. "Hold this."

Willet gently took the paper and whispered aloud. "What are we doing?"

As Willet studied the photo, she became slightly aware that the old woman was lighting candles and burning herbs and incents. Soon the old woman began to whisper chants. Willet's focus was on Mother Hazel's activities.

"Are we going to do a séance or something?"

Mother Hazel turned to the young girl. "When you had your vision, what were you doing right before it happened?"

"I was asleep, I guess."

"What were you doing right before you fell asleep?"

"I don't know, maybe skimming through that notebook you gave me."

The old woman stood upright with her cane for a moment as if she were in deep thought. "Do you remember what you were reading?"

"It's a blur!"

"I suspect you were reading about shammas and subconsciously memories from the hotel invaded your thoughts. Were there any particular sounds or smells that stuck out that evening at the hotel?

"Her scream woke me up from sleep, and the hallway had this scent. I've smelled it in town as well."

"Well, we need to recreate the event, just to make sure what actually did occur!"

"So you don't believe me? I mean, is there is no way a half breed could possibly do what a faigal can do?"

"Silence child! It is late, and you are improperly in my bedchamber, and yet here I am listening."

Willet quickly decided to close her mouth, as she knew Mother Hazel was the only person who would get what was happening. She was the only person she could turn to at the moment. Even the police were sketchy at best. She had met the constable, and it wasn't on the best of terms. When she thought about the reality of the situation, how could she sound credible trying to explain this?

Yes, officer, I astroplaned into the middle of the crime scene and I witnessed flying people and flying monsters with human heads.

The more she thought about the police, the less logical the idea sounded, especially with the real possibility that this witch with the eyepatch could drift to her. *What will happen when she discovers what happened to one of her harpies? Would she come after me?*

Mother Hazel had to tap Willet, who was in her mind creating several scenarios in which she could defeat Aquila. Willet jerked around. "You startled me."

"Ok, lie on the bed, facing up at the ceiling."

Willet did as instructed. She stretched across the small, quilted bed. Almost immediately, the scent of old crept into her nostrils. *Wow, it really smells like an old person's bed.* There were other aromas that assaulted her nose as well. Some were familiar, others not so much. The hint of mothballs, and face cream mixed with burning sage and methyl were some she recognized.

Thankfully, the bed was extremely soft, more so than her bed. As she looked up, she saw several strange symbols and markings on the ceiling. In the center of them was a large round picture frame with a mirror inside. Willet turned her head slightly.

"Hey, you're missing a picture in that frame!"

Mother Hazel stood over her as she softly responded. "The viewer fills in the picture."

"What does that mean?"

"Quiet, you talk too much."

Willet had forgotten she was holding the flyer. "Where do you want me to put this thing?"

"I want you to hold it close to your heart and focus on her spirit while you stare into the mirror."

"But, I don't know her."

"There is nothing more intimate than to bear witness to someone's transition."

Willet did as she was told and stared up at herself. There wasn't a lot going on up there. Willet found herself making exaggerated faces at herself. At one point, Mother Hazel snapped at her.

"Pay attention and focus!"

"Ok, I'm trying."

"Breathe in rhythm."

"I've never been good at this, but I'll try."

Willet took a deep breath and stared blankly at the frame. She noticed that the inside of the bottom was peeling. Mother Hazel sat in her rocking chair and proceeded to gently hum while she slowly rocked.

The situation reminded Willet of when she was little. Her mother used to sing to her. Whether it was the rhythm of the constant rocking, or the gentle hum combined with the flat boring view, after a few minutes, Willet started to get tired. She looked into the eyes of her own reflection, and for a moment, got lost. After several yawns, she called out to Mother Hazel.

"Well, how much longer do I stare?"

Willet waited for the answer, but there was none. She could still hear the chair rocking, so she knew the old woman hadn't fallen asleep.

"Mother Hazel, did you hear me?"

There was still no answer. Willet turned her head slightly to see what was going on with the old woman. She glanced over at the rocking chair, it was still rocking. However, she realized that Mother Hazel was no longer sitting in the rocking chair; in her place sat a young woman.

Chapter 38: The Black Cottage

Willet immediately jerked up. She was no longer sleepy. What in the Franken berry? The girl in the rocking chair continued to rock but kept her head down. It was as if she were in a trance. Her hair was so long that Willet couldn't see her face. She did notice the girl was wearing a long white flowing gown and nothing else. The girl turned her head to Willet.

"We didn't mean to startle you, Willet."

"Well, you did."

Willet was speechless as she looked around the room. She started to notice that everything looked quite different. The girl kept rocking at a steady pace.

"Wait a moment, how did you know my name?"

"It's so nice to see you again."

Willet realized they had sort of met. "Ryn, is that you? You can't be standing here, you were murdered yesterday!"

The ghostly girl calmly responded. "That's peculiar; I have no recollection of that."

"Wait! This is a dream, none of this is real."

Ryn was dressed in a thin nightgown, and her blonde hair hung down, partly blocking her face. Her skin was ghostly pale. Large delicate wings extended from her back over the sides of the chair's armrests. As she slowly looked up, Willet noticed her eyes were empty black pools of nothingness. Before Willet could react, Ryn spoke again. "We have been waiting."

"What do you mean, we?"

Ryn continued to rock and smile without answering.

"What did you do to Mother Hazel?"

"Who?"

Suddenly, Willet realized that she was no longer in Mother Hazel's room. Everything was wood, the floor, the wall, and even the ceiling, which was now free from the mirror frame that Willet was staring at just a few minutes ago.

There was a small, quaint cabinet on the other side of the room and a small wood-burning stove in the opposite corner by a large thick latched wooden door. The stove was lit and there was a reddish glow from the red embers inside.

"Where am I? What is this place?"

Before Ryn could answer, several strange sounds erupted from the other side of the wooden door. The sounds were a hybrid of coarse breathing, squawking, and feral-like grunts all at once. Willet shrank back. Perhaps the harpy had found her here, in this strange place.

This commotion was followed by deep knocking on the other side of the wooden door. This was repeated once more as Ryn stood to attention. "They're here."

"Who?"

Ryn abruptly crossed the room and headed for the door. Her wings folded in and out, allowing Willet to marvel at how majestic they seemed, and undamaged from the previous night.

"Where are you going?"

"They are calling me."

Willet had the urge to run and stand in front of the door, but she froze with fear. She didn't want to be near the door when she had no idea who could be on the other side.

Ryn lifted the latch, and the door slowly creaked open by itself. A thick fog of cold mist poured inside the room, obscuring Willet's view briefly. Voiceless whispers within the wind seemed to speak a single word: "transcendence."

As Willet looked out the open door, her eyes widened. She could see trees and underbrush, instead of a hallway. Why should she even be surprised? Ryn stepped out into the mist as the door shut itself behind her.

Willet called after her. "Ryn, don't!"

She got up and ran to the door, then paused. She could not just go out without a weapon or something. She looked about the room until her eyes spied the wood-burning stove. There was a long, dusty fire poker leaning beside it, against the wall. She reached out and got a good grip on the iron handle. She lifted it in front of her chest and reached for the door. She wasn't taking any chances outside.

She couldn't stay here by herself, she had to find out how to get back to her own home, wherever that was. She quickly opened the door and bolted into the mist. As she stepped outside, she soon realized the room she was just in was some sort of old wooden log cabin. As she looked back, she beheld the small black cabin. From outside, she realized it didn't appear to have any windows, just a single door and a pipe in the roof for the stove inside.

She looked around the perimeter and realized that the cabin was completely surrounded by trees. She was in a forest. Her panic level rose to ten as she voiced her thoughts aloud. "Where am I?"

She didn't see Ryn anywhere. There were just the trees that led into the vast darkness beyond. A glowing mist seemed to permeate the air outside. She tightened her grip on the fire poker as she walked toward a group of trees directly in front of her.

"Ryn? Ryn, where did you go?"

Willet's voice echoed into the misty nothingness. The air was still and listless as if the forest itself was in a vacuum. A sudden uneasiness invaded Willet's mood. Somehow, it felt as if the woods were carefully studying her.

"Ryn!"

Strange primal grunts and howling seem to respond to Willet's pleas. Fear started to drown her senses as she looked around frantically. Glimpses of movement from behind the ancient husk of a nearby tree trunk gave Willet the impression of something large and alien slithering. Within the ghastly shadows, a few yards away, she could feel a presence.

She saw glimpses of what appeared to be tusks, claws, and something resembling tentacles in some exaggerated creation hiding within the visible tree line. However her glimpse was so brief with all the mist, she wasn't even sure if something was really there. Perhaps her mind was playing tricks on her. After all, it was just moments ago; she was in a log cabin talking with a dead girl who was eaten by a pack of harpies.

Surely, nothing like that was real. Willet focused intently on the spot, but the supposed boogeyman was gone. Whatever she had imagined seemed to vanish into the nightmarish ether from whence it came.

A fluttering sound like large wings passed by her face and she swung the poker in the air, shrieking with fear. She turned her head back and eyed the door of the cabin. It was still open. Without hesitating, Willet did an about-face and ran back toward the open door.

Behind her, she could hear all manner of monstrosities. In her mind, they were quickly closing in after her. As she reached the door of the cabin, she quickly sprinted inside and latched the door behind her. No sooner had she done this, a series of inhuman groaning, snarling, and scratching began at the door.

Terrified, Willet backed up so far that she was practically lying on the bed. She started to breathe in and out quickly, as if trying to will herself someplace else. Loud scratching started again. Willet covered her ears to block out the noise and yelled at the door. "Stop it already!"

Suddenly, Willet was lying on her back. She was on the bed again and looking up at the fading image of a cabin in the framed mirror. She quickly sat up. She was back in Mother Hazel's room. The old woman was steadily rocking as Willet turned in her direction.

"Was that real?"

Mother Hazel stopped rocking and looked at her. "Was what real?"

"So, I didn't leave this room?"

"Not at all, you fell asleep and woke up yelling."

"Man, I had the craziest dream."

"How can you be sure it was a dream?"

"It was too crazy to be real."

"Well, what happened?"

"Don't laugh, but this wasn't a room anymore, it turned into some sort of a cabin."

"Did you say a cabin?"

"Yeah, like an old log cabin, except it was completely black!"

Mother Hazel's eyes widened, and she moved forward in a rapt state. "Did you say a black cabin?"

"Yeah, do you know the place?"

Mother Hazel cut her off. "Tell me more!"

"That girl, Ryn, was there. She knew my name."

"This is the dead girl?"

"Yes."

"And she was talking to you?"

"She said they were waiting for her."

"Who?"

"I don't know, she never said, but she was waiting for them to take her somewhere!"

"Where was this cabin?"

"It was in a forest, in the middle of nowhere. Though there was something vaguely familiar about it. It was like Deja Vu. It was as if I had been there before."

Mother Hazel removed her glasses and rubbed her face, as if she were worn and tired. Willet noticed the shift in her mood.

"Well, what is the deal. Is this cabin an actual place?"

"From what I've heard, the Black Cottage is very real."

"This place is called the Black Cottage? Is it here, in Meadowlark?"

"Yes and no."

"Ok, what does that mean? The half-truths and mystery puzzles are not helping!"

Willet hopped up from the bed and onto her feet, when something dropped off the bed with a loud clang. Mother Hazel looked down, mystified.

"What is that thing?"

Willet's eyes widened as she knelt to pick it up. "I brought it back with me."

"What do you mean, you brought something back?"

Willet held the dusty fire poker in Mother Hazel's face. "This was in the cabin. I swear I'm telling the truth. It was against a wood-burning stove. Across the room was a small bed, and in the middle of the room ..."

Mother Hazel quietly finished her words. "...sat a rocking chair."

"Yes!"

Mother Hazel sat with a sincere expression. "I believe you, Willet. Please continue."

Feeling encouraged to share her adventure, Willet poured out everything she experienced. "Ryn was sitting there rocking just as you were before. Her eyes were so empty. I don't even know if she could see me. There were these creepy sounds at the door, then she got up, opened the door, and left."

"Please, tell me you didn't follow after her."

"Look, I picked this up, and I did follow Ryn outside. That's when things got really weird."

"What did it look like outside?"

Willet had trouble verbalizing what she experienced, it seemed indescribable. "I know it was a forest, but I couldn't see much, there was so much mist."

"Was it a glowing mist?"

"Yes!"

"What happened next?"

"Ryn vanished, and I was alone in the fog. Or at least I thought I was. I can't really describe what I saw and heard, but there was something out there with me. I freaked out and ran back into the cabin and locked the door. Whatever was in the mist, it followed me back. I heard them clawing at the door, trying to get at me. Then suddenly, I was back here."

"Did you do anything right before you came back?"

"Well, I held out my hand and started screaming."

"Did you say anything while you were screaming?"

"I don't think so. Wait, I said, stop it already!"

"Did you use any of these same words when you returned from your first incident on Martin Bridge. What did you say then?"

"I don't remember. The entire incident is cloudy."

"Please, try to remember, it's important!"

Willet closed her eyes and thought hard. "I was upset and tired. I know I wanted it to stop, and I probably said something along those lines. Maybe... please stop."

Mother Hazel clasped her hands triumphantly. "Ah, then that is your safe word."

"What is?"

"Stop!"

"Stop is my safe word?"

"What's wrong with that?"

"Stop sounds kind of boring."

"It's simple, simple is always best. Many weavers spend years trying to find their word. Whenever you find yourself in one of these states again, the word stop is a trigger to disengage yourself back into this reality."

"So, you think this will happen again."

"I believe these altered states will become more frequent."

"Oh, well, that's just great."

"Just don't forget that word!"

Willet grimaced at the insulting advice. "I'll try very hard to remember the word, stop!"

"Be thankful. Some weavers have very long phrases to recite."

Willet looked to the old woman solemnly. "What's going on? I'm scared."

"Do you believe that something could be in two places at once?"

"Do you mean like when I was just dreaming?"

"The Namvula sisterhood refer to it as drifting. It's the ability to project one's consciousness. Drifting is just one of the 7 Kalas bestowed upon a weaver. You obviously have this ability!"

"But I'm not a weaver!"

"Are you sure?"

"I don't know what to think anymore."

"Sometimes other types of entities can share the same Kalas as weavers; a tree, a river, a house. The Black Cottage is an example of this."

"You're talking about this place as if it were alive or something!"

"Perhaps it is. Deep within the Greywood, this dwelling hides. I say hides because it moves around. It's never in the same place or location."

"To other parts of the world?"

"Perhaps even other worlds!"

"Does anyone live there?"

"This is not a place for living, it's just a place of transportation. Over the years, many have searched through the woods for this ancient structure. Very few have ever beheld it with their eyes. Only those with whom the cabin can commune can enter."

"So, are you saying this cabin is some sort of portal?"

"My, you're quick!"

"I'm right!"

"The Cottage is like a beacon. A spiritual antenna of a sort."

"What does it do?"

"Transmit and receive all sorts of energy."

"This is insane. Just a week ago, things were so ordinary."

"Things still are, you are just more informed about the world around you, not quite as ignorant."

Willet frowned. "Really?"

"If it makes you feel better, many faigal don't know much about this aspect of their lore and culture."

"So this Black Cottage is a faigal thing?"

"We are not human, so when our earthly vessels, and by that, I mean bodies, expire, our spirits use the Black Cottage as a means of transportation through the Fathom Black, and into the Illumination Divide."

"Illumination Divide, is that like heaven?"

"You would call it a god realm or the Mother Prime."

"What about this fathom world you just mentioned?"

"Well, the Fathom Black is not a real world, but more like an anti-world. It's a hallway that leads to all the other worlds. To enter any other world, one must cross through the Fathom Black."

"So, are there many other worlds?"

"There is more than what I even know. We need to get back to what's important for you to know now. There are an endless number of questions you could ask, but what do you need to know right now?"

"Well, what do we do now?"

"You have school in a few days. You need to focus and prepare."

"School, are you serious? How can I possibly manage to concentrate on school with all of this interdimensional madness going on?"

"All of this will still be here when I get back."

"Wait! Get back? Where are you going?"

"I need to talk to my mother sister; she is a priestess in Essex. This is a matter I need her counsel on."

"So, this is like some major stuff?"

"It's nothing to laugh about."

"Well, what do I do about the murder of Ryn? This is a small town, eventually, I will see the very people who murdered her!"

Mother Hazel touched her shoulder. "You must be strong and patient."

"Strong and patient! You might as well say, keep a stiff upper lip, kiddo!"

I understand there is no profit for the wise, but I will return as soon as I can. In the meantime, don't tell anyone about these episodes. If you find yourself drifting into a state, remember your safe word and leave immediately."

"The Black Cottage called to me for a reason, though."

"Mother Hazel grew agitated. "Perhaps not the reason you wish. Listen to me, I don't want you to go back to that cabin, or anywhere near those woods. It is too dangerous!"

"Wait, if this is such a sacred place, why is it so dangerous?"

"You do not understand. As I said before, to enter the Black Cottage, you had to commune with one another. This is a spiritual link, but not for you. When each occupant's time comes, they briefly visit before transcending. During this time, the occupant and dwelling both share of themselves. If you were able to walk about freely inside and even allowed to take something with you, you have most likely unwittingly shared something of yourself."

Willet looked down at the fire poker uneasily. "Should I be afraid?"

"I knew of another young lady, much like you, who courted the Black Cottage several times, until it drove her mad. You really don't want mysterious entities like that having access to your thoughts and dreams."

Willet took a deep breath. "My god, why did it choose me?"

"Unfortunately, because you were listening. Most of the world is asleep even now. There is a world beyond this world that few experience. You have just entered upon the cusp of this awareness. However, I sincerely warn you, be oh so careful where you tread. You don't honestly think you're the only one out there drifting about in the spiritual ether?"

"I never gave the matter much thought before."

"Well, you should. The last thing you want is to attract attention from anything in the Fathom Black."

"What do you mean? I thought you said it was an anti-world?"

"Yes, I did."

Willet could sense hesitation from the old woman. "Mother Hazel, what's in the Fathom Black?"

Mother Hazel glanced about her dimly lit bedroom. "It is not wise to speak of such things when shadows are ever so close."

"You're scaring me!"

"That is the intended purpose, girly. My point being, there are things far more insidious than a flock of hungry harpies. But that's enough talk for tonight, you have a busy week ahead of you. From what I have heard, public education can be a horror in itself!"

"Come on, you can't just leave me hanging like this!"

"Promise me, you will stay away from those woods and that cabin!"

"Ok, I promise!"

Willet looked at the fire poker in her hand, and then looked to Mother Hazel. "What should I do with this thing?"

Mother Hazel shrugged her shoulders. "Well, it appears to be yours."

"Mine? Really? Do you think it's dangerous?"

"I think it very well could be dangerous, but if it had any surprises for us, I think it would have shown us by now."

"Yeah, I guess so."

"You need to be getting to bed, Ms. Swift."

Willet nodded as she carefully opened the door and looked out into the dim hallway. Various night shadows covered the long corridors' interior surfaces. Upon learning what she had that evening, the darkness suddenly took on another, more sinister meaning. The night was alive, and all around her, observing.

Willet felt a chill run down her spine as she cautiously tiptoed across the cold marble floor. When she finally worked up enough courage, Willet took a deep breath and sprinted down the hallway and up the stairs to her bedroom.

Chapter 39: Intruder

When Willet finally reached her bedroom door, she was relieved to see it was still shut. However, as she grabbed the doorknob and pushed it open, she was greeted by darkness, as she had neglected to turn on the lights. She closed the door, thinking her eyes would adjust. Before that could happen, she became aware of a chill in the air. *Why was it so cold?*

She looked about the room until she saw the open blinds and the open window beneath them. *Crap, I left the window open this morning!*

The room was completely dark, except for the glowing moonlight streaming in the window. She was about to put down the fire poker when she noticed that the handle suddenly felt warm, as if it were heating up. She glanced down, just before she heard a slight ruffle to her left.

She didn't have time to react to the ruffle before a menacing voice from across the room cackled. "Good evening, dear tenderloin. You left the window open tonight for us, darling. How sweet of you."

Willet turned quickly to her side. On the large vanity in the corner of the room, it was just sitting there, watching her. The particularly large harpy had been waiting for her to return to bed, so it could attack her. Willet's eyes widened at the grotesque spectacle fanning its rather large wings. She took a deep breath to calm herself. *Don't panic!*

A stream of saliva dripped from the intruder's puffy lips as it grinned. Its long, wrinkled claws shifted slightly as it flexed its shoulders to keep balanced. The vanity creaked as it shifted its hulking body to get a better vantage point of its prey.

"You killed our sister, you didn't think we would just forget?"

Willet's response was quick. "Well, for a brief moment, I kinda did!"

Willet scanned about the room while keeping an eye on the enormously large beast. She was too far from the door to make it back out. Even if she did, she wouldn't be able to shut it back in time.

"What are you looking for? There is nowhere to hide from me, meat."

Where are the other harpies? They have had plenty of time to attack me. I wouldn't be surprised if one was in the bathroom or behind me, ready to pounce.

Willet quickly glanced back behind her, then she looked back at the open window. *I can't believe I was so careless about the window.*

Willet had to keep the harpy occupied till she figured something out. She continued to talk to her feathery guest. "Didn't your sister give you my message about what would happen to all of you?"

"Yes, we received your threat. You may have fooled my sisters, but not me."

"So, you have come alone?"

"Don't worry, this won't take long, meat."

Willet was still afraid, but the reality of one monster opposed to the daunting task of dealing with an entire flock gave her hope, especially given the heaviness of her foe. She would be much quicker.

Perhaps there is some fear within the harpy. Why would it not attack when I first entered the room? It's feeding off my fear.

This caused her to release a relieved sigh. Which was quite visible to the night visitor, and as a matter of pride, it violently flapped its wings. Showing its massive wing spread. "I need no one else to deal with you!"

The impatient harpy suddenly leaped from the edge of the dresser and dove straight at Willet's head. She was anticipating its move, and she ducked down. She then rolled to her side and countered, swinging the poker down across its back, as it flew overhead. There was a flickering spark as the poker struck the beast.

Without warning, the harpy exploded into flames. It was now a flying ball of fire. Willet gasped at her screaming intruder. She jumped backwards in such shock that she voiced aloud, "Holy Hell!".

She looked down at the fire poker that was now glowing a bright red ember. The harpy was just as shocked. Its eyes bulged as it looked at her in disbelief. It began to panic as an unearthly fire engulfed its body. It resembled some sort of fiery phoenix as it dove about, trying to extinguish the flames by creating enough wind. It knocked several items off the shelves and the nightstand in its futile attempt. Its blood-curdling screams filled the air as it desperately fanned the air.

It was filled with rage and fear, as it eyed Willet through a smoke-filled haze. The flaming beast flapped its massive wings. It raced toward Willet again, in a final desperate attempt to get her. Willet stood upright and held her ground. She had both hands wrapped around the handle of the fire poker like a glowing baseball bat.

Anticipating that it was overmatched, the large beast darted to the side and flew desperately out the very window it had come in. Willet was quick as she ran to the window and with her free hand, pulled it shut. Her fingers fumbled at the latch until it was locked. She then released the steel blinds and watched them crash down, blocking her view of the night.

Everything happened so quickly that she didn't have time to react. She stood shaking while tightly holding the poker. Her heartbeat was frantic. She moved her face against the side of the window and peeked through the blinds, at the outside world. There was no sign of anything now, but the moonlit night.

Her entire body was quivering. Even her knees felt weak as she steadied herself against the wall. Willet had almost calmed her breathing when there was a loud knock on her door. The abrupt thumping startled her into action. She quickly intercepted the door, cracking it slightly. Her mother was there in her nightgown.

Willet released a low sigh of relief. "Yeah?"

"Willet, what is all that commotion. Are you ok, dear?"

Willet glanced around the room. There was still a slight hint of burn in the air, and the dresser in the corner had a few superficial scratches from her visitor's claw marks. Other than that, everything looked normal. Willet turned back toward the crack in the door.

"Fine Mama, I had a nightmare."

"Nightmare! Do you need me?"

"I'm sorry if I was loud." Willet ended her conversation with a fake yawn. She followed this with their nighttime catch phrase. "Well, goodnight ma, sweet dreams."

Willet shut the door before Laraline could respond. She then waited to see if her mother was going to buy it. Apparently, this time, she did, as she could hear her mother head back down the hallway. Willet took a deep breath as she tried to gradually slow her heartbeat.

Willet looked down at the poker, which was now normal again. It appeared to be as dusty as before. She surmised it must be enchanted, since it came from such a dark, enchanted place.

Chapter 40: Departures

True to her word, Mother Hazel had booked a seat on the Elysium. It was one of three remaining ocean liners that still travelled internationally. Since New Essex was on another continent, her departure had to be discreet.

Right before dawn, Uncle Merle drove her and her bags to Monticello: the largest port beyond Meadowlark. Even though she could have boarded a private boat much cheaper in town, the chances of the Bransons finding out she left would be high.

Monticello itself was another coastal city with a heavy faigal population. Many of the business communities were aware of the Bransons and the Adlers as well. However, it was doubtful that anyone would know of Mother Hazel's existence.

This gave her the freedom to travel incognito. As far as Meadowlark knew, Mother Hazel was still at home. Since her appearances in the community were sporadic at best, no one from the outside world would be the wiser. Not even certain members of the family would be aware of her absence. Patsy and Phoebe were told nothing of her departure, just in case word got back to Aquila somehow.

Willet slept in late that morning, as her ability to sleep soundly was labored at best. Even though the night visitor didn't return, the encounter had shaken her. She spent the rest of the late morning reading and meditating on the faigal notebook. She could already feel the old woman's absence. During her practice, she felt herself slowly glance over at the fire poker, wishing that she could tell her about the flaming encounter.

Soon she found herself heading downstairs. Most of the house was already bustling with activity. Gardening, cooking, and washing the car had become frequent routines since the days had gotten quite warm. Like a ghost, Willet carefully avoided any detection as she crept down the hallway, into the aviary.

As soon as she shut the door to the outside world, she felt an instant calmness. Suddenly, it became deathly silent. The birds had stopped chirping. She walked across the terrain and found a mossy spot near the built-in watering hole. No sooner had she sat down than the light chirping and bird songs began again.

A voice from above suddenly called down. "They have grown accustomed to your scent."

Willet recognized Sirenna's voice. She gave a slight grimace but kept her head down. She didn't want to show her obvious disappointment at the old woman's company. Aunt Sirenna was hidden near the top of the rafters, dressed in a peach nightgown, and perched at the base of a branch that extended several yards above the young girl. Her red and gold wings were slowly fanning the air, trying to keep her body cool. As Evelyn had remarked, they were truly magnificent to behold. A handful of cardinals sat perched on Sirenna's shoulders and forearms as she studied Willet from above.

"After a while, they may let you touch them!"

Willet just nodded quietly. before she responded. "Do you mind if I sit in here for a while?"

Sirenna, instead of answering her directly, asked a most unusual and uncharacteristic human-like question that almost shocked the young girl.

"You miss her, too, don't you?"

Willet didn't know how to respond. Instead, she just looked up. Sirenna continued to talk as if she needed to confess her sins.

"Our father was a powerful and cruel creature who didn't so much like the company of females, so we didn't have a mother growing up. Our older sister Oriole tried to take care of us, but she was a child herself. Soon, it became fashionable to hire weavers from the Namvula, so he hired Mother Hazel. She was like the mother we never had."

"How did Grandma Oriole die?"

"What?"

"No one ever talks about her."

Sirenna considered the question for a while before answering. "One day, she stepped into the Greywood and never returned!"

Deep lines of grief covered Sirenna's face. She spoke with such frank conviction that Willet felt a hint of sadness. A single tear dropped on Willet's shoulder from above. She pretended not to notice, as she realized that Sirenna obviously didn't want her to. After a moment, Sirenna changed the subject. "I understand you had a few run-ins with the night visitors, and you killed one. "

"Actually, I killed two."

Willet suspiciously looked up. Expecting a verbal attack of some sort, what came back was again unexpected. "Good for you."

The calmness of Sirenna was unnatural and she wanted to take advantage of the situation. "How long will Mother Hazel have to be gone?"

Sirenna stared blankly at her for a moment; her large, lush wings gently swishing away the handful of red cardinals, as she descended, gliding gently past Willet as she landed on the tips of her toes. Willet could just make out the curve of her wings folding in as she rose to her feet. Sirenna took a deep breath as any semblance of wingspread disappeared into her shoulder blades.

It was the first time Willet had seen anyone from her family with wings. This moment reminded her of Ryn, but also solidified the nature of what she was herself. Sirenna never answered her question. Instead, with a hushed voice, she whispered as she headed to the door that led into the hall. "Please shut the door before you leave."

"Yes, ma'am."

With that, Sirenna disappeared beyond the door, leaving Willet to contemplate what her role was going to be, going forward. *Who exactly was she?*

She reached back with her hand and rubbed her own shoulder blades. They seemed ordinary and human, and yet there was a feeling that there was something more. Even though she was blood-related, she still felt like a human girl. She was her father's daughter.

She knew everything would change if she grew wings. She was afraid of the inevitable situation of either outcome. She was afraid that she would grow wings. She was also afraid that she would not grow wings. It was a terrifying dichotomy. She would have to choose who she wanted to be. Above all things, that scared her more than the return of the harpies or even the Black Cottage itself.

Chapter 41: Beach Party

Laraline finally agreed to let Willet and Adelie go to the beach party for a few hours. This meant they had to shop for new swimsuits and beach towels. Willet felt a bit uneasy about showing so much skin to total strangers. She wore her short combat cutoff shorts and a black tank top to compensate. She wore some semblance of a swimsuit underneath, just in case she got the nerve.

Adelie embraced her new curves in an aqua blue one-piece with a plunging V-line. The truth be told, with her overdeveloped look, everything would appear a bit revealing. As Laraline drove them across the bridge, passing the outskirts of the Greywoods, Willet realized two things immediately. She hadn't been on this side of the town physically, and she recognized the bridge from the other night. She didn't know exactly what part Ryn was thrown from, but she could tell this was the stretch of road.

A bizarre feeling overcame her as the Dodge sped on beneath the treetops that flanked them on either side of the road. It was almost as if she knew the trees, but worse still, the trees knew her. Technically, she wasn't in the forest, but it was close enough.

The very wind seemed to be whispering her name as they passed beneath. Of course, she could be imagining it. Sleep seemed more like an absent friend as of late. It did not help that as they travelled across Martin Bridge, the car was deathly silent.

There was a kind of unspoken reverence as everyone waited patiently for the forest to be behind them. When they did pass through, it was as if a veil of tension was lifted. Willet could even feel herself exhaling, as bright sunlight bathed the car once more. She was about to comment to her mother but thought against it.

When they arrived at the beach, it was mid-afternoon. The white sand gave the illusion that the entire world was washed out, because it was so bright. Willet quickly donned a pair of rose-colored glasses and a camouflage hunting fedora.

Laraline gave Willet an odd look as she parked the car. "Dear, you look like you're ready to storm the beach at Normandy. All you need now is a dog tag and combat boots!"

Adelie looked cross. "Really, Willie! You're going to embarrass us!"

"No, I'm not!"

Willet did get a thrill out of making her sister socially uncomfortable. She saw it as payback for when Adelie used to do the same to her. Willet bent down and retrieved the fire poker from the floor mat at her feet. Adelie's eyes widened.

"Mama, Willie is being weird!"

Laraline went into action. "Dear, you can't be serious. Why do you need that?"

"Protection!"

"Willet, I don't even know if you are allowed to bring that thing on the beach."

Adelie protested. "Mama, make her stop, she's trying to embarrass me on purpose!"

"Look, you're too young to have a boyfriend anyway. Idiot!"

Adelie's eyes bulged. "Shut up!"

"We all know that's why you push up your cleavage, so the boys will look at your boobs!"

Adelie quickly leaped out of the car and stopped just long enough to glare at her older sister. Her face was beet red. It was a look that Willet recognized. She was mortified as she hissed through her tears. "I hate you!"

Laraline looked back at Willet sternly. "Take off those shades for a moment."

Willet slowly complied as she slid down the sunglasses to expose the bright day. Wow, she felt like a vampire in the light. "What, Mama?"

"I know things have been difficult with your sickness, but please try to consider your sister's feelings a bit." Translation: You need to fix it, now.

Willet looked around to see that Adelie was already walking toward the beach from the parking lot. "Sure, Mama."

"Now, I will be back around seven to pick you two up at this very spot. Don't make me hunt you two down."

"Ok, Mama. Love ya!"

"Love you too, and be careful!" Willet hopped out of the car and blew her a kiss as she walked after her sister.

As soon as the car drove off, Willet tied the fire poker around her waist in a sash. She proceeded to search for Adelie, who was trying to keep a distance. Carrying a fire poker on one's hip at the beach might appear odd. Even Willet agreed. Considering the fact that she was attacked twice by mythical monsters this week, she felt her pride would survive.

The beach was semi-full. Pockets of people gathered here and there in various group activities. She carefully trekked across the sandy dunes, avoiding the various gatherings. She had lost sight of Adelie somewhere near a large red umbrella. Willet was scanning the groups when a large sunhat flew between her knees. She was quick and snatched it with her free hand.

She curiously looked around to see if she could see the owner. As luck would have it, a small pale woman waved her hand furiously in her direction. Willet held up the hat in the air.

"Does this belong to you, miss?"

"Thank you so much, I didn't have the energy to retrieve it. The wind is just furious today."

No sooner had the woman finished speaking than she weaved slightly backward. Willet quickly grabbed her shoulder, preventing her from falling.

"Are you ok, miss?"

"I'm just a bit weak today, but the sun helps me so much. Thank you again!"

Willet didn't know who the woman was, but she appeared to be quite fragile and weak. She was about to offer to help her back, then she thought of Adelie. She still hadn't found her. She was about to start yelling her sister's name, which would have been a most futile attempt, with the noise of the crowds and the ocean.

Finally, she recognized an aqua blue swimsuit from a distance. Adelie was near the water. She took a deep breath and glanced at the woman with the sunhat before she disappeared. "Hope you feel better."

Willet quickly darted across the beach in Adelie's direction. She was vaguely aware of the heat on her feet as she crossed the sand. Adelie was walking parallel to the tides, following a seagull that was a few feet ahead of her. Willet cut the distance between her and Adelie by a few dozen yards. She was about to call her sister when she heard her own name being called.

"Willet!"

She spun around, and a familiar face greeted her. "Jae?"

Jae's skin was extremely brown in her tiny two-piece swimsuit. Her hair was tied up into a red bandanna.

"So glad you could make it out today, we're all over there, under the canopy!"

She pointed to a distant blue tent with a handful of people who seemed to be playing music. Almost immediately, Willet felt a little more at ease.

"Well, let me collect my sister, and we will meet you guys over there."

When she reached her sister, Adelie was staring across the ocean. A couple of sailboats were playing chicken with one another in the midday sun. As Willet got close, Addle gave a quick, accusing glance back at her sister.

Willet was out of breath as she tried to express that she had found the party. "Hey, Addie, the party is down the other side of the beach!"

"Ok!"

"Are you still mad at me?" Her sister was silent. "Look, I'm sorry for what I said before."

Adelie quickly changed the subject. "Do you ever think of Daddy?"

"Well, not as much, but sometimes."

"You know, I hadn't thought about him since we got here, then I looked and saw the boats. I'm actually trying to look and see if he is out there sailing. I know he's dead, but sometimes it doesn't feel real. That sounds crazy, right?"

Willet put her hands on her sister's shoulders. "No, it doesn't."

"I was always jealous of how you and Daddy would spend all that time sailing!"

"Really? I thought you hated the water!"

"I still do, but you guys had this incredible connection!"

Willet didn't really know what to say, she suddenly felt guilty and sad, as she embraced her younger sister from the back.

Adelie finally turned slightly. "Do you ever miss the ocean?"

"Wow, I haven't thought about it. I think I've been trying so hard not to think about him and all the sadness. I feel like I blacked out how much I like being on the ocean." Willet looked ahead at the two boats that seemed to be going out further.

In the distance, Willet could see what appeared to be a series of tiny islands. It was most likely that both sailboats came from one of those islands. In Key West, there were several private inlets. For a moment, Willet wondered what type of people might live all isolated out there.

After a long silence, Adelie slid on her sunglasses. She pulled away from her sister and started to stroll along in her best, "look how cute I am" walk. She looked back at Willet, who was standing still, shaking her head at the spectacle. Adelie noticed Willet's reaction.

"What?"

"You're amazing Addie!"

"So, how long do we have Willie?"

"Well, knowing Mama, I would say till about around 7."

"That early!"

Chapter 42: Anyone for a S'more?

Tori Ingram and another girl with red curly hair were sitting curled by a bonfire that was just simmering. Across from them sat a boy with gold and brown locks. He was playing an old acoustic guitar. Jae was roasting marshmallows beside him, while two other guys were trying to help her put together a few ingredients for s'mores.

On the other side of the tent, four other girls were dancing to some new pop hit. Willet was somewhat familiar with the music, but not very. When they reached the tent, Tori's eyes widened.

"My god, it's the new girls. Are you ok now?"

"What?"

"You were so sick the other day."

Willet was suddenly on the spot. She forgot she had her incident in front of Tori. She quickly played it off. "Yeah, much better, thanks."

"What did you say your names were again?"

Jae turned her head from the marshmallow that was still rather undercooked, as she interjected. "This is Willet Swift and her little sister Adelie. Willet is the girl I was telling you about the other day."

Tori's eyes got even wider as she hopped up from her spot to properly greet Willet. "You're the girl."

Willet looked confused. "What did I do?"

"You gave that pompous Phoebe Crane a black eye, that's what you did, girl. Everybody is talking about the girl who punched Phoebe Crane out!"

"I didn't actually punch her."

"You didn't? What did you do?"

Jae answered for Willet. "She just kind of threw her."

Tori grinned. "That makes it even better!"

The girl who was sitting beside Tori moved in Willet's direction to get more information. "You look kind of small, do you work out or something?"

"Not really."

"What happened?"

Willet looked up from behind her sunglasses. She hated being the center of attention. Her eyes met Jae's, and she finally answered. "I'd rather not talk about my issues with my cousin, if it's all the same to you guys."

Tori immediately nodded. "Sorry if we made you feel uncomfortable. We are starving for gossip here in nowhere land. Phoebe Crane getting manhandled is quite the news."

Tori eyes danced mischievously as she continued. "I've never known any Adler personally, I mean, I worked for them, but I don't really know them."

"I'm not an Adler, I'm a Swift!"

"Same difference in this town!"

Jae turned to Willet. "That's what I was trying to tell you; your family is royalty around here."

Tori flipped into a handstand and attempted to walk on her hands. "Well, I'm glad you two could make it today."

Willet frowned. "We can only stay a few hours."

"It's cool, I just got called in to work tonight, so I have to leave by seven thirty anyway!"

Jae suddenly looked up, frustrated. "Really, why didn't you warn me!"

"I'm sorry, J.J., I just found out."

Willet had moved beside the acoustic guitar crooner. There was an open cooler filled with an assortment of soft drinks. She reached down and grabbed a fizzy seltzer drink. Mama very rarely let them drink soft drinks, and she was going to take full advantage. She popped the lid and took a squat by Jae, who sitting with her hands under her chin. "What's wrong, Jae?"

"Tori was my ride home, so that means I have to leave with her, unless I can bum a ride with one of you guys!"

Tori laughed. "Well, you could see if Jonas will let you take his skateboard."

"I should throw this s'more at your face, Toridora."

Tori's expression soured. "I told you not to call me that!"

"It's your name."

Jae looked over at Adelie, who was now with the dancers. She and another girl were trading off dance moves and laughing. Tori, who was in mid-handstand, fell over and laughed in front of Willet and Jae. "Oops!"

She pulled herself up and started to dust off the sand. That's when she eyed the fire poker that Willet had placed beside her. "What is that?"

Willet calmly responded. "A fire poker."

"Yeah, I can see that. What is it doing here?"

"I thought it would come in handy."

Tori furrowed her brow. "Are you going to be like one of those strange homeless broads who carry around miscellaneous crap and talk to buildings?"

Willet was taken aback. "Are you serious?"

The guy with the blonde hair stopped playing long enough to comment. "Dude, why did you bring a fire poker to the beach?"

She was now exposed. How she responded would determine the outcome of her entire social life in school. It was important to be cool and confident, no matter how foolish ones actions may appear.

"Perhaps it's for the bonfire." Willet stood and stuck the edge of the poker into a few coals before sitting down.

The guitar hippie had a confused look before he went back to his strumming. "Huh?"

Her candid explanation wasn't working, so she had to pivot. "It's a long story of heartbreak and terror you're not ready for."

Tori quickly dismissed her aloofness and sat down beside Willet. "I can definitely tell we're going to be friends!"

Chapter 43: Offering

Aquila sat on her back patio and watched the lights from the beach. Her condo was in Celandine, away from the sight of Branson Manor. As much as she wanted to run things, she hated the feel of the manor itself. It reminded her of a prison.

She patiently mixed the last few ingredients into a potion she had been secretly working on. All she had to do was let it cool outside in the moonlight. She had a lot of items belonging to Meena, several strands of her hair, nail clippings, lipstick, and a feather from her last blooming. The last item was difficult since she had been banned from Ephron's home. However, she always had other means of acquiring things.

She stared into the approaching night. Many of her young victims came from the beach. The last one, however, Gavin had known personally. She should have lasted much longer than the others. But they were hungry again, and their numbers were starting to increase.

Her children had developed voracious appetites. Once or twice a month wasn't going to be enough to feed them anymore. What would she do then? They had already started to acquire a taste for goats, sheep, and even dogs.

Even as she nursed her hot green tea, she could sense them approaching. The hot summer breeze had the sweet odor of something slightly spoiled. As she anticipated their arrival, she recognized the sound of the buzzer at the front door. Impatiently, she hopped up and went inside. Who was it? She wasn't expecting anyone. As she opened the door, she was greeted with a most curious sight.

"Headmistress, what on earth! What are you doing at my door this time of evening? Aren't you supposed to be preparing for the new semester?"

"You think you're so clever!"

"Actually, I do."

"Whatever devilment you have my sister up to; I ask that you release her."

"Devilment? I assure you, miss, when it comes to you or any member of your family, I think very little of either you or your halfwit sister. If she has insinuated herself into my family affairs, it's on her head."

"Is that a threat?"

"It's a fact."

"I have enough information about what you have been up to, I could go to the constable!"

"We both know, you wouldn't dare, or you would be out of a job immediately, Rhea. It's rather difficult for lonely old spinsters to find gainful employment."

Rhea nervously cleared her throat.

Aquila added, "Now that is a threat, headmistress. Do you understand the difference?"

Rhea frantically whispered in defiance. "You leave my family alone!"

"Concerning your sister, I have a message for you to give to her. Whatever she may think she knows. I know how she spends her nights, and with whom. If she wants things to be kept discreet, I suggest she forget whatever she thinks she knows, or all of Meadowlark will discover quite a lot more about her!"

Rhea stood solemnly as she took in the obvious threats. Aquila was growing impatient with her company. "I have company flying in for dinner tonight, so I suggest you leave now, unless you wish me to invite you to join the dance as well."

Rhea stood silent with a deep, angry frown.

"No? I didn't think so."

Aquila slammed the door in her face before she could respond. She doubted she would have any issues with her anymore, but still, it vexed her that her nephew would allow such a ninny to get so involved in their situation.

As she walked back to her patio, she entertained the idea of teaching lessons across the board to all her foes. The sun had lowered even more by now. When she returned to her patio, her expected guests had arrived.

As she reached the center of the patio, she realized that she was surrounded. Thirteen harpies stood perched on the railing. Each one, with its head slightly bowed before her. In the middle of the patio floor lay a dead harpy curled up on the floor before Aquila.

She was instantly irritated. Aquila tapped at the dead carcass with her bare foot. She realized that its exterior was almost charred beyond recognition. "What is the meaning of this on my patio?"

The closest visitor bowed its head and arched its vulture-like torso back. It cleared its throat and began to speak. "This is how we found her, mother."

"What happened?"

"She went to confront the meat."

"The meat did this?"

"It calls itself Willet."

Aquila looked closer at the burnt, tortured husk. "This is the work of the half breed?"

"Yes, mother."

"This isn't the first time she has taken one of your sisters!"

"Mother, we seek guidance on how to deal with this one. She is not like the other meat."

"She does appear to be a bit more resourceful than I expected."

"What should we do?"

Aquila's eyes closed, as her thoughts went to the image of Avis choking her. "Nothing, my children."

There was a sudden rumbling as the flock fell into shocked disbelief. Aquila opened her eyes and held her hands out, and her voice boomed. "Silence!"

The coven hushed and waited for her to speak. "For the moment, you are to do nothing against her."

Unrest and disbelief met her response. "Nothing?"

"Your failure to quickly get rid of any of these new visitors has caused a bit of a backlash. So... for the time being, you are to wait until the time is right!"

"Mother, we can't just wait. We grow so hungry. We need meat."

"Incidentally, I've noticed that your numbers are increasing. Why is this? You know the law."

It suddenly became silent as if they all knew they had committed a cardinal sin. The feathered creatures lowered their heads looking from one another, until she spoke again.

"Didn't think I would notice? I distinctly told you to keep your numbers low. The more of you there are, the more difficult it is to feed you. As I told you, it is still so important we remain discreet about your growing presence."

"Aren't we all equal, mother?"

Aquila nodded her head. "My poor, foolish children, you are all equal to a point."

"If that is the case, who is less equal to have life? Perhaps you can decide, mother."

Aquila dismissed the question. "Nonsense!"

There was a rumbling again amongst the crowd. Aquila finally reached down and lifted the dead harpy over her head. The small group immediately grew silent as they watched her actions in bewilderment.

Aquila gritted her teeth, then began to pull the wings apart. As she ripped and tore into the burnt carcass, a dark stream of blood sprayed the tiled marble floor. Aquila's bare feet were now completely stained red as she flung the body across the patio. Aquila addressed the agitated crowd in a low growl.

"Your sister sacrificed herself for the greater good. Eat of her body, so you may find nourishment to breathe another day!" Aquila glared intently at the feathered brood as she raised her arms triumphantly into the sky. "Blessed bounty!"

Instantly, the entire congregation descended upon the carcass. Aquila moved away from the scene as the pack of hungry harpies tore into the barbequed flesh of their sister.

Chapter 44: School Day

Regardless of her threats, Laraline did in fact drive the girls to their first day of school. When Adelie got out of the car, she nervously looked at Willet. They both were in the required uniform dress, and both felt rather foolish. It was the first time in their school career, that they had ever attended an actual uniform school.

The quad was completely different from the empty campus they had visited during their interview. There were pockets of students and faces everywhere. Many of them Willet had not seen in town anywhere.

All of them attired in the same white dress shirts and dark blue pants or skirts that were right below or above the knee. This outfit was capped off with a matching dark blue blazer. One look at the various black and brown loafers and they could only be described as sensible footwear.

Willet could see that she was a bit out of step with her own leather-bound Chuck Taylors. Most students didn't even notice, other than the occasional odd glance at her feet.

Willet looked at her schedule and tried to make sense of the thing. So, she had three classes a day. Two morning classes, a lunch break, and an afternoon study lab.

Her first class was with Ms. Faber, who taught class on myths and ancient religions. It was pretty much an overview of the world's religions and some beliefs of various cultures. It was a politically correct, watered-down view of history. That was the one class she had with her sister. Several other younger teens were in that class. In fact, Willet was one of the older kids in that class.

Faber was one of those teachers that was really into films and presentations. This was the type of class that Willlet and Adelie usually found themselves falling asleep. They didn't sit by one another, as Adelie was finally at the age that she wanted her own friends and life. There was a list of books Ms. Faber recommended that would be important to be successful in her class. Willet was sure that if she watched the films and wrote down the notes from the board that she could easily squeak by.

Her second class was a bit more interesting, however, it was twice as hard. Mr. Castor taught science and world alchemy for those wishing to go further in that discipline. There were a lot of faigal upperclassmen present. From what Willet had heard, Castor's classes were very popular and filled up rather quickly.

She recognized her cousin Phoebe, who pretended not to see her. She was sitting beside another girl whom everyone seemed to flock about. She had spicy, long red hair and an unusual amount of black mascara. *This Queen Bee seems to be holding court.* She had long fingernails that were painted black, and she wore a strange black top hat on her head. After a few spirited exchanges with the instructor about her hat, it was revealed that this girl was Raven Rose Branson. Raven Rose was one of the most popular girls in the entire school and heir to the Branson legacy.

Raven Rose was gorgeous. She could have easily been a model, and she took the cold femme fatale vibe to a completely new level. She was what Phoebe wanted to be when she grew up. Willet shook her head as she watched her cousin, along with a few others, fawn over this girl, as if she were candy. As entertaining as the situation was, it was nothing compared to the situation that happened next.

A young man strolled in with a tightly cropped blazer and eyeliner that matched Raven's. The reaction he got was quite similar to Miss Queen Bee. Phoebe batted her eyes in his direction, trying to get his attention. As Willet watched him pass Phoebe without as much as a glance, she chuckled.

In fact, he seemed passively ignorant. This was a guy who was used to having females throw themselves at him. To Willet, something was unsettling about him. She couldn't place what it was, then she looked at his eyes. She recognized him. He was the kidnapper from the other night. She turned her head away as her heart began to beat quickly. *Just relax!*

He doesn't know who I am, we have never actually met!

The young man strolled past the redhead's desk, while the lecture was underway. He quickly made his way discreetly to the seat beside Willet. Her heart sank. *Are you frickin' kidding me. All the seats in this class, he has to sit right beside me!*

She was instantly uncomfortable. She tried to ignore the fact that he had chosen to sit beside her. She tried her best to act calm. He threw her a glance, and in that moment, she could see he had the most extraordinary eyes. They were green and piercing. She nodded and quickly turned away.

He spent the next few minutes trying to get the attention of Raven Rose. When he finally did, she reached into her top hat and pulled out a pen, and tossed it in his direction. Willet felt it heading toward her head and instinctively caught it midair. She casually handed it over to the young man without looking up.

"Thanks!"

Willet grunted in response. She was trying her best to write down all the gibberish that was filling up the board. The young man leaned into Willet, and his hand brushed her knee. This jostled her focus as she felt her space suddenly violated. She tensed up and looked at him with a very queer expression on her face. He immediately apologized. "Sorry, my bad!"

Is he trying to screw with me, or flirt with me?

He leaned close to her ear. Willet could feel his breath as he seemed to be trying to decide what words to form. His warm breath caused a chill down her spine. He may be a murderer, but he was hot. He finally whispered in her ear.

"Where did he start? I think I missed that part."

Willet sighed and politely turned her page backward and slid it over so that he could copy her earlier notes. She could smell the familiar scent from the hotel as he moved away. A wave of nausea overcame her. She was able to contain herself as he rapidly began to copy her notes. There was a moment when he glanced at her curiously. She could feel his stare.

"Wow, you have great handwriting!"

Dr. Castor impatiently addressed the young man. "Would you like to share something with the class, Mr. Branson?"

"Excuse me sir?"

"I said, would you care to share what's on your mind?"

"You're doing a fine job with our tax dollars, sir!" The class exploded into hushed laughter.

"What about you, young lady?"

Willet realized that he was talking to her, and that all eyes were suddenly on her.

"Excuse me?"

"You and Mr. Branson seem so chummy. What were you two discussing?"

"I didn't say anything. I don't even know him, sir."

"Are you calling me a liar?"

Willet was pissed and before she could contain herself, her mouth opened. "You're calling yourself a liar, cause I didn't say a word!"

The entire class gasped. The instructor furrowed his brow and walked over to where she sat. The room was silent as he approached her desk. The only thing one could hear was the sound of his shoes walking.

Mr. Castor stood directly in front of Willet's desk. "Get up!"

The young man beside her protested. "Mr. Castor, she really didn't say anything!"

"Silence Mr. Branson, I'll deal with you later. What is your name, young lady?"

Willet immediately folded her arms. This time, she could feel Phoebe's stare. She was no doubt grinning to herself.

Willet looked at him impatiently, but not directly. That's one thing she learned not to do. Some teachers never like students to look them directly in the eyes. He reached down, picked up her notebook, and snatched her paperwork from between the pages.

"Willet Swift, what kind of name is that?"

"Is that a rhetorical question?"

"What?"

"I mean, do you actually want me to answer that question, or are you just trying to pistol with me, since you have a captive audience?"

The class rolled with laughter. However, Mr. Castor wasn't laughing, and neither was Willet.

"Who is your family in town?"

"With whom I'm related shouldn't matter!"

"Well, it does if you wish to return to my class. You may get your stuff and leave, Ms. Swift!"

"You're kicking me out? This is so stupid."

Willet was beyond mortified as she grabbed her things and stomped out of the classroom. She left the class and wandered around the campus until she reached the map room bulletin board. It was like returning to the scene of a crime. There was a batch of new flyers spread over the board. She still recognized some of the older ones. She found herself on the lawn to the side of the labs. She dropped down on her back and looked up at the sky. She opened her mouth and let out a shrill proclamation.

"I hate this stupid school!"

A voice responded to her call. "I second that emotion!"

Willet sat up, startled. "Who is that?"

"Sorry, I didn't mean to startle you. I was just agreeing with you!"

In a large oak tree near the side of the lab door, she first glimpsed the boy. He was sitting high in a group of branches looking down at her. Willet had to cup her eyes to soften the glare as she peered up into the tree.

"What are you doing up there?"

A rather striking young man with curly hair and earplugs was staring down at her. He calmly answered her question while nibbling on a green apple.

"Trying to get a better perspective on the world!"

"Does it help?"

"Not really. But it's a great view."

"Can you see the town?"

Suddenly, the young man held his hand out. "Why don't you give it a try?"

Willet stepped back in hesitation. "I don't know."

"You got a point, a strange guy calling you up a tree, can't be safe. Remember what happen to Eve when she reached for the tree of knowledge and wisdom."

Willet let out a snorted laugh. "Yeah. You already have the fruit. She motioned his partially eaten apple."

"Yeah, it does have a kind of eerie symmetry."

Suddenly a voice from across the campus called out. She recognized the voice immediately as Tori's. "What's up girl? I thought you had class?"

"I got thrown out of class."

"Mr. Castor?"

"How did you know?"

"Don't worry, just change to a different class."

"I can do that?"

"Of course, just do it before your class meets again, and you'll be fine. You can still get into Mrs. Platy's class. She doesn't even take roll."

That suited Willet just fine. She didn't know if she could handle a class with Phoebe and that Branson kid. Sitting in the same room with him gave her the creeps, much less sitting beside him.

Tori changed the subject. "You wanna get some lunch?"

"I guess so."

Willet looked up at the boy in the tree and waved. "Well, see you around, Lucifer!"

He nodded in response, as he put his head back and closed his eyes. "Later, Eve!"

By the time Willet got back to the main quad area, classes had ended. She sat with Tori, and they nibbled on noodles and baby carrots. They both got an iced coffee from the lunch quad.

Jae had classes during that time, so they could never have lunch with her. However, she always took an extended bathroom break, so she could at least visit for a few minutes. Willet was taking a sip of coffee when she saw Raven Branson pass. At least two boys and two girls seemed to be following her. Willet ducked down so she wouldn't see her.

Willet's afternoon ended in the study lab with Professor Dyveke on quantum physics. It was one of those classes where attendance was a mixed bag. Sometimes it was filled, but today it was very sparse. There were only seven students in the class. The makeup of the class was faigal and human.

Tori and another girl named Alouette sat together near the front. Willet immediately recognized someone from the beach party, the guy with the locks playing the guitar. There was a group of girls who were friendly with Phoebe. Not that they were friends, but acquaintances that you speak to, but don't hang with or think about. She remembered one of them from Castor's class. Instead of pointing and whispering about her, she just gave Willet a slight wave. This rather surprised her. Perhaps she hadn't made too much of a fool of herself. Finally, the boy from the tree rushed inside the door, right before the final bell.

Dr Dyveke threw him a curious look and then looked at his watch. Dr. Nathon Dyveke was an odd bird. He spoke as if he were from some place in India and had a wealth of knowledge, as he meandered about absolutes. He was also the only teacher who introduced the class and himself, which made Willet a little more engaged. The main thesis he presented before the class today was that, according to quantum physics, death is an illusion.

This concept was completely intriguing to Willet, because it deconstructed everything she had learned and experienced this year about death. The only problem was that the previous night's adventure had taken its toll, and she was starting to drift. She had an image of the black cabin. There was the wooden rocking chair, and her father sat rocking. Willet shook herself awake. Did she have a wishful thought, or was this a vision? Perhaps it was a little of both.

Chapter 45: While the Cats Away

When Meena answered the doorbell, she was surprised to find Aquila standing there. She had a pleasant smile on her face as she greeted the young woman. Meena herself had a most curious stare when she saw the older woman. She knew that Ephron did care for Aquila, so she had always tried to be polite to her.

"Ephron is gone at work, I can tell him you came by, Lady Branson."

"I'm sure you could, but I came to call on you!"

"Me?"

"Well, I figure it's been a while since you had some company, and nothing is as exciting as having a house call with gifts." Aquila held up a large red gift bag. It dangled in front of Meena as if it were a play toy for a cat.

"What's that?"

"It's some pretties for you, dear."

"For me, why?"

"You're practically a newlywed. I'm sure these items will do well for your marriage."

Meena was almost in tears as she listened to Aquila go on. "My marriage."

"Can I come inside?"

"Please, Lady Branson, this way." Meena extended her hand as Aquila stepped across the threshold.

"Call me Auntie, dear child."

"Ok, Auntie, please come into the parlor. I will have Millie make us some peach tea and treats."

Aquila gently smiled. "On such a warm day, it sounds quite delightful."

"Well, please make yourself at home, let me get myself a little more together."

Meena's voice cracked as she feebly called out for the house girl. A year earlier, she could have been outside and called for the house girl. It was little things like this that were disheartening about her condition. "Millie."

Promptly, a young island girl ran up to the mistress. "Yes, Lady Meena."

"We have company."

Millie was shocked at the appearance of Aquila. She had been given strict orders by Ephron to never let this woman into the house. She didn't care much for Aquila herself. There was something a bit superficial about Lady Branson. However, this was Meena's guest.

The truth be told, she didn't care for Ephron either. She had witnessed his several indiscretions in the brief time she had been in their employ. She had seen his fits and his tantrums directed at his sick wife. The way she saw it, the poor sick thing spends most of her days all alone in this house, if she wants a little companionship, I won't say a word.

Millie gently nodded in compliance. "Yes, my lady."

Both women sat in the parlor with hot ginger peach tea in delicate rose tea cups. Meena was excited about her company, but she was obviously very sick. Her eyes darted about, trying to avoid any direct light shining through the windows. She spied the gift bag and salivated. At times, peeking at the red bag as it lay curiously beside the chair that Aquila had seated herself in.

"So... what's in the bag?"

Aquila smiled gently. "Oh, I almost forgot. I have some gifts for you, the latest Paris fashions!"

"Paris?"

Aquila pulled out a flask with a greenish liquid. She watched the frail Meena reach out for the bottle. Aquila quickly grabbed her hand. "Let me see your hand!"

At first, Meena was taken aback until Aquila explained the situation. "Just smell the latest fragrances on your skin!"

Meena relented and allowed Aquila to spray a delicate mist across her wrist. The young woman quickly pulled her arm back and held her wrist up to her nose. "Oh my, it smells so divine!"

Aquila studied the young woman's expression before speaking. "Would you like more?"

"Yes, please."

Aquila looked down in the bag before removing a pale powder cream with a single black feathered brush. "Well, what do we have? Ah, yes, here is some blush from India. The finest ingredients."

She quickly moved close to Meena, who was beaming through her sickly stare. "Let's try a little on the check." Aquila gently rubbed the feather across her face as a gentle wave of euphoria overcame Meena.

As Aquila brushed a light rouge application on her cheeks, there was a striking appeal that was rather alluring to Meena. The idea that Ephron would find her desirable again despite her sickness was exciting. Aquila finished off with lipstick and eyeliner.

"Have you used this blush before, Auntie?"

"Why?"

"It feels a bit itchy."

"That happens at first. It's because the feathers in the brushes are so special."

"Special? What kind of birds?"

"They are harvested from the most unusual wildlife. Within a day or so, it will feel as if the makeup is just a part of you."

"Permanent?"

"More than you know."

"Well, I can hardly wait."

"Aquila mused to herself. "Neither can I."

Chapter 46: Der Komisar

That afternoon, when Willet and Adelie made it home, they immediately saw that the gate was open, and the constable's police cruiser was in the driveway. A steady dread overcame Willet. *Why was he here?* As they got closer, she could see Evelyn and the officer talking. They were waiting for them to get home from school. Willet sighed aloud. "Great, we have company."

Adelie viciously responded. "What does he want?"

"I bet it has something to do with me."

She surmised that Mother Hazel had shared some information with Evelyn and Mama, and now she decided to tell the police. Laraline emerged from the front door. She had been waiting for them as well. She soon joined the two girls as they approached the house. Laraline finally spoke, as if nothing was wrong.

"So, how was your first day?"

Willet stopped walking and surveyed the scene. "Is this an intervention or something?"

"This is Constable Fletcher, he just wants to ask you some questions, dear."

"Why me?"

The constable walked about two steps before he carefully spoke. She could tell he recognized her from the other week. "Your mother said you may have some information for me."

Laraline quickly spoke up. "I told him about the creep in the apartment, and you said you saw some of the same cars in town as you did at the hotel. *Nice going, Mama! So much for staying low profile!*

Willet turned to her sister. "Adelie saw the same thing I did."

Adelie was quick to correct. "No, I didn't."

Willet looked at her sister. "Really?"

"You went down the hall to the door."

311

The constable eyes widened. "So, did you meet the occupant?"

"No, I just heard movement, so I ran back to my room."

The constable continued. "You voiced some concerns that you recognized a car from the hotel here in town."

She sighed. "Yeah, that's the truck I tried to tell you about the other day."

The officer turned beet red as he uncomfortably changed the subject.

"Could you tell me what you saw?"

"I saw a big jeep. It was lime green."

Fletcher's eyes narrowed. "Lime green, are you sure?"

Willet still wasn't sure that she had imagined the truck, but she was sure about the murder. "I believe so."

Constable Fletcher sighed. "We currently have a missing girl about your age, who owned a lime green jeep."

Willet had already deduced this fact from the missing flyer.

"Did you see who was driving?"

Unfortunately, that was something she couldn't get a bead on. This seemed all academic to Willet. She was already dead. What she needed to do was implicate Gavin and the Blonde.

"I did see another car from the hotel here."

"On the same night?"

"Yes, a maroon Oldsmobile with red flames on the side."

"Where?"

Willet had to be careful, or she would be brought in as a witness. "Just around town, near the bridge."

"Did you see who was driving?"

Willet had to bite her tongue. "Not exactly."

"Well, I have a good idea already. Are you sure you saw this car at the motel at the same time the other car was there?"

Willet thought for a moment. She couldn't tell them that she saw what really happened, or she could become a target. *Yeah, officer,*

I saw a girl with wings being cut up and butchered by my classmate. I believe he and another older blonde woman kidnapped the girl and dumped her body off the Martin Bridge the other night under the guidance of an older woman, with an eye patch!

"Yes, they were parked beside one another."

"For right now, don't tell anyone what you saw. I already have a few leads."

Willet mused to herself. *Leads, isn't that what the cops say when they don't have a clue?*

Laraline nervously fumbled with her blouse. "Is my daughter in any danger?"

"No, but if there are any future concerns, please give me a call." Constable Fletcher reached into his pocket and removed a small business card with his name, title, city, and phone number.

Laraline snatched it impatiently as Constable Fletcher added. "The biggest plus, so far, is that no one really knows who you or your daughters are."

Willet looked at him queerly. *I doubt that!*

Chapter 47: In Full Bloom

The moon was high in the night sky. It glowed like a distant beacon in the countryside. Willet couldn't sleep, and she found herself outside on the front steps. She carried the fire poker by her side for protection. She had constructed a leg strap that allowed it to gently nestle along her thigh. Even though somehow, she felt that she wouldn't have any visitors tonight, it made carrying it more convenient.

The visit by the police unnerved her. She had to face the fact that she was the sole witness to a kidnapping murder, and the guilty were free and walking about like they had done nothing. It reminded her of her father's mysterious death.

Willet's eyes were drawn to the darkness of the Greywood. She promised Mother Hazel to stay out of the woods, but she felt a fascination growing within her. Not that she had any desire to act on any feelings she might have, but she thought of the dream often. *Is this the place where her dream took place?*

As she studied the dark wood, a strange feeling started to overcome her. Her muscles started to twitch all over her body. Her skin suddenly felt itchy, and she began to feel quite agitated.

A sensation of pent-up rage overcame her as she held back the urge to scream. She was covered in a light sweat as she headed out further onto the lawn. Her face and chest were clammy, while her hair stuck in wet clumps on her neck and face. It was as if her fever had returned.

The vast moonlit landscape stood before her, and she felt completely lost. She closed her eyes and focused on the sky. She could hear the rustling of the wind over the ocean tide. She couldn't see the ocean, however, the smell of driftwood was deep in her lungs as she inhaled sea air.

She stood still, listening to her breathing. Her heartbeat was speeding up. She was starting to question if she was having a heart attack. She clutched her chest as immense pressure overcame her. Willet grasped her chest, she realized that her body suddenly felt alien to her. As her fingers rubbed across her breasts, it was as if she didn't recognize her own body anymore. She felt twitching throughout her entire being.

Her head began to throb as if a migraine was trying to insinuate itself onto her. She could hear the sound of her blood pulsing through her veins. Something was happening to her. Was she sick again? The only problem was she was awake this time, conscious of everything.

The bones in her spine began to crack involuntarily. She doubled over as a muscle cramp seemed to rip across her lower back into her neck, and down into her chest. She was almost in tears as she was starting to spasm. She stretched her hands out and felt a shock as her fingers were changing into long, dagger-like claws. Strange veins and muscles contracted about her forearms.

There was a sudden ripping from the muscles on her back, as if a pulled muscle had just been released. She doubled over, with her hands outstretched, digging her fingers into the dirt. That's when she suddenly felt a strange draft of air running down the spine of her back.

Willet glanced at her own shadowy figure reflected on the lawn. She squinted her eyes in disbelief. She could hardly recognize her own shadow. The shape of two large wings were protruding from her shoulder blades. Willet frantically reached back with her hands. She groped the base of the protruding appendages in horror.

"Oh no, this can't be frickin happening to me!"

She grabbed at a handful of feathers and snatched them from her left wing, as if that would remove them. The sharp pain that shot through her body was unbearable. She let out a cry that was neither human nor bird but somewhere in the middle. She released the bloody feathers and doubled over in pain. She was almost in a fetal position as she contemplated her situation. Tears streamed down her face as she realized that her wings were real and part of her now.

It was the equivalent of pulling out one's hair by the root. She somewhat recovered as she stood upright. She looked down at the bloody pile of feathers on the ground. They were slick, black, and oily. As she used the wrist of her clawed hand to wipe her face, the question popped in her head frantically: *Why me?*

Such questions were fleeting, however, as instinct quickly dominated her thinking. She picked up a familiar scent in the air. Her eyes now scanned the dark sky with the intensity of a predator. Several hundred yards away, she could pick out several flying shapes. She went into an instinctual rage.

She leaped headfirst into the air. She coasted about four feet before gravity took over. Willet quickly tumbled down on her face. She jumped up again, and this time her wings started to flap violently. Before she realized it, she had ascended into the air. She had caught shallow air and remained hovering about 9 to 10 feet above the ground.

She would have to get her footing. There was a rhythmic ebb and flow to flying. She swooped down, almost crashing, and at the last moment, she twisted her body to the side. The tall grass tickled her belly as she rolled several feet before crashing again. *I can do this, I just have to focus.*

Willet took a deep breath and allowed her wings to bloom fully. They were large, and at times it seemed as if they had a mind of their own. They extended far past her arms. She could feel the muscles rooted at the base of her shoulder blades.

I just have to figure out how to control them independently of the rest of my body. This is not unlike sailing sideways.

Willet tried a half a dozen unsuccessful flying leaps into the air, before she had her ah-ha moment. She realized that as she exhaled with her chest, her wings flapped downward; as she inhaled, they flapped upward. The key was to focus on breathing and relax. She closed her eyes and tried to relax as she allowed herself to breathe in a steady rhythm with her wings.

Taking a running start, Willet breathed steadily before she leaped. She anticipated a gradual descent back into the tall grass again with a resounding crash. However, her descent never quite came.

Soon, the air was silent about her, and she opened her eyes. She was much higher this time. Willet looked down, she could see the roof of the Greywood manor below. She scanned the landscape and could see some of the town lights from this height.

There was a subtle calm that was unlike anything she had ever felt. The higher she was, the easier it was to control her wings. It was like floating and gliding at the same time. The entire experience was exhilarating and frightening at the same time. Her experience at sailing had indeed helped her understand how to use the wind to her advantage. She suddenly realized she had no idea how to land. If she crashed, she could very well kill herself from her current height.

As she contemplated the best plan to land, her instincts kicked in again. She picked up that scent again. She had a better vantage point now and spied those dark shapes flying about 20 yards ahead. Acting on impulse, she frantically began to fly toward the dark shapes in the distance. It was a primal urge she didn't quite understand. It was as if she had a second brain controlling her.

She could feel the wind rushing past her as she soared upward into the darkness. She could see them now. They were still some way off, but she could tell they were not heading in her direction. They hadn't even noticed her yet.

The committee of harpies were busy scanning the air for some hint of death. Those who were vulnerable or near death were preferable, this included small animals, and sometimes random livestock. Once in a while, if it was warm, a mother would leave a window open to a nursery. However, this had become increasingly rare. They had been regulated to such dismal feeding patterns in recent days by order of mother.

Blue Jay Way was their normal flight pattern. Sometimes they would veer right to the Greywood estate. Quite often, they would visit other places where they could be more discreet. Had they known of the events that were to transpire that night at Greywood Estates, they would have either flown in greater numbers or not gone at all. They were blindsided as the winged girl swooped down on them.

In reality, they were all capable of dealing with one flying faigal. However, she had the element of surprise, and some enchanted fire stick that seemed to cause them to burn, as it came into contact with their bodies.

Willet was still a few yards away, when she felt heat on her right thigh. She quickly looked down the side of her leg. The fire poker was starting to glow. She took a deep breath and quickly slid it from its leather straps that had already begun smoldering. As she held it out in front of her, it acted as a ghostly nightlight.

The illumination was bright enough to startle the flock just below her. However, Willet had already gotten within striking distance. She slashed down with the firestick across the face of one of the harpies. It immediately screamed in terror as its body was engulfed in some unholy blue flame. The other three scattered. The flaming harpy did an about-face and headed toward the direction of the beach. Willet was close behind. Her large wingspan propelled her quickly against the warm northerly breeze.

As they flew over the treetops, Willet clawed within inches of her foe. Realizing it would not make it to the water, the harpy decided on the woods below. It dove quickly as its wings struggled against the smoldering flames. Willett's hands grabbed a handful of burning feathers and she immediately recoiled. The only chance it had to escape was to shake her within the branches. It frantically swooped below the tree line. It looked back and for a moment, there was no sign of its pursuer.

"Where did she go?"

The flames were starting to die out from the wind speed. The harpy looked about and was about to surmise that her pursuer had given up the chase. Then she felt two arms grab around its neck. The weight was too much as they both tumbled in a chaotic tailspin. Several branches gave way as they ripped through them on the way down.

Suddenly, they both slammed into the ground. Willet was dazed and slowly lifted herself. The world was blurry, but not her rage. She looked for her prey. The harpy was trying to crawl away. It had been shocked by the sudden attack and hence decided it wanted to retreat. Willet extended her chest, as her massive black wings beat angrily at the humid air. Leaves from the forest floor pushed aside from the wind she created.

The harpy was out of breath. "Leave us alone."

"You started this, sister. Look at what you have done to me, look at me!"

Willet pointed to her wings. They were large and black, very similar to the harpies. They had the same gleam and constancy. They were a result of the sickness. "You turned me into a winged freak!"

"Willet, stop!"

Willet heard the voice, but it seemed so surreal. It was her mother. She was standing behind her with her own large, majestic green wings. Willet gazed at her in awe. Laraline seemed like some mythical goddess, with her great wingspan.

Willet looked at her own dark wings, claws, and vein-filled arms. She began to cry at the realization of what she had become. "Mama, I don't know who I am?"

"The wings are an expression of the soul. The more you kill, the more you become like your victims!"

Willet looked down, despondent and partially depressed. Laraline ran and put her arms around her daughter's shoulders. "It can be fixed, dear!"

"How?"

"Wings are an expression of one's aura. In time, your feathers will change shape and color."

Willet considered what she said as she beheld her mother's shiny, vibrant bloom.

"Please take my hand and let me take you home."

Laraline extended her claw-like fingered right hand. Willet quickly took it out of desperation. Willet took a step before falling to her knees. The wounded harpy quietly scrambled deeper into the forest away from the distracted young girl and her mother.

Chapter 48: Bitter Tea

• • • •

WILLET WOKE SOON AFTER sunrise. She immediately noticed that her wings were gone. She quickly reached around, touched her bare shoulder blades, and surprised herself with a deep, reflective sigh.

Evelyn was sitting with her mother by her bedside. Willet sat up as Laraline stroked her daughter's shoulder.

"What happened to my wings?"

"They have receded into your spine."

"I don't understand what happened to me."

"You started full bloom last night. It's a change that all faigal experience during adolescence."

"I thought... I'm not exactly faigal!"

Evelyn walked to the window. "You're not exactly sleeven either. Your mother said you have experienced this before."

"When?"

Laraline touched her head, Willet pulled away slightly. She felt the rumblings of anger and irritation towards her mother. Laraline noticed but pretended not to see.

"You were much younger; around the time you started nursery school. You got really sick and started to have spinal problems, especially balance issues. Sometimes the act of just walking caused you so much pain. We took you to a human doctor, and they found that you had four extra vertebrae in your spine. You were in braces and on pain medicine all the time, and eventually, we had to take you out of school. During that time, you and your father tried every type of oddball therapy and cure you could imagine. Naturally, we started to homeschool you, until your sister expressed interest in public school. By then, your issue had corrected itself!"

"I don't remember any of this."

"It doesn't surprise me; you were in a lot of pain during that time. I think you blocked a lot of those memories. That's when you started having all your nightmares."

Willet looked at her, suddenly embarrassed. "How did you know?"

"I'm your mother."

Willet seemed calm as Laraline tested the water with questions. "Do you ever dream of people or places that you don't understand?"

An image of the strange feather-filled forest popped into Willet's head. "Sometimes."

Evelyn egged her on. "What do you see?"

"An autumn forest covered in leaves, which eventually turn into feathers. There is a woman dressed in white, she is waiting for me."

Evelyn was visibly concerned. "This woman, is she from the Greywood?"

"I don't really know, perhaps."

"Think hard!"

"What does it mean?"

"Mother Hazel will have more of an idea."

"Have you heard from her?"

Evelyn frowned. "Not yet, but she should be returning soon. Just promise, you won't return to the woods for any reason."

"So, you can't kill the night visitors or you become one, that's quite a curse."

"It is. Quite a pickle of a curse."

"Mama, you said my condition could be undone?"

Laraline sighed. "Yes, but for now, we need to see how you feel about school today."

"School sucks!"

"You just started. Besides, school is the safest place for you, until we get things sorted out."

Willet murmured. "That's what you think."

"What did you say?"

"If I don't go, will I have to stay in bed?"

"Definitely."

"Then I guess I'll go to school."

Laraline rubbed Willet's back, as if she were checking her spine. "Good girl. If you can get through the week, perhaps we can talk about missing a day."

"Please, don't say a word to Adelie, Mama!"

"Not a word."

Laraline gave her a peck on her forehead and headed toward the door. Willet caught her as she was leaving. "Has Addie been dealing with anything like this?"

"No, you're the oddball, my dear!"

"Great!"

"Just joking, you're a couple of years older. She still has time before she has to experience the change. Don't worry, we will all figure this out together."

Evelyn tried to lighten the mood. "From what I heard, your first attempt at flying was quite impressive."

Willet had a sideways smirk. "I have to admit, it was pretty bitchin'. I just wish I could figure out the landing part."

Sirenna would be the one to ask about that.

"Really?"

"Don't be deceived by her off-putting manner. She was definitely the more accomplished of the Adler clan when it came to flying."

"I don't know if I want to risk it again."

"Don't be discouraged. It takes most faigal a few weeks to really understand their body and how it works differently than on the ground. Some faigal never feel quite comfortable in the air. Aunt Patricia is afraid of heights. She never uses her wings. Mother Hazel doesn't even want to go upstairs these days. I find it quite humorous.

I can't blame them. You have to be oh so discreet in these times we live in.

Willet whispered to her mother. "Who is Aunt Patricia?"

"Aunt Patsy, dear!"

Bitter recognition overcame Willet's expression. "Oh! What about Uncle Merle?"

"Well, that's another matter. At one time, he was quite adept at the art of flying. Merle could have given Sirenna a run for her money in his day."

"I can't picture him as the flying type. What happened to him?"

"He developed a phobia of flying. Now the only highs he sees are from the inside of a bottle."

Evelyn glanced at Laraline for a moment before turning to Willet. "Please, do not repeat what I am about to share with you."

Willet was ecstatic. She was finally going to learn a family secret. She quickly nodded. "Cross my heart!"

"Several decades ago, Merle fell in love with a pretty young girl named Merisol Bruges. Her family was from Paris, and because of this, she was rather a free spirit. She was a ray of sunshine. Even Sirenna could find no fault in Merisol, though not without trying. You know, she had these bright, beautiful yellow feathers. Her bloom was just magnificent."

Laraline interjected with a knowing look at Willet. "You know the color of the feathers reflects the condition of the spirit."

Evelyn continued as if she hadn't been interrupted. "Merisol had the brightest soul. She pulled Merle out of his comfort zone and timid inclinations, which he developed after some childhood trauma. The Merle you see today is just the shell of what he was with that girl. Her family was favorable of a union, as it would have given them international clout. I think they were going to make Merle an ambassador. Can you believe that?"

"I have a hard time seeing Uncle Merle as an ambassador!"

"Life is so strange. They were to be married in the summer of 1930. The invitations were all sent out. The Bransons, the Corbetts, and the Montagues would all be attending. Two days before, dear Marisol foolishly headed out alone into the countryside, before sunrise, to pick a bouquet of wild flowers. She was to have a dress fitting that morning, and she lost track of time. When she realized she was tardy, she absent-mindedly took to the sky, as she probably had done a dozen times. A group of sleeven were out deer hunting and spotted her. Their reaction was predictable and swift. It took five shots to bring her down. The local sleeven community lost their minds. Word spread across the country of the nymph with bird wings. Her body was sold to a German Firm called the Einin. They had people involved in the government whose job it was to expose the faigal threat."

"The government thinks we're a threat?"

"Just let me finish. Weeks passed before we discovered what exactly had happened to her. The next thing you know, there were pictures of her in the paper. She was sold as an oddity to be displayed at the World's Fair. A winged freak for the sleeven population to marvel and gawk at. Merle was devastated. That very night, Merle, Sirenna, Tom Bolen, and I, along with a few others, travelled to Chicago. We broke into the fairground, located her tank, stole her body, and cremated it properly. We made sure there was no evidence that she had ever existed."

"The world's fair photo that you showed me, that is why you were all visiting?"

Evelyn nodded. "Officials scrambled to put together some makeshift display, made from all types of taxidermy parts. It was generally viewed as a charlatan exhibition by most sleeven scientific experts and news outlets. The display was dismantled two days after that picture was taken." Evelin sighed. "That summer, Merle started to drink, and his desire for flying died at the bottom of a bottle." The room got silent.

Willet sat in disbelief. "Wow!"

Evelyn was holding back tears. "I have very strong feelings about sleeven, after I saw what they did to that poor girl. What they did to her was unconscionable. They sliced her up like some lab project, removed her eyes and inner parts. They stuffed her with paraffin and other manufactured crap, and sewed her up with wire and mesh. Do you know what they did to her beautiful yellow wings? They painted them this dull plaster white. Then glued on artificial feathers. Gawky red and blue to make her corpse appear more patriotic."

As Willet listened to the graphic depiction, she felt a hint of rage and pity. Everything was so confusing.

Chapter 49: Hazing

Willet was numb as she headed out with Adelie to school. She didn't see Jae that morning. It was probably for the best, as she really wasn't in the mood for any conversation. Several minutes had passed when Adelie turned to her sister. "What's wrong Willie?"

There was no answer, instead, Willet just put her shades on and tried to tune out the world. The walk to school was actually a bit therapeutic. The quiet morning stroll helped to calm her a bit. She was able to prepare for another day of school. The first two classes were a blur as she kept thinking about her night flight.

During lunch break, Willet was sitting with Tori and another girl. They were pretty much background noise at this point. They were talking about the new couples and the latest gossip regarding teachers and other peers. Willet couldn't add anything to the conversation, since she was a newbie, so she just zoned out into her own little world.

A cold hand gently touched the back of her neck, and she jerked up. "Hey!"

There stood Gavin Branson. He had that same devil-may-care expression that he had in the classroom. "You're pretty jumpy."

"I don't like people creeping up behind me!"

"You're Phoebe's cousin, right?"

Suddenly, Raven was right beside him. "Yeah, you're the one who just moved here from Florida."

Willet felt like she was being double-teamed. They were sizing her up. She decided to play it cool as she stayed aloof. "You seem to know a lot about me, who are you two supposed to be?"

Gavin and Raven glanced at each other and snickered. Raven put her shades over her eyes as she passively replied. "You'll find out soon enough, dear!"

A chill went up Willet's spine at Raven's words. She was just as creepy as he was.

Gavin snapped his finger. "Have we met before? You seem so familiar."

Willet was nervous as he was trying to focus on how he knew her. Raven popped Gavin on his head. "Come on, let's get going, I don't want to be late!"

Gavin leaned close to Willet. "Sorry about Mr. Carver. That was a pretty jerky thing for him to do to you."

Willet was still in shock that the twins had approached her and was a bit speechless. All she could say was something inane. "Well, what are you going to do? Teachers!"

"You were great though, wasn't she, sis?"

Raven impatiently rolled her eyes at his back. "She was freakin' hilarious, a regular Dr. Seuss! Are you ready, bro? I'm going to be late for archery again."

"To be continued."

Soon the two celebrities and their entourage left the table. Tori were speechless as they left.

Willet stared at them as they crossed the parking lot. "Are they leaving school?"

Tori yawned. "Yeah, it's time for clubs, and the Branson twins are Talomore's biggest stars."

Willet watched them as they walked away, her curiosity piqued. "How so?"

"Raven is the regional archer champion for two years running, and Gavin is the state fencing runner-up from last year, plus they both are in gymnastics. Don't you do that defensive stuff?"

"Defensive stuff?"

"Yeah, maybe you should trade in your fire-stick and get a sword so you can join the fencing team."

Willet rolled her eyes at Tori. Just about that time, Jae popped by on her way back to class from the restroom and commented on the group of popular kids leaving the table. "What was all that about?"

"Gavin is trying to stake his claim on Willet now!"

"Shut up!"

"All that flirting!"

"As if I would be interested in that murderer!"

Jae perked up. "What do you mean, murderer?"

Willet quickly backtracked on her comment, as she realized what she had let slip. "I mean, he acts like a criminal!"

Jae warned. "Well, if Phoebe finds out he came over to talk to you, she will try to murder you. Speaking of murder, you know people are saying Jonas had something to do with that missing girl?"

Willet unconsciously blurted out. "Are you talking about Ryn?"

"I didn't know you knew Ryn!"

Willet tried to play it off again. *Damn, my big mouth!*

"I don't, I just heard her name, and what were you saying?"

"Well, you know they went out twice. Then she just disappeared. This girl in my class said her sister's boyfriend said that Ryn broke up with Jonas. He got so mad he buried her in the Greywood."

Willet listened with vexation. "That's nonsense!"

"Well, she's the second girl he's gone out with that went missing."

Willet's aggravation grew as the image of Gavin dragging Ryn's body in the plastic bag flickered in her mind.

Willet shrugged off the comments. "Silly gossip."

Tori was trying to fix the braid on one of her pigtails when she changed the subject. "Hey, Willet, what are you doing this weekend?"

"I don't even know what I'm doing this afternoon."

Well, my uncle might let me take one of his boats out. I didn't know if you wanted to come?"

"I'd love to."

Jae interjected. "You know how to sail a bit yourself, don't you?"
"Well, it's been a while."

Tori snatched the iced coffee from her and took a long sip.
"Cool, then you have to come. Bring your sister if you want!"

The three of them talked about possible weekend plans, when
Willlet suddenly realized that despite the rough start, she was indeed
starting to make friends.

She was starting to feel pretty good until she got to her locker.
There was a crowd standing around her locker. She could smell the
putrid scent, even before she got close. The words, LEK STANK,
were written in big, bold, bloody letters on the front of her locker.

The headmistress was standing with Mr. Carver in front of the
locker, waiting. When Willlet arrived, Ms. Faulkner confronted her.
"What is the meaning of this?"

"What are you talking about?"

"That awful smell! Open this locker immediately!"

Willet complied as quickly as she could. As soon as she popped
open the door, several dead Knook fish poured out onto the hallway
floor. Willet's eyes opened wide, as everything in her locker poured
out with the slimy fishy goo.

"What is the meaning of this, Ms. Swift?"

"How would I know? I haven't even been to my locker?"

"I want this mess cleaned up immediately, and when you are
done, I want you to report to the cafeteria. I think a little afternoon
work detail should be in order."

"You think I did this to myself? that's the dumbest thing I've
ever heard!"

There was an immediate hush among the growing crowd.

"Watch your tongue!"

"You're serious! Someone did this to me, and I'm being
punished?"

"If you are innocent of this, then who is responsible?"

"I don't know!"

"That's what I thought."

"Why would I put dead fish in my locker? Everything I own in that locker is destroyed."

"I don't know how you do things where you're from. Perhaps you crave the attention that you aren't getting at home. Go to the broom closet and get a mop, child. I expect this mess to be cleaned up before the end of the day!"

"I'm a vegan!"

"Then I guess you have a good incentive to get it clean!"

Willet could hear several fits of laughter in the background. She heard the headmistress, but her focus was on who did this to her. She had strong suspicions. One thing was for sure: most of the staff seemed ambivalent toward her. Since she had been at school, it seemed to her that many people were going out of their way to make her feel unwanted.

Chapter 50: The Perfect Storm

A s soon as Willet finished cleaning out her locker, she grabbed her smelly, fish-ridden things and headed home on foot. Willet had decided she could not deal with any more school today, even though she still had another class.

Tears streamed down her face as she stomped back toward home. She could hardly breathe with the rage that was building in her chest at the idea that she was forced to clean fish guts. Her clothes, now tainted with the scent of dead fish, kept her latest humiliation fresh in her mind.

Although she didn't see her around, this had Phoebe Crane written all over it! She would see it as payback for their fight, among other things. Ms. Faulkner was another matter. Perhaps she had even invited the vandalism of her locker. She clearly didn't like Willet.

Willet had just crossed Martin Street to West Sabine. In hindsight, it might have been easier to just head east on Blue Jay Way. After all, it was a more direct path. However, there were fewer windows to pass on Sabine, so her sudden exodus from school wouldn't be detected as easily.

No sooner had she reached the sidewalk than a silver Rolls-Royce pulled up to the edge of the curb. The window rolled down, and a pale blonde woman popped her head out.

"Hello again!"

Willet looked suspicious. "Yeah?"

"You don't remember me. You saved my hat the other day."

"Oh, you're the lady from the beach. I didn't recognize you at first."

"Oh goodness, I never properly introduced myself. My name is Meena. Are you ok, dear?"

"I'm not having the best day."

"You look as if you need a ride home."

Willet wanted to, but she kept her distance because of the fish smell. "I'm fine, ma'am. I'm a bit dirty!"

"It's no problem, dear. It's the least we can do?"

The woman's pleasant demeanor had all but thawed Willet's resolve, and she was rather excited about the prospect of riding home in such an elegant car. That was until Meena's travelling companion, a young man wearing a suit and tie, stuck his head out the window to get a better look.

"Who are you talking to, Meena?"

"Ephron, this is the girl who helped me the other day. I didn't get your name, dear."

"Willet Swift, we just moved into my aunt's house. She lives on Blue Jay Way."

The young man furrowed his brow. "There aren't too many homes in that direction. Your family must be of some importance. Who is your aunt?"

"Aunts. I have two aunts."

The young man's expression suddenly changed. His face became cold and unflinching.

"Are you the new guests of Greywood Manor?"

"Yes!"

"Then I pity you, child!"

Meena looked confused. "What's wrong? What did she do?"

"She is an Adler, come on!"

No sooner had he uttered the words than the automobile quickly sped off, leaving Willet more confused than ever. She was transported back to the incident with the fish again.

I wonder if Gavin and Raven were part of the plan to do that crap to my locker? Perhaps I am being targeted. So this is being "safer at school"? Thanks mama!

She finally crossed back to Blue Jay Way and gave a hard stare at the silver caddie that was almost gone. She then glanced back at the observation tower of Talomore and mumbled to herself. "I hate this stupid place, I wish we had never moved here." She stomped back down the empty road, stewing about the rough morning.

Willet was about halfway home when she first noticed the storm clouds brewing overhead. The sky looked angry. Thinking aloud she looked at the rumbling clouds.

"So now you're going to rain down on me, why don't you strike the stupid school instead?"

Almost instantly, there was a flash of lightning, and a crack of thunder soon followed. The sudden spitefulness of the storm caused Willet to flinch. Looking up again, she noticed the clouds moving briskly past her. She glanced up several times at the dark shapes sliding at a frantic pace across the murky sky.

She paused in astonishment as the clouds appeared to be settling over the entire school campus. *What is happening?* The sky over Talomore was black. Large gusts of wind slammed against the main dorm area. Sheets of rain poured down from the clouds, yet it was completely dry where Willet was standing. Suddenly, several more streaks of lightning lit up the sky, followed by deafening cracks of thunder.

Willet began hyperventilating between the explosions of thunder as she felt a strange tingling after each lightening flash. The tingling ran up her spine, invading her nervous system. She tried to slow her breathing, but before she realized it, she was starting to rise. She was slowly ascending above the ground, her feet were at least three feet off the ground when Willet began to panic.

She was partly crying, partly screaming as she looked up at the blackened sky. It was too much for her to take, as she put her hands to her head to drown out the sound of the swirling storm clouds and lightning strikes.

"What's happening to me? What's happening? Please, make it stop already!"

No sooner had she spoken the words than she tumbled down to the ground. Willet fell flat on her back, knocking the wind out of her chest. She looked up at ominous sky, wheezing for air like a feeble old woman. She turned on her side and frantically sucked in the moist summer air. As she lay on the ground, she realized that she was actually barefoot. She had, quite literally, fallen out of her shoes. She closed her eyes and took several breaths before she could sit up comfortably.

It was now silent. The swirling wind and thunder had stopped completely. Willet could hear birds starting to chirp. The clouds were dissipating in the distance over the school. She looked down at her shoes and noticed that her soles were smoking. Steam was rising from the inside of her heels.

She waited on the ground for another two minutes, contemplating what she had just witnessed while allowing the air to return to her lungs. Finally, she rose to her feet, picked up her shoes, and finished the long trek home barefoot.

Chapter 51: Auntie Dearest

By the time she reached the driveway, she had convinced herself it was just an hallucination. In any case, she headed straight up to her room and tore off her clothes. Ever since the fever incident, she had developed an irrational fear of her bathtub. Regardless, she had a quick shower to relieve the sickly stench of dead fish and the disgust she felt.

Willet climbed into her bed, pulling a thick quilt around her damp body. She still smelled a faint hint of fish in her nose. She reached under her pillow, pulled out the book that Mother Hazel had given her, and started reading. She really missed her.

How was she going to navigate everything that was happening? It was too much of a burden, so she closed her eyes and started to breathe. Perhaps she could call for Mother Hazel to return. *Please come back. I need help!* She was in a deep concentration when her door creaked open. Sirenna's voice followed.

"I just received a message from your school; apparently, you left without so much as a word."

Willet looked up curiously, wondering how she knew. Then she saw Dadu sitting on the dresser across the room. Its magnificent white wings fluttered as if it were showing off.

Willet hissed at the great owl. "Snitch!"

Sirenna had her arms folded behind her back as she leaned against the wall. She wore a form fitting bodysuit that was a strange mix of violet and blue. She wore the expression of someone slightly bothered. Her eyes focused on Willet directly.

"Trouble with the headmistress?"

"That woman is a godless witch!"

Willet attempted to compose herself a bit before she continued to speak. "Auntie Sirenna, I regret to inform you that I will not be returning to that place."

"Is that so?"

"Yes ma'am!"

Willet was anticipating a stiff upper lip kind of lecture, or you poor dear, you're over reacting, and you can do it lecture. However, this wasn't Laraline Swift, this was Sirenna Adler.

"So you're going to let them break you!"

"Look, I am not a faigal and I am not a human, I'm a lek and they will never let me forget it!" Sirenna slowly leaned in with a most deliberate stare, which Willet hadn't seen before.

"Then don't let them forget either!"

"Excuse me?"

"You heard me. I am not in your shoes, but I've had my fair share of adversity. Those who wish to destroy me. I'm an Adler. I'm a survivor, and somehow you have to know what and who you are. You will never survive this world if you don't figure that out."

"I'm not an Adler!"

"No, you're a Swift, if you honor the blood in your veins, you need to get off your ass and head back down to that school tomorrow and correct those who try to define who you are meant to be!"

Willet looked intently at her. "Why are you telling me this?"

"What do you mean?"

"The way you have treated me and my family from the moment we got here, you have made it clear that we don't belong, that I don't belong!"

"You're right, you don't belong, but perhaps none of us do, including the very swine that you let dominate you."

Willet looked up at Sirenna. "Does my mom know yet?"

"No, and it's not my place to tell her."

Sirenna then abruptly left. Willet watched the open doorway, halfway expecting her to return. Dadu abruptly hopped off the dresser and flew down the hallway. Willet wondered where the great beast was headed now.

She contemplated the older woman's words as she sat alone by herself. After several moments of silence, the sound of the dogs started up. The barking shook her from her daze.

Willet opened the window to smell the fresh country sea air. The occasional breeze reminded her of the night that the harpy crept into her window. She wouldn't dare be that foolish again with the windows.

Willet returned to the book that Mother Hazel had given her. She thumbed through the weaver manual, occasionally looking out the window at the clear sky. The book read partly like an instruction manual, partly like an encyclopedia. It had so many historical references to people, events, and things she did not know of.

She turned to one page that shared the same symbol, which was on the cover of Evelyn's Asclan bible. There were references to the seven Holy Kalas. Willet's memory triggered. She remembered that term, Kala, from Mother Hazel. There was a definite list of all seven Kalas and the descriptions, but it was in the faigal tongue, so she couldn't decipher this part. Several pages filled with symbols caught her fancy.

Many of them seemed like variations of religious symbols she had seen before, triangles with overlapping crosses, infinity signs, eyes with a trio of parallel lines, and dozens of wing ikons with eyes. There was very little of the book that was in English. The parts that were seemed involved and overly wordy.

She must have been studying the book in her room for a while, as she almost didn't hear when Adelie came tearing into her room. "What happened to you, Willie?"

"What?"

"We were worried!"

"Worried? I was sick and came home early!"

Willet had almost forgotten that she left school without saying a word to anyone. She expected she would have to give an explanation to Adelie about the fish locker incident that was probably notorious by now. Instead, her sister's desired subject went somewhere completely unexpected.

"You missed it, there was this horrible storm that came from out of nowhere!"

An uneasy feeling started to overcome Willet, as she tried to sound innocent.

"Storm, what storm?"

"I can't believe you missed it all."

"Well, what happened?"

Willet sat in horrible anticipation as Adelie spun the events of the day. "In a nutshell, the wind smashed the auditorium windows, tore down a tree, and we all had to evacuate into the gym!"

Willet nervously whispered. "Did anyone get hurt?"

"I think a few students had to be taken to the hospital."

"Oh Crap!"

Willet's eyes were as wide as they were guilty. She listened intently as Adelie described her firsthand account of what she witnessed.

"I don't know what to say, I feel so horrible."

"Say about what, it's not like it's your fault?" Willet stared blankly at her sister.

Chapter 52: Namvula

The white ethereal light bathed the pool of clear liquid at the edge of the bank. The sisters sat sunning themselves as their wings gently fanned the humid air. Gertrude Pence motioned for Sephora Hazel to approach her.

"Let us commune, sister mother."

The Etherglyde was a hidden part of the greater monastery where the Namvula congregated into several small flocks, to meditate on issues within the faigal world. It was a large handmade pool consisting of faigal birth yolk and clear afterbirth. It was supposed to contain healing powers that allowed a steady stream of communication. Since very often, no verbal communication was needed within the Etherglyde.

"Yes, Mother Pence."

As both faigal lay in the pool of deep concentration, the mother sister began to speak to Mother Hazel's mind.

You have come a long way, sister mother.

I have urgent matters to discuss!

Patience, we already know why you have come.

Mother sister.

Why have you not brought the child, if this matter is so important?

She is not my child to bring; besides, she is under sanctuary.

Is the birth mother of any consequence to us?

No, she is nobody.

This is not exactly true, sister mother.

The mother's existence is shrouded in shades of deception.

Mmmm, what about the child's father?

The father was a sleeven.

Was?

Quite recently, he departed the mortal coil.

So, this child is a lek?

I know this is most unusual.

It's not like it's an unfamiliar situation. It happens from time to time.

How often does this occur?

There are always exceptions. Besides, from what you told me, we have already convened on the matter. We have gathered nothing new from the previous home visit.

How is that possible? I have witnessed her exercise powers to manipulate matter and enter the ether of events and worlds. She is able to do things I cannot begin to understand.

Dear sister mother, this counsel has already concluded from our previous home visitation that this child is indeed a tempest.

Mother Hazel's eyes widened.

"*This is not the explanation you were expecting?*"

Are you sure?

Even as we speak, there has been a steady increase of temporal disturbances back and forth throughout the Fathom Black. These psychic tremors are reacting to the sudden energy surges permeating the natural ecosystem of Meadowlark. She is not very subtle!

She is just discovering her powers!

She needs self-discipline, before she exposes herself!

So, her power is growing?

You seem surprised.

I've never heard of a lek tempest, mother sister.

There have been a few others over the years.

Why were we not informed?

It's not something the order likes to advertise.

You said there were others. How many others?

Enough to monitor such movement and energy. Most of our brethren are unaware of the possible threat that cross-mixing species has created over the centuries.

Mother sister, I thought a tempest creation is rare, even among faigal.

It is very rare. It's not that half breeds aren't capable. It's just the human side of them has a lust for power, and it's harder to balance. Usually, such creatures are destroyed by the Namvula during the first seven years of life, when this anomaly is first discovered.

Destroyed?

However, this is a more delicate situation, as the child is almost an adult, which complicates the situation. Now, its inception has been embraced within the faigal community as an act of sanctuary. She is naturally protected from harm until sanctuary is revoked or she departs from this mortal coil.

What do you suggest?

She needs to be properly trained; someone with her power could be quite invaluable to us, if she were instructed by the right teacher. As I see, she is already familiar with you, and would be more accepting of guidance from you.

I understand, mother sister.

When you return, you are to immediately take on the half breed as your sire.

I already have one. Lady Sirenna Adler is my current sire.

You have done well with her, but it is our assertion that Sirenna has reached her limits of understanding of the arts. Your obligation to sire the Adler twin has effectively ended as of now. Your focus is to sire the half-breed, until her knowledge is beyond your comprehension.

What then, mother sister?

At such time, you will bring her here to finish her training. Then, you will remain here, as a permanent resident, as a new mother sister.

I understand, thank you, mother sister!

There is something else you wish to share, sister mother?

What of those who wish to violate the sanctuary, there seems to be a conspiracy afoot.

Plans within plans. We suspected as much. The House of Branson is divided within itself!

Divided?

This imposed sanctuary is a great source of the conflict.

Is it possible for a weaver, who has been bound, to still practice?

Ask, sister mother.

I inquire about a possible former student who may have been excommunicated. She goes by another surname now.

What does she call herself?

Selandria Aquila Branson. formally from the house of Corbett.

Mmm, that name is vaguely familiar. What reasons do you have charge against this creature, other than she is a member of your rival clan?

I believe she hides a binding ring around her neck.

Believe, but not certain. Why do you feel this?

Just a feeling. An energy of deception.

Is that all?

They have outsourced a weaver from a distant land.

Many great clans do the same. Sourcing out is good for trade and creates stronger political alliances. The Adler house would be wise to diversify!

I understand, but he acts as a private liaison for the Lord of the House. It's very discreet.

Mmm, we will look into this allegation. Be careful of burning bridges prematurely, sister mother. There is a lot of moving parts that even you can not comprehend.

Mother Hazel was suddenly nervous. *What do you see, mother sister?*

Hard to tell, things are always in motion. We see a great eruption between both houses very soon. We sense a shift of power rising, even you have never felt this much.

Perhaps, what should I do?

Nothing, the past has taken root in the present, and the future is inevitable.

Chapter 53: Crecheland Connection

The main road of Crecheland was like an empty ghost town, even though it was a mere seven miles from the more scenic tourist havens of Meadowlark. Driving onto Teal Street from East Sabine, there was a feeling of being transported into another world.

Though not as depressed as some areas of the country, anyone from the outside would surmise that Crecheland was the poor side of town. Somewhere between a ghetto and a food desert. Most of the utility apartment units were hidden in the deepest corners here. Some of the more seedy nightclubs sat like empty spectral buildings, waiting for the sun to go down so they might reanimate themselves for evening mischief. That's not to say there weren't plenty of reputable businesses in Crecheland. Unfortunately, because of their geographic location, the association tainted them.

Arlis Greenbaum owned a bar on the beach called Kuzz. Kuzz was a seafood slash, brewery that was a family-owned, sleeven establishment. It was the kind of place that even affluent faigal patrons frequented or made large orders for delivery and catering.

Kuzz, along with a few other places, were popular despite their location. They had managed to create a niche for themselves in Meadowlark. A place where the locals went to avoid tourists.

Because of the boom in demand for seafood catering, as of late, Greenbaum had to diversify. This led to a joint enterprise with Ephron Branson, under his father's approval.

However, when it came time to renew their partnership, Avis found their once lucrative enterprise not an option, with a newly signed international deal helmed by local business lawyer Nester Crane.

Instead, Avis gave him the contact information of several local and regional fishermen whom he could recommend. This led to an eventual arrangement with Langston Swift, a regional seaman who was familiar with the town already, especially since he was once a native.

Laraline and Evelyn pulled up into a small gravel parking lot with a bland grey trailer-style building. These were the business offices of Kuzz and Benny's golf madness, a putt-putt tourist trap that offered 36 wild holes on an ever-shifting obstacle course. Benny's golf was also owned by Arlis. It was probably a way of tapping into the more family-oriented dollars he was losing with Kuzz.

As Laraline got out of the car, a sense of familiarity pricked her consciousness. The roads were almost as she remembered. As she looked about Teal Street, she recognized a rather large three-story Tudor-style home. The lights were on. However, they always were, at the Crecheland Inn. Laraline nudged Evelyn and pointed, as if she were speaking some dirty secret.

"I thought they closed the Crecheland Inn."

Evelyn nodded. "Yes, it's been closed many times, as it has been reopened again many more. It's still one of the more popular attractions here in town."

"I remember, you were afraid I would end up there, because you said, and I quote, I was so promiscuous."

Evelyn widened her mouth as if she were shocked. "That is not true; I said you were just too curious about everything!"

"Sounds like you're describing Willet."

Evelyn just smiled as she headed to the ramped walkway that led up to the offices. Laraline was close behind. As they made their way, she saw the front door of the Crecheland Inn open. A small, older woman with long dark hair in a large overcoat stepped out with a bag of trash. Laraline found herself studying the curious woman as she carried the trash around the back of the house.

Their eyes locked with one another for a moment before the woman disappeared. Laraline wondered if the woman was indeed the infamous Madam Tuludge. She recalled a rumor that Uncle

Merle had a thing for her in his day. That's the thing about small towns, there are always so many secrets. She came to her senses and followed Evelyn into the tiny office.

Arlis was a curious-looking fellow. Truth be told, he resembled a bushy bearded lumberjack. Heck, he even had the large red and black plaid shirt. This huge, hulking fellow sat behind a small, cheap wooden desk. A small index file sat on the desk with an old rotary phone. There was nothing inside that screamed décor. Even the windows were covered with cheap olive-colored blinds. The type you see in old school buildings. The inside was so small and cramped that Arlis seemed out of place here.

He looked at both women suspiciously as they approached. He squinted even more as Laraline walked briskly up to his desk. "What can I do for ya?"

"I understand you did some work with my husband several months ago. I'm trying to find information about his last whereabouts."

Arlis snapped at her sarcastically. "Ask him yourself!"

"I would, sir, but he is dead. Found murdered running a job for you, as I understand!"

His demeanor quickly changed from an arrogant ass to a paranoid ass. "Ok lady, I don't know nothin' bout him."

Evelyn impatiently cut him off. "Listen, little man, my name is Evelyn Adler and the information about you was given to us by Lord Avis Branson, and let me assure you, neither of us is in the habit of getting the runaround."

After her selective name-dropping, he immediately became more cordial to both women. "I wasn't meaning any disrespect. It's just I don't recall either of your faces."

Laraline was curt as she replied. "Well, you were familiar with Langston Swift. You worked with him during the winter and spring!"

Arlis's eyes widened at the name, Langston Swift. "Yes, Langston! Sorry for your loss. I never actually met you, Mrs. Swift, but he talked about his family a lot."

She had the urge to ask him what he said about his family, but she realized it didn't matter at this point. Instead, she continued to grill him. "Can you tell me about the last time you worked with him?"

"He mainly made a lot of deliveries. We do a lot of catering outside of the mainland. I think he was bringing a shipment of shellfish to a private party on one of the islands!"

"What islands?"

Evelyn turned to Laraline. "There are a handful of small, uncharted, privately owned cays and islets that are off the coast, close to the beach. "

Laraline turned her attention back to Arlis. "Who are these privately owned residents?"

"You mean like names?"

"Yeah, could you jot down a few names and addresses?"

Arlis sat back and rubbed the back of his head. "I can't just give that information."

"Look, I believe it's highly probable someone murdered him at one of these deliveries."

"Still, there are confidentiality laws!"

"Is there any way you could just give us a hint?"

"What you are asking is unethical, not to mention illegal, Mrs. Swift!"

"Mr. Greenbaum, please!"

"Look, I would love to help you, but I can't."

It remained painfully silent for several moments. Arlis, in fact, was about to rise and tell them he had things to do when Laraline interrupted.

"Wait, do you still need someone to do deliveries and catering?"

"Why?"

"Perhaps you could hire me to deliver to these islands."

"Are you insane? That's basically the same thing!"

"No, it's not. You wouldn't have to actually give me the names, just the addresses where the delivery goes!"

"Why are we even having this conversation?"

"Because my aunt is Evelyn Adler, and the amount of business she could bring your way could be staggering, provided that you can be helpful. You know I'm right!"

"That's plain bribery!"

"You call it bribery, we call it a favor."

Arlis stood up as if offended.

Evelyn stepped closer and cleared her throat. "Look, I can make an offer now. My sister has two large events happening this fall. Both events have over 300 guests. You could be paid handsomely for the rest of the season!"

Arlis looked at both women as if he were considering their proposal.

"Even if I did, there is no guarantee when they will order again, or if they will order again. Island folks keep to themselves, and they like it that way."

Evelyn quickly corrected him.

"You're making excuses. I'm pretty sure anyone from the islands is a regular. It's not like they get out to the mainland a lot."

Arlis looked at Laraline in desperation. "You have to have a second-class sailing license to even navigate these waters?"

"My daughter does."

Evelyn looked curious. "She does?"

"One of the things she inherited from her father was her love of the ocean. She's had her license since she was 15."

Arlis cut her off. "Look, I'm not hiring your daughter!"

"So, you're hiring me."

"Wait, that's not what I said!"

"It would make sense to have someone to assist in unloading deliveries. This way, you wouldn't have to pay a bodyguard to watch over me."

"My boaters don't need bodyguards!"

"Then why hasn't someone filled this position? My guess is no one wants the job. Especially after a well-established boater is mysteriously found dead doing a job for you. It is the type of thing to scare off potential employees. Word gets around."

Suddenly, Arlis realized he had shown his hand. "Do you have any other skills?"

"Well, I used to bartend, so if things get slow, I am still pretty useful."

Greenbaum raised his eyebrow.

"What do you have to lose?"

He finally sighed, then reached over into his file cabinet and pulled out a stack of papers. "Fill out this paperwork and have it back by Monday."

"Thank you, Mr. Greenbaum."

To save face, he bellowed defiantly. "This is only on a trial basis. Right now, I can use you sporadically as a third bartender to see how things work out. If you don't know how to handle yourself, the deal is off!"

Laraline turned to Evelyn as she clasped her hands excitedly. "Now I'm employed!"

Arlis was quick to correct her. "Well, you still need a rig!"

"What do you mean?"

"How are you going to transport the goods? You need to have a boat that is insured, and you're not using one of my boats?"

"Well, I still have Langston's old boat!"

Chapter 54: Aftermath

Willet saw the damage from the storm and was quickly reminded of the consequences of her actions and lack of control. Several classrooms had yellow tape across their doors, while puddles of water and shards of glass were scattered across the floors. There were signs on many of the doors providing directions to alternate classroom options. Her new class with Ms. Platy was moved to the chemistry labs since most of them started about midday.

As she passed across the quad, she saw the flashing lights of the constable's car. Fletcher was standing on the sidewalk with another officer, talking to the headmistress. The conversation appeared to get dramatic. At one point, Ms. Faulkner broke down into tears.

Willet walked along the edge of the building, so she wouldn't be seen. She was about the clear their line of sight, when she heard Tori from behind her. "What happened to you?"

"Jeez, you scared me!"

"Sorry. Where did you go yesterday? You just disappeared."

"Yeah, I didn't feel well, so I went home!"

"Are you ok?"

"It's complicated."

"I heard what happened to your locker!"

"So everyone knows?"

"Pretty much!"

"I don't like being the center of attention."

"So, who did it, I mean, pranked your locker?"

"I'm pretty sure it was Phoebe, though I haven't seen her since it happened."

"Yeah, that's quite convenient."

"Quite."

"So, what are we going to do to her?"

"We?"

"Yeah, I mean, I know Phoebe. There is no way she orchestrated that by herself. She knows a lot of people, but I do too."

"This is a family matter; if you get involved, it may spill over. Besides, the less you know, the better."

"Well, it sounds like you have a plan."

"I have a few ideas, but they're still brewing. What's all this with the police?"

"I think it was about the storm yesterday!"

"Really?"

Suddenly, the school bell rang. Like a beacon, the entire campus hurried to their designated classes. Fortunately, only one of Willet's classes moved. Over the course of the day, rumors and several theories of what had happened with the storm crossed Willet's ears. Some of them were ridiculous and far-fetched, while others seemed plausible.

By the time the first lunch bell rang, Willet had picked up a few universal facts. The first fact was that one of the offices destroyed by the storm was the headmistress's. Apparently, a strong wind blew her windows in and most of her important paperwork out the window. The stuff that wasn't taken by the wind was waterlogged.

The second and more troubling event was the fact that the only student taken to the hospital was Phoebe Crane. Apparently, she was taken to the hospital soon after the event happened. Willet could not exactly get the actual details. All she knew was it was a lightening-related incident.

When she found out, a bittersweet sickness overcame her. It was too ironic that the two people whom Willet wanted revenge on were the main victims of the storm. The whole incident had a bizarre sort of symmetry.

I mean, she wanted to get her, but the idea that she may have killed or maimed her was unsettling. The very storm that Willet had inadvertently spawned seemed to purposely seek out those whom she had a personal vendetta against. She wasn't exactly thinking about them at the moment. It was like the storm just knew to seek them out instinctively, as if it were actually a living, breathing entity. Whatever was happening to Willet, it was getting stronger.

She sat quietly eating her yogurt when Jae ran up to the table, trying to hold back laughter. Willet was distracted from her guilt long enough to look up. Jae, out of breath, finally got her question out. "Where is Tori?"

"Her class had a timed exam this morning, she should be here at any moment!"

"An exam, really?"

"I know, right. What's so funny?"

"Wait till Tori gets here; I want to see her face when I tell you guys!"

"More juicy gossip?"

"You don't know the half of it. Man, she needs to hurry. I have to get back to class."

"Well, have a seat till she gets here."

Jae complied as she knelt on one of the stone, bleached slabs beside the marble tables. She wore a single braid, which she delicately moved to the left side of her back. Willet was about to ask if she knew anything about Phoebe, when the brief silence was interrupted by a familiar voice.

"Dr. Amerge is a frickin' Nazi." Proclaimed Tori as she stomped up to the table. "I mean, who gives an exam on the first week of school, the day after a school-wide trauma, no less!"

Willet's pragmatic mind took over. "Was the test hard?"

"Well, I got my name right."

Willet winced. "Ouch!"

Jae interjected. "I heard all the computed test forms were on Faulkner's desk, so they wouldn't be able to record them anyway!"

Tori suddenly came to a realization. "Hey, aren't you late for your class again?"

"Well, I had to tell you guys some insane news!"

"What is she talking about?"

Willet shrugged her shoulders. "She wouldn't tell me until you got here."

Tori twirled to face Jae. "Well, hit us with the news, big daddy war bucks."

Jae stood up with a big smile. "So, you guys heard that Phoebe went to the hospital yesterday."

Willet nodded soberly. "Yeah."

"Well, I was talking to Alice Myers."

Tori frowned. "Which Alice?"

"She's the girl who is always smoking in the bathroom."

"The one with the greasy black hair?"

"Exactly!"

Willet was on the edge of her seat as she impatiently blurted out. "Well, what happened?"

"Well, Alice was in the bathroom when Phoebe came in. Phoebe was taking a big poo when it first started to rain. Alice said it was stinky, so she left."

Willet grimaced. "Some of us are eating."

"As soon as Alice stepped out of the bathroom, lightning struck Phoebe's bathroom stall. The walls collapsed and she was knocked unconscious."

Willet looked relieved. "She wasn't struck by lightning?"

"No, her mother spread that rumor because the truth was too embarrassing."

Tori popped Jae's shoulder. "What's the punch line?"

"Well, when she crawled out of the wreckage, her skirt was still around her ankles, and she had a stream of tissue still attached to her bum. The paramedics put her on a stretcher bare butt."

Jae paused a moment before the entire table exploded with laughter. Even Willet had to admit, the irony was a lot more cruel and funnier. Tori fell over and started choking on a potato chip she had previously stuffed into her mouth. Willet was in tears as she imagined the scene in her head. Jae snorted as a stream of snot dripped from her nostril. Tori finally rose, trying to compose herself.

Jae finished. "From what I understand, the paramedics had to calm her down with a sedative. They took her to the hospital at Celandine Springs. She was discharged twenty minutes later. Everyone thinks she is still in the hospital. She is just too embarrassed to return."

As Tori looked at Willet, she noticed that her expression had changed. She seemed suddenly bothered. Tori, confused, called out her conflicted mood. "Hey, five minutes ago, you were plotting revenge. What happened?"

Willet rose to her feet and looked out across the vast sky. "I don't know, sometimes life just seems a bit complicated."

"We make it complicated!"

"Well, sometimes it does it all by itself!"

Jae looked at both girls, confused. "Sounds like a deep conversation, but I gotta dip, bye guys!"

Tori slapped her own cheek, responding in a pompous aristocratic dialect. "Well, smooches, darling!"

Willet followed suit. "Alright, see you later!"

Jae gave a peace sign and smirked. "Later girl!"

With that, Jae quickly ran down the walkway back to her class. Jae had the perfect bathroom scheme, and she had perfected it. Whenever she wanted a break from class, she would just ask to go to the restroom.

It started innocently enough with a doctor's note she received 2 years earlier for a UTI issue she had. Things quickly worked themselves out, however, she kept the note and just kept recycling the same note every semester with minor date adjustments. She was able to copy the same letterhead, so the notes all looked official. Add the fact that she brought a thermos of water and cranberry juice everywhere with her. It was just assumed by most of the staff that she had a bladder issue.

Jae, of course, did very little to dissuade them otherwise. If her mother ever got wind of just how far her deception had gone, she would be mortified. Mrs. Weever was a proud woman who, despite being seen as a sleeven servant, was quite an honest woman. She was fond of quoting a famous religious poet she had learned about in school. Lies are the devil's unraveling of faith.

As Willet made it to Professor Dyveke's class. She discovered that he had paired everyone into groups. Since she left early, Tori had to pair up with one of the other girls. In fact, everyone was in their groups quietly discussing the lesson.

She soon discovered that she was paired up with Jonas Branson, the strange tree boy that had all the rumors circulating around about him. Willet breathed uncomfortably at the situation. She would just try to be pleasant until this assignment was over. She noticed quite quickly that he was unlike his other siblings. He was more withdrawn and almost clinically sad. His notebook had haiku and pictures doodled all over the cover.

Dyveke had some notes on the board that made almost no sense to Willet. She leaned into Jonas discreetly. "So, what did I miss yesterday?"

His response was deadpan. "Class."

Willet rolled her eyes. "Don't be a smart ass."

"Then I'll be a dumb ass."

"Come on."

"Here!"

He promptly opened up his notebook and slid it over to her desk. Willet took one look and shook her head. "I can't get my head around this quantum physics. You see, this makes no sense to me!"

"Well, you need to relax first."

"Relax? You don't know me. I'm fine!"

"Well, understand this. Understanding physics is kind of like meditation."

"So you mediate?"

"I try."

"Is that why you like to climb trees?"

"Well, there is so much noise on the ground."

"So go to a quiet bench in a secluded forest!"

"No, I mean it's like everyone in the world feeds into a collective radio wave, and the frequencies are becoming more and more polluted every day."

Willet was intrigued. "Polluted by what?"

"Thoughts, emotions, fears. There is a lot of negativity in the world. Therefore, I try to go high enough to focus. Does that make sense?"

"I didn't know you would try to go all Zen guru on me."

Jonas rolled his eyes. "I'm not a guru."

"I know, that's why I said trying, and trying too hard."

"Is it that obvious?"

Willet shrugged as she pushed his notes away. "No offense, but you give off a very negative vibe."

"Life is complicated!"

"That sounds like an excuse."

"Not when you belong to the type of family I do!"

Willet had a curious look. "Huh? Well, if we are to be lab mates, it would be proper to at least know one another's names."

Jonas extended his hand. "How foolish of me, let me introduce myself. Jonas Branson."

Willet took his hand without thinking. "Willet Swift!"

Willet looked around, suddenly realizing that Jonas was the only person she had connected with in class besides Tori. It made sense to pair up with him anyway.

"So, are you related to the Branson twins?"

"Yes, my little brother and sister are infamous around campus. Sometimes, I hate being tied to the name Branson!"

"Who are you telling? I'm a niece to the Adler clan. It's like I'm supposed to fill this role of what's expected, and if I don't please everybody, there will be dire consequences!"

"It's the opposite with me. I'm expected to fall below the rest of my exceptional family. The truth be told, I am nothing like any of them."

"Really!"

"You know, my older brother Ephron was still a legend around here when Gavin and Raven first enrolled. There is nothing particularly exceptional about me, I'm a lot like my mother, just different!"

"To think everyone says you're this murderous creep, in reality you're just a pissed off middle child!"

"That's what people say about me?"

He stared at her for a moment through his thin-rimmed glasses and curly hair. Willet suddenly realized what she said and tried to walk it back. "Look, I don't know you, I shouldn't have said that. Of all the kids I've met, you've actually been pretty cool."

"No, you're being honest. I appreciate that. I don't run into that too often. As to your observation, you're probably right. Perhaps I do have a negative vibe and actually add to this collective noise with my own issues. Which is why I mediate."

"Hey, that conversation went full circle!"

"Yes, and that is how quantum physics kind of works!"

Willet grinned at him, despite herself. "I have to admit that was clever."

"I have my moments."

"Don't get too cocky, I wouldn't want you to get the wrong idea about us."

"No, of course. After all, I'm just a lowlife murderous creep."

"And I'm an undisciplined, foul-mouthed bourgeois child!"

They both looked at each other and broke into a series of silent snickers and chuckles, while trying to make sure Professor Dyveke wasn't watching.

"So, the meditation thing, is there any other reason why you meditate?"

"There are several other reasons. I could show you how. It's not hard."

"I know how, I just don't."

"Why not? You seem capable of abstract thought, more than most of the others in town."

"Life kind of gets in the way."

"Now that's a lazy excuse."

"You're probably right, but I've spent my whole life around modern technology. What do you expect?"

"That doesn't make any logical sense."

"I'm a girl. I don't have to make sense."

"Ok."

"Seriously, can I ask you something? Do you have a phone in your house?"

"Of course."

"Well, I was informed that my aunts preferred to communicate by bird."

"You must mean specters."

"How does it actually work? I mean, do they tie notes on their legs like passenger pigeons?"

"You're pretty funny."

"I haven't even gotten started."

"Ok, let me see your hand."

"Excuse me?"

Jonas impulsively grabbed her wrist and gently pushed her fingers open to expose her palm.

"Relax. Specters share a type of universal consciousness with other species. When the master at point A communicates with their specter, the impressions of ideas and thoughts are transferred through several different birds until they reach a specter belonging to the master at point B."

With his index finger, he gently moved across her palm from one end to another. Willet felt a queer tingle in her stomach as she slowly pulled her hand away.

"Ok, I think I sort of understand."

Jonas was suddenly embarrassed and tried to dismiss his attempt at flirting. "Actually, it's a lot more complicated and nuanced than that. My aunt has a specter that she uses primarily to eavesdrop and find out bits of gossip around town. She has even taken to spying on us. She is really into blackmail."

"Jeez, that's disturbing."

"That's not the half of it. Her specter is a big, nasty crow she calls Nevermore!"

"My aunt Sirenna has an owl called Dadu. It's so creepy because you never know where it is. I went to the bathroom the other day, and it was on the windowsill in the corner of the room, just watching me."

"That's why they're called specters."

Chapter 55: The Cat

Willet was withdrawn on the walk home. The conversation with Jonas was rather pleasant. Against popular opinion, she found him sort of cute, in a pompous kind of way. She even enjoyed their playful flirting during class.

The reality of the situation was that he wasn't a good option. After all, he was for all accounts her mortal enemy. It was a pip, of all the guys she found intriguing, not only was it a Branson, but the black sheep of that family!

Jae and her younger sister joined them today. Deryn was a year younger than Adelie and they both quickly paired off away from the older girls and distanced themselves by walking several yards behind Willet and Jae.

Willet commented on Jae's presence. "This is the first I've seen you on the walk."

"Well, I gave Tori some gas money if she could take us home the first week."

"What happened?"

Jae huffed. "Her schedule changed. She has to go to work right after she gets out of Dyveke's class. I'm not looking forward to these long walks home."

Willet felt a bit insulted. "You walked passed my house the other day."

Jae rolled her eyes. "Not every day!"

"Are you ok?"

"Why do you ask?"

"You seem bothered."

"I'm fine."

They walk silently for several minutes. Things felt awkward, so Willet tried to strike up another conversation. "What do you think of Jonas?"

"Jonas Branson?"

"Yeah."

"I don't."

"He's in my class!"

"Yeah, Tori said you got stuck with him as a lab partner for the semester."

"I wish I hadn't skipped class. I wanted to be paired with Tori, but I guess he's not too bad.

Jae added. "Well, he's nothing like his brother or sister."

Willet concurred. "No, he's not, they don't even get along."

Jae looked dismissively. "I don't think he gets along with any of his family."

"Speaking of family, my aunt Sirenna actually tried to make me feel better about school."

"How?"

"It's complicated."

"Is that your favorite word, complicated?"

Willet was about to respond with some smart comeback when suddenly Daryn started to scream for her sister. "Jae, it's another one!"

Jae quickly turned around and ran back toward the younger girls. Willet was close behind. As they reached Daryn and Adelie, they saw them both standing still on the road, looking into the tall grass. Willet noticed they were all focused on something that had caught their eye.

Daryn continued to frantically yell. "She killed him!"

Jae quickly grabbed her sister and embraced her. "Come on, honey. He is in a better place now."

When Willet finally joined the group, she peered into the grass. Lying on its side, was a dead cat. A mound of flies covered its upper body. At closer inspection, there appeared to be a hole in its chest. Willet turned her head away as Adelie looked horrified.

"Willet, what happened!"

Jae glanced back with an irate tone. "Raven Branson!"

Willet looked confused at the answer. "She did this?"

"Well, she has a thing about cats."

"A thing?"

Willet was almost livid at the implications. "You mean to tell me; she just kills cats on purpose?"

"Pretty much."

"And no one does anything?"

"Well, she is kind of protected."

"Because her last name is Branson?"

"Of course."

"What is wrong with this town?"

"You mean what's wrong with the world, cause it's always been this way. The golden rule is that whoever has the gold makes the rules, so you Adlers and Bransons can do whatever you want. You get a free pass, Willet!"

"Do you believe that I think that way?"

"It comes with the territory. It doesn't matter what I think."

Willet grabbed Adelie by the arm and quickly led her past Jae and her sister. "Well, I'm sorry my presence is so offensive!"

Willet was almost in tears as she quickly rushed down the road. At first, she thought she heard Jae call after her, but she wasn't sure, and she wasn't about to turn around. Adelie was confused as usual.

"What's going on?"

"We need to get home."

"I like talking to Daryn, she's nice."

"Well, you can't right now!"

"I don't understand."

"Sometimes life can be complicated, Adelie!"

By the time the girls reached the driveway, Willet was brooding about the Jae and dead cat affair. The entire thing didn't make any sense. She kept trying to rewind her conversation with Jae as if she could find where everything went awry.

Adelie was the first to notice the large grey caddy parked in the driveway. Uncle Merle was pulling large bags out of the trunk. She motioned to her sister at the unusual activity beyond the gate. "Look!"

Willet was instantly excited. "Mother Hazel is back from her trip!"

Without hesitation, she quickly ran toward the house. Whatever may have happened paled in comparison to the fact that Mother Hazel was back. Willet ran past the grey caddy and up the steps to the front door.

Instinctively, she tore down the hall to Mother Hazel's room. She stopped just a few feet before she reached her destination. "Stop!"

Mrs. Weever's voice boomed from behind her. "She just went to bed; she is very tired from her trip. She will come to fetch you when she is ready."

Willet nodded politely. "Yes, Mrs. Weever, I'm very sorry."

The older woman paused at Willet's behavior. Perhaps her sadness of late caused her to be extra polite to Jae's mother. She wasn't sure, but she quietly headed back up the long stairwell that led upstairs to her room. When she got to the entrance of her room, her mother was waiting for her.

"Mama, what are you doing here?"

"I just need to talk about a few things."

"What now?"

Adelie ran down the hallway and hugged her mother before turning to Willet. "Willie, can you play with me on Sirenna's chessboard in the back yard?"

"Get lost, I'm busy!"

Adelie clinched her teeth and stormed down the hallway to her room. "You're just like everyone else!"

Laraline's jaw dropped at the exchange. "Willet, don't talk to your sister like that. If you have an issue, don't take it out on her. She looks up to you. One day, you will really need her in your corner."

Willet rolled her eyes emphatically as she yelled down the hallway. "Sorry, Addie, maybe later!"

"What's wrong, tough day?"

"Tough week, is there any other school I could attend?"

"What's wrong?"

"All the kids at Talomore have issues!"

"And you don't?"

"Jeez, Mama, thanks for the encouraging words."

"You know what I mean. We are all damaged one way or another!"

"I just can't seem to fit in."

"Of course not, you don't know how to just fit in!"

"Huh?"

"You heard me. You are like this bright, glowing peacock, Willet. The problem is that everyone can see your bright, beautiful plumage, except for you!"

"A peacock?"

"You are so worried that you aren't normal. Guess what, you aren't, you never have been. You don't realize how exotic you really are!"

"A frickin' peacock?"

"Ok, I get the point."

"I'm just kidding. It was cute, ma. I love bird references. Hey, where is everyone?"

"Well, the aunts both left right after Mother Hazel got back. They went to visit your Aunt Patsy."

"Why on earth would they visit that flake?"

"Well, she is their younger sister and apparently, her daughter got injured pretty badly at school, with all those sudden strong winds."

Willet snickered to herself, recalling what she had learned. "More like breaking wind."

"Is that funny?"

"It's just that her injuries are a bit exaggerated. The truth has been bent out of proportion a tad."

"She was hospitalized! I don't think that is a laughing matter, Willet!"

Willet could see that it was better to just listen. Her mother wasn't going to hear anything she had to say, even if she had an eyewitness account. She refrained from saying anything else and waited for her mother's self-imposed lecture to finally end.

When the dust settled, Laraline finally explained why she was camped out in her daughter's room. "We need to talk about something else, Willet."

Willet's heart sank; whatever it was, she knew she wouldn't be happy after hearing about it. However, before Laraline could continue, Adelie came in to ask where everyone had gone. Laraline had to sit her down beside Willet for her big reveal.

"OK, listen up girls. When your father passed, there were certain things I didn't want to discuss. I'm sure that it seemed like I was shutting you out, but I was trying to protect you."

"What are you saying, Mama?"

"Your father didn't die of a heart attack. He was very healthy. He was found aboard his boat, which had been adrift for at least three days." Laraline began to tear up as she began to relive the incident. "The police and I feel your father was murdered, because of the condition of his body." Willet and Adelie looked at one another with the same concerned expression.

Willet fearfully probed. "What condition, Mama?"

"There were wounds all over his body. I hadn't seen anything like that before, except once. When I was a child, I wandered into the Greywood over the hill. I saw a woman's body with similar wounds."

Willet pushed harder. "What kind of wounds?"

"Willet, please."

"What happened to his body, Mama?"

"Stop talking!" Adelie covered her ears. "I don't want to hear anymore!"

Willet still pushed. "What kind of wounds, ma?"

"Bite marks. Something had started to eat him."

Willet abruptly stood up and then stumbled to her knees, hyperventilating. Adelie was steadily crying with her hands covering her ears. Laraline pushed Willet to help carry Adelie to her room. By the time they got her in bed, she had all but passed out. Laraline rubbed her head. "She will sleep for a while."

Willet eyed her mother as they carefully left Adelie's room. As soon as they got to the hallway. Willet started to grill her mother.

"So, you came here to find who or what killed Father?"

"Why do you have to make everything so dramatic and insidious?"

"Well, it kind of already sounds that way. Is there something after us, mother?"

Laraline felt fragile, so she gave a simple, yet blunt answer. "I don't know."

In that moment, Willet understood why her mother was so tight-lipped about the whole affair. Just getting the footnotes gave Willet a sickness in her stomach. She looked at her mother. "Thank you, Mama."

Laraline could see Willet needed the truth, so she expanded. "So far, all I know is that he did a lot of work here in town off-season. He did some catering work for a series of private islands off the coast. I believe he came across someone or something nefarious on one of those islands."

Willet sat patiently listening to her mother's words. It was the first time Laraline could remember her daughter this attentive and still.

"The only way I can find out is to sail to one of these islands. However, I'm not very good at sailing."

Willet completed her thought process before it was expressed. "Obviously, you think I can." Willet looked concerned at her mother. "This is what you wanted to ask me?"

"Your father taught you everything he knew about boating. You have that gift."

"Even if I could, we don't have a boat."

"Technically, I still have the deed to your father's rig."

"Yeah, back in Florida!"

"That's the problem. None of us can leave this town to go pick it up."

"Why not?"

"To ensure all of our safety, I had to ask for sanctuary."

"I've heard you refer to that term several times. What exactly does it mean?"

"I had to agree that we would live under certain conditions and codes for complete protection across the entire faigal community."

"Protection? You mean the protection that allows monsters to come into your window and attack you in your sleep?"

"Look, it's not perfect, but my concern isn't harpies. A damn harpy didn't kill your father."

"Are you telling me we can't physically leave town?"

Laraline grimaced. "Not at this time."

"What happens if we sneak out and bring the boat back?"

"If we were discovered, the bargain would be broken, and we would become fair game."

"So basically, you're telling me we are prisoners here in this town?"

Laraline was about to correct her, but her point was irrefutable. It wouldn't make a difference in her daughter's eyes, and she couldn't argue about what it had become.

Willet exhaled a nervous breath after being clued in to their situation. "Well, that sucks!"

"Yes, yes it does!"

"So, we need someone to help us bring the boat back into this port safely."

"Someone we can trust."

"Provided that it is still docked where we left it, Mama."

"It hasn't been that long, but whatever we do, it needs to be done pretty soon!" Laraline touched her daughter's shoulder. "Look, I don't want you to worry about that, I will worry about getting it here. I just need to know if you're ok helping me sail it to one of those islands, when the time comes?"

"When?"

"It could be anytime from three to six months."

"That long?"

"It's complicated, Willet."

"I guess I now know why I've been using the word complicated so much."

"What?"

"Nothing. I promise, when the time comes, you can count on me."

Chapter 56: Mother Hazel's Return

In celebration of Mother Hazel's return, Sirenna held a dinner party and invited many friends within the faigal community. Even the Cranes were invited. Patsy, Nester and Phoebe would surely attend, as it would be a social gathering. Nester had secured a deal with Avis, that would put Patsy in a better bargaining position with her older sisters. Even Arlis Greenbaum was given a bone, as they used his catering services to whet his appetite.

Of course, the Swifts were expected since they were the honorary sanctuary guests of the Adlers. Today, Sirenna made sure the appropriate attire was set out for them. Even if they weren't the exact type, they could at least look the part. Laraline spent almost an hour in the dressing room working on Adelie's hair, which had turned a darker shade of red due to the difference in the weather.

Willet's hair was the same midnight black color with perpetual curls, so there shouldn't have been much to do. However, tonight Evelyn insisted that she have her hair tied up into a type of bun called a casque. According to Auntie Evelyn, it would make her appear more refined.

As the guests made their way to the great table. Willet experienced a feeling of Deja vu. She felt the same feeling from that fateful dinner several weeks ago. It was the day she first became acquainted with her extended family.

She would take her same seat at the large table, decorated in the most glorious gold and crimson colors. Mother Hazel loved those colors as she said that gold and crimson were delectably pagan. Willet quickly took a sip of water. There was a wine glass beside her dish filled with a reddish substance. She would be allowed to drink tonight.

She looked about the table, and immediately she could feel Phoebe's stare as she entered the room. Willet could not resist the chance to get up and mingle, as guests were still spilling into the dining area.

Willet quietly got up from her chair and casually walked to the other side of the room. There were red and gold flowers arranged about a large fireplace. Phoebe was near the hearth, trying not to notice Willet heading in her direction. Phoebe was finally forced to address her.

"Cousin, you're here?"

"You seem surprised."

"I didn't think this was your type of scene. Wouldn't you be happier in the company of your sleeven friends?"

Willet leaned ever so close to Phoebe. "I know it was you who vandalized my locker, pip!"

Phoebe's response was quick. "I'd like to see you prove it, lek!"

"You know, we never did get to finish our little dance, cousin."

"Well, this is not the time or the place for mindless violence."

"Really, I should like to know if Mrs. Broom sees your point of view, especially after you deliberately maimed her."

"She was an incompetent old fool, maybe next time she will watch where she is going."

Sirenna's voice suddenly boomed loudly across the room. "Everyone, find your seats. Dinner is served."

Willet turned to walk back to her seat when Phoebe grabbed her arm. "Let go of me before I break your wrist!"

Phoebe was close to her face. "Remember one thing, cousin, no matter how you dress or whom you know, you will be nothing more than a half breed lek."

Willet's eyes glared with an uncontrollable urge to strike her.

Phoebe could see this in her eyes and egged her on. "You would like to hit me. Go ahead, so everyone will see what an animal you truly are."

Willet took a deep breath and smirked. "Well, at least I'm toilet-trained."

An instant look of embarrassment overcame Phoebe. "What did you say?"

"You heard me, Phoebe poopy pants!"

Phoebe's face flushed bright red, as she tried to hold back tears. "Shut up!"

Phoebe looked as though she could run and hide. Willet found the moment to be exhilaratingly satisfying as she walked back to her seat. However, she knew eventually, things would come to a head between them.

When everyone had settled into their seats, Sirenna quickly addressed the crowd by tapping on the outside of a large goblet with her dagger-like fingernails. The loud bell-like clanging tempered the crowd as she cleared her throat.

"Family and friends, thank you for this wondrous occasion. When our father placed the first stone at Adler Estate, he wanted to build an empire that was formidable to every great house that had come before. Not only on the outside but also with the personnel he surrounded himself with on the inside. Mother Hazel Sephora is a prime example of what I speak. Presently, she is the oldest member of the Adler house. She has been a pillar of strength for this family. She was by my father's side as they fought many battles: the Sleeven Raids of the 1810's, the Griskin plague of 1872, the Degas Crusades at the beginning of the 20th century. Recently she took a trip back to her homeland. We feared that she might decide she wanted to stay, but alas, she has returned to Adler Estate, back to where she belongs."

Sirenna lifted her goblet high. "Since I have known this creature, she has acted as mentor, tutor, counselor, and mother to every one of us. Please, raise your glasses for dear Mother Sephora Hazel!"

Sirenna extended her drink towards the old woman as the room exploded with cheering and clapping. Mother Hazel herself seemed to be lost about how to respond. It was hard tell her exact expression behind her rose-colored glasses.

As the room died down, the ancient weaver stood. "Well, I am an old woman with not a lot to say. I am deeply touched. Thank you all." There was more applause, and this time, a slicked-up Merle called to her from across the room.

"Do you have any plans this year, mother?"

"It's funny that you asked that question. After my time in New Essex, I was offered the chance to return to the Namvula and live out the rest of my days. After much deliberation, I have decided to do just that. As much as Greywood Estate has meant to me over the years, this year will be my final cycle here as your mother sister. "

There was a sad hush among the crowd.

Sirenna's eyes were wide with disbelief. "You're leaving Meadowlark?"

"This is a different era, and my kind are growing out of touch with today's needs. The next generation must forge ahead with their own ideas and plans."

Evelyn's hand flew to her heart. "I'm speechless."

"I'm not gone yet, I have another cycle still ahead of me."

Patsy called out in detached amusement. "Well, who will be the new house weaver?"

"It's ironic that you should mention that, I have already started training my replacement this year." Another great hush fell over the room. Most of the faces looked astonished, including Sirenna.

"What do you mean, this year?"

"It's no big secret, she has come to our household, under the most dubious of circumstances, and has had to learn to adjust to our sometimes-arcane way of life. In such a short time, she has exercised a voracious aptitude for competent learning, with a rare intuitive knowledge of the craft itself. Because of these reasons, I have chosen to take on Willet Gale Swift, as my new sire. When I depart this mortal coil, she will take on and exercise all duties of this great household!"

Sirenna gasped as did the rest of the room. Laraline looked at Willet, whose eyes were wide and confused. She shook her head in defiance. "Oh no."

Patsy was in disbelief. "This is just not right, mother!"

The old woman glanced over at Willet and gave a mischievous wink. "As someone once said to me, life can be complicated."

Sirenna finally spoke. "That's impossible, she is a half breed, the Namvula wouldn't stand for this."

"The Namvula fast-tracked this replacement in particular. It was the one condition of my being able to return home. I am sorry, Sirenna, but they were quite insistent."

Sirenna was almost speechless. "What about me?"

Evelyn quickly rose to her feet, sensing a conflict, and quickly called to her sister. "Perhaps this delicate subject should be discussed in private. I'm sure there are many questions that need to be addressed."

Sirenna's nostrils flared. "That's the first sound idea I have heard today." Evelyn and Mother Hazel abruptly got up from their large throne chairs. Evelyn looked at Laraline and then toward Willet. "Both of you need to come along. This matter concerns both of you, as well."

Willet still had a look of concerned disbelief. "What just happened?"

Sirenna addressed the remaining guests at the table before she stormed out the door. "I regret to inform you all that we have some rather urgent matters to iron out. Mrs. Weever will be serving dessert in about seven minutes. Please talk freely until we return."

The party of five silently headed down the hallway. Willet was trying to make sense in her head of what was happening, as they all continued to the study. As soon as Evelyn locked the doors behind them, Sirenna erupted into a tirade.

"I've never been so humiliated in my own home. It's a slap in the face to the House of Adler and to me. How can you do that to me, at my own table?"

Mother Hazel calmly responded. "The sisterhood feel as if you have reached your full potential."

Evelyn finally spoke. "It's not the news but how it was delivered, mother. You could have easily brought us into this room earlier. To make this grand proclamation in front of half of the family is a bit tacky."

"Under the circumstances, I felt it necessary."

Sirenna glared at Willet. "Are you happy? You have taken everything from me, you horrible little troll!"

Willet protested the sudden attack. "Look, I never agreed to this, you can have your old weaver position. I don't want any of this!"

Sirenna pointed her finger at the young girl. "She doesn't even want this!"

Mother Hazel quietly corrected Sirenna. "She will in time. Besides that, none of us are getting younger. Right now, you and Evelyn are the youngest eidolon, unless you expect Uncle Merle to succeed!"

Evelyn rolled her eyes. "Oh, that is a frightening thought."

Willet cleared her throat. "I can't handle this. Tell them it's too much for me."

Mother Hazel sighed. "This is a great honor."

Sirenna piggybacked right behind her comment. "If it's such an honor, why don't they train her themselves?"

"As a matter of fact, when I discharge my duties here, they request that she finish her training with them."

Willet was quite bothered and voiced her position. "Excuse me, but don't I have a say, I mean, it's my life. I have plans!"

Evelyn soberly corrected the young girl. "A life that your mother has forfeited under the rite of sanctuary. If you wish to live under faigal sanctuary, you must abide by faigal law."

Willet looked at her mother. "Is that true, mother?" Laraline barely looked up.

Willet snarled. "Not only am I trapped here, but apparently I can't even decide what I'm going to do with my own life."

Sirenna scoffed as she pointed at the young girl. "And they actually want you to train that. I don't understand. This is madness!"

Laraline finally reacted. "Silence old woman, that, as you are referring to, is still my daughter!"

Sirenna shouted back. "How dare you raise your voice to me!"

Willet covered her ears and began to yell. "Shut up, shut up, shut up, everyone!"

Willet's eyes raised bitterly in Sirenna's direction. They were distant and dead, as Sirenna caught the young girl's gaze, she noticed that her eyes were now completely black. A chill went up the older woman's spine.

Suddenly, a cold breeze drifted through the study. The ghostly wind hushed out the desk candles. Frost began materializing on the wooden desk. The globe was instantly encased in a thin layer of December frost. The window curtains swayed open as Willet clenched her hands into fists.

The entire inside of the study was bitterly cold. As the group looked about the room, they could see one another's breath as the air left their lips. Ice crept up the sides of the window, walls, and door. As ice encased the doorknob, there was a steady cracking sound.

Everyone turned in Willet's direction. Mother Hazel had begun to gently speak to her. Her voice was calm and soft as she tried to calm Willet.

"It's ok, Willet. Take a deep breath. Remember your safe word."

Laraline joined Mother Hazel. "It's ok, honey. Calm yourself."

Evelyn and Sirenna stepped back, as if uncertain of the young girl's motives. Willet closed her eyes and began to slowly breathe. It was obviously a conscious attempt to calm herself. Whispering to Sirenna, as if she were about to explode. A deep voice poured out of her throat as if completely alien.

"Please stop fighting."

Sirenna was speechless as Willet finally took a deep breath and exhaled. The breeze quickly dissipated, as Willet's rage tempered down to a slow, dull irritation. As she finished her calming breath, her normal breathing pattern resumed.

"I'm very tired, I think I'll retire for the evening."

Willet slowly looked about the room as if she were in a trance. She then abruptly left as a final breeze slammed the door behind her. The study remained silent for several moments before Mother Hazel whispered to Sirenna.

"Now do you understand?"

Sirenna turned to Laraline. "What kind of abomination have you brought into our home?"

"Shut your disgusting lips, before I shut them for you, auntie!"

Sirenna grimaced in shock at her niece's response. She decided instead to turn her venom on Mother Hazel. "And you, how long have you been training her?"

"Long enough to know that her powers are growing and she needs to learn to control them."

Laraline was visibly worried. "I need to go check on her."

"No, let her rest. Exercising such power has a caveat: it can temporarily deplete the body of energy. She will need to rest for a few hours." Mother Hazel hobbled with her cane to the window. "Four hundred years of rule and the Adler dynasty has finally spawned an actual tempest, do you know how rare that is?"

Evelyn looked at Mother Hazel. "You used this event as an opportunity to show her off like some new toy."

Sirenna quickly dismissed Willet. "She is too young and green!"

"Too green? Look at this room. May I remind you she has only been here a few weeks? Imagine what she will be like in another year or so."

Laraline's voice quivered. "You exposed my daughter, and now she is a target. It will only be a matter of time before everyone knows your plans."

"Wake up, woman! Your child was already a target. She has been since you first arrived here. My motive tonight was to protect her. If they see her as an institutional threat backed by the Namvula, they may be less likely to go after her."

Evelyn's head snapped towards Mother Hazel. "Great Arke! That's why you announced it at this public gathering!"

"Do you think someone will try to hurt her?"

Sirenna folded her arms. "The question is, will she hurt someone else?"

Laraline ignored Sirenna's comments as she questioned Mother Hazel's logic. "That's all very well, but wouldn't we need to at least tell the Bransons for this plan to work?"

Mother Hazel calmly responded. "We already have, dear."

Laraline glanced at Evelyn, perhaps thinking she had spoken to Branson already. However, Evelyn didn't share her gaze. "What do you mean?"

Sirenna's eyes were distant as she calmly answered. "She is saying we have a traitor among us."

Laraline seemed quite surprised. "Who?"

Mother Hazel looked at Laraline with a dry, whimsical look. "It's not really a surprise. Evelyn and Sirenna already know, they have known for years. Unfortunately, the time is nye and lies no longer become us, children."

Chapter 57: Sire

After the last of the guests staggered home, Mother Hazel made her way up the stairwell to check on Willet. Regardless of Mother Hazel's advice, Laraline had already checked on her daughter soon after they left the study. Sirenna and Evelyn returned to try to salvage the evening with their visitors. Laraline had found her quite knocked out and almost impossible to stir.

Willet had fallen asleep without getting undressed. As she lay in her wrinkled dress clothes, images of the dinner and the reality of what was becoming her life unnerved her. She was starting to stir and turn over when she felt a strange presence in her room. Mother Hazel moved beside her and sat at the end of the bed.

"I know you're not sleeping. I can hear it in your heartbeat. How are you feeling?"

"What happened? I was so tired."

"Kali is activated by the physical body, much like a battery. When you use it all up, you must rest to recharge. However, your endurance will grow in time."

"Crazy, everything is sort of a blur. Has everyone left?"

"Yes, and everyone has gone to bed except Sirenna and Uncle Merle."

"Sirenna is pretty angry at me."

"It's more the situation. She'll get over it in time."

"Why are you here?"

"I'm just checking to see how you're feeling."

"Before you say anything. I have a life plan, and it does not include Meadowlark Downs."

"Are you sure about that? You seem to wield Kali so effortlessly."

"I don't appreciate being ambushed."

"In hindsight, I should have informed you. I apologize."

"I never said I wanted to be a witch, much less the house witch."

Mother Hazel took a deep breath. "The correct term is weaver. A witch is a sleeven term."

"My bad. It's hard to remember."

"The term 'witch' is akin to a racial slur."

"Sort of like calling someone half breed or lek?"

"Touché. I stand corrected."

"Speaking of terms, you referred to Aunt Sirenna as an eidolon. What exactly is that?"

"As I told you before, since the Adler family is in possession of a part of the first light, we have a responsibility. Our entire bloodline is charged with the duty of watching and guarding the gateways of Greywood."

"So that is why you all choose to live here in Meadowlark, because of the woods? You're all stuck here, like I am? We are all prisoners?"

"There are times when I can't recall what came first, the forest or the town!"

"That's pretty messed up."

"You and your sister are also eidolon."

"Now I get your angle. You just want to unload this job onto me! Well, I ain't biting!"

"Let me try another approach. If you do not comply with the Namvula expectations, you will be deemed a threat, and you and your sister will be destroyed. Do I have your attention now?"

Willet was wide awake now. She looked intently at the older woman. "Why, I haven't done anything?"

"They are afraid of what you may become. You are a threat to both races. At least this way, it protects you and your loved ones."

"I keep thinking this is all a nightmare and it will soon end. But every morning, it gets worse."

"Then it's up to you to change the narrative. Become the very thing that they fear. Then you will have some control back."

Willet was silent as she carefully thought about what her next move would be. "How do I know I can truly trust you. I mean, I could be another pawn to get you what you want."

"Do you realize what I did tonight, what I lost because I went out on a limb for you? By becoming my sire, you cannot be touched while I am still living. Any attack on you will be visited on me. If you fail in your training, you will not be the only one to suffer. This entire clan will be erased from faigal memory, and I will be the first to go."

"They can just do that?"

"They have done it before!"

"That's rather cold-blooded. I thought the faigal were supposed to be these truly enlightened angelic beings. From what I see, you all are not that different from the petty thieves and hoods in the human world."

Mother Hazel's response was soft and controlled. "I will overlook that comment, as long as you get your bum up and let's start your formal training.

Chapter 58: Meena's Final Ice Bath

That morning, after Mother Hazel's coming home gathering, the paramedics rushed Meena Branson to Celandine Medical Tower. It was one of the few hospitals that had deep faigal pockets invested in it. Originally built to reap the benefits from the rising medical costs in the human world, it soon became a quick band-aid for those faigal families who wanted quick and discreet treatment.

Ephron was at the hospital when Meena was wheeled into the emergency room. Her skin was puffy with small psoriasis-looking whelps across her face and body. She had pretty much been drifting in and out of consciousness for the last ten minutes. Avis and Shahaf arrived shortly after. As they entered the waiting room, Ephron looked up from his chair. His arms were folded, and his face was stained with exhausted tears.

"I don't know what happened. She was doing so well the other day. We even went to the beach."

Avis glanced at his son, and instantly he was transported to the moment when they learned of Meadow Branson's eventual fate. Even the expression on Ephron's face was similar.

"What did the doctor say?"

"They just wheeled her into the room. They originally told us she may have been in a temporary remission."

Avis put his hand on his son's shoulder. It was the first time Shahaf looked at both men with concern.

"Perhaps I could try to find out some information on how this advanced so quickly."

Avis looked in his direction and nodded in agreement. "Please do that, Shahaf!"

Ephron looked at an empty gurney as he tried to contain himself. "She started running a fever last night, and we couldn't get it down. Her skin was like fire!"

Avis sat with his son until an orderly emerged through the doors. "Are you the husband?"

"Yes, I am."

"Please come with me. The doctor wants to see you."

Ephron quickly followed the young orderly. As they reached the room, a rather gaunt-looking fellow met him at the door.

"Mr. Branson?"

"Yes."

"I'm Dr. Parish, the floor doctor."

"Well, what's happening?"

"We did all that we could, but her condition had accelerated to the point that I'm afraid her body can't take the stress of the heat. Her body is starting to shut down."

"Just last week, the doctor told us she was on the road to remission. Was that a lie?"

"I can't explain the change. Perhaps she experienced some type of inner trauma."

"She stays shut up all day long in bed reading books, what trauma could have befallen her?"

"Well, it's all in Ark's wings now."

The orderly popped his head through the door. "Doctor, she doesn't have much time."

Ephron peered his head impatiently inside the door. From this distance, he could see they had her placed in an ice bath. She was conscious as he approached her. Ephron knelt beside the tub. Steam hissed from the warmth of her body.

Ephron looked up at the physician with blurry eyes. "Could I have a few minutes alone with my wife?"

The word, wife, for the first time, had a powerful meaning. It was the first time he could ever remember actually referring to her as his wife. Before that, she was always his Meena. That moment of finality was sobering. The weight of his words rang heavy as both the doctor and the orderly left the room. Dr. Parish paused at the door. "Take as long as you need."

Meena looked in his direction and gently smiled. The stare on her face terrified Ephron. He recognized that same look on his mother's face as she lay on her deathbed. There was a strange calmness about her which unnerved him.

"I'm sorry, I've been so much trouble lately."

"Please don't Meena. You're going to be ok!"

"I really tried to stay a bit longer, but now I feel so tired. Please allow me to see the sunrise once more. The sun makes me so happy."

"They say you're shutting down. You will be in so much pain soon."

"I simply don't care, as long as you're with me, till the sunrise."

He suddenly felt a twinge of anger, but he took a deep breath and nodded. Ephron quickly grabbed her hand and kissed her forehead in quiet desperation. Almost immediately, his lips were scalded by the extreme heat of her fever. He splashed some water across his mouth to ease the burn, then he whispered so gently to her.

"Darling, just try to relax."

"What's wrong? What are you doing?"

"Goodbye Meena."

Ephron suddenly looked about the room cautiously. They were alone. He cupped his hands inside the sleeves of his coat jacket and stood up. He took a deep breath and, without warning, shoved Meena down to the bottom of the tub. He wrapped his covered fingers about her throat and squeezed. Her clawed hands reached up to him instinctively. Her fingers dug into his face.

As much as she fought, he wouldn't let her up. Tears streamed down his face as he fought against his fragile wife. Her wings popped up out of either side of the tub as she struggled helplessly to stay alive. Finally, her wings stopped flapping, and her body gave out.

He watched the water for a few moments before he pulled his arms out. His fingers were completely numb with blisters, as he wiped his face. He was still breathing hard as he removed his coat. he glanced at his reflection in the mirror wall beside the tub. For some reason, he didn't even recognize his face. He quickly looked away, straightened his tie and headed out of the room in tears.

Chapter 59: Morgue

Later that evening, the Branson family announced Meena's death. The family gathered at the Bransons' home with several visitors giving empty condolences to the grieving family. Avis hovered over Ephron with sadness and pity, as guests paid their respects. Many community leaders dropped by with gourmet food in one hand and lucrative business deals in the other.

Back at the hospital, Shahaf found himself alone with the coroner. The doctor gave him Meena's final results to the intrepid weaver.

"Meena's body, by all accounts, was normal other than the diastasis." The doctor frowned. "I don't know what to tell you and Lord Avis. Usually, it doesn't act this abruptly. I myself thought she had at least another two years. I mean, you were here all evening, and you saw her alert. I don't know what happened in the space of thirty minutes. Something doesn't add up."

"Please, doctor, tell me what you think, personally."

"Off the record, if I had to guess, I would say she caught some sort of infection. This isn't diastasis. I think whatever she contracted sped up her condition."

"What kind of infection?"

"We just don't know, and I am aware her husband doesn't want her cut up. He said as much when I talked to him on the phone. I can't blame him."

"Well, her family has the last say. Her uncle wants her on ice in case they have to do an inquiry."

"I suppose that's for the best."

Shahaf shrugged his shoulders. "Well, Lord Branson personally wanted me to find out what happened. Her death could become political if she did die of nefarious causes. The last thing we need is to have a mirror danser roaming our streets."

"Unless there is a reason for a formal inquiry, I don't see the point. I mean, she was terminal anyway."

"Well, thank you, doctor. I guess there is nothing else."

"Tell Avis I will be up that way to pay my respects in the morning."

"I will inform him, blessed Arke!"

"Blessed Arke!"

As the weaver was about to leave, he recognized something peculiar about Meena.

"Wait, doctor. What's that on her neck?" He was pointing to a dark brown bruise.

"Oh my, I saw that earlier, but it was deep red. That is strange, I'm sure I would have noticed when I was with her. It looks like burns from the inside. My Arke, her entire body now has them."

"So, that isn't diastasis."

"No, this is different."

"Could it have been a topical infection?"

"It's highly possible, granted she was exposed to something recently."

Shahaf squinted suspiciously. "What about feathers?"

"Feathers, my good fellow, she's faigal. That doesn't make sense. You might as well say she is allergic to her skin."

Shahaf put his hands in his pockets as his eyes focused on her neck. As if something clicked in his thoughts. *Perhaps they weren't her feathers.*

"These wouldn't be ordinary feathers."

"You weavers understand that type of earth science alchemy. I'm a bit of a layman when it comes to that sort of stuff."

"They could be from some rare bird."

"Are these tropical species?"

"Not at all, the breed I'm thinking of is of the local variety, native to only the Greywood."

"Well, you seem to have some ideas. I hope you find what you're looking for."

Shahaf leaned close to Meena's hair and took a deep breath. "I recognize this aroma. This particular species wears a very unusual fragrance, blue jasmine."

Chapter 60: Griskin

The two women sat in the constable's office. One of the other officers patiently tried to calm the younger one until her statement was recorded. When Fletcher arrived, he immediately recognized the other woman sitting in his office. The initial officer approached Fletcher and gave him the clipboard. Fletcher frowned.

"What do we have?"

"Another missing child, but this one says she saw the perp!"

Fletcher was instantly excited. "Really?"

"I don't know, you really need to talk to her, sir."

"What do you mean?"

"I think she has had some breakdown or something, cause what she said doesn't make much sense to me!"

Fletcher looked back at the two women and then at the officer. "Why is Koko here?"

"She drove the mother here."

"Is she one of Koko's girls?"

"Not as far as I can tell."

Fletcher headed into his office. As soon as he stepped in, both women stood and began talking. He immediately responded. "Please, don't get up."

Fletcher first addressed the elephant in the room. "Mrs. Tuludge, what do you have to do with this?"

"Ms. Evema needed a ride. I'm just here for moral support."

"Moral support, so you're just a helpful neighbor?"

"You can get bent, Fletcher."

"Usually when you're here, it's because of other matters."

"Look, someone took her child, and you're wasting time, Constable."

"Of course, my apologies, Ms..." Fletcher snatched up the clipboard that the assisting officer handed him. After skimming the report he addressed the young woman. "Ms. Evema Persing. Is that is your name?"

She nodded through tear-stained eyes.

"I know this is difficult, but we're going to do everything we can to get your child back safely. Could you explain to me exactly what happened this morning?"

Evema burst into tears. Fletcher waited patiently for her to compose herself. She had been the fourth mother, of whom he had to witness overwhelming grief. It didn't get any easier. As soon as she calmed a bit, he looked down at the clipboard for basic facts.

"Ok, you claim someone took your son."

She nodded.

"Dom Leon Persing, age three."

She nodded again.

"Ok, Ms. Persing, you told the officer that you saw what happened. Could you, in your own words, explain?"

She almost immediately had a sour look on her face. "What mean this?"

It was at this time that he realized how thick her dialect was. She was from one of the eastern European countries. As she talked, it was at times unclear what she was saying. The language barrier would be an issue. Luckily for her, Koko was there to help explain things. Which is why, Fletcher quickly discovered, she had chosen to drive the woman.

Koko leaned into her. "Tell him what you told me, dear!"

As soon as KoKo explained, her face said she understood. She began nodding her head.

In a rather thick accent, she started to explain a narrative that described an incident in which she was planting tomatoes in her garden. Her son was playing close by. She was on her knees, crawling through some bramble bushes, when she saw her son being dragged into the underbrush. She followed after, but lost them.

Fletcher cut off her story to ask questions. "So, did you see who took your son?"

Her answer was quick and clear, but it was nonsensical all the same. "Griskin!"

Fletcher repeated. "Who?"

Koko answered for her. "The griskin took him!"

"Is that the name of one of your neighbors, the one who took him? I'm not familiar with anyone in town with that name."

Koko was impatient. "Look, her little boy was stolen, are you going to help or not!"

Fletcher looked at the young woman who seemed barely able to contain herself. His cynicism quickly dissipated as he again began to address the woman. "This griskin, a male or female?"

Koko spoke in the strange dialect, and Evema responded.

Koko answered for her. "She said it was a woman!"

"Well, what did this woman look like?"

She slowly tried to explain in simple words. From what he was able to pick up, she had black eyes and a large, wide grin that went from ear to ear. When she opened her mouth, several tongues spewed out like tentacles. She said the woman was naked, but her skin was shiny and covered in needles.

This detailed vexed Fletcher. "Needles?"

"Yes, needles!"

"Do you mean like hypodermic needles?"

Koko inserted herself in the conversation again. "She means her skin was fuzzy."

"Like fur?"

The woman insisted. "No fur!"

Starting to get frustrated, Fletcher continued. "We'll come back to that. What else can you tell me? Did she have any distinguishing marks?"

"Marks?"

"Was there anything unusual or different about her?"

The woman held her arms in the air as if she were being arrested. She then leaned forward at the constable and blurted out, "Four!"

Koko repeated the response. "She has four."

The woman started to make claw-like motions and chomp her mouth. Fletcher tried to ignore the charade-like motions as he tried to listen to Koko.

"What does she mean, four?"

"She says she has four arms with large claws."

Fletcher looked at them both oddly. "You mean four actual arms?"

Koko studied the woman chomping her mouth about, before adding more details.

"And she had sharp teeth!"

"Of course, we have to have sharp teeth in such a wide mouth. It would be incomplete without that!"

Koko finally addressed him. "I know this may sound strange to you. But she is not crazy, Constable!"

"What does she mean by griskin? It sounds like she's talking about some wild animal."

"That is the spirit, she feels, that took her child!"

"A spirit?"

"She is from the old country. As am I and many members of this community."

Since Fletcher had arrived in Meadowlark, he had been inundated with what could only be described as a wide range of religious communities. There were Catholics, Hindus, Muslims; and the strangest religion that was dominant here in town was alien to him. They referred to one another as faigal and kept to themselves.

They did interact with those outside their belief, but they were very tight-lipped about some of the customs and beliefs. He had to twist a few arms just to get what little he knew about it. There was a regimented, rigid quality that reminded him of the Amish. Especially the working-class ones. The Adlers, Bransons, and a few others with money seemed more open and even worldly to a degree. However, there were still hints of the culture that seemed to extend even to them.

Fletcher, with a straight face, addressed Koko Tuludge. "So, is she saying a ghost took her child?"

"Not a ghost, a spirit."

"What's the difference?"

"A spirit can take physical form."

"Why did it take her child?"

Evema continued to explain, using exaggerated hand gestures and facial movements. As extensive as her explanation was, the language barrier was difficult. Koko had to explain to Fletcher that the woman was hiding at the edge of the yard and began to crawl through the tall grass like a snake to get close to him. She then seduced the boy from her!

"How can a complete stranger seduce a child from its mother? Did she have a bag of candy?"

"Perhaps he thought she was his mother."

"What?"

"A Griskin is supposed to be a changeling."

A very frustrated Fletcher turned to Koko. "Did you see this woman?"

"No, I didn't?"

"When you got there, what did you see?"

"I saw Evema digging around in the bushes, screaming. It was early afternoon, and I was taking out the trash. I remember because I saw Evelyn Adler with her niece across the street at Greenbaum's office."

"Are you sure you saw Ms. Adler?"

"Yes, I know what she looks like."

"It's just that she usually doesn't hang out in Crecheland."

"Everyone in town eventually makes their way to Teal Street. You might even have an itch to visit us one evening, Constable."

Fletcher slightly blushed at the older woman's proposal. Koko ran the Crecheland Inn, a local brothel that employed the most exotic faigal girls. This made it quite popular with the faigal and sleeven clientele who were upwardly mobile. Even the mayor's brother was rumored to have frequented it when he was younger.

Because of the deep-pocket popularity, it was virtually impossible to shut down the Crecheland Inn. It had been closed several times and received several fines over the years. However, mysterious donors would always cover any fines and waive any legal issues they may have had.

Koko herself was easy on the eye for her age. In actuality, if she wasn't seen as so morally corrupt by the community, she would have a line of men trying to court her. There were even rumors that when she was younger, she dated Merle Adler.

Fletcher's eyes wrinkled at the prospect. "Are you sure you saw Evelyn?"

"I saw what I saw!"

"Did she see you?"

"I don't know, I didn't talk to them."

"We'll get back to that later as well. Ms. Persing, what exactly happened next?"

"I call deme, but deme no answer. Then I know, she take him!"

Fletcher turned to Koko for additional clarification. Koko explained. "Deme means son in the native tongue."

Evema continued speaking, oblivious to the conversation between the officer and her neighbor.

"My deme say, he see her before!"

"Your son saw this griskin, prior?"

"He say she hide in bushes at night, then she flies away when sun come."

Fletcher's eyes widened. "You said flies, so she has wings?"

Suddenly, Fetcher stood up and walked across the room to a dusty file cabinet. Both women looked at one another in puzzlement as he started to silently thumb through a variety of files.

Koko herself was growing claustrophobic just being in the station. She took a deep sigh before she finally addressed Fletcher. "Look, Constable, I really need to get back."

Fletcher's response was quite frank. "What's wrong? Got a customer waiting?"

"Actually, I was baking fruitcake and didn't want to burn it up!"

"People actually eat those things?"

"The people I know love them."

Fletcher turned back to his files until he seemed to find the one he was looking for. He quickly moved back to his seat.

Evema glanced at Koko, concerned. "Did I say something wrong?"

He pulled a sheet from the file. It appeared to be a drawing. He held it out to Ms. Persing. The moment she saw it, she got emotional.

Fletcher signed. "So, does this mean something to you?"

Koko looked confused at Fletcher. "Where did you get that drawing, Constable?"

Fletcher cleared his throat and sat up in his chair. "We had a missing person about two years ago. She was one of the few children that we actually found alive. According to the child, she was abducted by a woman from the Greywood. She did escape and drew a few pictures of the woman. However, soon after, she lapsed into a catatonic state. This is one of her drawings. I don't know why I kept it. Something about them stuck with me."

Koko looked down at the worn paper. It was a simple, rudimentary drawing, but what it expressed was far from a simple child's drawing. It showed three stick people lying dead at the bottom of the paper. High above in the air was another person with long hair, like a woman. The body had multiple segmented legs and long wings like some sort of flying insect. A red crayon scribbled across all three bodies on the ground, and on the lips of the flying woman. The obvious intention was that the red crayon represented blood. The eyes of the people on the ground were large x marks, while the flying woman's eyes were darkened black circles.

Fletcher looked hard at Evema. "Did she look like this?"

Chapter 61: A New Day

The morning was somewhat crisp and chilly for a change. Willet stepped out into the morning air and took a deep breath. She was starting to like the fresh country vibe. The backdrop of the trees against the sunrise was devastatingly beautiful.

As beautiful as the world looked, she was tired. Her training with Mother Hazel had gone a bit long. However, she was starting to get used to the regimen. For the most part, things had settled a bit.

The only issue was the long walk to school. At times, it was kind of boring, as neither of the girls were happy about the distance they had to walk to go to school and then back home. It was about two miles coming and going. Willet tried to come to terms with the situation. At least she did have time to think to herself.

Adelie, on the other hand, pretty much just complained about how long the walk was until she grew tired of talking. As they headed down the driveway, Willet could hear Adelie several yards behind starting her quips. They were nearing the street when Adelie blurted out loudly. "This sucks Wille!"

Willet spun around to see what her sister's daily gripe was. She managed to catch a glimpse of something white in the far distance, over Adelie's shoulder. Several yards away in the grassy field that faced the entrance into Greywood, she saw a figure just standing there, watching them.

The figure was dressed in a white robe and cloak and had the natural build of a woman. The mysterious woman was at the edge of a clump of trees, peering intently at them. Willet was sure she didn't know her at all. However, there was something slightly familiar about her. They made eye contact, and a chill went up Willet's spine as she recalled the phantom's identity. It was the same woman from her nightmares. The one in the woods that confronts her over and over.

There she was, standing about 40 yards from them, as bright as day, watching. Willet tossed her book bag down in front of her and slowly began to dig through the contents. These days, she was always transporting her fire poker with her. This morning was no different. Her fingers swept about her school books, Mother Hazel's feather, a textbook on shammas, and a diary, until she retrieved her iron weapon from her book bag.

Adelie could sense the tension immediately. "What's wrong, Willie?"

As soon as Willet pulled it out and looked up, she noticed that the woman was gone. There was nothing there. Just the gentle breeze from the trees where she was once standing. She brushed by Adelie and scanned the field. *Was she even really there?*

The fire poker was not hot, glowing, warm, or anything. She looked about the perimeter again, now she couldn't even sense anything. She took a deep breath and began to second-guess herself. Adelie followed her sister's lead. "What is it?"

"Nothing, I thought I saw something."

Adelie had a nervous look on her face. She didn't ever remember seeing her sister so afraid. "Are we safe, Willie?"

"Safe is a relative term in this town, and please stop calling me Willie!"

"What's wrong?"

"You have noticed that I'm not a boy?"

As Willet leaned down to put her poker away, a green Volkswagen slowly crept up around the bend. The car stopped right beside the driveway with an abrupt screech. Willet, who was zipping up her bag, looked up with a casual, yet surprised glance. "Morning."

"What are you doing?"

"Trying to get my fire poker to fit back into my bag, without poking a hole in the damn side."

Tori laughed. "Swift, you are so mental. I'm not sure that's even legal on campus."

"What's up?"

"I'm here to pick you guys up for school. I was talking to your mother the other day when she came into the shop. She mentioned that you have a hard time staying in school the entire day. She wanted to make sure you got escorted to your class."

Willet gave a rolled glance back at the manor. She was almost about to be insulted; however, a ride was not necessarily a bad thing. Especially considering what she had just experienced.

"Isn't this out of your way?"

"Shut up and get in, girl. Addie, put your bag in the trunk."

Adelie's eyes widened with excitement. "Yes, my prayers have been answered."

As soon as Willet got in, she smiled. "Thank you so much."

Tori quickly pulled off as Willet shut the door behind her. Tori turned on the radio and started playing some obscure pop song that they all knew.

"Where have you been, Swift? I haven't seen you at lunch!"

"Jae and I had a falling out, and I didn't want to make things awkward for you guys."

"Seriously?"

"What?"

"I should kick your ass for ditching me. Aren't we friends?"

Willet was taken aback. All this time, she hadn't even considered the idea that she had any friends; she quickly answered. "Of course!"

"Look, Jae is pretty cool, but she has that Crecheland mentality."

Willet wasn't sure if she should be offended for Jae. "What do you mean?"

"Just because you're born into a certain situation, you shouldn't let that define who you are, or what you can and can't do!"

Willet added. "Or who you can be friends with!"

"See, you're the only one in this town whom I can talk to about anything real! I really missed you. I thought you had gotten fed up and gone back to Key West or something!"

Willet felt a tear in her eye, which she quickly wiped away. "Well, I thought I might just bum around town a bit longer. I mean you guys would be lost without my fire poking skills."

Adelie suddenly interrupted. "Hey, what did you see back there, Willie?"

Willet had forgotten about the woman. Her response was quickly dismissive. "I don't know, probably nothing."

As the car entered the school parking lot, Willet's mind focused on the possible apparition of a woman. She was reminded of something Mother Hazel had told her this week. Many spirits and entities existed in Meadowlark. Though most folks don't know about them. Only those few in tune with nature are aware and can see them. She also told Willet that as her powers grew, she would most likely start to see some of these very spirits. They would sense her and reveal themselves to her, whether she wanted them to or not. There was a world hidden beneath the ordinary world that most of us never see unless we pay close attention.

Fini

E.J. Gambles

Don't miss out!

Visit the website below and you can sign up to receive emails whenever E.J Gambles publishes a new book. There's no charge and no obligation.

https://books2read.com/r/B-A-PPWBE-ZAAPG

BOOKS 2 READ

Connecting independent readers to independent writers.